New York Times and *USA TODAY* bestselling author **Heather Graham** has written more than two hundred novels. She is pleased to have been published in over twenty-five languages, with sixty million books in print. Heather is a proud recipient of the Silver Bullet from Thriller Writers and was awarded the prestigious Thriller Master Award in 2016. She is also a recipient of Lifetime Achievement Awards from RWA and *The Strand*, and is the founder of The Slush Pile Players, an author band and theatrical group. An avid scuba diver, ballroom dancer and mother of five, she still enjoys her South Florida home but also loves to travel. Heather is grateful every day for a career she loves so very much.

New York Times and *USA TODAY* bestselling author **B.J. Daniels** lives in Montana with her husband, Parker, and three springer spaniels. When not writing, she quilts, boats and plays tennis. Contact her at bjdaniels.com, or on Facebook or Twitter, @bjdanielsauthor.

New York Times Bestselling Author

HEATHER GRAHAM

TANGLED THREAT

**HARLEQUIN
BESTSELLING
AUTHOR
COLLECTION**

HARLEQUIN®
BESTSELLING
AUTHOR
COLLECTION

Recycling programs
for this product may
not exist in your area.

ISBN-13: 978-1-335-49837-3

Tangled Threat
First published in 2019. This edition published in 2022.
Copyright © 2019 by Heather Graham Pozzessere

Hijacked Bride
First published in 2003. This edition published in 2022.
Copyright © 2003 by Barbara Heinlein

For questions and comments about the quality of this book, please contact us at CustomerService@Harlequin.com.

Harlequin Enterprises ULC
22 Adelaide St. West, 41st Floor
Toronto, Ontario M5H 4E3, Canada
www.Harlequin.com

Printed in U.S.A.

CONTENTS

TANGLED THREAT

Heather Graham

For Roberta Young Peacock, a true Florida girl,
with lots of love and best wishes.

Prologue

The History Tree

"They see her...the beautiful Gyselle, when the moon is high in the sky. She walks these oak-lined trails and sometimes pauses to touch the soft moss that drips from the great branches, as if she reaches out for them to touch what is real. In life she was kind and generous. She was beloved by so many. And yet, when brought so cruelly to her brutal and unjust death at the infamous History Tree, she cast a curse on those around her. Those involved would die bitter deaths as well, choking on their own blood, breath stolen from them as it had been from her," Maura Antrim said dramatically.

The campfire in the pit burned bright yellow and gold, snapping and crackling softly. All around them, great oaks and pines rose, moss swaying in the light breeze. The moon overhead was full and bright that night, but cloud cover drifted past now and then, creating eerie shadows everywhere.

It was a perfect summer night, and perfect for storytelling. She was glad to be there, glad to be the storyteller and glad of the response from her audience.

Maura's group from the resort—teenagers and adults alike—looked at her, wide-eyed.

She refused to smile—she wanted to remain grave—though she was delighted by the fascination of the guests assembled around her. She had been grateful and pleased to be upgraded to her position of storyteller for the Frampton Ranch and Resort, an enterprise in North Central Florida that was becoming more renowned daily as a destination. The property had been bought about five years back by billionaire hotelier Donald Glass, and he had wisely left the firepit and the old riding trails as they were, the History Tree right where it grew, the ruins of the old plantation just as they lay—and amped up the history first, and then the legends that went along with the area.

Maura wasn't supposed to be on tonight—she shared the position with Francine Renault, a longtime employee of Donald Glass's hotel corporation, probably second in command only to the main resort manager, Fred Bentley. The two of them were known to argue—but Francine stayed right where she was, doing what she wanted. Despite any arguments, Donald Glass refused to fire either Francine or Fred, who, despite his stocky bulk, moved around the resort like a bat out of hell, always getting things done.

Fred Bentley had watched Maura at the start of the

evening; she thought that he was smiling benignly—that he approved of her abilities as a social hostess and storyteller.

It was hard to blame him for fighting with Francine. She was…a difficult personality type at best.

And sharing any job with Francine wasn't easy; the woman had an air of superiority about her and a way of treating those she considered to be "lesser" employees very badly. Francine was in her midthirties—and was a beauty, really, a platinum blonde, dark-eyed piece of perfection—and while Maura had turned eighteen, Francine considered all of Donald Glass's summer help annoying, ignorant children.

The young adults—or "camper" summer help—were fond of gossiping. It was rumored that Francine once had an affair with Donald Glass, and that was how she held on to her position—and her superiority.

Glass was married. Maybe Francine was blackmailing him, telling him that if she wasn't given a certain power, she'd tell his wife, Marie, and Marie—or so rumor had it—could be jealous and very threatening when she chose to be. Hard to believe—in public Marie was always the model of decorum, slim and regal, slightly younger than Donald but certainly older than Francine.

Teens and young adults loved to speculate. At Maura's age, the thought of any of the older staff together—all seeming so much older than she was at the time—was simply gross.

Tonight, by not being there, Francine had put herself in a bad position.

She hadn't shown up for work. A no-show without a

call was grounds for dismissal, though Maura seriously doubted that Francine would be fired.

Maura looked around, gravely and silently surveying her group before beginning again.

She didn't get a chance—someone spoke up. A young teenager.

"They should call it the Torture Tree or the Hangman's Tree...or something besides the History Tree," he said.

The boy's name was Mark Hartford, Maura thought. She'd supervised a game at the pool one day when he had been playing. He was a nice kid, curious and, maybe because he was an adolescent boy, boisterous. He also had an older brother, Nils—in college already. Mark's brother wasn't quite as nice; he knew that many of the workers were his own age or younger, and he liked to lord his status as a guest over them. He was bearable, however.

"The Torture Tree! Oh, lord, you little...heathen!"

Nils had a girlfriend. Rachel Lawrence. She was nicer than Nils, unless Nils was around. Then she behaved with a great deal of superiority, as well. But, Maura realized, Nils and Rachel *were* at the campfire that night—they had just joined quietly.

Quietly—which was amazing in itself. Nils liked to make an entrance most of the time, making sure that everyone saw him.

Rachel had her hands set upon Mark's shoulders—even as she called him a heathen. She looked scared, or nervous maybe, Maura thought. Maybe it was for effect; Nils set his arm around her shoulders, as a good, protective boyfriend should. They made a cute family picture, a young adult male with his chosen mate and a young one under their wings.

Maura was surprised they were on the tour. Nils had said something the other day about the fact that they were too mature for campfire ghost stories.

"Torture Tree—yes, that would be better!" Mark said. He wasn't arguing with Rachel, he was determined that he was right. "Poor Gyselle—she was really tortured there, right?"

Mark and the other young teens were wide-eyed. Teenagers that age liked the sensational—and they liked it grisly.

"She was dragged there and hanged, so yes, I'm sure it was torture," Maura said. "But it was the History Tree long before a plantation was built here, years and years ago," Maura said. "That was the Native American name for it—the Timucua were here years before the Spanish came. They called it the History Tree, because even back then, the old oak had grown together with a palm, and it's been that way since. Anyway, we'll be seeing the History Tree soon enough," she said softly. "The tree that first welcomed terror when the beautiful Gyselle was tormented and hanged from the tree until dead. And where, so they say, the hauntings and horrors of the History Tree began."

Maura saw more than one of her audience members glance back over the area of sweeping, manicured lawn and toward the ranch, as if assuring themselves that more than the night and the spooky, draped trees existed, that there was light and safety not far away.

The new buildings Donald Glass had erected were elegant and beautiful. With St. Augustine just an hour and a half in one direction and Disney and Universal and other theme parks just an hour and half to the south—not to mention a nice proximity to the beaches and racetrack at Daytona and the wonder of Cape Kennedy being an hour or so away, as well—Frampton Ranch and Resort was becoming a must-see location.

Still, the ranch had become renowned for offering Campfire Ghost Histories. Not stories, but histories—everything said was history and fact...to a point.

The listeners could hear what people claimed to have happened, and they could believe—or not. And then they'd walk the trails where history had occurred.

"You see, Gyselle had been a lovely lost waif, raised by the Seminole tribe after they found her wandering near the battlefield at the end of the Second Seminole War. She was 'rescued' by Spanish missionaries at the beginning of the Third Seminole War, though, at that point, she probably didn't want or need rescuing, having been with a Seminole family for years. But 'saved' and then set adrift, she found work at the old Frampton plantation, and there she caught the eye of the heir, and despite his arranged marriage to socialite Julie LeBlanc, the young Richard Frampton fell head over heels in love with Gyselle. They were known to escape into the woods where they both professed their love, despite all the odds against them—and Richard's wife, Julie. Knowing of her husband's infidelity, Julie LeBlanc arranged to poison her father-in-law—and let the blame fall on Gyselle. Gyselle was hunted down as a murderous witch, supposedly practicing a shaman's magic or a form of voodoo—it was easy to blame it on traditions the plantation workers didn't really understand—and she was hanged there, from what was once a lover's tree where she had met with Richard, her love, who had promised to protect her..."

She let her voice trail. Then she finished.

"Here, in these woods, Gyselle loved, not wisely, but deeply. And here she died. And so they say, when the moon has risen high and full in the night sky—as it is now—those who walk the trails by night can hear her singing softly 'The Last Rose of Summer' with a lovely Irish lilt to her voice."

"What about the curse?" a boy cried out.

"Yeah, the curse! That she spoke before she died—swearing that her tormenters would choke on their own blood! You just said that she cursed everyone, and there are more stories, right?" Mark—never one to be silent long—asked eagerly.

Maura felt—rather than saw—Brock McGovern at her side. He was amused. Barely eighteen, he'd nevertheless been given the position of stage manager for events such as the campfire history tour. He'd been standing to one side just behind her as she told her tale with just the right dramatic emphasis—or so she believed.

He stepped forward, just a shade closer, nearly touching her.

"Choking on their own blood? Kind of a standard curse, huh?" he teased softly and for her ears alone.

Maura ignored him, trying not to smile, and still, even here, now, felt the rush she always did when Brock was around.

Brock was always ready to tease—but also to encourage and support whatever she was doing. He had that ability and the amazing tendency to exude an easy confidence that stretched far beyond his years. But he was that sure of himself. He was about to leave for the service, and when he returned, he planned to go to college to study criminology. Barely an adult, he knew what he wanted in life. She was sure he was going to work hard during basic training; he'd work hard through the college or university of his choice. And then he'd make up his mind just where he wanted to serve—FBI, US Marshals, perhaps even Homeland Security or the Secret Service.

He shook his head, smiling at her with his unusual eyes—a shade so dark that they didn't appear brown at times, but rather black. His shaggy hair—soon to become a buzz cut—was as dark as his eyes, and it framed a face that was, in Maura's mind, pure enchantment. He had already had a fine, steady chin—the kind most often seen on more mature men. His cheekbones were broad, and his skin was continually bronzed. He was, in her mind, beautiful.

He'd often told the tales himself, and he did so very well. He had a deep, rich voice that could rise and fall at just the right moments—a voice that, on its own, could awaken every sense in Maura's body. They had known each other for three years now, laughed and joked together, ridden old trails, worked together…always flirting, nearly touching at first, but always aware that, when summer ended, he would head back down to Key West and she would return to West Palm Beach— about 233 miles apart, just a little too far for a high school romance.

But this summer…

Things had changed.

She had liked him from the time she had met him; she had compared any other young man she met to him, and in her mind, all others fell short. He'd been given a management job that summer, probably because he was always willing to pitch in himself, whether it came to working in the restaurant when tables needed bussing or hauling in boxes when deliveries arrived. He'd gained a lean and muscular physique from hard work as much as from time in the gym, and he had a quick mind and a quicker wit, cared for people, was generous with his time, and was just…

Perfect. She'd never find anyone so perfect in life again, Maura was certain, even though she knew that her mother and father smiled indulgently when she talked about him in glowing terms—she was, after all, just eighteen, with college days and so much more ahead of her.

This summer they'd become a true couple. In every way.

A very passionate couple.

They'd had sex, in her mind, the most amazing sex ever, more meaningful than any sex had ever been before.

Just the thought brought a rush of blood to her face.

But…she believed that they would go on even through their separation, no matter the distance, no matter what. People would think, of course, that she was just a teenager, that she couldn't be as madly in love as she believed she was. So she was determined that no one would really realize just how insanely fully she did love him.

She turned to Brock. He was smiling at her. Something of a secret smile, charming, sexy...a smile that seemed to hint that they always shared something unique, something special.

She grinned in return.

Yep. He had become her world.

"Take it away," she told him.

"The curse!" he said, stepping in with a tremor in his voice. "It's true that while being dragged to the tree—which you'll see soon on our walk—the poor woman cried out that she was innocent of any cruel deed, innocent of murder. And she said that those who so viciously killed her would die in agony and despair. The very woods here would be haunted for eternity, and the evil they perpetrated on her would live forever. They had brought the devil into the woods, and there he would abide."

He smiled, innately charming when he spoke to a group, and continued, "I think that storytellers have added in the choking-on-blood part. Very dramatic and compelling, but...there are records of the occasion of the poor woman's demise available at the resort library." He set his flashlight beneath his chin, creating an eerie look.

"And," Maura said, "what is also documented is that bad things continued to happen on the ranch—under the same tree, the condemned killer, Marston Riggs, tortured and killed his victims in the early 1900s, and as late as 1970, the man known as the Red Tie Killer made use of the tree as well, killing five men and women at the History Tree and leaving their bones to fall to the ground. But, of course, we don't believe in curses. The

History Tree and the ranch are perfectly safe nowadays…" She looked at Brock. "Shall we?" she asked.

"Indeed, we shall," he said, and the sound of his voice and the look that he gave her made her long for it to be later, when they had completed the nighttime forest tour—and were alone together.

They walked by the grove, where there was a charming little pond rumored to invigorate life—a handsomely written plaque commemorating the Spaniard Reynaldo Montenegro and his exploration of Florida.

Brock said to the tour group, "Here we are at the famous grove where Reynaldo Montenegro claimed to have found the Pond of Eternal Youth."

It was as great tour; even the adolescents continued to ask questions as they walked.

"I'm happy to have been the tour guide tonight," Maura murmured to Brock. "But I can't believe that Francine just didn't show up."

"If I know Francine, she'll make a grand entrance somewhere along the line, with a perfect reason for not being on time. She'll have some mammoth surprise for everyone—something way more important than speaking to the guests. Hey, what do you want to bet that we see her somewhere before this tour is over? Here, folks," Brock announced, "you'll see the plaque—an inquisition did come to the New World!"

The copse, illuminated only by the sparkling lights that lit the trail, offered a sadder message—that of tortures carried out by an invading society on the native population it encountered.

They passed the ruins of an old Spanish farm and then they neared the tree.

The infamous History Tree.

The tree––or trees––older than anyone could remember, stood dead center in the small clearing, as if nothing else would dare to grow near. Gnarled and twisted together, palm and oak suggested a mess of human limbs, coiled together in agony.

Maura stopped dead, hearing a long, terrified scream, then realizing that she'd made the sound herself.

From one large oaken branch, a body was hanging, swaying just slightly in the night breeze.

She didn't need to wonder why Francine Renault had been derelict in her duty.

She was there…part of the tour, just not as she should have been.

Head askew, neck broken. She was hanging there, in the place where others had been hanged through the years, again and again, where they had decayed, where their bones had dotted the earth beneath them.

Brock had been right.

Francine Renault had indeed shown up before the tour was over.

The police flooded the ranch with personnel, the medical examiner and crime scene technicians.

The rich forest of pines and oaks and ferns and earth became alive with artificial light, and still, where the moss sagged low, the bright beams just made the night and the macabre situation eerier.

Detective Michael Flannery had been put in charge of the case. Employees and guests had been separated and then separated again, and eventually, Maura sat at the edge of the parking lot, shivering although it wasn't cold, waiting for the officer who would speak with her.

When he got there, he wanted to know the last time

she had seen Francine. She told him it had been the night before.

Where she had been all day? In the office, in the yard with the older teen boys and at the campfire.

Had she heard anyone threaten Francine?

At least half of the resort's employees. In aggravation or jest.

The night seemed to wear on forever.

When she was released at last, she was sent back to her own room and ordered to stay there until morning.

When morning came, her parents were there, ready to take her home.

She desperately wanted to see Brock.

Her parents were quiet and then they looked at each other. Her father shook his head slightly, and her mother said softly, "Maura, you can't see Brock."

"What?" she demanded. "Why not? Mom, Dad— I'm about to leave home. Go to college, really be on my own. I love you. I'm going to come home. But... I'm eighteen. I won't go without seeing Brock."

Her father, a gentle giant with broad shoulders and a mane of white hair, spoke to her softly. "Sweetheart, we didn't say that we wouldn't let you see Brock. We're saying that you *can't* see Brock." He hesitated, looking over at her mother, and then he continued with, "I'm so sorry. Brock was arrested last night. He was charged with the murder of Francine Renault."

And with those words, it seemed that her world fell apart, that what she had known, that what she had believed in, all just exploded into a sea of red and then disappeared into smoke and fog.

Chapter 1

"I'm assigned to go back to Florida. To stay at the Frampton Ranch and Resort—and investigate what we believe to be three kidnappings and a murder. And the kidnappings may have nothing to do with the resort, nor may the murder?" Brock McGovern asked, a small note of incredulity slipping into his voice, which was surprising to him—he was always careful to keep an even tone.

FBI Assistant Director Richard Egan had brought him into his office, and Brock had known he was going on assignment—he just hadn't expected this.

"Yes, not what you'd want, but, hey, maybe it'll be good for you—and perhaps necessary now, when time is of the essence and there is no one out there who could know the place or the circumstances with the same scope and experience you have," Egan told him.

"Three young women have disappeared from the area. Two of them were guests of the Frampton Ranch and Resort shortly before their disappearances—the third had left St. Augustine and was on her way there. The Florida Department of Law Enforcement has naturally been there already. They asked for federal help on this. Shades of the past haunt them—they don't want any more unsolved murders—and everyone is hoping against hope that Lily Sylvester, Amy Bonham and Lydia Merkel might be found."

"These are Florida missing persons cases," Brock said. "And it's sad but true that young people go to Florida and get caught up in the beach life and the club scene. And regrettable but true once again—there's a drug and alcohol culture that does exist and people get caught up in it. Not just in Florida, of course, but…everywhere." He smiled grimly. "I go where I'm told, but I'm curious—how is this an FBI affair? And forgive me, but FBI out of New York?"

"Not out of New York. FDLE asked for you. Specifically."

"I see."

Egan didn't often dwell on the emotional or psychological, but the assistant director hesitated and then said, "You could put your past to rest."

Brock shrugged. "You know, one of the cooks committed suicide not long after the murder. Peter Moore. He stabbed himself with a butcher knife. He'd had a lot of fights with Francine Renault—the victim found at the tree. They suspected he might have killed himself out of remorse."

Egan offered him a dry grimace. "I know about the

cook, of course. You know me—I knew everything about you on paper before I took you into this unit. I'm not sure anyone would have made a case against him in court. That's all beside the point—the past may well be the past. But there's the now, as well. They're afraid of a serial killer, Brock," Egan said. And he continued with, "The badly decomposed remains—mostly bones—of another young woman who went missing several months ago were recently found in a bizarre way—they were dumped in with sheets from several hotels and resorts at an industrial laundry that accepted linens from dozens of places—Frampton Ranch and Resort being one of them."

"I see," Brock said.

He didn't really see.

That didn't matter; Egan would be thorough.

"Yes, this may be a bit hard on you, but you're the one in the know. To come close to a knowledge of the area and people that you already have might take someone else hours or days that may cost a life… You're the best man for this. Especially because you were once falsely accused. And, I believe, you may just solve something of the mystery of the past. And quit hating your own home."

"I don't hate my own home. Ah, come on, sir, I don't want to play any cure-me psychological games with this," Brock said.

Egan shook his head and leaned forward, his eyes narrowed—indicating a rise in his temper, something always kept in check. "If I thought you needed to be cured, you wouldn't be in my unit. Women are missing. They might be dead already," he said curtly. "And then again, they might have a chance. You're the agent with a real sense for the place, the people and the surrounding landscape. And you're a good agent, period. I trust in your ability to get this sorted."

Brock greatly admired Egan. He had a nose for sending the right agent or agents in for a job. Usually.

But Brock was sitting across from Egan in Egan's office—in New York City. He, Brock, was an NYC agent.

And while Brock really didn't dislike where he came from—he still loved Florida, especially his family home in the Keys—he had opted to apply to the New York office of the Bureau specifically because it was far, far away from the state of his birth.

The New York City office didn't usually handle events in Florida, unless a criminal had traveled from New York down to the southern state. Florida had several field offices—including a multimillion-dollar state-of-the-art facility in Broward County. That was south—but Orlando had an exceptional office, close enough to the Frampton place. And there were more offices, as well.

Even if the Frampton Ranch and Resort was in a relatively isolated part of the state, a problem there would generally be handled by a more local office.

"Frampton Ranch and Resort," he heard himself say. And this time, years of training and experience kicked in—his voice was perfectly level and emotionless.

It was true: he sure as hell knew it and the area. The resort was just a bit off from—or maybe part of—what people considered to be the northern Ocala region, where prime acreage was still available at reasonable prices, where horse ranches were common upon the ever-so-slightly rolling hills and life tended to be slow and easy.

There were vast tracts of grazing ground and great live-oak forests and trails laden with pines where the sun seemed to drip down through great strands of weeping moss that hung from many a branch. It could be considered horse country, farm country and ranch county. There were marshes and forests, sinkholes and all manner of places where a body might just disappear.

The Frampton ranch was north of Ocala, east of Gainesville and about forty-five minutes south of Olustee, Florida, where every year, a battle reenactment took place, drawing tourists and historians from near and far. The Battle of Olustee was won by forces in the state; the war had been heading toward its final inevitable conclusion, and then time proved that victory had been necessary for human rights and the strength and growth of the fledgling nation, however purposeless the sad loss of lives always seemed.

Reenactors and historians arrived in good numbers, and those who loved bringing history to life also loved bringing in crowds and many came for the campgrounds. The reenactment took place in February, when temperatures in the state tended to be beautiful and mosquito repellent wasn't as much a requirement as usual. During the winter season—often spring break for other regions—the area was exceptionally popular.

The area was beautiful.

And the large areas of isolation, which included the Frampton property, could conceal any number of dark deeds.

He'd just never thought he'd go back to it.

Certainly, time—and the path he had chosen to take in life—had helped erase the horror of the night they had come upon the body of Francine Renault hanging from the History Tree and his own subsequent arrest. He'd been so young then, so assured that truth spoke for itself. In the end, his parents—bless them—had leaped to the fore, flying into action, and their attorney had made quick work of getting him out of jail after only one night and seeing that his record was returned to spotless. It was ludicrous that they had arrested him; he'd been able to prove that it would have been impossible for him to have carried out the deed. Dozens of witnesses had attested to the fact that he couldn't have been the killer, he'd been seen by so many people during the hours in which the murder must have taken place. He could remember, though, sitting in the cell—cold, stark, barren—and wondering why in God's name they had arrested *him*.

He discovered that there had been an anonymous call to the station—someone stating that they had seen him dragging Francine Renault into the woods. The tipster had sworn that he would appear at a trial as a witness for the prosecution, but the witness had not come to the station. Others had signed formal protests, and the McGoverns' attorney had taken over.

So many people had come forward, indignant, furious over his arrest.

But not Maura. She had been gone. Just gone. He couldn't think of the Frampton Ranch and Resort without a twinge of pain. He had never been sure which had broken him more at the time—the arrest or the fact that

Maura had disappeared as cleanly from his life as any hint of daylight once night had fallen.

They had been so young. It had been natural that her parents whisked her away, and maybe even natural that neither had since tried to reach the other.

But there were times when he could still close his eyes and see her smile and be certain that he breathed in the subtle scent of her. Twelve years had gone by; he wasn't even the same person.

Egan was unaware of his reflections.

"Detective Michael Flannery is lead investigator now. He was on the case when you were arrested for the crime, but he wasn't lead."

"I know Flannery. We've communicated through the years, believe it or not. I almost feel bad—he suffered a lot of guilt about jumping the gun with me."

"He's with the Florida Department of Law Enforcement now, with some seniority and juice, so it seems," Egan informed him. "Years ago, when the murder took place, the federal government wasn't involved. Flannery doesn't want this crime going unsolved. He knows you're in this office now. His commander told me that he keeps in touch with you." Egan paused. "It doesn't sound as if you have a problem with him—you don't, right?"

"No, sir, I do not."

Even as a stunned kid—what he had been back then—Brock had never hated Detective Flannery for being one of the men who had come and arrested him.

Flannery had been just as quick to listen to the arguments that eventually cleared Brock completely of any wrongdoing. While Brock knew that Flannery was furious that he had been taken and certain that there had been an underlying and devious conspiracy to lead him and his superiors so thoroughly in the wrong direction, he had to agree that, at the time, Brock had appeared to be a ready suspect.

He'd had a fight with Francine that day, and it had been witnessed by many people. He hadn't gotten physical in any way, but his poor opinion of her, and his anger with her, had probably been more than evident—enough for him to be brought in for questioning and to be held for twenty-four hours at any rate.

"I'm curious how something that happened so long ago can relate to the cases happening now," Brock said.

"It may not. The remains of the dead girl found in the laundry might have been the work of one crazed individual or an acquaintance seeking vengeance, acting out of jealousy—a solitary motive. It might be coincidence the way she was found—or maybe a killer was trying to throw suspicion upon a particular place or person. But…a lot of the same individuals are still there now who were there when Francine Renault was killed."

"Donald Glass—he's around a lot, though he does spend time at his other properties. Fred Bentley—I imagine he's still running the works. Who else is still there?" Brock asked.

Egan handed him a pile of folders. "All this is coming to your email, as well. There you have those who are in residence—and dossiers on the victims. Yes, Glass and Bentley are still on the property. There are other staff members who never left—Millie Cranston, head of Housekeeping. Vinnie Marshall, upgraded to chef—after Peter Moore's death, I might add. And then…" He paused, tapping the folders. "You have some old guests who are now employees."

"Who?"

"Mark and Nils Hartford," Egan told him. "Both of them report directly to Fred Bentley. Mark has taken over as the social director. Nils is managing the restaurants—the sit-down Ranch Roost and the Java Bar."

Brock hadn't known that the Hartford brothers— who'd seemed so above the working class when they'd been guests—were now employed at the very place where they had once loved to make hell for others.

"Flannery said this is something he hadn't mentioned to you. One of your old friends—or acquaintances— Rachel Lawrence is now with FDLE. She's been working the murder and the disappearances with him."

"Rachel? Became…a cop?" Brock shook his head, not sure if he was angry or amused. Rachel had never wanted to break a nail. She'd been pretty and delicate and… She'd also been a constant accessory of Nils Hartford.

"I guess your old friend Flannery was afraid to tell you."

"I don't know why he would be. I'm just a little surprised—she seemed more likely to be on one of those shows about rich housewives in a big city, but I never had a problem with her. That the Hartford brothers both became employees—that's also a surprise. They made me think of *Dirty Dancing*. They were the rich kids—we were the menial labor. But the world changes. People change."

"Flannery's point, so it appears, is that a number of

the same players are in the area—may mean something and may not. There have been, give or take, approximately a thousand murders in the state per year in the last years. But that's only about four percent per the population. Still, anything could have happened. Violent crime may have to do with many factors—often family related, gang related, drug related, well...you know all the drills. But if we do have a serial situation down there—relating to or not relating to the past—everyone needs to move quickly. Not only do you know the area and the terrain, you know people and you know the ropes of getting around many of the people and places who might be integral to the situation."

"Yes. And any agent would want to put a halt to this—put an end to a serial killer. Or find the girls—alive, one can pray—or stop future abductions and killings."

Egan nodded grimly and tossed a small pile of photos down before him. Brock could see three young, hopeful faces looking back at him. All three were attractive, and more grippingly, all three seemed to smile with life and all that lay before someone at that tender age.

"The missing," Egan said. He had big hands and long fingers. He used them to slide the first three photographs over.

The last was a divided sheet. On one side was the likeness of a beautiful young woman, probably in her early twenties. Her hair had been thick and dark and curly; her eyes had been sky blue. Her smile had been engaging.

"Maureen Rodriguez," Egan said. He added softly, "Then and now."

On the other side of the divided sheet was a crime scene photo—an image of bones, scattered in dirt in a pile of sheets. In the center of the broken and fragmented bones was a skull.

The skull retained bits of flesh.

"According to the investigation, she was on her way to Frampton Ranch and Resort," Egan said.

Brock nodded slowly and rose. "As am I," he said. "When do I leave?"

"Your plane is in two hours—down to Jacksonville. You've a rental car in your name when you arrive. I'm sure you know the way to the property. Detective Flannery will be waiting to hear from you. He'll go over all the particulars."

Brock was surprised to see that Egan was still studying him. "You are good, right?" he asked Brock.

"Hey, everyone wants to head to Florida for the winter, don't they?" he asked. "I'm good," he said seriously. "Maybe you're right. Maybe we can put the past to rest after all."

"I love it—just love it, love it, love it! Love it all!" Angie Parsons said enthusiastically. She offered Maura one of her biggest, happiest smiles.

She was staring at the History Tree, her smile brilliant and her enthusiasm for her project showing in the brightness of her eyes and her every movement. "I mean, people say Florida has no history—just because it's not New England and there were no pilgrims. But, hey, St. Augustine is—what?—the oldest settlement continually…settled…by Europeans in the country, right? I mean, way back, the Spaniards were here. No, no, the state wasn't one of the original thirteen colonies. No, no Puritans here. But! There's so much! And this tree... No one knows how old the frigging oak is or when the palm tree grew in it or through it or with it or whatever."

Angie Parsons was cute, friendly, bright and sometimes, but just sometimes, too much. At five feet two inches, she exuded enough energy for a giant. She had just turned thirty—and done brilliantly for her years. She had written one of the one most successful nonfiction book series on the market. And all because she got as excited as she did about objects and places and things—such as the History Tree.

The main tree was a black oak; no one knew quite how old it was, but several hundred years at least. That type of oak was known to live over five hundred years.

A palm tree had—at some time—managed to grow at the same place, through the outstretched roots of the oak and twirling up around the trunk and through the branches. It was bizarre, beautiful, and so unusual that it naturally inspired all manner of legends, some of those legends based on truth.

And, of course, the History Tree held just the kind of legend that made Angie as successful as she was.

Angie's being incredibly successful didn't hurt Maura any.

But being here... Yes, it hurt. At least...it was incredibly uncomfortable. On the one hand it was wonderful seeing people she had worked with once upon a time in another life.

On the other hand it was bizarre. Like visiting a mirror dimension made up of things she remembered. The

Hartford brothers were working there now. Nils was managing the restaurants—he'd arrived at the table she and Angie had shared last night to welcome them and pick up their dinner check. Of course, Nils had become management. No lowly posts for him. He seemed to have an excellent working relationship with Fred Bentley, who was still the manager of the resort. Bentley had come down when they'd checked in—he'd greeted Maura with a serious hug. She was tall, granted, and in heels, and he was on the short side for a man—about five-ten—but it still seemed that his hug allowed for him to rest his head against her breasts a moment too long.

But still, he'd apparently been delighted to see her.

And Mark Hartford had come to see her, too, grown-up, cute and charming now—and just as happy as his brother to see her. It was thanks to her, he had told her, and her ability to tell the campfire histories, that had made him long to someday do the same.

The past didn't seem like any kind of a boulder around his neck. Certainly he remembered the night that Francine had been murdered.

The night that had turned *her* life upside down had been over twelve years ago.

Like all else in the past, it was now history.

Time had marched on, apparently, for them—and her.

She'd just turned eighteen the last time she had been here. When that autumn had come around, she'd done what she'd been meant to do, headed to the University of Central Florida, an amazing place to study performance of any kind and directing and film—with so many aspects thrown into the complete education.

She'd spent every waking minute in classes—taking elective upon elective to stay busy. She was now CEO of her own company, providing short videos to promote writers, artists, musicians and anyone wanting video content, including attorneys and accountants.

Not quite thirty, she could be proud of her professional accomplishments—she had garnered a great reputation.

She enjoyed working with Angie. The writer was fun, and there was good reason for her success. She loved the bizarre and spooky that drew human curiosity. Even those who claimed they didn't believe in anything even remotely paranormal seemed to love Angie's books.

Most of the time, yes, Maura *did* truly enjoy working with Angie, and since Angie had tried doing her own videos without much success, she was equally happy to be working with Maura. They'd done great bits down in Key West at the cemetery there—where Maura's favorite tomb was engraved with the words *I told you I was sick!*—and at the East Martello Museum with Robert the Doll. They had filmed on the west coast at the old summer estates that had belonged to Henry Ford and Thomas Edison. And they'd worked together in St. Augustine, where they'd created twenty little video bits for social media that had pleased Angie to no end—and garnered hundreds of thousands of hits.

Last night, even Marie Glass—Donald's reserved and elegant wife—had come by their dinner table to welcome them and tell them just how much she enjoyed all the videos that Maura had done for and with Angie, telling great legends and wild tales that were bizarrely wonderful—and true.

Maybe naturally, since they were working in Florida, Angie had determined that they had to stay at Frampton Ranch and Resort and film at the History Tree.

Maura had suggested other places that would make great content for a book on the bizarre: sinkholes, a road where cars slid uphill instead of downhill—hell, she would have done her best to make a giant ball of twine sound fascinating. There were lots of other places in the state with strange stories—lord! They could go back to Key West and film a piece on Carl Tanzler, who had slept with the corpse of his beloved, Elena de Hoyos, for seven years.

But Angie was dead set on seeing the History Tree, and when they'd gotten to the clearing she had started spinning around like a delighted child.

She stopped suddenly, staring at Maura.

"You really are uncomfortable here, aren't you? Scared? You know, I've told you—you can hire an assistant. Maybe a strapping fellow, tall, dark and handsome—or blond and handsome—and muscle-bound. Someone to protect us if the bogeyman is around at any of our strange sites." Angie paused, grinning. She liked men and didn't apologize for it. In her own words, if you didn't kiss a bunch of frogs, you were never going to find a prince.

"Angie, I like doing my own work—and editing it and assuring that I like what I've done. I promise you, if we turn something into any kind of a feature film, we'll hire dozens of people."

Angie sighed. "Well, so much for tall, dark—or blond—and handsome. Your loss, my dear friend. Anyway. You do amazing work for me. You're a one-woman godsend."

"Thanks," Maura told her. She inhaled a deep breath.

"Could you try not to look quite so miserable?"

"Oh, Angie. I'm sorry. It's just…"

"The legend. The legend about the tree—oh, yes. And the murder victims found here. I'm sorry, Maura, but… I mean, I film these places because they have legends attached to them." Angie seemed to be perplexed. She sighed. "Of course, the one murder was just twelve years ago. Does that bother you?" Staring at Maura, she gasped suddenly. "You're close to this somehow, right? Oh, my God! Were you one of the kids working here *that* summer? I mean, I'd have had no idea… You're from West Palm Beach. There's so much stuff down there. Ah!" It seemed that Angie didn't really need answers. "You wound up going to the University of Central Florida. You were near here…"

"Yes, I was here working that summer," Maura said flatly.

"Your name was never in the paper?"

"That's right. The police were careful to keep the employees away from the media. And since we are so isolated on the ranch, news reporters didn't get wind of anything until the next day. My parents had me out of here by then, and Donald Glass was emphatic about the press leaving his young staff alone."

"But a kid was *arrested*—"

"And released. And honestly, Angie, I am a little worried. Even if it has nothing to do with the past, there's something not good going on now. Haven't you watched the news? They found the remains of a young woman not far from here."

"Not far from here, but not *here*," Angie said. "Hey," she said, frowning with concern. "That can't have anything to do with anything—the Frampton ranch killer committed suicide, I thought."

"One of the cooks killed himself," Maura said. "Yes, but… I mean, he never had his day in court. Most people believed he killed Francine—he hated her. But a lot of people disliked her."

"But he killed himself."

"Yes. I wasn't here then. I did hear about it, of course."

Angie was pensive for a moment, and then she asked, "Maura, you don't think that the tree is…evil, do you?"

"*Trees*—a palm laced in with an oak. And no. I'm quite accustomed to the spooky and creepy, and we both know that places don't become evil, nor do things. But people can be wicked as hell—and they can feed off legends. I don't like being out here—not alone. There will be a campfire tonight with the history and ghost stories and the walk—we'll join that. I have waivers for whoever attends tonight."

"What if someone doesn't want to be filmed?" Angie asked anxiously. "You tell the story just as well as anyone else, right? And the camera loves you—a perfect, slinky blonde beauty with those enormous gray eyes of yours. Come on, you've told a few of the stories before. You can—"

"I cannot do a good video for you as a selfie," Maura said patiently.

"Right. I can film you telling the story," Angie said.

"Just that part. And I can do it now—I think you said that the stories were told by the campfire, and then the historic walk began. I'll get you—right here and now—doing the story part of it. Oh, and you can include... Oh, God!" Angie said, her eyes widening. "You weren't just here—you saw the dead woman! The murdered woman... I mean, from this century. Francine Renault. And they arrested a kid, Brock McGovern, but he was innocent, and it was proved almost immediately, but then... Well, then, if the cook didn't do it, they never caught the killer!"

Maura kept her face impassive. Angie always wrote about old crimes that were unsolved—and why a place was naturally haunted after ghastly deeds had occurred there.

She did her homework, however. Angie probably knew more than Maura remembered.

She had loved the sad legend of the beautiful Gyselle, who had died so tragically for love. But, of course, she would have delved as deeply as possible into every event that had occurred at the ranch.

"Do they—do they tell that story at the campfire?" Angie asked.

Maura sighed. "Angie, I haven't been here since the night it happened. I was still young. My parents dragged me home immediately."

She was here now—and she could remember that night all too clearly. Coming to the tree, then realizing while denying it that a real body was hanging from it. That it was Francine Renault. That she had been hanged from a heavy branch, hanged by the neck, and that she dangled far above the ground, tongue bulging, face grotesque.

She remembered screaming…

And she remembered the police and how they had taken Brock away, frowning and massively confused, still tall and straight and almost regally dignified.

And she could remember that there were still those who speculated on his guilt or innocence—until dozens of people had spoken out, having seen him through the time when Francine might have been taken and killed. His arrest had really been ludicrous—a detective's desperate bid to silence the horror and outrage that was beginning to spread.

Brock's life had changed, and thus her life had changed.

Everything had changed.

Except for this spot.

She could even imagine that she was a kid again, that she could see Francine Renault, so macabre in death, barely believable, yet so real and tragic and terrifying as she dangled from the thick limb.

"Oh," Angie groaned, the one word drawn out long enough to be a sentence. "Now I know why you were against doing a video here!"

Angie had wanted the History Tree. And when she had started to grow curious regarding Maura's reluctance to head to the Frampton Ranch and Resort—especially since the resort was supposedly great and the expense of rooms went on Angie's bill—Maura had decided it was time to cave.

She hadn't wanted to give any explanations.

"Angie, it's in your book, and you sell great and your video channel is doing great, as well. It's fine. Really.

But because they did recently find what seems to be the remains of a murder victim near here, I do think we need to be careful. As in, stay out of these woods after dark."

"There is a big bad wolf. Was a big bad wolf... But seriously, I'm not a criminologist of any kind, but I'd say the killer back then was making a point. Maybe the bones they found belonged to someone who died of natural causes."

Angie wasn't stupid, but Maura was sure that the look she gave her tiny friend at that moment implied that she thought she was.

"Maybe," Angie said defensively.

"Angie, you don't rot in the dirt on purpose and then wind up with your bones in a cache of hotel laundry," Maura said.

"No, but, hey—there could be another explanation. Like a car accident. And whoever hit her was terrified and ran—and then, sadly, she just rotted."

"And wound up in hotel sheets?"

Maura asked incredulously. Angie couldn't be serious.

"Okay, so that's a bit far-fetched."

"Angie, it's been reported that the remains were found of a murder victim. Last I saw, they were still seeking her identity, but they said that she was killed."

"Well, they found bones, from what I understand. Anyway," Angie said, dusting her hands on her skirt and speaking softly and with dignity and compassion, "I wish you would have just said that you were here when it happened. Let's get out of here. I'm sorry I made you do this."

"You didn't make me do it. If I had been determined

not to come back here, I wouldn't have done so. But it's going to get dark soon. Let me shoot a bit of you doing your speech by the tree while I still have good light."

Maura lifted her camera, looked at the tree and then up at the sky.

They wouldn't have the light much longer.

"Angie, come on—let's film you."

"Please—you know the stories so well. Let me film you this time."

"They're your books."

"But you'll give me a great authenticity. I'll interview you—and you were here when the last crime occurred. I'm surprised they haven't hacked this sucker to the ground, really," Angie said, looking at the tree. "Or at the very least, they should have video surveillance out here."

"Now, that would be the right idea. They have video surveillance in the lobby, the elevators—and other areas."

"But for now, please?"

They were never going to be able to leave.

"All right, all right!" Maura said. She adjusted the camera on its lightweight tripod and looked at the image on the camera's viewing screen. "I've got it lined up already. I'll go right there. You need to get it rolling. The mic is on already, and you can see what you're filming."

"Hey, I've used it before—not a lot, but I kind of know what I'm doing," Angie reminded her.

Maura stepped away from the camera and headed over to the tree. Angie had paid attention to her. She lifted her fingers and said, "In three..." and then went silent, counting down the rest by hand.

Maura was amazed at how quickly it all came back to her. She told the tale of the beautiful Gyselle and then went into the later crimes.

Ending, of course, with the murder of Francine Renault.

"A false lead caused the arrest of an innocent young man. But this is America, and we all know that any man is innocent until proved guilty, and this young man was quickly proved innocent. He was only under arrest for a night, because eyewitness reports confirmed he was with several other people—busy at work—when the crime took place. Still, it was a travesty, shattering a great deal of the promise of the young man's life. He was, however, as I said, quickly released—and until this day, the crime goes unsolved."

She finished speaking and saw that Angie was still running the camera, looking past her, appearing perplexed—and pleased—by something that she saw.

"Hello there! Are you with Frampton Ranch and Resort? You aren't, by any chance, the host for the campfire stories tonight, are you?"

Angie was smiling sweetly—having shifted into her flirtatious mode.

Curious, Maura turned around and started toward the path.

If a jaw could actually drop, hers did.

She quickly closed her mouth, but perhaps her eyes were bulging, as well. It seemed almost as if someone had physically knocked the breath from her.

Brock McGovern was standing there.

Different.

The same.

A bit taller than he'd been at eighteen; his shoulders had filled out and he appeared to have acquired a great deal more solid muscle. He filled out a dark blue suit and tailored shirt exceptionally well.

His face was the same...

Different.

There was something hard about him now that hadn't been there before. His features were leaner, his eyes...

Still deep brown. But they were harder now, too, or appeared to be harder, as if there was a shield of glass on them. He'd always walked and moved with purpose, confident in what he wanted and where he was going.

Now, just standing still, he was an imposing presence.

And though Angie had spoken, he was looking at Maura.

"Wow," Angie said softly. "Did I dream up the perfect assistant for you—tall, dark and to die for? Who the hell... The storyteller guy is wickedly cute, but this guy..."

He couldn't have heard her words; he wasn't close enough.

And he wasn't looking at her. He was staring at Maura.

"That was great," he said smoothly. "However, I don't consider my life to have been *shattered*. I mean— I hope I have fulfilled a few of the promises I made to myself."

Maura wanted to speak. Her mouth wouldn't work.

Angie, however, had no problem.

"Oh, my God!" Angie cried.

Every once in a while, her Valley girl came out.

"You—you're Brock McGovern?" she asked.

"I am," he said, but he still wasn't looking at Angie. He was locked on Maura. Then he smiled. A rueful smile, dry and maybe even a little bitter.

"Here—in Florida," Angie said. "I mean—at the History Tree."

He turned at last to face Angie. "I'm here for an investigation now. I'm going to suggest that you two head back to the resort and don't wander off alone. A woman's remains were found at a laundry facility not far from here, and there are three young women who have gone missing recently. Best to stay in the main areas—with plenty of people around."

"Oh!" Angie went into damsel-in-distress mode then. "Is it really dangerous, do you think? I'm so glad that you're here, if there is danger. I mean, we've seen the news…heard things, but seriously, bad things aren't necessarily happening here, right? It's just a tree. Florida is far from crime-free, but… Anyway, thank God that you're here. We didn't really think we needed to be afraid, but now you're here…and thank God! Right, Maura?"

Maura didn't reply. She'd heard Angie speaking as if she'd been far, far away. Then she found her voice. Or, at least, a whisper of it.

"Brock," she murmured.

"Maura," he returned casually. "Good to see you. Well, surprised to see you—but good to see you."

"Investigation," she said, grasping for something to say. She seemed to be able to manage one word at a time.

"I just told you—they found a woman's remains, and

three young women who have been reported missing had a connection to the Frampton Ranch and Resort. The FDLE has asked for Bureau help," he explained politely.

"Yes, we were just talking about the young woman's remains—and the missing girls. I, uh, I think I'd heard that you did go into the FBI," she said. "And they sent you…here." There. She had spoken in complete sentences. More or less. She'd been almost comprehensible.

"Yes, pretty much followed my original plans. Navy, college, the academy—FBI. And yes, I'm back here. Nothing like sending in an agent who knows the terrain," he said. "Shall we head back? I am serious. You shouldn't be in the woods alone when…well, when no one has any idea of what is really going on. We're not trying to incite fear. We're just trying to get a grip on what is happening, but I do suggest caution. Shall we head back?"

He was the same.

He was different.

And she was afraid to come too close to him. Afraid that the emotions of a teenager would erupt within her again, as if the years meant nothing…

If she got too close, she would either want to beat upon him, slamming her fists against his chest, demanding to know why he had never called, never tried to reach her and how it had been so easy to forget her.

Either that, or she would throw herself into his arms and sob and do anything just to touch him again.

Chapter 2

"The soil—clay based, some sand—like that covers most of the north of the state," Rachel Lawrence said.

She was seated across from Brock with Michael Flannery in the Java Bar on the Frampton property.

Rachel had changed. Her nails were cut short, clean of any color. Her hair was shorter, too. She still wore bangs, but her dark tresses were attractively trimmed to slide in angles along her face.

Everything about her appearance was serviceable. The girl who had once cried over a broken nail or scuffed sneakers had made an about-face.

She had greeted Brock politely and gravely, and seemed—like Flannery—to be anxious to have him working on the case with them.

"There's the beginning of a task force rumbling around," she'd told him when they'd first met in the coffee bar. "I'm lucky to be working with Michael Flannery—very lucky. But at this moment, while our superiors are listening, and they were willing to accept FBI involvement, they don't necessarily all believe that we are looking at a serial killer and this situation is about to blow up and get out of hand. It's great to have another officer who knows the lay of the land, so to speak."

"Yes, I do know it. And I've got to say, Rachel, I'm happy to see that you are working for the FDLE—and that you're so pleased to be where you are."

She made a face. "Oh, well, there was a time when I thought I wanted to be rich and elite, own a teacup Yorkie in a designer handbag and be supported in fine fashion. But I do love what I do. Oh—I actually do have a teacup Yorkie. Love the little guy!"

It had been far easier to meet back up with Rachel—and even Nils and Mark Hartford—than Brock had expected.

Time.

It healed all wounds, right?

Wrong. Why not? He believed he was, as far as any normal psychology went, long over what had happened regarding his arrest for murder at such a young age—he'd barely been in jail before his parents arrived with their attorney, his dad so indignant that the icy chill in his eyes might have gotten Brock released before the attorney even opened his mouth.

Truly, he had seen and heard far worse in the navy. And, God knew, some of the cases he'd handled as an agent in a criminal investigation unit had certainly been enough to chill the blood.

Still…the haunting memories regarding the forest and the History Tree clung to him like the moss that dripped from the old oaks.

"A Yorkie, huh?" he asked Rachel, remembering that she was there.

They both grinned, and he assured her that he liked dogs, all dogs, and didn't have one himself only because it wouldn't be fair to the animal—he was always working.

Rachel went on with the information—or lack of it—that she had worked to obtain.

"Some of our elegant hotels have special bedding, but…lots don't. The sheets around the remains might have come from five different chain hotels that cover North Florida, Central Florida and the Panhandle, all of which have twenty to forty local franchises. That means that Maureen Rodriguez might have been murdered anywhere in all that area—buried first nearby or somewhere different within the boundaries—and then dug up and wrapped in sheets."

"You checked with the truck drivers making deliveries that day, naturally?" Brock asked her.

She gave him a look that was both amused and withering. "I did go to college—and I majored in criminology. I'm not just a piece of fluff, you know."

Detective Michael Flannery grunted. "She's tailing me—I'm teaching her everything I know. And," he added, "how not to make the same mistakes."

Brock nodded his appreciation for the comment and asked, "Were you able to narrow it down by the drivers and their deliveries?"

"The way it works is that they pick up when they

drop off," Rachel said. "So it's not as if they're kept separately. It's almost like recycling receptacles—the hotels have these massive canvas bags. The sheets are all the same, so they drop off dirty and pick up clean replacements. The laundry is also responsible for getting rid of sheets that are too worn, too stained, too whatever. But the driver drop-offs do narrow it down to hotels from St. Augustine to Gainesville and down to northern Ocala. I have a list of them, which I've emailed and…" She paused, reaching into her bag for a small folder that she presented to Brock. "Here—hard copy."

He looked at the list. There were at least thirty hotels with their addresses listed.

"All right, thank you," he told her. "I'd like to start by talking to Katie Simmons—the woman who reported Lydia Merkel missing. And then the last person to see each of the missing young women."

"Cops have interviewed all of them. I saw Katie Simmons myself," Flannery told him. "I'm not sure what else you can get from her."

"Humor me. And this list—I'd like you to get state officers out with images of all the women. Let's see what they get—they'll tell us if they find anyone who has seen any of them or thinks they might have seen someone like them. We need the images plastered everywhere—a Good Samaritan could call in and let us know if they saw one of the women walking on the street, buying gas…at a bar or a restaurant."

"The images have been broadcast," Flannery said. "I asked for you, but come on. We're not a bunch of dumb hicks down here, you know."

Brock grinned. "I'm a Fed, remember?"

Flannery shrugged. "You're a conch," he reminded Brock, referring to the moniker given to Key West natives.

"I get you, but I'm not referring to local news. I mean, we need likenesses of the young women—all four of them—out everywhere. We need to draw on media across the state and beyond. And we need to get them up in all the colleges—there are several of them in the area. All four of the women were college age—they might have friends just about anywhere. They might have met up with someone at a party."

"I'll get officers on the hotels and take the colleges with Rachel. She and I can head in opposite directions and cover more ground." Flannery hesitated. "I've arranged for us to see the ME first thing, so we'll start all else after that—I assumed you wanted to see the remains of Maureen Rodriguez."

"Yes, and thank you," Brock told him. "Do I meet you at the morgue?"

"No, we'll head out together—if that's all right with you. I have a room here and so does Rachel. I'm setting mine up as a headquarters," Flannery said. "I'll start a whiteboard—that way, we can keep up with any information any of us acquires and have it in plain sight, as we'd be doing if we were running the investigation out of one of our offices."

"A good plan," Brock said. "But tomorrow I would like to get started over in St. Augustine as quickly as possible."

"All right, then. We will take two cars tomorrow morning. Compare notes back here, say, late afternoon. Get in touch sooner if we have something that seems of real significance. It's good that you decided to be based here. Easier than trying to come and go."

Flannery hesitated, looking at Brock. Then he shrugged. "Mr. Glass actually came to me." He lowered his voice, even though there was no one near them. "On the hush-hush. Said his wife didn't even know. Seems he's afraid himself that someone is using this place or the legends that go with it."

Brock drained his cup of coffee. "Can you set me up with Katie Simmons for some time tomorrow?" he asked Rachel.

"Yes, sir, I can and will," she assured him. "She's in St. Augustine."

Brock stood.

They looked up at him.

"And now?" Flannery asked.

"You wanted me here because I know the place," Brock said. "I'm going to watch a couple of the people that I knew when I worked here. See what's changed— and who has changed and how. I'm not leaving the property tonight. If there's anything, call me. And I'll check in later."

"You're going to the campfire tales and ghost walk?" Flannery asked.

"Not exactly—but kind of," Brock said. He nodded to the two of them and headed out, glancing at his watch.

He did know the place, that was certain. Almost nothing on the grounds had changed.

His father had heard about the place—that it was a great venue for young people to work for the summer during high school. There was basic housing for them, a section of rooms for girls and one for boys. They weren't allowed off the grounds unless they had turned eighteen or they were supervised; any dereliction of the rules called for immediate dismissal. The positions were highly prized—if anyone broke the rules, they were damned careful not to be caught.

Of course, fraternizing—as in sex—had not been in the rules.

Kids were kids.

But with him and Maura...

It had felt like something more than kids being kids.

He still believed it. He wondered if, just somewhere in her mind, she believed it, too.

Mark Hartford proved to be excellent at telling the stories—despite the fact that he'd told Maura that he was afraid that night. Well, not afraid but nervous.

"You were so good!" he had said to Maura when he saw that she and Angie were going to be in his audience. "So good!"

He'd been just about fourteen when she knew him years before; he had to be about twenty-five or twenty-six now. He'd grown up, of course, and he still charmed with a boyish energy and enthusiasm that was contagious. His eyes were bright blue and his hair—just slightly shaggy—was a tawny blond. He'd grown several inches since Maura had seen him, and he evidently made use of the resort's gym.

Angie was entranced by Mark. But she'd always been unabashed about her appreciation of men in general— especially when they were attractive. Maura didn't consider herself to be particularly suspicious of the world in general, but she did find that she often felt much older and wiser when she was with Angie—warning her that it wasn't always good to be quite so friendly with every good-looking man that she met.

"I'm sure you're just as good a storyteller," Angie had told Mark.

"I try—I have a lot to live up to," he'd said in return, answering Angie, smiling from one of them to the other.

Maura was somewhat pleased by the distraction. Angie had been talking incessantly about Brock and she'd finally stopped—long enough to do a new assessment of Mark Hartford.

She had decided that she liked young Mark Hartford very much, as well.

They'd already seen Nils in the restaurant. Mark and Nils were easily identifiable as brothers, but Mark's evident curiosity and sincere interest in everyone and everything around him made him the more naturally charming of the two.

"Ooh, I do like both brothers. But the other guy…the FBI guy… Hey, he was the one they arrested—and he turned out to be FBI! Cool. I appreciate them all, but that Brock guy…sexier—way sexier," Angie had said.

Actually, Maura found Angie's honesty one of the nicest things about her. She said what she was thinking or feeling pretty much all the time.

Now the tales were underway. Mark was telling them well. Maura allowed herself to survey his audience.

There were—as there had always been, so it seemed—a group of young teens, some together, some with their parents. There were couples, wives or girlfriends hanging on to their men, and sometimes a great guy admittedly frightened by the dark and tales and hanging on to his girlfriend or wife or boyfriend or husband, as well. There were young men and women, older men and women—a group of about twenty-five or thirty in all.

She couldn't help but remember how her group had been about the same size that night twelve years ago— and how they had all reacted when they reached the History Tree.

She had screamed—so had several people.

Some had laughed—certain that the swinging body was a prop and perhaps part of a gag set up by the establishment to throw a bit of real scare into the evening.

And then had come the frantic 911 calls, the horror as everyone realized that the dead woman was real and Brock trying to herd people away and, even then, trying to see that the scene wasn't trampled, that as a crime scene it wasn't disturbed...

Only to be arrested himself.

Tonight, Maura had her camera; she also had waivers signed by everyone in the group. She'd been lucky that night—everyone had been happy to meet her and Angie and they all wanted their fifteen minutes of fame. They were fine with being on camera with Angie Parsons.

They were still by the campfire.

She was thinking about Brock.

Determining how much she was going to video after Mark's speech, she looked across the campfire to the place where the trees edged around the fire and the storyteller and his audience.

Brock was leaning against a tree, arms crossed over his chest, listening.

He was no longer wearing a suit; he was in jeans

and a plaid flannel shirt—he could pass himself off as a logger or such. Her heart seemed to do a little leap and she was angry at herself, angry that she could still find him so compellingly attractive.

Twelve years between them. Not a word. They weren't even friends on social media.

He must have sensed her looking at him. She realized that his gaze had changed direction; he was looking at her across the distance.

He nodded slightly and then frowned, shaking his head.

He didn't want to be on camera; she nodded.

She turned away, dismissing him.

She tried to focus on the words that Mark Hartford was saying.

The stories were the same. Until they came to the History Tree.

There, a new story had been added in. Mark talked about the tour that had come upon Francine Renault.

He wasn't overly dramatic; he told the facts, and admitted that, yes, he had been among those who had found her.

The story ended with the death of the cook, Peter Moore, who had stabbed himself and been found in the freezer, his favorite knife protruding from his chest.

A fight had gone too far, or so the authorities believed, and Moore had killed Francine. And then later, in remorse or fear that prison would be worse than death, he had committed suicide.

On that tragic note, the story of the History Tree ended. As did the nightly tour.

Mark then told his group that they needed to head

back—there had been some trouble in the area lately and the management would appreciate it if guests refrained from being in the forest at night and suggested that no one wander the woods alone.

As they began to filter back, Maura saw that Brock didn't go with the others.

She might have been the only one to note his presence; he had apparently followed silently at a bit of a distance, always staying back within the trees.

She turned when the group left. As they headed back along the trail, Brock stepped from his silent watching spot in the darkness of the surrounding foliage. He walked to the History Tree.

He stood silently, staring up at it, as if seeking some answer there.

Mark was asking if the tourists wanted coffee or tea or a drink before they called it a night.

Angie had already said yes.

Maura turned away from Brock purposefully and followed Angie and Mark. Once they reached the lodge, she would beg off.

All she wanted to do that night was crawl into a hole somewhere and black out.

Her room and her bed would have to do—even if she didn't black out and lay awake for hours, ever more furious with herself that she was allowing herself to feel…

Anything about him. Anything at all.

"I've seen some strange things in my day," Rita Morgan, the medical examiner, said. She was a tall, lean woman, looked to be about forty-five and certainly the no-nonsense type.

"Many a strange thing, and some not so strange. Too many bodies out of the ocean and the rivers, a few in barrels, some sunk with cement." She pursed her lips, shaking her head. "This one? Strange and sad. As long as I've done this, been an ME, it still never ceases to amaze me—man's inhumanity to fellow man." She looked up at Brock and Flannery and shook her head again. "Thing that saves me is when I see a young person get up and help the disabled or the elderly—then I get to know that there's as much good out there as bad— more, hopefully. Yeah, yeah, that doesn't help you any. I just… Well, I can show you the remains. I can't tell you too much about them. No stomach content—no stomach. I had disarticulated bones with small amounts of flesh still attached—and a skull."

She stepped back to display the gurney that held the remains of a young woman's life, tragically—and brutally—cut short.

"It looks as if she was killed a long time ago— but from my brief, she was only missing about three months," Brock said, looking from Flannery to the medical examiner.

And then to the table.

Bits of hair and scalp still adhered to the skull.

"Decomposition is one of those things that can vary incredibly. I believe she was killed approximately two months ago. Particular to situations like this, the internal organs began to deteriorate twenty-four to seventy-two hours after death. The number of bacteria and insects in the area have an effect on the outer body and soft tissue. Three to five days—you have bloating. Within ten days, insects, the elements and bacteria have been busy and you have massive accumulations of gas. Within a few weeks, nails and teeth begin to go. After a month, the body becomes fluid."

"The skull retains a mouthful of teeth," Brock noted.

"Yes, which is why I believe decomp had the best possible circumstances. Lots of earth—and water. Rain, maybe. Even flooding in the area where the body was first left. As I said, there's no way to pinpoint an exact time of death. It's approximately two months' time. I also believe, per decomp, that she was left out in the elements—maybe a bit of dirt and some leaves were shoveled over her. It's been a warm winter, and the soil here can be rich—and as we all know, this is Florida. We have plenty of insects.

"The question is, after all that decomp in the wild, how in the world did she come to be in sheets at an industrial laundry? But that's your problem. Mine is cause of death. Not much to go on, as you can see, but enough." She pointed with a gloved hand. "That rib bone. You can see. The scraping there wasn't any insect—that was caused by a sharp blade. There's a second such mark on that rib—would have been the other side of the rear rib cage. In my educated estimation, she was stabbed to death. Without more tissue or organs I can't tell you how many wounds she sustained—exactly how many times she was stabbed—but I do imagine the attack would have been brutal, and that she probably suffered mortal damage to many of her organs. There's no damage to the skull."

"Were there any defensive wounds you were able to find on the arm bones?" Brock asked.

Flannery was standing back, letting Brock ask his

own questions, since the detective had already seen the remains and spoken with the ME earlier.

"No, there were no defensive wounds, Special Agent McGovern," Dr. Morgan said. "She was stabbed from behind. She might never have seen her killer. Or she might have trusted him—or her. It was a violent assault, I can tell you that. But—I am assuming that she didn't want to be stabbed to death—she had to have been taken by surprise. She never had a chance to fight back at all. Some of what I've been saying I'm assuming, but I am making assumptions based on education and experience. I'm the ME—you guys are the detectives. Can't help having an opinion."

"Of course, that's fine, and thank you," Brock said. "The sheets are at the lab? Still being tested?"

"Yes. They can't pinpoint the sheets to a certain hotel because too many of them buy from the same supplier."

She covered the remains.

She looked at Brock curiously, studying him. Then she smiled broadly. "You came out all right, it seems." She glanced over at Flannery. "Despite what you did to him."

"Hey, I acted on the best info I had at the time," Flannery said.

"Rash—hey, he was a newbie at the time. Didn't know his—oh, never mind. But good to see you—as a law enforcement officer, Agent McGovern."

"Well, thank you. I'm sorry, did we meet before?" he asked her.

She shook her head. "I was new in this office. But I assisted at the autopsies for both Francine Renault and the cook, Peter Moore..." She left off, shrugging. "I knew that they'd brought you in—one of the summer kids. Because you were seen in some kind of major verbal altercation with her. And arrested, from what I understand, on a *tip*."

She didn't exactly sniff, but she did look at Detective Flannery with a bit of disdain.

"I say again, I acted on the best info I had at the time. And yeah—I guess he came out all right," Flannery said with something that sounded a bit like a growl in his voice. He eyed Brock, as if not entirely sure about him yet.

"I spent only one night in jail. Trust me, I spent many a worse night in the service," he assured Dr. Morgan and Flannery.

Flannery looked away, uncomfortable. Dr. Morgan smiled.

"Thank you," he told her. "If there's anything else that comes to mind that might be of any assistance whatsoever..."

"I'll be quicker than a rabbit in heat," she vowed solemnly.

He arched his brows slightly but managed a smile and another thank-you.

Brock and Flannery left the county morgue together. They'd come in Flannery's official vehicle; it would allow them to bypass heavy traffic if needed, Flannery had said.

Brock preferred to drive himself, but that day, while Flannery drove, it gave him a chance to look through his notes on the victim.

"She stayed at the Frampton Ranch and Resort three months ago," he murmured out loud. "Her home was St.

Pete. She wasn't reported missing right away because she was over eighteen and had been living alone in St. Augustine, working as a cocktail waitress—but hadn't shown up for work in over a week. Says here none of her coworkers really knew her—she had just started."

"The perfect victim," Flannery said. He glanced sideways at Brock. "The other missing girls… You have the information on them, too, right?"

"Yeah, I have it online and on paper. I have to hand it to Egan. He believes in hard copy and there are times it proves to be especially beneficial."

"And saves on eyestrain," Flannery muttered. He glanced Brock's way again. "You know, I asked for you specifically. Hope you don't mind too much. Can't help it. Still think there's something with that damned resort, even if I can't pin it. Well, I mean, back then, of course, it had to do with the ranch. Francine Renault worked there—and died there. But…that tree has seen a lot of death."

He said it oddly, almost as if he was in awe of the tree. Brock frowned, looking over at him. Flannery didn't glance his way, but apparently knew he was being studied.

"Well, bad stuff happens there," Flannery said.

"Right—because bad people like the aspect that bad things happened there."

"You think it should be chopped down."

"It might dissuade future killers."

"Or just cause them to leave their victims somewhere else," Flannery said. "Or create a new History Tree or haunted bog or…just a damnable stretch of roadway."

"True," Brock agreed.

"What drives me crazy is the why—I mean, we all study this stuff. Some killers are simply goal driven—they want or need someone out of the way. Some killings have to do with passion and anger and jealousy. Some have to do with money. Some people are psychotic and kill for the thrill or the sexual release it gives them. Years ago, it was just Francine. Now, that Francine—I didn't find a single soul who actually said they liked her, but it never seemed she'd done anything bad enough to make someone want to kill her. She seemed to be more of an annoyance—like a fly buzzing around your ear."

"Maybe she was a really, really annoying fly—buzzing at the wrong person," Brock said. Then he reminded the detective, "Peter Moore committed suicide. There was no note—but maybe he did do it, because he was afraid of being apprehended, or felt overwhelming remorse or was dealing with an untreated mental illness that led him down a very dark path. Seems to me that everyone accepted the fact that he must have done it—though he sure as hell didn't get his day in court."

Flannery glanced his way at last. "But you don't think that Peter Moore killed Francine any more than I do."

Brock hesitated and then said flatly, "No. And I knew Peter Moore. He hated Francine, but he held his own with her—he didn't really have to answer to her. He was directly under Fred Bentley. I don't think he killed Francine. I don't even think that Peter Moore killed himself."

Flannery nodded. "There you go—see? There was a reason I needed you down here. Damn, though, if it doesn't seem like homecoming somehow."

"What do you mean?"

"I mean, I can't just buy the theory that Peter Moore did it, either. In my mind, the killer might have helped him into that so-called suicide. No prints but Peter's on the knife in his gut, but hell, the kitchen is filled with gloves."

"So it is."

"That beauty is back, as well," Flannery said, glancing his way once again.

Brock didn't ask who Flannery meant. That was dead obvious. Maura.

"Did you ask her up here?" Brock asked him.

"Me?" Flannery was truly surprised. "I barely met her back in the day, and she was fairly rattled when I did… Well, you were there. You didn't ask for her to be here? I'd have thought, at least, that the two of you would still be friends. You were hot and heavy back then, so I heard—the beautiful young ones!"

"I hadn't seen her since that night until I saw her again late yesterday afternoon—out by the tree."

"Ah, yes, she's with that web queen or writer—or whatever that little woman calls herself," Flannery said. He looked over at Brock. "Is that what they call serendipity?"

Brock didn't reply. He was looking at his portfolios on the missing women. He'd already read through them on the plane, but talking things out could reveal new angles.

"All right," Brock said. "Maureen Rodriguez was out of the house and just starting a new life. So she wasn't noted as missing right away. But Lily Sylvester was supposed to check in with her boyfriend. She'd come to the Frampton ranch because she wanted to see it. She stayed at a little hotel on the outskirts of St. Augustine one night after her visit, and then she was supposed to meet with a girlfriend at a posh bed-and-breakfast in the old section of the city. She never showed that day and her friend called the cops right away."

He flipped through his folders.

"Friends and family were insistent about Lily," Flannery told him. "She was as dependable as they come. Is," he added. "We shouldn't assume the worst."

But it was natural that they did.

"All right, moving on to Amy Bonham. She stayed at the Frampton ranch. She told one of the waitresses that she was excited about a surprise job opportunity the next day. She was supposed to be heading in the other direction—toward Orlando and the theme parks. She also stayed at a chain motel the night right after she was at the Frampton ranch and disappeared the next day. I know you certainly looked into her 'job opportunity.'"

Flannery nodded. "We've had officers interviewing people across more than half the state."

"But no one knew anything about it."

"No. But the waitress at the Frampton ranch—Dorothy Masterson swears that Amy was super excited. Dorothy believed that she was looking for work at one of the theme parks."

"And you checked with all the parks."

"Of course. Big and small."

Brock went on to his third folder. "Lydia Merkel."

Flannery nodded; he'd already committed to memory most of what Brock was still studying.

"Lydia. Cute as a button."

"You met her? You knew her?" Brock asked, frowning.

"I met her briefly—I was in St. Augustine. The wife had her nephews down and I was taking them on one of the ghost tours. Lydia was on our tour. All wide eyes and happiness. Can't tell you how stunned I was when the powers that be called me in and told me that we had another missing woman—and that I recognized her." He glanced quickly at Brock. "You know how it goes with missing persons reports. Half of the time someone is just off on a lark. There's been a fight—a person has taken off because they want to disappear. But I just don't think that's the case." He was silent. "Especially since we found the remains of Maureen Rodriguez."

"And you can't help but think that Frampton Ranch and Resort is somehow involved."

Flannery nodded grimly.

"Lydia had told a young woman she was working with—Katie Simmons—that she wanted to take her first days off to drive over and see the History Tree. We're not just working this alone. I have all kinds of help on this. We do have officers from the Florida Department of Law Enforcement out all over—not to mention the help we've gotten from our local police departments. I keep feeling like I'm looking at some kind of puzzle with pieces missing—except that the frame is there. Because there was only one thing the girls—or young women—had in common."

"They had left or were coming to the Frampton Ranch and Resort," Brock said.

He felt a sudden pang deep in his heart or maybe his soul—someplace that really hurt at any rate.

He glanced over at Flannery. "The four of them

are between the ages of twenty-two and twenty-nine," he said.

"Lydia Merkel was—is—twenty-nine. On the tour, she talked about loving ghost stories—and how excited she was going to be to see the infamous History Tree."

Seriously—the tree should have been bulldozed.

Not fair—the tree wasn't guilty. Men and women could be guilty; the tree was just a tree—two trees.

"Funny, isn't it?" Flannery asked. "I mean, not ha ha funny, just…strange. Maybe ironic. The History Tree is two trees. Entwined. And you're here—because I asked for you particularly because I knew you were FBI, criminal section—and I'm here. And Miss Maura Antrim is here. We're all kinds of entwined. And I can't help but think that we still know the killer—even if twelve years have gone by."

"Yep. We're all tangled together somehow, like that damned tree. And so help me God, this time I really want to have the answers…and to stop the killing," Brock said quietly.

"You don't disagree with me?" Flannery asked him.

Brock shrugged grimly.

"But you don't disagree—you don't think I'm being far-fetched or anything?" Flannery pressed.

"No, I just wonder what this person—if it is the same killer—has been doing for twelve years," Brock said. And then added, "Although…maybe he hasn't been lying dormant. It's a big state filled with just about everything in one area or another. Forests, marshes, caverns, sinkholes, the Everglades—a river of grass—and, of course…"

"That great big old Atlantic Ocean," Flannery said.

"So, there you go. My puzzle. Are there pieces missing? Did the three young ladies who disappeared just run off? Or…"

"Has someone been killing young women and disposing of corpses over the last twelve years?" Brock finished. He took a deep breath. "All right, I guess I'm going to do a lot of traveling. There will be dozens of people to question again. But I think I'll start at the library at Frampton ranch."

Angie was a late sleeper, something Maura deeply appreciated the next morning. She wanted some on-her-own time.

She had gotten a lot of great footage for Angie's internet channel on the tour the night before.

Mark had ended up loving being on camera—and it had loved him. They were going to do the campfire again that night, get more video and put together all the best parts.

She'd behaved perfectly normally, even though she was ready to crawl out of her own skin. While on the tour, she'd expected to see Brock materialize again.

It hadn't been until the very end that she'd realized he'd been there all along—watching from the shadows, from the background.

But he'd never approached her. She'd seen him later in the lounge, briefly, when she and Angie walked in after the trek through the woods. He'd been deep in conversation with a slightly older man in a suit—she'd seen him earlier and remembered him vaguely. He was a cop of some kind; he'd been there the night that Francine Renault was killed. She had seen him earlier in the day as well, walking around the ranch with a woman. Maura hadn't seen the woman's face, just the cut of her suit, and for some bizarre reason she had noticed the woman's shoes. Flat, serviceable.

And she'd thought that perhaps the woman was a cop or in some form of law enforcement, too.

Angie hadn't seemed interested in talking to any of them—Maura had been glad. She'd left Angie in the lounge, waiting for her appointed drink with Mark, and Maura had slipped quickly upstairs, wanting nothing more than to be in her room, alone.

Once there, she'd lain awake for hours, wondering why something that had happened ages ago still had such an effect on her life—on her.

Why... Brock McGovern could suddenly walk back into her life and become all that she thought about once again. So easily. Or why she could close her eyes and see the man he had become and know that he was still somehow flawed and perfect, the man to whom she had subconsciously—or even consciously—compared to everyone else she ever met.

He hadn't so much as touched her.

And he hadn't looked at her as if he particularly liked her. He'd simply wanted her—and Angie—to be safe. Nothing more. Stay with people. He was a law enforcement officer, a Fed. He worked to find those who had turned living, breathing bodies into murdered, decaying bodies—and he tried to keep all men and women from being victims. His job. What he did.

A job he always knew he wanted.

She had to stop thinking about him, and that meant

she needed to immerse herself in some other activity—
research. Books, knowledge, seeking...

She had always loved the library and archives at
the Frampton ranch. One thing Donald Glass did with
every property he bought was build and maintain a library with any books and info he had on that property.
It was fascinating—much of it had been put on computer through the years, but every little event that had
to do with the property was available.

The hotel manager—solid, ruddy little Fred Bentley—had never shown any interest in the contents of
the library.

Nor, when she'd been alive, had Francine Renault.
But the libraries were sacred. No matter what else the
very, very rich Donald Glass might be, he loved his
history and his libraries, and anyone working for him
learned not to mess with them.

For this, she greatly admired Glass. Not that she
knew the man well—he'd left the hands-on management to Francine and Fred when Maura had been working there. And back then, she and Brock had both spent
hours in the library—often together—each trying to
one-up the other by finding some obscure and curious
fact or happening. It was fun to work the weird trivia
into their presentations.

That had been twelve years ago.

But Brock was suddenly back in her life.

No, he wasn't in her life. He just happened to be here
at the same time.

Because a woman had been murdered—and others
had disappeared.

Concentrate... There was a wealth of information

before her. Bits and pieces that might offer up something especially unusual for Angie Parsons.

The library room was comfortable and inviting, filled with leather sofas and chairs, desks, computers—and shelves upon shelves of files and books.

Donald Glass had acquired an extensive collection; he had books on the indigenous population of the area, starting back somewhere between twelve and twenty thousand years ago. Settlers had arrived before the end of the Pleistocene megafauna era. The Wacissa River—not far away in Jefferson County near the little town of Wacissa—had offered up several animal fossils of the time, and other areas of the state—including Silver Springs, Vero, Melbourne and Devil's Den—had also offered up proof of man's earliest time in the area.

Way back that many thousands of years, there had been a greater landmass and less water, causing animals—and thus hunters—to congregate at pools. Artifacts proving the existence of these hunter-gatherers could be found in countless rivers—and even out into the Gulf of Mexico.

Mammoths had even roamed the state.

By 700 AD, farming had come to the north of Florida. There were many Native American tribes, and many of those were called Creek by the Europeans and spoke the Muskogee language. But by the time the first Frampton put down roots to create this great ranching and farming estate, Florida Indians of many varieties—though mostly Creek—were being lumped together as Seminoles, largely divided into two groups: the Muskogee-speaking and the Hitchiti-speaking.

There were wonderful illustrated books describing

fossils and tools found, creating images of the people and the way they lived.

According to the one she pulled from the shelf there had been a colony of Seminole living in the area when Frampton first chose his site.

They had held rites out at what was already a giant clearing in the forest. It was the Native Americans who had first called it the History Tree. The Timucua had first named it so; the Seminoles in the area had respected the holiness of the tree.

Maura—like the writer of the book—didn't believe that the Native American tribes had practiced human sacrifice at the tree. But as war loomed with the Seminole tribe, the European populace had liked to portray the native people as barbarians—it made it easier to justify killing them.

So the tree had gotten its reputation very early on.

Gyselle—who became known as Gyselle Frampton, since no one knew her real surname—had arrived at the plantation soon after it was built in the late 1830s. Spanish missionaries had "rescued" her from the Seminole, but she was fifteen at the time and had been kidnapped at the age of ten—or that was the best that could be figured. Oliver Frampton—creator of the first great mansion to rest on the property—had been a kind man. He'd taken her in, clothed her, educated her and had still, of course, given her chores to do.

She was a servant and not of the elite. She was not, in any way, wife material for his son.

That hadn't stopped Richard Frampton from falling in love with his father's beautiful servant/ward.

But Richard had underestimated his wife. Back then,

a wife was supposed to be a lovely figurehead, wealthy to match her husband and eye candy on the arm of her man. Unless she was very, very, very rich—and then it wouldn't matter if she was eye candy or not.

But Julie LeBlanc Frampton had been no fool and not someone to be taken lightly.

She discovered the affair—and knew that her husband loved Gyselle deeply. Perhaps she was angry with her father-in-law for not only condoning the affair but perhaps finding it to be fine and natural. Wives weren't supposed to get in the way of these things after all.

Or maybe the situation was just convenient for her plan.

She hid the taste of the deadly fruit of the manchineel tree in a drink—one that Gyselle usually made up for the senior Mr. Frampton right before he went to bed made up of whiskey, tea and sugar.

The old man died in horrible pain. Julie immediately pointed the finger at Gyselle.

She created such an outcry and hysteria that the other servants immediately went for poor Gyselle. The master had been well loved. And without trial or even much questioning, they had dragged Gyselle out to the History Tree—thought to surely be haunted at that time and also a place where the devil might well be found.

Gyselle died swearing that she was innocent—and cursing Julie, those around her and even the tree.

After she was hanged, she was allowed to remain there until she rotted, until her bones fell to the ground.

Three years later, Julie Frampton died. At the time no one knew what her ailment was—tuberculosis, it sounded like to Maura.

But in the end, the true poisoner did die choking on her own blood—and confessing to the entire room that she had murdered her father-in-law.

"Maura!"

She had become so involved in what she was reading that the sound of her name made her jump.

She'd been very comfortable in one of the plush leather chairs, feet curled beneath her, the book—*Truth and Legends of Central Florida*—in her arms.

Luckily, she didn't drop it or throw it as she was startled. It was an original book, printed and bound in 1880.

"Mr. Glass!" she exclaimed, truly startled to see the resort's owner. He usually kept to himself; Fred Bentley was his mouthpiece.

She quickly closed the book and stood, accepting the hand he offered to her.

Donald Glass, in his early sixties now, Maura thought, was still an attractive man. He kept himself lean and fit—and had maintained a full head of salt-and-pepper hair. His posture was straight; his manners tended to be impeccable. He'd never personally fired anyone that she knew of, in any of his enterprises. He left managers—like Fred Bentley—to do such deeds. He was customarily well liked and treated kindly by magazines when he was included in an article.

Donald Glass used his money to make more money, granted. That was the American way. But he did it all in one of the best possible manners—preserving history and donating to worthy causes all the while.

Whether he was into the causes or simply into tax breaks, no one really looked too closely.

But he tended to do good things and do them well.

"Miss Antrim, how lovely to have you here again," he said, smiling. "And I'm delighted that you've brought Angie Parsons with her incredible ability to show the world interesting places—and provide wonderful publicity for those places!"

"I'd love to take the credit, Mr. Glass," Maura told him. "Angie heard the story about the History Tree. She couldn't wait to come."

"Well, however you came to be here, I'm most delighted. Still sorry—and I will be sorry all my life—about Francine. She was..."

He paused. Maura wondered what he'd been about to say. That Francine Renault had been a good woman? But she really hadn't been kind or generous in any way.

"No one deserved to die that way," he said. "Anyway... I did consider having the tree torn out of the ground. But I thought on it a long time and decided that it was the *History Tree*. They didn't burn down the building when a famous woman died in a room at the Hard Rock in Hollywood, Florida, and..." Again, he paused. "I decided that the tree—or trees—should stay. Not to mention the fact that the environmentalists and preservationists would create a real uproar if we were to cut it down. It's hundreds of years old, you know. And yes—as you learned last night, we do tell the story at the campfire and continue the walk by the tree."

"Trees aren't evil," Maura said.

She wondered if she was trying to reassure him—or if it was something she said but doubted somewhere in a primal section of her heart or mind.

"No, of course not. A tree is a tree. Or trees are trees," he said and smiled weakly. "Anyway, I'm delighted to see you. And thankful for the work you're doing here with Miss Parsons."

"I'm not sure you need us. You've always had a full house here."

He didn't argue.

"I'm sure Marie will be delighted to see you, too."

"A pleasure to see her," Maura murmured.

Marie was perhaps ten years younger than her husband; they had been together for thirty years or so. Like her husband she kept herself fit, and she was an attractive and cordial woman. Her public manner was pristine—every once in a while, Maura had wondered what she was *really* thinking.

Glass lifted a hand in farewell and said, "Enjoy your stay." He started to walk away and then turned back. "I don't mean to be an alarmist, but…be careful. I'm sure you heard. Remains were found nearby. And several young women have disappeared, as well. Whether they ran away or…met with bad things… I know you're smart, but…be wary."

"Yes, I've heard. And I'll be careful," Maura said.

She watched him for a moment as he headed out of the room and then she opened the book again. Words swam before her as she tried to remember where she'd left off.

She heard Glass speaking again and she looked toward the door, thinking that he had something else to say.

But he wasn't speaking to her.

Brock was at the doorway, his tone deep and quiet as he replied to whatever Glass had said.

The length of Maura's body gripped with tension, which angered her to no end.

She hadn't seen or heard from him in twelve years.

He and Glass parted politely.

Brock headed straight for her. He smiled, but it seemed that his smile was grave.

His face seemed harder than the image of him she'd held in her mind. Naturally. Years did that to anyone.

And he'd always wanted to be law enforcement. But that job had to take a toll.

"I thought I'd find you here," he said softly.

"Yes, well, I... I'm here," she said.

She didn't invite him to sit. He did anyway. She wondered if he was going to talk about the years between them, ask what she'd been doing, maybe even explain why he'd just disappeared after the charges against him had been dismissed.

Elbows on his knees, hands folded idly, he was close—too close, she thought. Or not really close at all. Just close because she could feel a strange rush inside, as if she knew everything about him, or everything that mattered. She knew his scent—his scent, not soap or aftershave or cologne, but that which lurked beneath it, particular to him, something that drew her to him, that called up a natural reaction within her. She knew that there was a small scar on the lower side of his abdomen—stitches from a deep cut received when he'd fallen on a haphazardly discarded tin can during a track event when he'd been in high school. She knew there was a spattering of freckles on his shoulders, knew...

"You really shouldn't be here—you need to pack up and go," he said. His tone was harsh, as if she were committing a grave sin by being there.

She couldn't have been more surprised if he'd slapped her.

"I beg your pardon?" she demanded, a sudden fury taking over.

"You need to get the hell out—out of this part of the state and sure as hell off the Frampton Ranch and Resort."

Why did it hurt so badly, the way he spoke to her, the way he wanted to be rid of her?

"I'm sorry. I have every right to be here. It's a public facility and a free country, last I heard."

"No, you don't—"

She raised a hand, aware she badly needed to leave the room.

"Excuse me, Special Agent—or whatever your title may be. You don't control me. I have a life—and things to do. Things that need to be done—here. Right here. Have a nice day."

She stood—with quiet dignity, she hoped—and headed quickly for the door.

How the hell could he still have such an effect upon her?

And why the hell did he have to be here now?

Another body. Another life cut tragically short. His job.

Brock was right; she was the one who shouldn't be here.

Chapter 3

To say that he'd handled his conversation with Maura badly would be a gross understatement.

But he couldn't start over. She was angry and not about to listen to him—certainly not now. Maybe later.

The library seemed oddly cold without her, empty of human life.

Brock needed to get going, but he found himself standing up, studying some of the posters and framed newspaper pages on the walls.

There was a rendering of the beautiful Gyselle, running through the woods, hair flowing, gown caught in a cascade.

Donald Glass didn't shirk off the truth or try to hide it; there were multiple newspaper articles and reports on the murders that had taken place in the 1970s.

And there was information on Francine Renault to be

found, including a picture of her that was something of a memorial, commemorating her birth, acknowledging the tragedy of her death—and revealing that, while it was assumed she had been murdered by a disgruntled employee, the case remained unsolved.

Going through the library, Brock couldn't help but remember how shocked he had been to find himself under arrest. He'd been young—and nothing in his life had prepared him for the concept that he could be unjustly accused of a crime. He'd known where he wanted to go in life—but his very idealism had made it impossible for him to believe that such a thing as his being wrongly arrested could happen.

The world just wasn't as clean and cut-and-dried as he had once believed.

Of course, he had been quickly released—and that had been another lesson.

Truth was sometimes a fight.

And now, years later, he could understand Flannery's actions. There had been an urgency about the night; people had been tense. The police had been under terrible pressure.

Brock had usually controlled his temper—despite the fact that Francine had been very difficult to work with. But the day she had been killed, his anger had gotten the best of him. He hadn't gotten physical in the least—unless walking toward her and standing about five feet away with his fists clenched counted as physical. Perhaps that had appeared to be the suggestion of underlying malice. Many of his coworkers had known that he was always frustrated with Francine—she demanded so much and never accepted solid explanations as to why her way wouldn't work, or why something had to be as it was.

Like almost everyone else, he had considered Francine Renault to be a fire-breathing dragon. Quite simply, a total bitch.

She had been a thorn in all their sides. He had just happened to pick that day to explode.

After his blowup, he'd feared being fired—not arrested for murder.

He didn't tend to have problems with those he worked with or for—but he had disliked Francine. In retrospect, he felt bad about it. But she had enjoyed flaunting her authority and used it unfairly. Brock had complained about her to Fred Bentley many times, disgusted with the way she treated the summer help. Her own lack of punctuality—or when she simply didn't show up—was always forgiven, of course, because she was above them all. That night, Brock had been quick to put Maura Antrim on the schedule—as if he had known that Francine wouldn't be there.

Until she was—dangling from the tree.

As the police might see it, after they'd been pointed straight at Brock by the mysterious anonymous tipster, he'd been certain to be on the tour when Francine's body had been discovered, a ready way to explain any type of physical evidence that might have been found at the History Tree or around it.

At the time, Brock had wanted nothing to do with Detective Flannery. He'd been hurt and bitter. He was sure that only his size had kept him from being beaten to a pulp during his night in the county jail, and once he'd been freed, he found that his friends had gone.

Including, he now thought dryly, the woman he had assumed to be the love of his life.

Maura had vanished. Gone back home, into the arms of her loving parents, the same people who had once claimed to care about Brock, to be impressed with his maturity, admiring of his determination to do a stint in the service first and then spend his time in college.

Calls, emails, texts, snail mail—all had gone unanswered. It hurt too much that Maura never replied, never reached out, and so he stopped trying. He had joined the navy, done his stint and gone on to college in New York.

And yet, oddly, through the years, he'd kept up with Michael Flannery. Now and then, Flannery would write him with a new theory on the case and apologize again for arresting Brock so quickly. Flannery wasn't satisfied; he needed an explanation he believed in. He explored all kinds of possibilities—from the familiar to the absurd.

Francine had been killed by an interstate killer, a trucker—a man caught crossing the Georgia state line with a teenage victim in his cab.

She had been killed by Donald Glass himself.

By college students out of Gainesville or Tallahassee, a group that had taken hazing to a new level.

She had even been killed, a beyond-frustrated Flannery had once written, by the devils or the evil that lived in the forest by the History Tree.

Frustration. Something that continued to plague them. But then, Brock had been told that every cop, marshal and agent out there had a case that haunted them, that they couldn't solve—or had been considered closed, but the closure just didn't seem right, and it stuck in his or her gut.

Standing in the library wasn't helping any; Francine Renault had been dead a long time, and regardless of her personality, she hadn't deserved her fate.

The truth still needed to be discovered.

More than ever now, as it was possible that her murderer had returned to kill again.

Brock left the library.

Before he left for his interviews in St. Augustine that day, he had to try one more time with Maura. He had to find her. He hadn't explained himself very well.

In fact, he had made matters worse.

He had known Maura so well at one time. And if anything, his faltering way of trying to get her far, far from this place, where someone was killing people had probably made her stubbornly more determined to stay.

He'd admit he was afraid.

Beautiful young women were disappearing, and with or without his feelings, Maura was certainly an incredibly beautiful woman.

And there was more working against her.

She was familiar with the Frampton ranch and many of the players in this very strange game of life and death.

"Maybe we should move on," Maura said. She and Angie were sitting in the restaurant—Angie had actually wakened early enough for them to catch the tail end of the breakfast buffet, a spread that contained just about every imaginable morning delight.

The place was renowned for cheese grits; savoring

a bite, Maura decided that they did remain among the best tasting she'd ever had. There were eggs cooked in many ways as well, plus pancakes, fruit, yogurt, nuts and grains and everything to cater to tastes from around the country.

Angie, too, it seemed, especially enjoyed the grits. Her eyes were closed as she took a forkful and then smiled.

"Delicious."

"Did you hear me?"

"What?"

"I was thinking we should move on."

Angie appeared to be completely shocked. "I... Yes, I mean, I know now about you—I mean, when you were a kid—but I thought we were fine. This is the perfect place to be home base for this trip. We can reach St. Augustine easily, areas on the coast—some of those amazing cemeteries up in Gainesville. I..."

She quit speaking. Nils Hartford, handsome in a pinstriped suit, was coming their way, smiling.

They were at a table for four and he glanced at them, brows arched and a hesitant smile on his face, silently asking if he could join them.

Angie leaped right to it.

"Nils! Hey, you're joining us?"

"Just for a minute. My people here are great—we have the best and nicest waitstaff, but I still like to oversee the change from breakfast to lunch," he said, sliding into the chair next to Maura. "You're enjoying yourself?" he asked Angie.

"I love it!" she said enthusiastically. "And last night—your brother was amazing. I mean, of course,

I know that Maura had his job at one time, and I know Maura, and I know she was fantastic, but I just adored your brother. Keep him on!"

Nils laughed. "Oddly enough, that would have nothing to do with me. My brother reports directly to Fred Bentley, as do I. Couldn't get him hired or fired. But he's loved that kind of thing since we were kids. I was more into the cranking of the gears, the way things run and so forth." He turned toward Maura and asked anxiously, "And you—you okay being back here?"

"I'm fine," Maura said.

"Well, thank you both for what you're doing." He lowered his voice, even though there was no one near. "Even Donald is shaken up by the way we keep hearing that young women have been heading here or leaving here—and disappearing. Seriously, I mean, a tree can't make people do things, but… I guess people do see things as symbols, but—we're keeping a good eye on it these days. We never had arranged for any video surveillance because it's so far out in the woods—and nothing recent has had anything to do with the tree, but… anyway, we're going to get some security out there.

"Donald has a company coming out to make suggestions tomorrow. We have cameras now in the lobby, elevators, public areas…that kind of thing. But dealing with security and privacy laws—it's complicated. I mean, the tree is on Donald's property and it's perfectly legal to have cameras at the tree. And with today's tech—improving all the time, but way above what we had twelve years ago—the tree can easily be watched. Anyway, it's great that you're helping to keep us famous."

"A true pleasure," Angie told him.

He smiled at Angie and then turned back to Maura, appearing a little anxious again. "I just—well, I know you thought I was a jerk—and I was, back then. I did feel superior to the kids who had to work." He laughed softly and only a little bitterly. "Then the stock market crashed and I received a really good comeuppance. Odd, though. It's like 'hail, hail, the gang's all here.' Me, Mark, Donald, of course, Fred Bentley, other staff...and now you and Brock and Rachel."

"Rachel?" Maura echoed, surprised.

"Oh, you didn't know? Rachel is with the Florida Department of Law Enforcement now—she's working with Detective Mike Flannery. They've stationed themselves here—good central spot—for investigating this rash of disappearances. I think it's a rash. Well, everyone is worried because of the remains of the poor girl that were found at the laundry."

"Oh! Are you and Rachel still...a twosome?" she asked.

"No, no, no—friends, though. I have a lot of love for Rach, though I was a jerk to her when we were teens. I'm grateful to have her as a friend. And can you imagine—she's like a down and dirty cop. Not that cops can't be feminine. But she made a bit of a change. Well, I mean, she has nice nails still—she just keeps them clipped and short. Short hair, too. Good cut. She's still cute. But I hear she's hell on wheels, having taken all kinds of martial arts—and a crack shot. Great kid, still. Well, adult. We're all adults—I forget that sometimes. And hey, what about you and Brock? I was jealous as hell of you guys back then, you know."

She certainly hadn't known.

"Of the two of us?" she asked. "And no—I hadn't seen him since that summer. I'm afraid that we aren't even social media friends."

"I'm sorry to hear that. But I guess that… Well, it was a bad time, what happened back then." He brightened. "But you're here now. And that's great! I believe you recorded a tour? And more, so far? I'd like to think that you could spend days here—"

"We *are* spending days here," Angie assured him. "I guess we're like the cops—or agents or officers or whatever. We're in a central location. We'll head to St. Augustine and come back here, maybe over Gainesville's way. It's just such a great location."

"Well, I'm glad. That's wonderful. If I can do anything for either of you…"

His voice trailed oddly. He was looking toward the restaurant entrance. Maura saw that Marie Glass had arrived and seemed to be looking for someone.

"Excuse me," he said, making a slight grimace. "Our queen has arrived. Oh, I don't mean that in a bad way," he added quickly. "Marie never meddles with the staff and she's always charming. I mean *queen* in the best way possible, always so engaging and cordial with the guests and all of us." He made a face. "She's even nice when she knows an employee is in trouble, never falters. Just as sweet as she can be—while still aloof and elegant. Regal, you know?"

"Yes, very regal," Maura agreed.

Marie was looking for Nils, Maura thought, and as she noted their table and graced them with one of her smiles, Nils stood politely, awaiting whatever word she might have for him.

But she wasn't coming to speak with Nils. As she approached them, she headed for the one chair that wasn't occupied and asked politely, "May I join you? I'll just take a few seconds of your time, I promise."

"Of course, Mrs. Glass, please," Maura said.

Marie Glass sat delicately. "My dear Maura, you are hardly a child anymore, and though I do appreciate the respect, please, call me Marie."

Maura inclined her head. It was true. She was hardly a child. Marie simply had an interesting way of putting her thoughts.

"I know my husband and the staff here have tried to let you know how we appreciate the publicity your work here will bring us—and free publicity these days is certainly wonderful," Marie Glass began. "But we'd also be willing to compensate you if you want to show more of the resort—if you had time and if you didn't mind." She paused, flashing a smile Maura's way. "We love your reputations—and would love to make use of you in all possible ways. I am, of course, at your disposal, should you need help."

"Oh, that's a lovely idea," Angie said. "I'd have to switch up the format a little—as you know, I bring to light the unusual and frankly, the *creepy*, so—"

"Oh, bring on the creepy," Marie Glass said. She grinned again, broadly. "We do embrace the creepy, and honestly, so many people visit because of the History Tree. But we thought that allowing people to see how lovely the rest of the resort is... Well, it would make them think they should stay here and perhaps not just sign up for the campfire histories and the ghost walk into the forest. If it's a bit more comprehensive, we could use your videos on our website and in other promotional materials."

"I'm happy to get on it right away. Well, almost right away," Angie said cheerfully. "We did have plans to wander out a bit today, but we'll start on a script tonight. Maura's a genius at these things."

Maura glanced over at Angie, not about to show her surprise. So far, she hadn't known they were wandering out that day, and she wasn't sure that she was going to come up with anything "genius" after they got back.

From wherever it was that they were apparently going.

"Thank you ever so much," Marie said, standing. Her fingers rested lightly on the table as she turned to Maura. "We always knew our Maura was clever—we'd hoped to have her on through college and beyond, but, well…very sad circumstances do happen in life. Ladies, I will leave you to your day." She inclined her head to Nils. "Mr. Hartford, would you come to the office with me?"

As soon as they were out of earshot, Maura leaned forward. "Where is it that we're wandering off to today?"

"Well, it was your idea—originally, I'm certain," Angie said.

"Where?"

"St. Augustine, of course. You said it wasn't much of a drive and that we could easily get there and back in a day. I want to head to the Castillo de San Marcos—did you know that it's the oldest masonry fort in the continental United States? And I'm not sure how to say this, but St. Augustine is the oldest city in the country *continually* inhabited by European settlers. Think that's right. I mean, the Spanish started with missions and then stayed and... I have it all in my notes. Though I know you—you may know more than my notes!"

Maura glanced at her watch. It wasn't late—just about ten. If they left soon, they could certainly spend the afternoon in the old city, have dinner at one of the many great restaurants to be found—perhaps even hear a bit of music somewhere—and be back for the night.

"Okay," she said. "I had thought you wanted to finish up around here today—maybe even leave here and stay in St. Augustine or perhaps head out to the old Rivero-Marin Cemetery just north of Orlando. I just had no idea—"

"I thought you loved St. Augustine."

"I do."

"So it's fine."

"Sure. But we don't have permits, and while people film with their phones all the time now, what you're doing is for commercial purposes and—"

"We'll film out in front of places where I might need a permit to film inside. And if you don't mind, when we get to the square, I'll have you tell that tale about the condemned Spaniard who kept having the garrote break on him so that they finally let him go. Now, that's a great real story."

"The square is called the Plaza de la Constitución."

"Right. Yeah, but it's still a square," Angie said, grinning. "It is a square, right?"

"The shape is actually oblong."

"Okay, technicalities are important. But the story is great. About the man."

"His name was Andrew Ranson and he wasn't a Spaniard. He was a Brit and he had been working on an English ship and was accused of piracy. He absolutely declared that he was innocent but met his executioner with a rosary clutched in his hands. While he was being garroted, the rope broke, and the Catholic Church declared that his survival was a miracle. He recuperated, but when the governor asked that he be returned to be executed, the Church refused to give him back. He was eventually pardoned."

"And it's real—proving my desire to show all these stories. We're back to truth being far stranger than any fiction. And there's so much more. It is okay to go today, right?"

"Yes, it is, sure—let's sign this tab and get going right away."

Maura asked for the bill, but as she did so, her old boss came striding over to their table, a massive smile on his face.

Fred Bentley was powerfully built, stocky, not fat, but to Maura, it had always seemed that a barge was coming toward her when he strode in her direction.

He still had a head full of dark hair—dyed? She didn't know, but he had to be over fifty now, and it was certainly possible. He kept a good tan going on his skin, adding to his appearance of being fit, an outdoor man who loved the sun and activity.

He hadn't been a bad man to work for—he had certainly been better than Francine, who had changed her mind on a dime and blamed anyone else for any mistake.

Maura lowered her eyes for a moment, feeling guilty. Francine had not been nice. That didn't make what had happened to her any less horrible. Maura had to shake the image of Francine's lifeless body hanging from the tree. It haunted her almost daily.

"Maura, Angie," Fred said cheerfully. "Please, not a bill to be signed," he assured them. "What you're doing—in the midst of all this—is just wonderful. We're so grateful, honestly. Anything, anything at all that we can do, please just say so."

Maura smiled, uncomfortable. Angie answered him enthusiastically, telling him how she loved the grounds, the beauty of the pool and the elegance of the rooms, and, of course, most of all, the extra and unusual aspect of the campfire tales and the history walk. She was delighted to tout such a wonderful place.

To her surprise, Maura stood and listened and smiled, and yet, inside, she found that she was suddenly wondering about Fred.

Where was he when Francine Renault had been hanged from the great branches of the History Tree?

St. Augustine was, in Brock's opinion, one of the state's true gems. Founded in 1565 by Pedro Menéndez de Avilés, the city offered wonders such as the fort, the old square, dozens of charming bed-and-breakfast inns, historic hotels, museums, the original Ripley's Believe It or Not! Museum, ghost tours, pub tours and all manner of musical entertainment.

The city also offered beautiful beaches.

But that day, he hadn't come to enjoy any of the many wonderful venues offered here.

As asked, Detective Rachel Lawrence had set up a meeting with Katie Simmons, the coworker who had reported the disappearance of one of the missing women, Lydia Merkel. She was possibly the last one to see Lydia alive.

They were meeting at La Pointe, a new restaurant near the Castillo—Katie hadn't wanted to talk where she worked, though Brock intended to go by after their meeting, just to see if anyone else remembered anything that they might have missed when speaking with officers before.

The restaurant was casual, as were many that faced the old fort and the water beyond, with wooden tables, a spiral of paper towels right on the table and a menu geared to good but reasonable food for tourists.

Katie Simmons was there when he arrived; if he hadn't seen a picture of her in his files, he would have recognized her anyway. She was so nervous. She saw him as he entered through the rustic doorway, and her straw slipped from her mouth. She quickly brought her fingers to her lips as iced tea dribbled from them. She was a pretty young woman with soft brown hair and an athletic build, evident when she leaped to her feet, sat and stood once again.

She must have realized who he was by the way he had scanned the restaurant when he had entered. Maybe it was his suit—not all that common in Florida, even for many a business meeting.

She waited for him to come to the table.

He smiled, offering her his hand, hoping to put her at ease quickly.

"Katie, right?" he said.

"Special Agent McGovern?"

"Call me Brock, please," he said as he joined her at the table. "And please sit, and I hope you can relax. I can't tell you how grateful I am that you've agreed to speak with me. I know you've already told the police about Lydia, but as you know, we're hoping that we can find her."

Katie sat and plucked at the straw in her tea, still nervous. It looked as if tears were starting to form in her eyes.

"Time keeps going by… It's been weeks now. I don't know how she could still be alive."

A waiter in a flowered shirt was quickly at their table. Brock ordered coffee and he and Katie both requested the daily special, a seafood dish.

"I don't want to lie to you, but I also don't think you should give up," Brock told her when the waiter had gone. "People do just disappear—"

Katie broke in immediately. "Not Lydia! Oh, you had to know her. She was so excited to have moved here. She loved the city, loved working here—and there was more, of course. Lydia is a wonderful musician. She's magic with her guitar. She has the coolest voice—not like an angel, more like… I don't know, unique. She can be soft, she can belt it out… I love listening to her! She was going around getting gigs—and our boss is a great guy. He does schedules every week and talks to us before he sets them up. That allowed Lydia to set up her first few gigs."

"She was performing before she left here?" he asked.

"Oh, she only had two performances. One was for a private party out on a boat—but good money. They just wanted a solo acoustic player. And then another was at a place called Saint, which is a historic house that just became a restaurant—or kind of a nightclub. Can you be both? Or maybe you could say the same of a lot of places here—restaurant by day, club, kind of, by night with some kind of musical entertainment."

"Thanks. Do you know who hired her for the boat?"

"Sure. An association of local tourist businesses—it's called SAMM," she said and paused to grin. "St. Augustine Makes Money. That's really the name. Only you don't have to be in the city to belong—people belong from all kinds of nearby locations. In fact, half of the members, from what I understand, are really up in Jacksonville. We're the cute historic place, you know—Jacksonville is the big city. And where most people come in, as far as an airport goes." She grew somber again. "But she wasn't working the night before she disappeared. We were out together that night. She was leaving in the morning. She was so excited. Her career—her musical career—wasn't skyrocketing, but it was taking off."

"And according to what I've learned, she did leave in her own car."

"Yes, and she loved her car. It was old, but she kept it up—she kept great care of it. Oh, and that's why she chose her apartment. She could park there for free. Right in this area—well, out a bit—but still in what we consider the old section. I mean, you could walk to her place if you had to."

"Her car was never found," Brock noted. He'd read everything he could about Lydia before coming here today. And, of course, one of the reasons it was easy for law enforcement to consider the fact that she might have disappeared on purpose had to do with the fact that her car had never been found.

Katie was instantly indignant. "I know that—and I'm so sorry, but it made me wonder if the cops are stupid. The state is surrounded by water—oh, yeah, not to mention swamps and bogs and sinkholes and the damned frigging Everglades! Someone got rid of her car. I'm telling you—there is no way in hell that Lydia left here willingly—that she just drove away. Okay, I mean, she did drive away that morning, but... I didn't worry until I didn't hear from her. I know she would have called and texted me pics of the History Tree. When she didn't... I swear, I didn't panic right away, but when I didn't hear from her by that night, I knew something was wrong. I called the ranch, and they told me that she'd never checked in. That's when I called the police. And they all told me she might have just taken a detour. I told them that her phone was going straight to voice mail, and they still tried to placate me. I had to wait the appropriate time to even report her as a missing person with people really working on the case. Then I found out that two other young women had disappeared, and then..."

She broke off.

Brock continued for her, "And then they found the remains of Maureen Rodriguez. Katie, as I said, I don't want to give you false hope. But don't give up completely. People are working very hard on this now, I promise you." He hesitated—an agent should never make a promise he couldn't guarantee he could keep, but...

"Katie, I promise you, I won't stop until we know what happened to her."

She smiled with tears welling in her eyes.

"I believe you," she said.

Their lunches arrived. As they ate, Brock allowed her to go on about her friend. They hadn't known each other that long; they had just hit it off. She loved old music and Lydia loved old music. They had loved going to plays together, too, and were willing to travel a few hours for a show, and they both loved improv and ghost tours and so on…

He thanked her sincerely when the meal was over; she had taken his business card, but also put his direct line into her phone. He promised to call her when he knew something—good or bad—and they parted ways.

He decided to stop by the offices of SAMM next, wanting a list of those involved in the boat event during which Lydia Merkel had played, and then he'd be on to the restaurant where she'd entertained at her one gig on the mainland.

Someone, somewhere, had to know something.

Her car hadn't been found.

She'd only had one credit card; it hadn't been used outside the city. No one disappeared without a trace. There was always a trace.

He just had to find it.

Chapter 4

"I am standing here on Avenida Menendez in historic St. Augustine in front of a home that was originally built in 1763. While it was in 1512 that Juan Ponce de Léon first came ashore just north of here, and 1564 when French vessels were well received by the Native population, it was in 1565 that Pedro Menéndez came and settlement began.

"It was while the Spanish ruled in 1760—nearly two centuries later—that Yolanda Ferrer's father first built the house that stands behind me. In 1762, Spain ceded Florida to the British in exchange for Cuba, and Yolanda and her young husband, Antonio, left for Havana. But in 1783, Florida was ceded back to the Spanish in exchange for the Bahama Islands. Yolanda came back to claim the home her father had built, and the governor granted the home and property to her. At that time, she was a young and beautiful bride, and she thought that she and her husband would live happily ever after—but it wasn't to be.

"Yolanda, deceived by her husband, argued and pleaded with him not to leave her—and then either fell to her death or was, perhaps, pushed to her death, in the courtyard behind the house, where, today, diners arrive from all over the world to enjoy the fusion cooking of one of St. Augustine's premier chefs, Armand Morena.

"Through the years, the house has changed. It stood for a while as an icehouse and as a mortuary. For the last fifty years, however, it has changed hands only once, being a restaurant for those fifty years. But it wasn't just as a restaurant that the building was haunted by images of the beautiful, young Yolanda, sometimes weeping as she hurries along the halls, sometimes appearing in the courtyard and sometimes in what was once her bedroom and is now the manager's office. Yolanda is known to neither hurt nor frighten those who see her. Rather, witnesses to her apparition claim that they long to reach out and touch her and let her know that her story is known and that, even today, we are touched by her tragedy."

Maura finished her speech and waited for Angie to cut the take on the camera. Angie did so but awkwardly, and Maura thought briefly about the editing she was going to have to do. She much preferred it when Angie did the talking, but Angie had already spoken in front of the Castillo and Ripley's, and at the Huguenot Cemetery, the Old Jail, the Spanish Military Hospital Museum and several other places. She had begged Maura to let her do the filming on this one and Maura had acquiesced.

The sun was just about gone. And Maura was tired. As much as she loved St. Augustine, she was wearying of seeing it as if she was reliving that old vacation movie with Chevy Chase.

"Ready for dinner?" she asked Angie.

"Oh, you bet. We're going to have to come back. I loved what I called the square—the Plaza de la Constitución. I mean, that's the whole thing, isn't it? Executions took place there once, and now it's all beautiful, and there is a farmer's market, and people come for musical events and more. I love the streets surrounding it, the beautiful churches and all. I'm so glad we came."

"I've always loved this city," Maura agreed. "But I'm tired and starving. Have you picked out a place you'd like to go?"

There were plenty of choices.

Angie hesitated. She winced. "If I picked a particular restaurant, would you think that I was being ghoulish?"

Maura arched a brow warily. "Ghoulish? I don't know of any new horrific restaurant murders in St. Augustine."

"The restaurant is quite safe—no blood and guts in the kitchen or elsewhere, as far as I know," Angie assured her. "But..." she said and hesitated again. "It is the last place one of the missing girls had a music gig—I think I saw some video—because Lydia Merkel was playing her guitar and singing there not long before she disappeared. It's called Saint."

"Oh," Maura murmured. "Really, I'm not—"

"You wouldn't have even known, I don't think, if I hadn't told you."

Maura had read news reports; she had seen videos

of the young women, including Lydia Merkel, who had worked here in St. Augustine, before her mysterious disappearance.

She hadn't remembered the name of the restaurant where the girl had played, nor even the name of the restaurant where she had worked.

"Please? I can't help but want to see it," Angie said.

Of course, Angie wanted to see it. If the poor woman's body was found and her murder was never solved, she would become another Florida legend.

She didn't have the energy to fight Angie, and besides, she doubted that the restaurant itself had been any cause of what had happened.

"Okay. Is it close? I'm sure you know. Are we walking? I don't think it existed the last time I was up here. I'll google it," she told Angie.

"Two blocks to the east and then one to the south," Angie said.

"We'll leave the car and walk."

Saint was like many restaurants in the historic district—once upon a time, it had been someone's grand home. Maura thought that it might have been built in the 1800s during the Victorian era; a plaque on the front assured her she was right: 1855. Originally the home of Delores and Captain Evan Siegfried.

Abandoned after the Civil War, it had become an institution for the mentally ill in the 1880s, a girls' school in 1910, a flower shop in the 1920s, a home again briefly in the 1950s before it was eventually abandoned—then recently restored by the owners of Saint.

The restaurant's original incarnation as a home was evident as they entered; there was a stairway to the second floor on the right, and on the left was what had once been a parlor—it now held a long bar and a few tables.

They were led around to what had probably been a family room; there, to the far rear, was a small stage, cordoned off now, but offering a sign that told them that Timmy Margulies, Mr. One-Man Band, would be arriving at 8:00 p.m.

As the hostess led them to their table, Maura stopped dead—causing a server behind her to crash into her with his tray and send a plate of gourmet french fries and something brown and wet and covered with gravy to go flying to the floor.

Maura was instantly apologetic, beyond humiliated, and—what was worse—she had stopped in surprise.

Brock McGovern was seated at a table near the door, deep in conversation with a woman who was wearing a polo shirt with the restaurant's logo but not the tunic worn by the waitstaff.

Of course, now he—like the rest of those in the place—was staring at her.

She truly wanted to crawl beneath the floor.

Apparently he admitted to the woman that he knew Maura; he was standing, about to head her way.

She winced and ignored him, trying to help the waiter whose tray she had upturned, stooping down to help.

"It's fine, it's fine—really!" the young waiter told her, smiling as he met her eyes, collecting fallen plates.

"Oh, dear," Angie murmured.

Then Brock was at her side with the woman who had been at his table.

"Miss, seriously, please, it's all right—this is a restaurant. We do have spills," the woman said.

"I know, but this one was my fault," Maura said.

She was startled when Brock took her arm. She looked up into his eyes and saw that she was overdoing her apology.

She was still looking at him, but she couldn't help herself.

"I am so, so sorry!" she said again.

"Maura, it's all right," he said quietly. And, looking back at him, she realized she was as attracted to the man he had become as she had been to the boy he had once been. And maybe, just maybe, she had been apologizing to him, and he had been telling her that it was all right.

But...

"You never tried to reach me," she blurted as the waiter and busboys—and whoever the woman with Brock was—all scrambled around, cleaning up.

His frown instantly assured her that something was wrong with that statement.

"I did try," he said. "Repeatedly. I called, and I wrote and... I guess it doesn't matter now. There's no way to change the past."

Angie cleared her throat, "Um, excuse me. I think that they want us to sit. Maybe get out of the way? Brock! Wow, weird coincidence. Nice to see you—want to join us? Maura, we really need to sit."

"Yes, of course," Maura said, wincing again—wishing more than ever that she could sink into the floor and disappear. Her mind was racing; she was stunned and felt as if she had been blindsided.

She had great parents. Loving parents. But had they decided that there was no proof that Brock had really been cleared—and that he shouldn't contact their precious daughter? What else would explain that he said he'd reached out but had never actually reached her?

She was still standing. And everyone was still looking at her.

She smiled weakly and took her chair, continuing to be somewhat stunned by Brock's words, wishing that they might not have been said under these circumstances. She supposed that was her fault. But she hadn't been able to stop herself.

"This is charming, absolutely charming," Angie said when they were seated, her eyes on Brock. "We had no idea that you'd be here—and even if we had, how convenient that we came to be in the same place! Have you had dinner? Will you join us for the meal?"

"I have not had dinner, though I did have a great lunch," he said.

"You were here investigating?" Angie asked.

"Yes."

"I know some of what's going on, of course," Angie said. "There's news everywhere these days—even on our phones. Hard to miss. I understand that the last girl who disappeared near the ranch had been living here in the city."

"Yes," Brock agreed. Angie frowned slightly; she'd obviously been expecting more info.

"Do you think there's any possibility of finding any of the missing women alive?" Maura asked him.

"There's always the possibility," Brock said.

"Ah," Angie said, studying him. "A politically correct answer."

"No," Brock said. "They haven't been found dead.

That means there is a possibility that they will be found alive."

"Even after the woman's bones were found in sheets?" Angie asked.

"Even after that. It's still unknown if the cases are connected. That three young women have disappeared in a relatively short period of time does suggest serial kidnapping, but whether they were connected to the murder of Maureen Rodriguez is something that we still don't know. But," he added, "as I tried to say, I think it's a dangerous time right now for any woman from the ages of seventeen to thirty-five or perhaps on upward. Frankly, I'd be much happier if all those I knew were in Alaska right now—or Australia or New Zealand, perhaps."

He glanced over at Maura and she felt bizarrely as if her heart stopped beating for a minute.

She had been so angry for so long.

And now she realized that he hadn't been trying to get rid of her, per se—he was worried about everyone.

And maybe, because of the past, *especially* about her.

"But I do say it's a good thing that you stick together," he said, offering them a smile. "So, did you enjoy your day?" he asked politely.

Maura didn't have to worry about answering—Angie had no problem excitedly telling him about all that they had seen and done.

Their waiter—the same man who had collided with Maura—came and suggested that they have the snapper; the preparation of it, a combo of lemon and oil and garlic, was simple but exceptional. The three of them ordered. Maura and Brock were both driving, but Angie was at her leisure, so she indulged in the restaurant's signature drink—the Saint. It came out blue and bubbly, and she assured the waiter she didn't care much about what was in it. It was delicious.

"Have you all finished up here for the day?" Brock asked.

"Oh, yes, Maura is amazing. She knew where to go, what to get—we don't do full-length documentaries, you know. Just little bits. There have been all kinds of surveys about the modern attention span. You'll have tons of people look at something if it only takes them briefly out of their scanning. Unless it's something they really want to see, they pass right by when things become long. Two to three minutes tend to work really well for me. I was doing terribly, then I started working with Maura. She edits, although half the time we get just about perfect in one take."

He glanced over at Maura. "Are you in business together?" he asked.

"No," Maura said.

"Are you kidding? She's in megapopular demand!" Angie answered. "Artists, authors, performers—Maura knows how to make everyone really show off in that two to three minutes," Angie said.

"And I should definitely put in," Maura said quickly, "that Angie is truly a shooting star—her books on truth being stranger than fiction, weird places and so on do amazingly well."

"I have some pretty generous sponsors for my video channel. Whoever knew that being a nerdy and somewhat gruesome kid would pay so well, huh?" Angie asked.

"We never do know where life will take us, I guess,"

Brock said, turning his attention to Maura once again. "But sometimes you pop before the camera?"

"When Angie wears out," Maura said.

"No, she's great," Angie said. "The video-cam thing loves her—and she's so smooth. A grand storyteller. She'd have been perfect in the old Viking days or in Ireland when history was kept orally and people listened around the fire. Of course, I keep telling her that it can't be her life. We've worked together about three years now and I'm always amazed that she never says no. Work, work, work, I tell her. I put things off when I'm in the middle of a relationship. Maura won't take the time for a relationship."

Maura glared at Angie, amazed that her friend would say such a thing—especially when she'd been flirting with Brock in front of Maura and was unabashedly interested in men. If not forever, for a night—as she had often said.

Maura wanted to kick her. Hard. Beneath the table.

And she might have, except that Angie was a little bit too far away to accomplish the task.

But Brock looked at Maura, something strange in his eyes. "Some of us do make work into everything," he said.

Angie pounced on that. "So—you're not married. Or engaged. Or steadily sleeping with anyone?"

Once again, Maura wanted to kick Angie. She damned the size of the table.

Brock laughed. "No, not married, engaged or sleeping with someone steadily. I think you only want to wake up every morning looking at someone's face on the other pillow when that person is so special that they know the good and the bad of you and everything in between. When you know… Well, anyway…my work takes up a lot of time. And it takes a special person to endure life with someone who works—the way I do." He sat back. "I'd like to follow you back to the Frampton ranch. Being perpetually, ever so slightly paranoid is a job hazard. I know you're fine, but…humor me?"

He was looking at Maura.

She still loved his face. His eyes, the contours of his cheeks, the set of his mouth. He'd been so determined and steady when they'd been young, and she had been so swept into…loving him. For good reason, she thought. He'd grown into the man she'd imagined somewhere in the back of her mind.

The man whose face she had wanted to see on the pillow next to hers when she woke up every morning.

"Maura?" Angie asked.

"Um, yes, sure," Maura said.

Brock stood, heading to find the waiter and pay the check.

"He is so hot!" Angie said. "He's got a thing for you. But if you're going to waste it—"

"Angie, he's working down here."

"You must have been the cutest kids."

"Oh, yeah, we were just frigging adorable, Angie. It was twelve years ago. Come on, let's get the car and head back. I have a lot of editing to do."

"No, you don't. Almost every take was perfect. I should have gotten that check—I'm really making money. Unless, of course, he has a budget for dinners out. I'd hate to ruin his budget."

"Angie, it's all right—look, he's motioning to us. We're all set to go."

Brock wasn't parked far away; he walked them to their car and then asked that they wait for him to come around on Avenida Menendez so that he could follow them.

As Maura waited behind the wheel, she thought about the years that had gone by.

She'd been stunned at first that things had ended so completely with Brock, but slowly, she'd felt that she was more normal—that heartbreak was a part of life. There had been other men in her life. But anytime it had gotten to *we're either going somewhere with this, or...*

She had chosen the "or."

She hadn't planned on making that choice forever, she'd just never met anyone else she wanted on the pillow next to hers every morning.

She wondered what it meant that he'd never found that person, either.

Brock drove up slightly behind her, allowing her to move into traffic. She headed out of the historic district of the city with him behind her, easily following.

"I wonder if I should have ridden with him," Angie said. She glanced over at Maura. "I mean, if you're going to waste a perfectly good man…"

Maura was surprised that she could laugh. "Angie, I rather got the impression that you liked Nils Hartford or Mark Hartford. Maybe even Fred Bentley…"

"Bentley? No, no, no!" Angie said. "I like them tall and dark—or a little shorter but with that ability to smile and charm, something in their eyes, love of life, of who they are…not sure what. But Bentley? Nah. He's

like a little tram coming at you—no, no. Although…"
She turned in the passenger's seat to extend her seat
belt, allowing her to look straight at Maura. "Now, I'd
love to find out more about Donald Glass. Power and
money! We all know that those are aphrodisiacs. Even
when a man is sexually just about downright creepy.
Somehow, enough money and power can change the
tide, you know?"

"Uh, you know he's married," Maura reminded her.

"Ah, well, I heard that didn't always matter to him
so much," Angie said. She laughed. "He even has a
younger wife—younger than him. But that's the
problem—there will always be younger, and younger
will always be replaced with younger still."

"See, a warning philosophy," Maura said.

"But I know plenty of couples where there's an age
difference—both ways!—who are happily going strong.
I mean, there are older men who stay in love, and even
older women who stay in love with younger men who
stay in love."

"Of course," Maura murmured. She wasn't really
paying attention to Angie anymore—she was only
aware of the car following her.

It seemed forever before they reached the Frampton
Ranch and Resort.

Angie talked the whole way.

It was all right. All Maura had to do was murmur an
agreement now and then.

At long last, she pulled into the great drive and out
to the guest parking. Brock was still right behind her,
turning into a parking space just a few down.

He headed over to them while Maura went into the back seat of her car to grab her camera bag.

"An escort all the way," Angie said, greeting Brock as he joined them.

"All the way to the lobby," he agreed.

As they walked, Maura realized that despite the fact that he had joined them for dinner, she had never asked him about the woman in the Saint shirt who had been his companion at his table before she and Angie arrived.

But oddly, she didn't want to ask him in front of Angie. She glanced his way as they neared the entrance to the lobby, once the great entry to the antebellum house. He glanced back at her and, for a moment, it was strangely as if no time had passed at all. She'd always been able to tell him with just a look if they needed to talk alone.

He seemed to read her expression. Or, at least, she thought that he gave her a slight nod.

They walked up the porch steps and then through the great double doors to the "ranch house."

That was rather a misnomer. When the house had been built, it had been based on the Southern plantation style.

The integrity of the plan had been maintained with the registration desk to the far side and the doors leading to the coffee shop and the restaurant on opposite sides—one having once been the formal parlor and one the family parlor. The floors were hardwood, polished to a breathtaking shine without being too slippery—a great accomplishment by maintenance and the cleaning crew. There were great suites in the main house on the second floor while the attic had been heightened and rooms added there. Two wings—once bunkhouses—had become smaller one-room rentals.

Angie had, naturally, taken one of the big suites on the second floor.

Maura just hadn't needed that much space; she'd been perfectly happy up in the attic, and though she enjoyed working with Angie, she liked her own room, her own downtime and her own quiet at times.

"Safely in," Brock murmured.

"Welcome back...did you all decide to hit the entertainments somewhere nearby together?" a voice asked.

Maura was surprised to see that Fred Bentley was behind the registration desk. There was someone on duty twenty-four hours, but it wasn't usually Bentley. He lived on the property, having something of an apartment at the far end of the left wing, and she'd never really figured out what he considered his hours to be, but he was usually moving about in different areas, overseeing tours, restaurants, housekeeping and everything else.

"Our night clerk didn't show," he said, apparently aware that they were all looking at him curiously. "Not appreciated," he added.

Maura didn't think that the night clerk would be on the payroll much longer.

"I ran into Maura and Angie in St. Augustine," Brock told him, answering Fred's earlier question. "It can be a surprisingly small world."

"That is a strange coincidence," Bentley said. "Well, as I said, welcome back. Oh, Angie, Mrs. Glass was hoping that you'd tour the place a bit with her tomorrow, get an idea of what you could do...more videos on the resort as a whole. The swimming pool and patio out back are really beautiful." He nodded toward Brock and Maura. "Those two used to love it—our summer employees have always been allowed use of the pool and gym during their off-hours."

"It was a great place to work," Brock said. "Well, it's been long day. I'm going to head up."

"I think we all are," Maura said. "Good night, Fred."

An elevator had been installed; Maura usually took the stairs, but Angie headed for them and she thought that maybe Brock was on the attic floor, as well. "Night, Angie," he said, heading for the elevator.

"Good night. But long day—I'll take the elevator, too!" she said, joining him and Maura, who pressed the call button.

"I'm in the Jackson Suite," Angie said. "Have you seen the suites?" she asked Brock cheerfully in the elevator. "You're welcome to come see my room."

"I've seen all the suites, and thank you, but tonight… I'm ready for bed," he told her.

Angie laughed softly and said, "Me, too."

Angie was always flirtatious—and she'd honestly stated what she wanted to Maura. Usually her easy way with come-ons didn't bother Maura in the least.

Tonight…

It wasn't the night. It was that she was coming on to Brock.

The elevator stopped on the second floor. Angie stepped out. "Well, lovely day, lovely dinner. Thank you both!"

"Thank you," Maura told her.

The elevator door closed.

"She's subtle, huh?" Brock murmured.

To her surprise, Maura smiled. "Very."

"So, what did you want to ask me?"

He could still read her glances. And in the small elevator, they were close. She wondered if it was possible for so much time to have gone by and there still be that something...

The elevator door opened. They stepped out into the hallway. Brock stood still, waiting for her to talk.

"None of my business really, but that was rather bizarre running into you. And you were with that woman at a table, and then just came on over with us so easily... I..."

"I went in search of Lydia Merkel," he said. "She had a coworker, Katie Simmons, who insists that Lydia didn't disappear on purpose. She'd gotten two gigs playing her guitar and singing, as well as working as a waitress. One of those gigs was at Saint."

"Oh! Well, yes, of course, you were working. And the woman you met... She hired Lydia Merkel?"

"Exactly. Lydia played there the Wednesday night of the week she disappeared. I was hoping to learn something more. But I pretty much gained the same information. The manager did have a few minutes to speak with Lydia. Katie said that she was the perfect entertainment for their night clientele—charming, speaking between songs, performing at just the right volume for diners. She asked her back for a few nights each week and Lydia was delighted. But she had a bit of a vacation planned. She was heading to the Frampton Ranch and Resort, and it was a long-held dream. The manager told her that was fine. Lydia could come in the next week and they'd discuss the future. Of course, as we all know, Lydia never went back."

He paused for a minute and said very softly, "I'm sorry. I never meant to come off the way that I did earlier. But a woman was murdered. Three young women are missing."

"I'm sorry, as well. I thought... Never mind. I don't know what I thought. But you seriously think that... there will be more kidnappings? And that the same person who murdered the poor woman whose remains were found at the laundry has taken these other women?"

He nodded grimly. "From what I've learned, there is no way Lydia Merkel just walked away from her life. I haven't had time for other interviews yet, but I imagine I will find that neither Lily Sylvester nor Amy Bonham just walked away, either. And—while other businesses had sheets and used the laundry and fall in place with other leads as well, the Frampton Ranch and Resort still comes out on top of every list. Maybe I am touchy as far as this place goes, but in truth, I was sent here because of my familiarity with not just my home state but with the Frampton Ranch and Resort. You...you need to be so careful, Maura."

"I will be—I always am. But I'll be very careful. And...thank you."

He nodded. He knew that she was thanking him for the warning—and for telling her just how hard he had tried to reach her years ago.

He still hadn't moved; neither had she.

There were five rooms in the attic. The space was small. The walls were old and solid, and they were speaking softly, but it had grown late.

There was nothing more to say.

And there were years and years of words that they might say.

And, still, neither of them moved.

"I, uh… I'm so sorry for the families and friends of those poor women. And it's truly horrible about that young woman who was murdered, but do you think that they're all related?"

"We don't know. But they did have this place in common. And there's the past."

Maura shook her head. "You mean Francine?"

"Yes."

"But…that was twelve years ago."

"Yes."

"Peter committed suicide," Maura said. "I remember reading about it, and I remember him fighting with Francine. But then again, I remember everyone fighting with Francine. Still, with what Peter did…killing himself. Peter was a bit of a strange man with intense religious beliefs. He also had a temper, which usually came out as a lot of screaming and boiled down to angry muttering. It wasn't hard to believe that he had gone into a rage and dragged her out to the History Tree—and then been horrified by what he had done and regretted his action. Committed suicide."

"That's what was assumed. Never proved," Brock told her. "He was stabbed in the gut, something someone else could have done. Wipe the knife…put it in his hand. Leave him in the freezer. Easy to believe he might have done it himself. Especially when there were no other solid suspects. Just as easy to believe he was stabbed—and that the scene was staged."

He took a slight step back—almost as if he needed a little space. "Well, I'm in room three. I guess we should call it a night. I…uh… Well, you look great. And congratulations. I understand that you're doing brilliantly with your career. But I guess we all knew that you would. You're a natural storyteller—easy to see how that extends to directing people, to making them look great on video."

"Thanks. And you're exactly what you wanted to be—an FBI agent." She paused and took a deep breath. "And… Brock, I never received any of your messages. I don't know if my parents thought they were protecting me… They're good people, but… I am so sorry. I really had it in for you for years—I thought you just walked away."

He shook his head. Shrugged.

"Well, where are you?"

"I'm the last down the hallway, in five," she said.

"I'll watch you through your door," he said with a half smile. "I mean, I'm here—might as well see it through to perfect safety."

"Okay, okay, I'm going. I… I assume I'll see you," she murmured.

"You will," he assured her.

She turned and headed down the short hallway to the end. There, she dug out her key, opened her door, waved and went in.

Finally alone and in the sanctuary of her room, she leaned against the door, shaking.

How could time be erased so easily? How could the truth hurt so badly…and mean so very much at the same time? What would have happened if she had received his messages? Would they have been together all these years with, perhaps, a little one now, or two little ones…

She could have turned to him, laughed, slipped her arms around him. She knew what it would feel like, knew how he held her, cupped her nape when he kissed her, knew the feel of his lips…

Time had gone by. She hadn't received his messages.

She hadn't known he'd tried to reach her; she should have. As soon as she was home, her parents had gotten her a new phone with a new, unlisted number. They'd insisted that she change her email and delete all her social media accounts—not referencing Brock specifically, so much as the situation and the danger that could possibly still come from it.

Maybe she should have tried harder to get in touch with him. But when she'd never heard from him, she'd given up. Tried to move on.

Now they were living different lives.

She pushed away from the door. It had been a long day. She was hot and tired and suddenly living in a land of confusion. A shower was in order.

Maybe a cold shower.

She doffed her clothing, letting it lie where it fell, and headed into the bathroom. And it was while the water was pouring over her that she felt a strange prickle of unease.

It was like a perfect storm.

She was here. Brock was here…

Nils and Mark Hartford were here. Donald and Marie Glass… Fred Bentley…

And then, today her and Angie in St. Augustine, Brock in St. Augustine.

In the same restaurant. At the same time.

She turned off the water, dried quickly and stepped back out to the bedroom. She knew that Brock was working—that they all needed to be concerned. One poor woman was beyond help. Three were still missing, and maybe, just maybe...

There was nothing that she could do except, of course, be smart, as Brock had warned. And suddenly she couldn't help herself. She was thinking like Angie.

A night, just a night.

As Angie had made sure they all knew at dinner, Brock wasn't sleeping with anyone now in his life. There was no reason that the two of them shouldn't relive the past, if only for a night, for a few hours, for...

Memory's sake. If Maura just revisited the past, she might realize that it hadn't been so perfect, so very wonderful, that Brock wasn't the only man in the world who was so perfect...for her.

She knew his room number. It was wild, but...

Yes. It was too wild. She forced herself to don a long cotton nightgown and slip into bed.

And lay there, wide-awake, staring at the ceiling, remembering the contours of his body.

Chapter 5

Brock closed and locked his door, set his gun on the nightstand, and his phone and wallet on the desk by his computer. He shrugged out of his jacket and sat at the desk, opened his computer, keyed in his password and went to his notes.

He quickly filled in what he had learned that afternoon.

The most interesting had not been his conversation with the manager at Saint.

It had been earlier, when he had visited the offices of SAMM.

The event Lydia Merkel had played had been a social for members of the society. It hadn't been a mere boat, but the yacht *Majestic*, and fifty-seven members of SAMM had been invited.

Donald Glass and his wife had been among them.

The contact at SAMM had known that Maureen Rodriguez—or her sad remains at any rate—had been discovered. Every hotel, motel, inn and bed-and-breakfast that used the laundry facility had been questioned upon that finding. But no evidence had led to any one property.

Donald Glass knew about the women who had disappeared. He had never mentioned that he had met any of them.

To be fair, he might not have known that he had met Lydia Merkel. She had been working under her performance moniker—Lyrical Lee.

And, of course, the proprietors of many of the properties that used the laundry service were among those who had been on the yacht.

It was still a sea of confusion.

Except that Frampton Ranch and Resort was the location where the missing girls had been—or been headed to.

Brock filled in his notes, then stood, cast aside the remainder of his clothing and got into his shower. He needed to shake some of the day off. His puzzle pieces were still there, but he was missing something that was incredibly important.

Hard evidence.

And back to the old question—what the hell could something that had happened twelve years ago have to do with the now?

And why, in the middle of trying to work all the angles of the crimes, concentrating on detail and logic, did he keep seeing Maura's face as she stood before him in the hallway?

He knew her so well. He smiled, thinking that she hadn't really changed at all.

She'd been polite, always caring, never wanting to hurt another person.

She'd been so stunned to see him in the restaurant and stopped short and then...

He smiled again, remembering her face. So mortified.

And then trying to clean up the mess herself because she'd caused it. When they had spoken...

She'd obviously been stricken, hearing that he had tried to reach her. He'd seen the pull of her emotions—she had to be angry with her parents, but they were good people and she did love them, and now, with the passage of time, she surely knew that they had thought they were doing what was best, as well.

He showered, thinking that washing away the day would help; sleep would be good, too, of course. He felt that learning about Lydia Merkel and her aspirations to be a full-time musician were another piece of the puzzle—not because she entertained, but because of who she had done entertaining for: the hospitality industry—including the Frampton Ranch and Resort.

Brock and Maura had once been part of that. And they had intended to work part-time through college. His future had been planned out—he'd known what he was going to do with his life. And he had done it.

But Maura had always been part of his vision for his life, and maybe the most important part, the part where human emotion created beauty in good times and sustained a man through the bad.

He wasn't sure he ever made the conscious decision to go to her. He threw on a pair of jeans and left his room, years of training causing him to take his weapon and lock the door as he departed.

Which made him look rather ridiculous as he knocked softly on her door. When she opened it—he hoped and assumed she'd looked through the peephole before doing so—she stared at him wide-eyed for a minute, a slight smile teasing her lips—and a look of abject confusion covering her features.

"Um—you came to shoot me?"

She backed into the room. He entered, shaking his head, also smiling.

"Can't leave a gun behind," he told her.

"I see," she said.

For a moment, they stood awkwardly, just looking at each other, maybe searching for the right words. But words weren't necessary.

He set his holster and Glock down, fumbling blindly to find the dresser beside the door. He wasn't sure if she stepped into his arms or if he drew her in. But she was there. And time and distance did nothing except heighten each sensation, make the taste of her lips sweeter than ever. Their kiss deepened into something incredible. He felt her hand on his face, her fingers a gentle touch, a feathery brush, something unique and arousing, incredible and just a beginning.

His hands slid beneath the soft cotton of her gown and their lips broke long enough for him to rid her of it. He felt her fingers, teasing now along the waistband of his jeans. A thunderous beat of longing seemed to pound between them; it was his own heart, his pulse, instinctive human need and so much more.

Her fingers found the buttons on his jeans.

He couldn't remember ever before stepping from denim so quickly or easily.

Nor did he remember needing the feel of flesh against flesh ever quite so urgently.

They kissed again, his hands sliding down her spine, hers curving from his shoulders and down to his buttocks. They kissed and fell to the bed, and as his lips found her throat and collarbone, she whispered, "I was on my way to you."

He found her mouth again. Tenderness mixed with urgency, a longing to hold the moment, desire to press ever further.

It had been so long. And it was incredibly beautiful just to touch her again, hear her voice, bask in the scent of her...

Love her.

Familiar but new.

Their hands and lips traveled each other. He loved the feel of her skin, the curves of her body, loved touching her, feeling her arch and writhe to his touch.

Feeling what her touch did to him, hands traveling over his shoulders and his back; hot, wet kisses falling here and there upon him; that touch, ever more intimate.

As his was upon her. The taste and feel of her breasts and the sleekness of her abdomen, the length and sweet grace of her limbs.

And finally moving into her, moving together, feeling the rush of sweet intimacy and the raw eroticism of spiraling ever upward together, instinct and emotion bursting upon them with something akin to violence in their power, and yet so sweetly beautiful even then.

They lay together in silence, and once again he heard

the beat, the pulse, his heart and hers, as they lay entwined, savoring the aftermath.

At last, he kissed her forehead, smoothing hair from her face.

She smiled up at him. "Twelve years," she said. And her eyes had both a soft and a teasing cast. "Worth waiting for, I'd judge."

"How kind. May I say the same?"

"Indeed, you may," she said, curling tighter against him. "You may say all kinds of things. Good things, of course. My hair is glorious—okay, so it's a sodden, tangled mass right now. My eyes are magnificent... Well, they are open. And, of course, you've waited all your life for me."

"I have," he said gravely.

She grinned at that. "You joined the FBI monastery?"

"I didn't say that. And I'm doubting you joined the Directors Guild nunnery."

She smiled, but she was serious, looking up at him. "I—I knew some good people."

"I would expect no less," he said softly.

"None as good as you," she whispered.

"Now, that can be taken many ways."

"But you know what I mean."

"I do. And don't go putting me on a pedestal. I wasn't so good—I was...a bit lost. The best way I had to battle it was to plunge head-on into all the plans I had made. Most of the plans I had made," he added softly.

"I am so sorry."

"Neither of us can be sorry," he assured her.

She kissed him again. For a while, their touching was soft and tender and slow.

But it had been so many years.

Somewhere in the wee hours, they slept. And when morning came, he awoke, and he saw her face on the pillow next to his. Saw her eyes open and saw her smile, and he pulled her to him, just grateful to wake with her by his side.

"Perfect storm," she murmured. "And I'm so sorry for the cause of it. So grateful for…you."

"We can't change what happened then. Now it's all right to be glad that we've…connected."

She nodded thoughtfully. "I keep thinking…there's something in history, something in the books, something that has to give us a clue as to what is going on."

"You need to stay out of it all," he told her firmly.

She rolled on an elbow and stared at him. "How? How would I ever really stay out of it? I was here when Francine was killed. That in itself…it's most horrible that a woman was so cruelly murdered, but, Brock…it changed everything. Changed us. And you do believe that what is happening now is related."

"There is really no solid evidence to suggest that," he said. "In fact, as far as profiling and evidence go, there is little reason to suppose that a killer might have hanged Francine—and then stuck around for over a decade to murder one young woman and kidnap three more. Really, the best thing would be for you to head to Alaska—as quickly as possible."

She smiled. "I would love to see Alaska one day. I haven't been. I'd love to see it—with you."

He was certain that, physically possible or not, his

heart and soul trembled. They had just come together—tonight. And, well, thanks to Angie, they were both aware that nothing else had ever really worked for either of them in the years that had been lost between them.

He had never found *her* again. And she had never found him.

He grinned, afraid to let the extent of his emotion show.

"I don't think I have vacation coming anytime soon. But how about Iceland? What an incredible place for you to do legends and stories."

She was next to him, the length of her body close, and she touched his forehead, moving back a lock of his hair. "I don't work for myself—well, I do, but I'm a vendor hiring out my services. We need to be realistic. This is your work and more than your work. And now I'm working here, too. And I can help. I'm not stupid, Brock, you know that. I lock doors. I stay where there are other people. Whoever is doing this—be it a new thing or a crime associated with the past—they're smart enough to work in the shadows. No one is going to be hurt in the resort. You're in room three, and I'm in room five, and I'm not worried at all about the nights. Brock, I'm all grown-up. Quite a bit older than the last time, remember."

"And around the same age—"

"The missing women weren't wary or suspicious. They were just leading normal lives, trying to work and survive and simply enjoy their lives. Brock, most people are wonderful. They will lend others a helping hand. They just want the same things. Maureen Rodriguez was probably a lovely person—simply expecting others to be like that, too. From the little I know, the three missing women were probably similar—expecting human beings to act as human beings, having no idea that a very sick person was out there. I know that there's a predator. I won't be led astray, into any darkness—or off alone anywhere with anyone."

"Okay," he said quietly. "But if we're apart, I'll be calling you on the hour. Oh, screw the hour. Every five minutes, maybe."

"That will be fine. But unlikely. I think most of your interviews and investigations will take more than five minutes. And you really don't need to worry about me today—we'll be videoing out at the pool, in the restaurants—and I'm sure Angie would like to show herself speaking with Marie Glass—maybe Donald, too."

He heard a buzzing from the floor and leaped up. Luckily—he hadn't thought about it when he had left his room with just pants and his Glock—his cell phone was in the pocket of his jeans.

He dug for his phone.

"Yeah, Mike," he answered, having seen the detective's name on his caller ID.

"I'd like you to come with me to the Gainesville County morgue," Flannery said.

Brock gritted his teeth; the morgue meant a body. A body meant that his actions thus far had failed to save anyone.

"One of the missing girls?"

"I don't think so—I believe—or the ME there has suggested—that the remains are much older. But… Well, I'll fill you in. How soon can you be ready?"

"Ten minutes," Brock said.

"Better than me. Meet you downstairs in fifteen. We can grab coffee and head out."

"I'll be there."

"First man to arrive orders the coffee. Never mind—Rachel will beat us both. She'll order it."

"I'll be down."

He hung up and slipped into his jeans, looking back at the bed. Maura was up, staring at him, her face knit into a worried frown.

"I have to go… Not sure when I'll be back. Keep in touch, please. And stick with Angie and Marie Glass—and don't go walking into any old spooky woods, huh, okay?" he asked.

She smiled. "I promise," she told him. "But—"

"Old bones—we have to see what they are. And no—not one of our three missing girls. You'll be here all day?"

She smiled back at him.

"I'll be here all day," she assured him.

He hurried out of her room, heading to his own, hoping he wouldn't run into anyone while he was clad in his jeans only—but not really caring.

He would shower, dress and be ready in ten minutes. He wasn't worried about that.

He did hate that he was leaving.

And hoped it was something he was going to have to get used to doing.

Maura was happy—and determined. No, she wasn't an agent. Or a cop of any kind. No—she wasn't even particularly equipped to defend herself should she need to do so.

But she was smart and wary and everything else that she had told Brock.

Like it or not, she had been at the ranch when Francine was killed. And she was here now, and she was a Floridian and these horrible things were happening in her state. Today she would be filming around the estate with Angie and Marie, and she'd be speaking with all those here as much as possible—especially Fred, Marie, maybe Donald and Nils and Mark.

Her reasoning might be way off. Just because they had all been here twelve years ago and were here now didn't mean a thing. The solution to Francine's murder and answers about the girls who were dead and missing now might be elusive. It was sad but true that an alarming percentage of murders went unsolved. She'd read the statistics one time—nearly 40 percent of all homicides in the US went unsolved each year.

Except on this, while it was in his power, she knew that Brock wouldn't let go.

So, in her small way, she would do her best. And maybe that meant going through the library again, finding out everything she could about the Frampton Ranch and Resort—and the people who were here.

Maura showered, dressed and set out to edit some of her video from the day before. At nine she decided to go down to breakfast; Angie, she knew, would wake up when she was ready and come down seeking coffee.

Maura took her computer with her, curious to see what various search engines brought up on the ranch. As with most commercial properties, the results showed every travel site on the planet first. And the history of North Central Florida didn't provide any better results.

She didn't find much that was particularly helpful—nothing she didn't know already.

Frustrated, she was about to click over into her email when she noticed a site with the less-than-austere title of Extremely Weird Shit That Might Have Happened.

Once there, she read about a strange organization that had sprung up in the area in the 1930s. Various local boarding schools and colleges had provided the members—usually rich young men with a proclivity for hedonistic lifestyles. They had created a secret society known as the Sons of Supreme Being, and considered themselves above others, apparently siding with the Nazi cause during World War II, dissolving after the war, but supposedly surfacing now and then in the decades that followed.

They had been suspected of the disappearance of a young woman in the 1950s, but it had been as difficult for police to prove their complicity as it had been to prove their existence. Members were sworn to secrecy unto death, and in the one case when a young man had admitted to the existence of the society and the possible guilt of the society in the disappearance of the girl, that young man had been found floating in the Saint Johns River.

"My dear Maura, but you are involved in your work!"

Startled, Maura looked up. Marie Glass had come to her table. She was standing slightly behind her.

Maura quickly closed her computer, wondering if Marie had seen what she'd been reading.

"I'm so sorry," she said. "Have you been waiting on me long?"

"No, dear, I just saw the fascination with which you

were reading!" Marie said, sliding into the seat across from her. "Today is still a go, right? You and Angie will shoot some of the finer aspects of the resort?"

"Oh, yes, we're all set," Maura said. "Or we will be, once Angie is down."

"That's lovely. I thought we'd start with the pool and patio area, maybe scan the gym so that people can see just how much the resort offers? I know that Angie's forte lies in a different sort of content—as does yours—but she does have such an appeal online. She reaches a big audience. I can't help but think it'd be good exposure."

"Of course. Whatever you'd like."

"It's lovely that Angie Parsons will use her video channel for us."

"She couldn't wait to come here. She's fascinated with the resort."

"Well, her fascination was with the History Tree—" She paused a bit abruptly, then smiled. "I've seen some of Angie's videos and heard her podcasts and I even saw her speak at a bookstore once. The tree does seem right up her alley. And, of course, since it does seem to draw much of our clientele, I do appreciate the tree. Or trees. But… Well, those of us who knew Francine can't help but take that all with a grain of salt. Anyway…when do you think we'll be able to get started?"

"I imagine Angie will be down anytime," Maura told her. "I don't want to see you held up, though. Do you want me to call you when she's had her coffee?"

"Well, dear, this is my plan for the day, but if you could… Oh, there she is now," Marie said with pleasure.

Maura turned toward the entry to the coffee shop.

Angie was walking in with Nils Hartford. She was her smiling, bubbling, charming self, talking excitedly.

She saw Maura sitting with Marie and waved, excused herself to Nils and came over. "Good morning. Mrs. Glass, you are bright and early."

Marie slowly arched a silver brow. "If one can call ten in the morning early, Angie, yes, I am bright and early." Apparently in case her words had been too sharp, she added, "But I'm certainly grateful for your work and ready whenever you are."

"Right after one coffee," Angie said. "One giant coffee!"

"Wonderful. I'll just check on the patio area and make sure someone's darling little rug rat hasn't made a mess of the place."

Marie rose and smiled again, perhaps trying to take the sting from her comment. "At your leisure," she said and sailed out of the coffee shop.

Angie made a face and sat. "If America had royalty, she'd be among it. If she hadn't been born into it, she would have married into it. Oy!"

"She is a bit…"

"Snooty?" Angie said

Maura shrugged.

"Kind of strange, don't you think?"

"What's that?"

"Donald doesn't seem to be as…well, snooty. Best word I can come up with."

"To be honest, I don't know either of them that well. I mean, I worked for them before, but I was among the young staff—they hardly bothered with us. Fred was our main supervisor at the time."

"Along with Francine Renault?" Angie asked.

"Yep."

"And wasn't your beau kind of like the ranking student employee here?"

"Yes."

Angie smiled and leaned toward her. "And?"

"And what?"

"What about last night?"

"What about it?"

"Oh, you are no fun. Details. Ouch! You can feel the air when you two are close together. I'll admit—well, I don't need to admit anything, I frankly told you that I was deeply into him."

"Angie, you're deeply into a lot of people."

"True. So I've turned my attention to Nils. He is a cutie, too. Maybe even more classically handsome. Not as ruggedly cool—not like fierce, grim law enforcement. But damned cute. And, hmm, we are here a few more days. I do intend to have some fun."

"Angie—"

"Yes, I mean get laid!" Angie laughed at Maura's reaction. "Too graphic and frank for you? Oh, come on, Maura, you know me."

"And I wish you luck in your pursuits. I'm sure you'll do fine."

"Ah, you see, I shall do as I choose, which is much better than fine." Angie frowned suddenly. "Where is your law-and-order man?"

"He's here working, Angie. He went off—to work."

"Well, I suppose we should work, too. Let me grab my coffee."

"Great. I'll run my computer up and grab the camera."

Angie didn't need to get up for her coffee; Nils arrived at their table with a large paper cup.

"Two sugars, a dash of cream, American coffee with a shot of espresso," he said, delivering the cup to Angie. Her fingers lingered over his as she accepted the drink.

"Thank you so much," Angie said, smiling at him brilliantly. "When we talk about the restaurants, you will be in the video with me, won't you?"

"My absolute pleasure," Nils assured her. He smiled over at Maura. "Morning. I saw you earlier, but you were so involved, I didn't want to interrupt."

"You can interrupt anytime," Maura told him. "I was really just web browsing."

"Anything in the news—or have Brock or that Detective Flannery made any progress on the missing girls? Or, wow, I keep forgetting—Rachel?"

"Not that I know about."

"Something is going on this morning. There was a discovery just south of the Devil's Millhopper," Nils said. "I saw it on the news. Human remains were found. A Scout troop discovered them during a campout."

"I—I probably should have started with the news," Maura said. "I didn't." She didn't tell him that she knew something had been found because Brock had taken off early with Detectives Flannery and Lawrence to investigate. "More human remains. How sad."

Angie didn't seem concerned. "The Devil's Millhopper?" she asked. "That's…a cool name. What the hell is it?"

"A sinkhole," Maura told her. "Devil's Millhopper Geological State Park—it's in Gainesville. It's a really beautiful place, a limestone sinkhole about 120 feet deep. The park has steps all the way down, a board-walk—sometimes torn up by storms—and beautiful nature plants and trees and all that."

"We need to go there," Angie said. "How did I miss a sinkhole?"

"I don't think it's haunted. But, hey, who knows? Anything can be haunted, right?" Nils asked. "It's not all that far from here—a cool place. Hey, I'd love to take you. I have a day off coming up, if you want to go."

"I'd love it if you could go with me... We'll need Maura, of course, for the video," Angie said.

"I'd love to go with both of you," Nils said.

While Angie smiled back at him, Maura found herself remembering the Nils she had known before—the young man who had thrived on being so superior. She tried to remember if she had noted any of his interactions with Francine. Francine most probably wouldn't have reacted to any of his behavior.

Could Francine have angered Nils...and could he, at eighteen, have been capable of murder?

Ridiculous. He'd been the same age as Brock; they'd all just been kids.

"Seriously, I love the park, too," Nils said, looking at Angie and then flashing a quick smile at Maura. "It's really a pretty place."

"Isn't Florida at sea level? Doesn't it flood?" Angie asked.

Nils looked at Maura again and shrugged. For a moment, he just looked like a nice—and attractive—man. One with a sense of humility—something he had once been lacking.

"Hey, we even have hill country in this area. But

honestly, I don't know. It's a sinkhole. It has something to do with the earth's limestone crust or whatever. Geology was never my forte. Hey, we really do have hills in the state—not just giant Mount Trashmores, as we call them. And we have incredible caverns and all kinds of things. Most tourists just want warm water and the beaches, but it's a peninsula with all kinds of cool stuff. I'll find a ghost there for you if you want!"

Angie laughed and even Maura smiled.

"Great—we'll set it up," Angie said.

Maura quickly stood. "Meet you by the pool," she told Angie.

She clutched her computer and ran up both flights of stairs to her room. Housekeeping had already been into her room, she saw.

It seemed so pristine now. Cold.

Maybe just because Brock was no longer there.

She shook her head, impatient with herself. And for a moment, she paused. Being with him again had been so easy, so wonderful, so…perfect.

And she was, perhaps, wrong to dwell so much on one night. Things had torn them apart before.

She was suddenly afraid that events might just tear them apart again.

"When remains are down to what we have here," Dr. Rita Morgan told them, "it's almost impossible to pinpoint death to months, much less days and weeks. The bones were found just south of the Devil's Millhopper, as you know, deep in a pine forest. The area was just outside a clearing where the Scouts set up often, but not in the clearing, and it was only because a boy went out in the middle of the night to avail himself of a tree—no facilities out there, camping is rugged—that he came across them. Of course, the kid screamed and went running back for his leader or one of the dads along on the trip, and the dad called the police and... Well, here we are. The bones were scattered and we're still missing a few. I believe that all kinds of creatures have been gnawing upon them, but...there are marks—here, there—" she pointed to her findings "—that were not made by teeth. This young woman—we did find the pelvis, so we can say she was female—was stabbed to death. Oh, these are rib bones I'm showing you with the knife marks. I guess you figured that."

Brock nodded, as did Michael Flannery and Rachel Lawrence.

They were all familiar with the human skeletal system.

"But you think that she was killed sometime in the last year?" Brock asked.

"The integrity of the bone suggests a year—and a few teeth were left in the skull," Dr. Morgan explained. "I'm going to say that she was killed sometime between six and twelve months ago. She was most probably buried in a very shallow grave in an area where the constant moisture and soil composition would have caused very quick decay of the soft tissue, and insects and the wildlife would have finished off the rest. We're still missing a femur and a few small bones. And I'm afraid so many teeth are missing I doubt we'll ever be able to make an identification. We can pull DNA from the bones and compare to missing persons, but as you know, that will take some time."

"She's not one of the three recently missing women,

though, right? We are talking at least six months?" Brock asked.

"At least six months," Dr. Morgan agreed. She indicated the pile of bones that were all that was left of a young life, shaking her head sadly. "I wish I could tell you more. She was somewhere between the ages of eighteen and thirty, I'd say. Again—the pelvis is intact enough to know that. We'll keep trying—we'll do everything that we can forensically."

They thanked the doctor and left the morgue.

Outside, Michael Flannery spoke up. "I think that whoever killed Francine Renault twelve years ago got a taste for murder—and liked it. I think that whoever it is has been killing all these years. Maybe slowly at first, fewer victims. I'm not a profiler, but I've taken plenty of classes with the FBI—and I'm sure that you have, too. He's speeding up—for years, he was fine killing once a year. Now—or in the last year—he's felt the need becoming greater and greater."

"It is a possibility," Brock said. "Michael, it is possible, too, that whoever killed Francine did so because she was really unlikable and made someone crack—and that these two dead women we've found have nothing to do with Francine's death. And that the kidnappings aren't associated, either."

Rachel shook her head. "You're playing devil's advocate, Brock."

He was. Brock didn't know why—maybe just too much pointed to the Frampton Ranch and Resort, and he didn't really want it to be involved. Despite what had happened, he had a lot of good memories from his time there.

They now had the bones of two women killed within the past year. Three women were still missing. He'd barely had a chance to scratch the surface of what was going on.

"Come on, Brock. I've been chasing this for twelve years," Flannery said. "I did something I came to learn the hard way simply wasn't right—and now I'm chasing the results of my mistake."

"It wasn't your mistake. You weren't high enough on the food chain back then to insist that the case not just remain open, but that it continue to be investigated with intensity," Brock said. "But say your theory is right. If the killer is at large, then the killer hanged Francine and stabbed Peter Moore to death to make it appear like a suicide and provide a fall guy. That may have been where the killer decided stabbing afforded a greater satisfaction than watching someone strangle to death."

"Where they got a taste for blood," Flannery agreed.

"And you think it's someone who was or is still involved with the Frampton ranch," Brock said.

Rachel watched them both. "Honestly, Nils Hartford was a bona fide jerk—but I don't believe he was a killer," she said, though neither of them had accused Nils. "He… I mean, he and I were never going to make it, but we did become friends. When his family lost all their money, he admitted to me that he loved restaurants and he loved the ranch and that he believed Fred might give him a chance. And as to Mark… Mark was just a kid."

"Kids have been known to be lethal," Flannery reminded her.

"Fred Bentley?" Brock asked, looking at Rachel. "He

wasn't a bad guy to work for—and I think he was well liked by the guests. He's still holding on to his position."

"And he'd oversee any laundry sent out by the hotel," Rachel said.

"If not Bentley…and you're right about the Hartford boys…"

"That leaves Donald Glass himself," Brock said.

Donald Glass—who was married. Who, it had been rumored, had been indulging in an affair with Francine Renault.

A man who had acquired quite a reputation for womanizing through the years.

But would a man brilliant enough to have doubled a significant family fortune have been foolish enough to commit murder on his own property—and leave clues that could lead back to him?

"Time to head back," Brock said. "I say we casually interview all of our suspects. Let them in a little on our fear that the three missing women are dead—and that there is, indeed, a serial killer on the loose."

"Can you get someone at your headquarters tracing the movements of our key possible suspects at the ranch?" Flannery asked Brock. "FDLE is good—but your people have the nation covered."

"Of course," Brock said. He hesitated. "I haven't spoken with Glass that much, but he expressed pleasure that we chose his place as a base. Of course, it's possible that such a man thinks of himself as invincible. Above the rest. But still, I'd say there's another major question that needs to be answered."

"What's that?" Flannery asked.

"Where are the missing women? There are no bodies. Of course, it's difficult for police when adults disappear—they have the right to do so, and often they have just gone off. But the woods were searched. Bodies weren't found. If it's Glass committing these crimes—or someone else at the Frampton property or someone not involved there at all—he might be taking the women somewhere. Keeping them—until he kills them. If we can find that place…maybe we can still save a few lives."

"And maybe we're all barking up the wrong tree," Rachel said. "And if we concentrate too hard in the wrong direction…well, there go our careers."

"We have to put that thought on hold—big thing now is to find the truth and hope that we can find the missing women. Alive," Brock said. "Agreed?"

Rachel winced. "Right, right. Agreed."

"Agreed. Oh, hell, yeah, agreed," Flannery said.

Brock didn't like what he was coming to believe more and more as a certainty.

A killer was thriving at the Frampton Ranch and Resort.

And Maura was there.

A beautiful young woman who had a history with the ranch.

A perfect possible victim.

Ripe for the taking.

Except that he wouldn't allow it. God help him, he'd never allow it.

He had found her again; he would die before he lost her this time.

Chapter 6

Maura and Angie wrapped up at the pool. Out in the back of the main house and nestled by the two wing additions, the pool was surrounded by a redbrick patio. While the many umbrellas and lounge chairs placed about the pool were modern and offered comfort and convenience, the brick that had been set artfully around managed somehow to add a historic touch that made it an exceptional area.

Maura didn't have to appear on camera; she took several videos of the pool itself and then several with Angie and Marie Glass seated together, sipping cold cocktails, with Marie talking about the installation of the pool twenty years earlier and how carefully they had thought about the comfort of their guests.

A young couple had come out while Maura was filming the water with the palms and other foliage in the background. They'd been happy to sign waivers and be part of the video—laughing as they splashed each other in the water.

When Maura's cell rang, she was so absorbed in detail that she almost ignored it—then she remembered that she and Brock had made a pact and quickly excused herself to answer the phone, leaving Angie and Marie to sit together chatting—just enjoying the loveliness of the pool and one another's company. It was evident that Marie did admire Angie very much. The two women almost looked like a pair of sisters or cousins sitting there, chatting away about the adults around them.

Maura turned her back and gave her attention to the call.

Brock sounded tense—he reminded her to stay with Angie and in a group at all times.

"I won't be leaving here," she assured him. "I'm with Angie and Marie. We're going to go film the restaurants and then the library. We'll probably record in Angie's suite. Are you heading back?"

He was, he told her.

She smiled and set her phone down and looked at Angie and Marie, who were watching her, waiting politely for her to finish her call.

"Onward—to the restaurant," she said.

"Perfect. They won't open for lunch for another twenty minutes," Marie said. "We can show all the tables and will let Nils describe some of our special culinary achievements."

"Yes. Perfect," Maura said.

"Oh, yes, that will be wonderful—we'll have the daily specials, and Nils can serve them. First, Maura can take the restaurant empty, and then some of the food—it's going to be great!" Angie said, always enthusiastic.

Angie and Marie went ahead of Maura; she collected her bag and the camera and expressed her appreciation to the young couple again.

They thanked her—they couldn't wait to send their friends to Angie's web channel when the video was posted.

Maura hurried after Marie and Angie.

The restaurant was pristine when they went in—set for lunch with shimmering water glasses and wine-glasses and snowy white tablecloths. The old mantel and fireplace and the large paned windows created a charming atmosphere along with all that glitter. Angie did a voice-over while she scanned the restaurant.

Nils stood just behind Maura; that made her uneasy, but she wasn't alone in the restaurant, she was with Marie and Angie, and a dozen cooks and waitstaff lingered just in the kitchen. She knew that she was fine.

She wondered if Nils made her nervous because she did suspect him of something, or...

If she was just nervous because she didn't like any-one at her back.

When Nils touched her on the shoulder, she almost jumped. "Sorry, sorry!" he said quickly. "I don't want to mess this up—if I do something wrong, you'll tell me, right? You'll give me a chance to do it over?"

"Nils, this is digital. We can do things as many times as you want, but I believe what we're trying for is very spontaneous, natural—just an easy appreciation for what the resort offers."

"Okay, okay —thank you, Maura," he said.

She smiled. "Sure."

Marie was going to sit with Angie. Before she could, there was a tap on the still-locked door. "Let me just tell them we'll open in a few minutes, right at twelve," Nils said.

Angie and Marie took a seat at a circular table for two right by a side window.

But Nils didn't come back alone.

Donald Glass, elegantly dressed in one of his typical suits and tall and dignified—as always—arrived with him.

"I'd thought it would be good if I popped into one of these videos Marie thinks will be such a thing. If you don't mind. Darling," he told Marie, "would you mind? I think I speak about our wine list with the most enthusiasm."

"No, darling, of course, you must sit in," Marie said.

She rose, giving up her seat. "I'd have thought you might want to do the library," she said. "You do love the library so."

He grinned. "Yes, I'm proud of my libraries. But even then…good wine is a passion."

"Okay, dear."

Maura thought that Marie seemed hurt, but she really didn't show anything at all. She smiled graciously, telling Nils, "They'll need the menus and wine lists."

"Already there, Mrs. Glass, already there," Nils said.

"Okay, then," Maura said. "In five, four…" She finished the count silently with her fingers.

"Angie Parsons here, and I'm still at the Frampton Ranch and Resort. After a day at the oh-so-beautiful pool—and before a night at the incredible historic walk—there's nothing like a truly world-class dinner. And I'm thrilled to be here with Donald Glass, owner of this property and many more, and—perhaps naturally—a magnificent wine connoisseur, as well."

"Thank you so much, Angie. Marie and I are delighted to have you here. I do love wine, and while we have Mr. Fred Bentley, one of finest hotel managers in the state, and Nils Hartford, an extraordinary restaurateur, manning the helm, no wine is purchased or served without my approval." He went on to produce the list, explaining his choices—and certainly saying more in a few words than Maura would ever know, or even understand, about wine.

But the video was perfect on the first take.

Nils came in as they discussed the menu. He spoke about the excellence of their broad range of menu choices. He suggested that Angie enjoy one of their fresh mahi-mahi preparations, and that Donald order the beef Wellington. That way they could indulge in bites of each other's food.

He might have been nervous, but he did perfectly.

"And now we really have to open the restaurant," he said.

Donald Glass smiled and nodded. "No special stops—we run a tight ship. But, of course, that will be fine, right, Maura?"

"That will be fine. I can avoid other tables, not to worry," she said.

But people were excited when they noted that something was going on.

Many had been at the campfire when she had filmed.

They wanted to be involved.

As she spoke to other diners pouring in, Maura knew that Marie Glass was watching her. She turned to her.

"Is that okay?" she asked.

"Yes, yes, lovely," Marie said. She glanced back at Donald, chatting away still with Angie at the table.

They were laughing together. Angie was her ever-charming self—flirtatious. She basically couldn't help it. Glass was enamored of her.

Marie looked back at Maura, her eyes impassive. "Indeed, please, if others wish to sign your waivers, it will certainly add on. Hopefully the food will come out quickly for my husband and Miss Parsons, and we'll be moving on. I can lock down the library, though, of course, Donald will want to be on the video then, too, as I suggested earlier."

"Thank you," Maura told her.

Marie was at her side as she chose a table close by to chat with the guests and diners who arrived—wanting to be on video.

She was startled when she accepted the last waiver and Marie spoke.

But not to her...

Not per se.

She spoke out loud, but it was as if she believed that her words were in her mind.

"And I have always vouched for him. Always," she murmured.

"Pardon?" Maura said.

"What? Oh, I'm so sorry, dear. I must be thinking out loud."

She walked away; Maura went to work.

The head chef himself, a new man, but well respected

and winner of a cable cook-off show, came out to explain his fusions of herbs and spices with fresh ingredients.

The videos were coming out exceptionally well, Maura thought.

But she couldn't help remembering the way Donald Glass had sat with Angie—and the way Marie reacted to her husband.

Brock was parking the car when he received a message from his headquarters. He hadn't contacted Egan. He had gotten in touch with their technical assistance unit and had reported on the remains that had been found, but it was Egan who called.

Egan wanted to know about the body that they had seen that morning; Brock told him their working theory, thinking that Egan might warn them against it.

He didn't.

Then he put Marty Kim, the support analyst who had been doing extra research for Brock's case, on the phone.

"I did some deep dives this morning," Marty told him. "Before coming to the Frampton Ranch and Resort, Nils Hartford was working at a restaurant in Jacksonville, Hatter and Rabbit. Trendy place. He left there for the Frampton resort, but there was a gap between jobs. I found one of the managers willing to talk. Nils resigned—but if he hadn't, he would have been fired. There was a coworker who complained about sexual harassment. Hartford was managing. The young woman was a waitress. She told the owner that she was afraid of Nils Hartford."

"Interesting. And do we know if the waitress is still alive and well?"

"Checking that out now," Marty told him. "I can't find anything much on Mark Hartford. He went to a state university, majored in history and social sciences, came out and went straight to work for Donald Glass."

"Fred Bentley?"

"He's been with Glass for nearly twenty years—at the Frampton Ranch and Resort for fifteen of them. Before that, he was working at a big spread that Glass has in Colorado."

"Anything on Donald Glass himself?"

"Nothing—and volumes. If you believe all the gossip rags, some more reliable than others, Glass has had many affairs through the years. Some of the women kept silent, some of them did not. He has been married to Marie for twenty-five years, and if I were that woman—I'd divorce his ass." Marty was silent for a minute. Then he added quickly, "Sorry, that wasn't terribly professional."

"You're fine. So...he's still playing the dog, eh?"

"One suspected affair he enjoyed was reportedly with Francine Renault. That hit a few of the outlets that speculate on celebrities without using their names—avoiding legal consequences. Over the years, he did pay off several women. One accused him of sexual assault—except, when it came to it, she withdrew all charges. There was a settlement. But most of these are confidential legal matters, and without due process and warrants, I can only go so far."

"Thanks. He's been spending most of his time and effort down at his property in Florida, right?"

"Oh, he travels. London, New York, Colorado and LA. But yes, most of the time he is in Florida. His trips to other properties tend to be weekends, just twice a year or so."

"Does Marie go with him?"

"It seems he does those trips alone. But, of course, paper trails can only lead you so far," Marty reminded him. "I'll keep searching. I'll naturally get back to you if I find anything else that might be pertinent to your investigation."

He'd parked the car. Detectives Flannery and Lawrence had waited for him.

He reported what he'd just learned to them.

Flannery shook his head. "A man with all that Glass has… Could it be possible?"

"We have nothing as yet, so let's not go getting ourselves thrown out of the resort before we have something tangible, okay?" Brock said.

"Of course not," Flannery said, and he looked at Rachel, frowning. "You should try to get some talk time in with Donald Glass," he said.

"Are you pimping me out?" she asked him.

"Never," Flannery said. "But maybe he'll respond more easily to you on many levels."

"You mean that you doubt that he takes me seriously," Rachel said.

"Rachel, Rachel, you have a chip on your shoulder," he told her.

Brock groaned slightly.

Rachel looked at Brock and he shrugged. "You never know."

"Yes, Rachel, I'm pimping you out—whatever

works," Flannery told her. "He might still think of you as the teenager who spent summers at the resort, instead of the whip-smart detective you are now. You might catch him off guard."

She grinned. "Okay, just so I know what I'm doing."

"Let's get lunch," Flannery said. "Oh, and feel free to flirt with your old beau, if need be. I'm sure you've got enough wiles to go around."

Rachel paused before they reached the house, looking at Brock. "Maybe Brock could get Maura on that one," she said.

"Maura is a civilian," he said, hoping he hadn't snapped out the words.

"Yes, but…" Rachel hesitated, glancing at Flannery, who nodded. "Everyone around here always had kind of a thing for Maura. I know that I'd be with Nils— and see him look after her longingly, even though she was a summer hire. And I'd see Glass looking at her, too, and I even think that Francine Renault was hard on her because the others seemed so crazy about her. If she could just draw Nils into conversation—with us around, of course, and see where that leads."

"We do remember that we are professionals, that we play by the book," Flannery said. "But come on, Brock, what led you to law enforcement was the knowledge that you had instincts along with drive. What made me follow your career as you moved on was…well, hell, like I said. You obviously have the instincts for it. Sometimes lines get a little blurred. I am not suggesting that we really use Maura. I'm just suggesting that she could help us chat some of these people up—with one of us right there."

Brock stared at the two of them. He didn't agree, and he didn't disagree. He was surprised by Rachel's words, but he'd been mostly oblivious to others back then. He shouldn't have been surprised by Michael Flannery's passion; he'd always known that Flannery was like a dog with a bone on this case.

Brock would never use Maura. Never.

But on the other hand she was in there interacting with all the persons of interest right now.

Twelve years ago, Maura had been with him; he had been with her. No room for doubt, and certainly, they had never thought to mistrust each other.

Now she had grown into an admirable professional—and a courteous and caring human being. And she was with him once again, although he reminded himself that they had been together just a night. There had been no promises. In the end, whether there was or wasn't a future for them didn't matter in the least. She was a civilian, and that was that.

He raised a finger in an unintentional scold. "She's never alone—never, ever, alone with any of them. With Fred Bentley, either of the Hartford brothers or Donald Glass."

"Right," Flannery said.

At his side, Rachel nodded grimly. He turned and they followed him.

"I'm starving," Rachel murmured as they entered the lobby and tempting aromas subtly made their way out and around them from the restaurant.

"Yeah, it's lunchtime," Flannery said.

"I'll join you soon," Brock told them. He headed to the desk; there was a clerk there he hadn't seen before.

"Good afternoon, sir. How can I help you?" he asked.

"You're new," Brock said.

"I am, sir."

"What happened to the young lady who was working?"

"I don't know, sir, and I don't know which young lady you might mean. Mr. Bentley gives us our schedules, sir. I'm doing split shifts, morning and night now, if I can be of assistance."

"Yes, I understand Angie Parsons is doing some filming here at the resort today. Can you direct me to where they're working now?"

"They're in the library, but they don't wish to be disturbed, sir. Sir!"

Brock turned and headed for the library.

"Sir! I shouldn't have told you. They don't want to be disturbed. Please, I have just been hired on—sir!"

Brock paused to turn back. "It's all right. I'm FBI," he said.

His being FBI didn't really mean a damned thing in this scenario. But he felt he had to say something reassuring to the clerk.

He went through the lobby and down the hallway that led to the library, in back of the café.

The door was closed.

There was a sign on it that clearly said Do Not Disturb.

Well, he was disturbed himself, so he was going to do some disturbing. He knocked on the door.

To his surprise, it opened immediately.

Marie Glass stood before him, bringing a finger to her lips. He nodded. She closed the door behind him.

Angie was holding the camera. He had arrived just

before they were to begin a segment. While she loved being the director and videographer, Maura was also a natural before the camera. She smiled right into the lens and said that she was in her favorite area of the resort—the library. She was with Donald Glass, who kept the library stocked, not just here, but at all of his properties, and that he bought and developed places specifically because of unique or colorful histories.

"A true taste of life, the good, the bad and the evil," Maura said, smiling.

"Exactly, for such is life, indeed, and history can be nothing less," Glass said.

Maura knew what she was doing; Glass had been interviewed so many times in his rich life that he was apparently well aware of a good ending.

"Cut! Perfect!" Angie said. "Marie, what do you think?"

Marie smiled—her usual smile. One that maintained her dignity—and gave away nothing of her real thoughts. "Excellent. If we can just do an opening at the entry…perhaps have Fred giving the guests a welcome along with Angie." She turned and looked at Brock. "Oh, would you like to appear in a video, Brock? This was once a home away from home for you."

"No, thank you—though I would enjoy watching," he said. He looked at Maura, who was looking at him then, too. He couldn't read what she was thinking, but she had that look in her eyes that indicated there were things she had to say—but to him alone.

He glanced at Marie. "Not sure my bosses now would like it," he explained.

"Well, we can finish up then," Marie said. "Donald, dear, would you like to find Fred? He has been our general manager now for over fifteen years. He should be shown greeting Angie."

"Good thinking, my dear," Glass told his wife. "Meet you out front."

Donald left. Brock smiled, excused himself and hurried after Glass.

"Sir!"

Glass stopped and turned around with surprise. "Oh, Brock, yes, what can I do for you?" He frowned. "Have you learned anything? I caught a 'breaking news flash' about thirty minutes ago. More remains have been discovered, but those over south of Gainesville. It wasn't… Did they find one of the missing girls?"

He seemed truly concerned.

"No, sir. Whoever they found has been missing much longer. They don't have an ID yet."

"You never know if that's true, or if it's what the media was told to say."

"It's true. They have no identity on the remains yet. Indulge my concern for a moment—there was a young woman working at the front desk here. She might have been just on nights, and I may be a bit overly cautious, but I noticed you have a new hire on the desk."

"We do?"

He appeared genuinely surprised. "You'd have to ask Fred about that. I must admit, I don't concern myself much with the clerks. I worry more about the restaurants and our entertainment staff. But Fred will be able to tell you."

"Thank you."

"Have you seen Fred?"

"No, I haven't, but—"

"He's probably at lunch. I'll take a look in the restaurant. Excuse me."

Brock watched him as he went on by. The man was polite to him—always had been. But he couldn't imagine that dozens of reports were all false—the man evidently had an eye for women and an appetite for affairs.

Did he leave for tours of his other properties because he just needed to work alone, or because he needed space for casual affairs?

Or maybe he didn't really leave every time he said that he was doing so, or go exactly when and where he said that he was going.

Power and money.

Maybe Glass lured young women with those assets.

Brock hurried out front.

Maura wasn't alone. She was with Marie Glass and Angie, and they were standing in broad daylight.

He was still anxious to be with her.

More anxious to hear what it was she might have to say to him alone.

It wasn't that her work was hard, but Maura was weary—ready to be done.

Most of the videos had gone very smoothly.

Angie spoke spontaneously, and they had needed no more than three takes on any one scene that day. Maura had known what she'd wanted to say—she truly loved any library, especially one as focused and unique as the library at the Frampton Ranch and Resort.

And still, she was tired.

The idea made her smile. She was happy to be tired—

because she was happy that she hadn't spent much of the previous night sleeping.

She didn't want to be overly tired that night, though!

Brock appeared on the steps of the porch before Donald Glass got there. He had an easy smile as he joined them and waited for Donald to appear with Fred Bentley.

"The Devil's Millhopper! Sounds like a place I have to see!" Angie said, smiling and looking at Brock.

He shrugged. "It's geographically fascinating—and has great displays on how our earth is always changing, how the elements and organic matter often combine to make things like sinkholes and other phenomena work. Sure—I love it out there." He laughed. "I love our mermaids, too. Weeki Wachee Springs and Weeki Wachee State Park. Absolutely beautiful—crystal clear water."

"Mermaids, eh?"

"Mermaids," he agreed politely and turned away; Glass was coming down the steps with Bentley. The stocky manager was beaming.

"I get to be in a video!" he announced.

"You do," Angie said.

"With the famous Angie Parsons," Fred said. He paused, frowning. "Or with our beautiful Maura—which is fine, too. Love our beautiful Maura."

Maura smiled. "No, sir—thank you for the compliment. You get to be with our famous and beautiful Angie."

"What do I say?" Fred asked.

Maura already knew exactly where she wanted them to stand for the afternoon light—and how she wanted them walking up the steps to the porch and the entry for the finale of the little segment.

"If you could give a welcome to the Frampton Ranch and Resort—and tell us how you've been here for fifteen years," Maura said. "Naturally, in your own words, and you can add in any bit of history you like."

She probably should have expected that something would go badly.

First, Fred froze and mumbled.

Maura smiled and coaxed him.

Then he went blank.

Then he forgot to follow Angie up the stairs at the end.

He apologized and said that he should be fired — from the video, not the property. He tried to laugh.

Maura encouraged him one more time, and they were able to get a decent video.

Brock stood nearby through the whole painful process, as did Donald and Marie. The owners—the married pair—did not stand next to each other.

Nor did they speak with each other.

And when they were done, Marie thanked Angie and Maura, bade the others good-afternoon and said that she was heading out for some shopping.

Donald thanked everyone and said that he'd be in his office.

Fred thanked Angie—then Maura.

"I was horrible. You fixed me. I guess that's what a good director does. Anyway, back to work for me. See you."

He lifted a hand and started up the steps.

"Fred," Brock said, calling him back.

"Yeah?"

"I noticed you have a new hire on the front desk."

"I do," Fred Bentley told him. "Remember when I was night clerk—well, I don't like being night clerk. Heidi didn't show up at all—and didn't call with an excuse. That's grounds for dismissal, and everyone knows it, so I left a message telling her not to come back."

"You never spoke with her?" Brock asked.

Bentley frowned. "No, I got her voice mail. She must have heard it. She never came back in."

"What's Heidi's last name and where does she live?"

"Heidi Juniper. She lives between here and Gainesville," Bentley told him. His frown deepened. "You don't think that—"

"I'll need her address and contact information," Brock said. "We'll just make sure that Heidi is irresponsible—and not among the missing."

"Of course, of course, I'll get it for you right away," Bentley told him.

When Fred was gone, Angie turned to Brock, repeating Bentley's concern. "You don't really think—"

"I don't know. I think we'll just check on her, that's all," Brock said. He looked at the two of them. "Lunch?"

"Are they still serving lunch?" Maura asked. "They do close for an hour, I think, between lunch and dinner."

"I bet they'll serve us," Angie said. She smiled broadly. "Oh, I do love it when people feel that they owe you."

She started up the steps. Maura was glad; she wanted a few minutes with Brock alone.

She believed that she'd have all night, but she needed a moment now.

But Angie stopped, looked back and sighed impatiently. "Come on! Let's not push our luck too hard, okay? I want them to keep owing me."

She was waiting.

No chance to talk.

Maura started up the stairs to the porch, grateful, at least, that Brock was with her.

Grateful, in fact, that he was simply in the world— and in her part of the world once again.

Chapter 7

Brock saw that Michael Flannery and Rachel Lawrence were still in the restaurant when he arrived—they had taken a four top, expecting him to join them.

They hadn't expected Maura and Angie, but Michael quickly grabbed another chair and beckoned them all on over.

Angie was happy to greet them both, offering to film some of the campfire fun again with them in it. She hadn't quite figured out that law enforcement officers didn't often want their faces on video that went around to the masses—especially when they worked in plain clothes.

Both politely turned her down.

"I feel like a terrible person," Angie said. "I mean, I'd seen the news. I knew that women had been kidnapped and one had been found dead...or her remains had been found. I just didn't associate it with worrying about the central and northern areas of Florida. And the state has a huge population… Not that having a huge population makes terrible things any better, but statistically, they are bound to happen. I had no idea that the FBI and the FDLE would be staked out at the resort. But I can't tell you how glad I am. Though we did finish here today. And we went to St. Augustine yesterday. I want to see this Devil's Millhopper—the big sinkhole. But I'm not sure if Nils can go right away, and he did say that he wanted to."

Nils must have been close; as if summoned, he was suddenly behind Angie's chair. "While you're waiting to go to the Devil's Millhopper, there's some other cool stuff for Maura's cameras not far from here. Cassadaga—it's a spiritualist community, and the hotel there and a few other areas are said to be haunted. There's a tavern in Rockledge that's haunted, a theater in Tampa… It goes on and on. We can find you all manner of places."

"You need permits for some of them, advance arrangements and all," Maura reminded him.

Nils grinned. "Well, there's more here, too. Hey, I know what we have—and near here! Caves. Yes, believe it or not, bunches of caves in Florida. Up in Marianna, but closer to us—not really far at all—Dames Cave. It's in Withlacoochee State Park, but…outside the state park, on the city edge, there's an area that's not part of any park system. Not sure who owns the land but you can trek through that area and find all kinds of caves."

Maura glanced at Brock; he knew from that look

that she definitely didn't want to go off exploring caves alone with Angie.

"Caves! Cool—haunted caves? Weird caves?" Angie asked.

"Oh, yes, there's an area called Satan's Playground. Not in a state park, and not official in any way. I know that Maura and Brock know it—they used to love to go off exploring when they were working here and they had a day off," Nils said. He smiled at Angie. "I'd truly love to explore the Devil's Millhopper with you, if you don't mind waiting."

Angie leaned toward him, smiling. "I don't mind at all. We'd intended to spend several days here."

Nils nodded, apparently smitten; they might have been a match made in heaven.

"Well, hey, Nils, can we still get lunch?" Maura asked.

"No," he said. "But yes, for you. Order quickly, if you don't mind. Chef saw you come in and he said that you're going to help make him more famous, so he'll wait. But he did have a few hours off before dinner, so…"

"I ate," Angie said, smiling. "Two of Chef's lunches would be great, but I just don't think I could manage to eat a second. I suggest the mahi-mahi."

Brock looked at Nils and then Maura. "Two hamburgers?" he asked.

Rachel cast Nils a weary gaze. "Mike and I had the hamburger plate. Chef makes a great hamburger."

"Yes, hamburgers sound good," Maura said.

"Done deal," Nils told them.

When he had walked away, Flannery leaned toward Angie. "I know how important your books and your videos are to you, but for the time being, please don't go off to lonely places on your own."

"I would never go on my own," Angie said.

"Good," Rachel murmured.

"I wouldn't be alone. Maura would be with me," Angie said. She turned to watch Nils. The chef had come out of the kitchen and they were speaking.

"Good-looking man," she murmured.

"So he is. Many women think so," Rachel said, studying something on her hand. "Anyway, the point is…"

"Don't go off anywhere alone as just two young women," Flannery said.

Angie smiled at him. "Detective Flannery, did you want to come along with us? Brock? It could be fun."

"Actually, if you want to see the caves, sure," Brock said.

Maura stared at him, surprised. She quickly looked away.

She knew that if he wanted to head out to the caves, there had to be a reason. And yes, he did have a reason.

Remains had been found not far from the caves.

And there were areas where more remains might be found, or where, with any piece of luck, the living just might be found, as well.

"Nice!" Angie said. "Great—it will be a date. Well, a weird threesome date," she added, giggling. "Unless, of course, Detective Flannery, Detective Lawrence, you two could make it?"

"We're working," Rachel reminded her sharply.

"Yes, of course," Angie said.

"And," Rachel added, "we don't want to be picking up your remains, you know."

Angie stared back at her, smiling sweetly. "Not to worry on my account. Brock will be with us, and when we go to the Devil's Millhopper, we'll be with Nils. Anyway! If you all will excuse me, I just popped in for a few minutes of the great company. We did such a good job with the video this morning that I'm dying to get into the pool."

She stood, motioning that Brock and Flannery didn't need to stand to see her go. "If you take work breaks other than food, join me when you're done."

Angie left them. When she was gone, Rachel stared at Maura.

"You *like* working with her?" Rachel asked.

"She's usually just optimistic about everything," Maura said. "And I guess she has that same feeling that most of us do, most of the time—it can't happen to me."

"Until it does," Brock murmured.

Maura glanced at Brock uncertainly. She had things to say that she hadn't been about to say in front of Angie.

"What is it?" Brock asked her. "We're working a joint investigation here—Rachel and Mike and I are on the same team."

"You want to go to the caves—really?" she asked.

She hoped he would just tell her the truth. "I want to go out to the area south of the Devil's Millhopper we talked about before. The remains today were found between the Millhopper and the caves. I think it might be a good thing to explore around there some more, though it could so easily be a futile effort," Brock told her. "People tend to think of Florida with the lights and fantasy of the beaches—people everywhere. There are really vast wildernesses up here. Remains could be… anywhere."

"It's so frustrating. Nothing makes sense, and maybe we're just creating a theory that we want to be true because we don't want more dead women, and we're all a little broken by Francine's murder. Maybe these cases are all different," Rachel said, looking over at Flannery. "One set of remains in a laundry, another in a forest where a Scout had to trip over them trying to pee. The one suggests a killer who wants to hide his victims. The other suggests a killer who likes attention and wanted to create a display. I mean, it's the saddest thing in the world, the way these last remains were discovered, by a kid…out on his night toilet rounds. Oh, sorry—you guys didn't get your food yet."

Brock waved a hand in the air and Maura smiled, looking down. She hadn't been offended.

But their hamburgers had arrived. And it wasn't how the remains had been discovered that was so disturbing—it was simply that now a second set had been found.

Rachel was looking at Brock with curiosity. "Do you think that the killer could be hiding kidnap victims in a cave or a cavern? Wouldn't that be too dangerous?"

"The better-known tourist caverns?" Brock asked. "Yes. The lesser-known caverns that are just kind of randomly outside the scope of the parks? Maybe. I don't know. He'd keeping them somewhere for days, maybe even weeks. Then there are also hundreds of thousands of warehouses, abandoned factories, paper mills…" He broke off. "I just know that there are three missing women somewhere, and I'd sure as hell like to find them while they're still just missing."

"And not dead," Flannery said grimly. He turned slightly, looking at Maura. "Do you remember anything, anything at all, from back then that might suggest anyone as being...guilty? Of killing Francine Renault."

Maura shook her head, then hesitated, glancing at Brock. He nodded slightly, and she said, "I was stunned—completely shocked—when we came upon Francine's body. When the news came out that Peter Moore had killed himself, I was already far away, and we were young and... I didn't know what else to believe. I—I was exploring on the internet today, though, and came across something that might—or might not— have bearing on this. It's a bit strange, so stick with me. There was a society in this area, decades ago, called the Sons of Supreme Being. They were suspected of the disappearance and possible death of a woman in the 1950s. That's why it struck me as maybe relevant. One of their members was supposed to testify in court—he died before he could. Now, I got this information from a random site—I haven't verified it in any way, but..."

Brock looked over at Flannery. "Have you ever heard anything about this group—this Sons of Supreme Being society or club or whatever?"

Flannery shook his head and then frowned. "Maybe, yes, years ago. I'm not sure I remember the name... When I joined the force, some of the old-timers were wondering during a murder investigation if the group might have raised its head again—a girl had been found in a creek off the Saint Johns River. She was in sad shape, as if she'd been used and tossed about like trash. But her murderer was caught—and eventually executed. Talk of rich kids picking up the throwaways died down. But as far as I know, nothing like that has been going on."

Maura was still looking at Brock.

"You have something else," he said.

She nodded and lowered her voice. "I don't think that Marie Glass realized that she was standing by me or that she was speaking aloud, but…she was watching her husband with Angie. And she said something to the effect that she shouldn't…cover for him. And she acted as if she hadn't said anything at all when she caught me looking at her. But in all fairness… Glass has always been decent to the people who worked for him, even if…"

"He's paid off a number of women through the years," Rachel said. "He was always decent to me. But there were rumors about him and Francine."

Glancing over at Maura, Brock said, "I want to find out if a young lady named Heidi Juniper is all right."

"Heidi Juniper?" Flannery asked him.

"She was working here. She didn't show up and Bentley left her a message that she was fired. He's supposed to be getting me contact information for her. Under the circumstances, I think it's important to know why Heidi didn't show up for work."

They had all finished eating. Flannery stood first. "Rachel and I will get to work finding out about Heidi Juniper. I was thinking you might want to talk to your old friends Donald and Marie Glass."

"Hardly my old friends," Brock said.

"I'm going to go to the library," Maura said. She

paused, looking at them all. "It really wouldn't make sense. Donald Glass may be a philandering jerk, since he is a married man. But he is so complete with his libraries, with his campfire stories...he included Francine's murder in the collection. Would he be so open if he was hiding something?"

"Being so open may be the best way of hiding things," Flannery said. He hesitated, glancing from Brock to Maura.

"Young lady, you are a civilian. You be careful."

"Not many people think that reading in a library is living on the edge," she said, smiling. "Brock will be near, and reading is what a civilian might do to help."

"We thank you," Flannery said. "Rachel..."

She rose and the two of them headed out.

"I'm going to the library with you," Brock told Maura.

"But I thought you wanted to speak with Marie and Donald," she said.

"What do you want to bet that they both show up while we're there—separately, but..."

"You're on," she said softly, standing.

Maura knew what she was looking for—anything that mentioned the Sons of Supreme Being. She delved into the scrapbooks that held newspaper clippings through the decades, aiming for the 1950s. Brock was across the room, seated in one of the big easy chairs, reading a book on the different Native American tribes who had inhabited the area. It was oddly comfortable to be there with him, even though she did find her mind wandering now and then, wishing that they could forget it all—and go far from here, someplace with warm ocean breezes and hours upon hours to lie together, doing nothing but breathing in salt air and each other.

Gritting her teeth, she concentrated on her research.

After going through two of the scrapbooks that went through the 1950s, she came upon what she was seeking.

The first article was on the disappearance.

In 1953, Chrissie Barnhart, a college freshman, had disappeared. She had last been seen leaving the school library. Friends had expected her to meet up with them at the college coffee shop to attend a musical event.

She had not returned to her room.

There was a picture of Chrissie; she had been light haired and bright eyed with soft bangs and feathery tresses that surrounded her face.

The next article picked up ten days later.

In a college dorm, a young man had awakened to hear his roommate tossing and turning and mumbling aloud, apparently in the grips of a nightmare. Before he had wakened his friend, he had heard him saying, "I didn't know we were going to kill her. I didn't know we were going to kill her."

The event was reported to the police and an officer brought the student who had the nightmare in for questioning; his name had been Alfred Mansfield. At first, Mansfield had denied doing anything wrong. He'd had a nightmare, nothing more. But the police had put the fear of God into him, and in exchange for immunity, he had told them about a society called the Sons of Supreme Being. Their fathers had been supportive of Hitler's rise to power in Germany. After the war, they had made their existence a very dark secret. Only the truly elite were asked to join—elite, apparently, being the very rich.

Alfred Mansfield hadn't known who he had been with, but he was certain he could help bring those who had killed Chrissie to justice. He had simply accepted a flattering invitation, donned the garments sent to him late one night and joined with a small group, also clad in masks, in the clearing.

All were anonymous—but he thought that their leader might have been Martin Smith, the son of a wealthy industrialist.

They hadn't killed Chrissie on the day she had been taken; Alfred didn't know where she had been kept. He only knew that he was in the clearing with the double tree when she had been dragged out, naked and screaming, and that the leader had spoken to the group about their need to make America great with the honor of those who rose above the others; to that end, they sacrificed.

Alfred had tried not to weep as he watched what was done to her and how she died. He didn't want to be supreme in any way. He wanted to forget what had happened.

He wanted the nightmares to stop.

He would serve as an informant for the police.

He was released, both he and the police believing that they had taken him in for questioning quietly and that he was safe out in the world. He'd done the right thing by letting the police know, and they would take it from there.

Alfred's body had been dragged out of the Saint Johns River twenty-four hours after his release. He had been repeatedly stabbed before being thrown into the water to drown.

The body of Chrissie Barnhart had never been found.

Maura turned a page to see an artist's rendering of Alfred's description of the murder of the young woman.

She gasped aloud.

It was a sketch created by a police artist. But it might have been the clearing by the History Tree, looking almost exactly as it did today.

Minus the masked men.

And the naked, screaming woman, appropriately hidden behind the sweeping cloaks of the men.

"Brock... Brock..."

Maura said his name, beckoning to him, only to hear him clear his throat.

She spun around. As they had both expected to happen, a Glass had come into the room.

Marie. Brock had risen and was blocking the path between Maura and Marie.

"Mrs. Glass," Maura said, rising. She felt guilty for some reason—and she must have looked guilty. Of something. She quickly smiled and made her voice anxious as she asked, "Did we miss something? I know that Angie will be more than happy to start up again with anything else you'd like."

"Oh, no, dear, I think we did a great job today. I just heard that someone was in the library—I should have known that it was you two! My bookworms. Still, in my memory, the best young people we ever hired for our summer program," Marie said.

"Thank you," Maura said.

Marie was looking at Brock. "Such a shame," she

said. "And I'm so sorry. What happened... Well, the mistake cost all of us, I'm afraid."

She did appear as if the memory caused her a great deal of pain.

"Marie, it's long over, in the past—and as far as things went, my life hardly had a ripple," Brock told her. Maura looked at him; he was so much taller than Marie that she could clearly see his face. His look might as well have been words.

She'd been much more than a ripple; losing her had been everything.

She lowered her head quickly, not wanting Marie to see her smile.

"It wasn't your fault," Maura assured her.

Marie was silent for a minute, and then said, "Maybe, maybe I could have... Um, I'm sorry. I didn't mean to disturb you. Get back to it—I have to...have to...do something. Excuse me."

She fled from the library.

"See?" Maura whispered to Brock. "See? There's something bothering her. She has, I think, been telling law enforcement that Donald was with her—*when he wasn't*. Brock, you have to come read this. Donald Glass didn't go to school here, but...if there was ever a candidate for the Sons of Supreme Being, he is one! Do you think that he could be resurrecting some old ideal? And look—look at the police sketch. Well, you have to read!"

Brock sat down where she had been. She set a hand on his shoulder, waiting while he went quickly through the clippings.

He was silent as he studied the pictures.

He turned back to her, rising, and as he did so, his phone began to ring. He pulled it from his pocket, glanced at the ID and answered. "Flannery. What did you find?"

His face seemed to grow dark as he listened. Then he hung up and looked at her.

"What is it?" she asked.

"I think we have another missing woman. Which frightens me. I just don't know how many this killer of ours keeps alive at one time."

"I'll be fine. I'll stay right next to Angie—and the group. We saw Mark Hartford in the hallway—he said that he had twenty people signed up for tonight. Oh, yeah—and Detectives Flannery and Lawrence are staying behind," Maura told Brock.

"I wish you'd just lock yourself in this room until I got back," he said, smoothing his fingers through her hair.

They hadn't slept; they weren't waking up. But they were in bed, and he was still in love with her face on the pillow next to his.

They'd left the library, making plans. But while talking, they'd headed across the lobby, to the elevator, up to her room.

And then talking had stopped, and they were kissing madly, tearing at each other's clothing, falling onto the bed, kissing each other's bodies frantically—very much like a pair of teenagers again, exploring their searing infatuation.

"Reminds me of staff bunk, Wing Room 11," she had told him breathlessly, her eyes on his as they came together at last, as he thrust into her, feeling again as he had then, as if he had found the greatest high in the world, as if nothing would ever again be as it was being with her, in her, feeling her touch and looking into her eyes.

And it never had been.

"I wonder if Mr. and Mrs. Glass ever knew how much the staff appreciated the staff room?" he'd asked later when, damp, cooling and breathing normally again, they had lain together, just touching.

Their current conversation had started with, "We have to get up. You have to go and see Heidi's family, and I'm taking my camera out for the campfire and ghost walk again."

"No. You're locking yourself in this room."

"No, that would be ridiculous. I'll be with about two dozen witnesses. No one would try anything."

The argument had been done; she did have logic in her favor. And so they dressed, reluctant to part, knowing that they must.

The evening had been decided.

Brock hesitated. "Do you think that Angie knows we're together again?"

"Probably, but…"

"But?"

"I'm not so sure she'd care. Angie is—Angie. Unabashed. Men are dogs—adorable dogs, and she loves them. But one of her great sayings is that if men are dogs, women definitely get to be bitches."

He frowned, thinking about Angie's behavior at lunch. "Does she know anything about Rachel and Nils having once been hot and heavy?"

"I don't think so. Why would she? She wasn't around way back then. Angie does like Nils. She likes you better, but…"

"I'm spoken for?"

"She might actually think that you're more interested in me—and that wouldn't sit well with her ego. She did tell me that if I wasn't interested, she'd move in."

He laughed. "Well, honesty is a beautiful thing."

"It can be—it can be awkward, too," Maura assured him. "So, are you leaving?"

"Not until I see you gathered with a large group of guests and Angie to head out to the campfire."

"Okay, then, we should go down."

He opened the door for her. They headed for the lobby. It was busy—people were gathering. One was a family, including a mom and a dad and three children: older boys and a girl of about five. The couple from the pool was going to be at the campfire that night; they greeted Maura warmly. A few people seemed to be alone. There were two more families, one with a little girl, one with twin boys who appeared to be about fourteen.

Angie was there already, chatting with Mark.

"Hey—are you coming out tonight?" Mark asked Brock. He seemed pleased with the prospect.

"No, duty calls," Brock said. "But hopefully I'll catch up by the end."

"You have to go?" Angie asked.

"I do."

"You can't send that other cop?"

"No—because Mike Flannery and Rachel Lawrence are coming here tonight. Rachel knows all about the campfire and the walk and the stories, but Mike has never had a chance to go. And there are things I like to do myself," Brock said.

"Ah, yeah, every guy thinks he's got to do everything himself," Angie said.

"Just on this. Mike and Rachel have really been taking on the brunt of the load. My turn for an initial investigation," he said pleasantly.

He saw that Mike and Rachel had arrived.

"I'll just have a word with Mike—maybe I'll see you later."

He walked over to join Flannery and Rachel, aware that they'd be heading to the campfire any minute.

"Thanks for doing the interview tonight," Flannery said. "Really. I know you don't want to leave. I swear, we'll watch her like a pair of parental lions."

"I think male lions just lie around," Rachel said.

"I'll be a good male lion," Flannery said. "I feel that I do need to do this. Everyone really knows the stories and the tree—or trees—but me."

Brock didn't want to admit that he really wanted to interview Heidi's parents himself; there were often little things that could be said but lost in retelling. It was always better to have several interviews with family, witnesses and more. And he did owe this one to Mike.

"I'll be back as soon as possible," Brock told them.

"And really, we don't know that you need to be worried."

"I don't know. Glass is looking like a more viable suspect all the time," Brock said.

"Glass won't be out here. No need to fear," Rachel

said. "And I may be small, but trust me—I am one fierce lioness."

Brock smiled. "I know," he told her.

He turned. Mark Hartford was deep in conversation with Maura. She wasn't looking Brock's way—she was listening.

He turned and headed out to the parking lot and his car. He knew he couldn't be ridiculous—he'd never keep his job that way.

It was a twenty-minute drive east to Heidi's home in a quiet neighborhood just south of St. Augustine. He noted that the girl lived in a gated estate.

The houses were about twenty years old and reflected an upper-working-class and family atmosphere.

Heidi's parents were eagerly waiting for him. Her mother, Eileen—a slim woman with curly gray hair and dark, tearstained eyes—was frantic. Heidi's father, Carl, bald and equally slim, kept trying to calm her.

"The police didn't even want to start a report until today—they said that she hadn't really been missing. I know my daughter—when she says she's coming home, she's coming home!" Eileen said and started to cry.

"When was the last time you spoke with her?" Brock asked gently.

"She was at work. She said she was leaving soon. It was right at the end of her shift—for that day. Shifts could change, and she didn't care at all. She sometimes worked double shifts, but she said that she wasn't going to work double that day. She was tired. She was coming home. But she never arrived. I waited up. I woke Carl. We drove all up and down the highway. I mean, nothing happened to her here—our community is very secure."

"Did you call her work—talk to anyone there?"

"Some man answered the phone—he just sounded irate. He said that they weren't a babysitting service and she wasn't even with the summer program. That she probably ran off with some friends!"

"You don't know the man's name?"

"He just answered the phone, 'Front desk, how can I help you?'" Eileen said.

"Rude. If I'd known how rude… You'll investigate, right? The detective who called us—Flannery—he was the first one who seemed concerned," Carl said.

Brock nodded. "We'll take this very seriously, I swear," he assured them, taking Eileen's folded hands. "This is important. Did she say anything else? Had she been having any trouble with anyone there? Had any of the other employees or guests been ugly to her—or come on to her inappropriately?"

"She loved her job," Carl said. "Loved it." He looked at his wife. "She said that Mr. Glass was nice, but she hardly saw him. Or Mrs. Glass. Fred Bentley was her supervisor, and he seemed to be fine. She said he was a stickler for time and the rules, but she was always on time, and she never broke the rules, so they got on fine. Oh, she loved the guy who was like a social director, and she was welcome to use the pool and the gym and go on the walks—as long as she wasn't disturbing or taking anything away from the guests. There wasn't anything she told you that she wouldn't have told me, right?" Carl asked his wife. "As far as I know, she simply loved her job."

"Yes, she did," Eileen agreed. "But…"

She frowned and broke off.

"Please, tell me what you're thinking," Brock said. "Even if it seems unimportant."

Eileen's frown deepened as she exhaled a long sigh before speaking. "Something odd... She was muttering beneath her breath. She said..."

"Yes?"

"Well, I think... I'm not even sure I heard her right. The last time I talked to her on the phone—before she left work and disappeared—she said something like... 'Supreme Being, my ass!' Yes, that was what she was muttering. I didn't pay that much attention—I thought she was talking about a guest—someone acting all superior. I didn't think much of it—people can act that way, when they think they're superior to those who are working. And my daughter would deal with it—and mutter beneath her breath. Yes. I'm almost positive, and honestly, I'm not sure what it can mean, if anything, but... Yes. She murmured, 'Supreme Being, my ass.'"

Chapter 8

"The beautiful Gyselle," Mark Hartford said, "is sometimes seen in the woods near the History Tree. Running from it. A ghost forced to live where she saw the end of her life. Or, as a spirit, does she remember better times? Is she running to the tree—where she would meet her lover and dream of the things that might have been in life?"

He told the tales well, Maura thought. And even after they had finished at the campfire, he spoke as they moved along the trails into the woods, and finally, to the History Tree.

Mark had asked her to speak twice and she'd obliged; she'd had the camera rolling again, too—she might as well since they were out there. Angie could decide later which night's footage she liked best.

Maura noted with a bit of humor that Mike and Rachel were being true to whatever promises they had certainly given Brock—they hadn't been ten full feet away from her all night.

But at the tree, she found that she wanted it on video from every angle. She kept picturing the police artist's rendering she had seen that day.

Creepy figures surrounding the tree, unidentifiable. The victim from the 1950s, Chrissie, caught in the arms of one of her attackers.

Were the current victims being held—as she had been held? And if so, how in the hell were they being hidden so well…until their remains were left to rot in the elements?

"You are getting carried away," Angie whispered to her.

"Just a little," Maura agreed.

"Questions—anything else?" Mark asked his group pleasantly.

Maura wondered if she should or shouldn't speak, but her mouth opened before her mind really worked through the thought.

"Yes, hey, Mark, have you ever heard of a group called the Sons of Supreme Being?" she asked.

He looked at her, a brow arching slowly.

His entire tour group had gone silent, all curious at her question.

"Yeah," he said. "I—yeah. I thought it was kind of a rumored thing." He lifted a hand. "No facts here, folks, just stuff I heard at college. They say they existed once. They were a pack of snobs—thought they were better than anyone else. They were never sanctioned by any of the state schools—in fact, I heard you got your butt kicked out if you were suspected of being one of them.

They were like an early Nazi-supporter group—seemed they watched what Hitler was doing in the 1930s. But, hey, nothing like that exists now, trust me!" He grinned at his crowd. "I'm a people person. Someone would have told me. Where did you hear about them?"

"Oh, I read something," Maura said. "I was just curious if it had been real or not."

"I can't guarantee it, but I heard that they did exist. No one I know has anything on who the members might have been or anything like that," Mark told her. "Although I did hear that while the rumors of the group started in the 1930s, it really went further back—like way, way back. It was the rich elite even in the 1850s— dudes who came to Florida from the north and all, and built plantations and homes and ranches after Florida became a territory and then a state. They considered themselves to be above everyone else—everyone! If you ask me—a theory I've never spoken aloud before— I have a feeling that Gyselle's death might have been helped along by members—even way back then. Those dudes would have thought that this tree was a sacred spot. And Julie Frampton could have easily whispered into someone's ear. Gotten them to do the deed."

"There is an idea for you," Maura murmured. "Thanks, Mark."

She felt Detective Flannery take a step closer to her.

"Okay, time to head on back, folks. No stragglers— no stragglers. We don't know what's up, but we're asking people to stay close." Mark pointed to the way out.

His group obediently headed back along the trail.

As they came out of the woods, she saw that Brock was walking from the parking lot toward them.

"Brock!" Angie called. "You missed new stuff—the beautiful Gyselle might have been killed by a secret society. Wild, huh?"

Brock frowned and glanced past her at Maura, Mike and Rachel.

"I asked Mark if he'd ever heard of the group," Maura said.

"Oh," he said. "Well, you got something new and fresh on a tour. Great."

He wasn't going to talk, not there, not then—not with others around them. She thought, too, that he seemed tense.

Maybe even with her.

Because, perhaps, she shouldn't have spoken.

But the day was done at last; she wanted nothing more than to get back and close out the world—except for Brock.

She knew that he'd meet first with Mike and Rachel. And, she knew, he'd probably had a rough last few hours—talking to the parents of another girl who had disappeared.

She yawned. "Long, long day—I'm going up to bed," she said. "Angie, we can head out to those caverns tomorrow—at least, I think we can. Brock, can you take the time?"

"Yes. In fact, I think that maybe Detectives Flannery and Lawrence can join us."

Flannery might have been taken by surprise; if so, he didn't show it.

"Yes, we'll all go. Search those woods—close to where the last remains were discovered. You okay with that, Angie?"

"You bet—that will be perfect. Oh, I do hope we

find something!" she said enthusiastically. "Oh, lord, that sounded terrible. Terrible. I mean, I didn't mean it that way. Except, of course, it would be cool to find a lair, a hideout—save someone!"

"That would be something exceptional," Maura said, looking at Brock. He still seemed disturbed. "So," she added, "Angie, an excursion tomorrow means you have to wake up fairly early."

"Oh, I will, I will. Meet in the coffee shop at 8:30 a.m.?" she asked.

"Sounds good," Brock said.

"Adventure day—nice break," Rachel murmured.

"You're really going to be there at eight thirty?" Maura asked skeptically.

"Ah, and I even have plans tonight! But yes, I'll be there," Angie said.

"You have plans tonight?" Brock asked her.

"Not to worry—I'm not leaving the property. I'm just meeting up with a new friend in the coffee shop—or not the actual coffee shop, you know, the little kiosk part that stays open 24/7. We'll be fine."

Maura wanted to get away from everyone.

"Okay," Maura said. "I am for bed." She didn't wait for more; she hurried past them and straight for the resort, anxious to get to her room.

And more anxious for Brock to join her.

Brock remained outside, just at the base of the porch steps, with Mike and Rachel—waving as Angie at last left them, smiling and hurrying on up the steps to meet her date.

He quickly filled them in on what Heidi's parents had told him.

Flannery shook his head. "It just gets more mired in some kind of muck all the time. I can see a serial kidnapper and killer, but… You think that there's some idiot Nazi society that has been going on for years—oh, wait, even before there were Nazis?"

"I know, I never heard of it before today—and then that's all that I've heard about. So there is a cult—or someone wants us all to believe that there is," Brock said.

"That could mean all kinds of people are involved," Rachel mused. She frowned. "I never heard what Mark was saying tonight before—that a really narcissistic group being 'supreme' might have existed as far back as the end of the Seminole Wars. Seriously, come on, think about it—and let's all be honest about humanity. At that time, males were superior, no hint of color was acceptable and no one had to say they were or weren't supreme. Society and laws dictated who was what."

"Okay, historically, we know that Gyselle was dragged out of the house to the hanging tree and basically executed there. History never told us just who did the dragging," Brock said. "I do believe that Heidi was taken by the same people who took the other girls—and I don't believe that she's dead yet, and we can only really pray—and get our asses moving—to find them."

"Brock, we have had officers going into any abandoned shack or shed, getting warrants for anything that was suspicious in the least. The state has been moving, but yeah, we need to get going on the whole instinct thing. You think that the caverns might yield something?"

"I think that remains were found very close to them,"

Brock said. "Anyway, I'm going up for the night. I'll see you in the morning."

"Yep. We'll say good-night and see you in the morning," Flannery said.

By then, the group from the campfire tales and walk had apparently retired for the night. The lobby was quiet as Brock walked across it.

The young man he'd met the night before was on the desk. Brock waved and headed for the elevator, but then noted that he didn't see Angie or the date she was meeting.

He headed to the desk.

"Yes, sir, how may I help you?" the young clerk asked.

"Miss Parsons was down here, I believe. I think she was meeting up with someone in that little twenty-four-hour nook by the entrance to the coffee shop. I don't see her."

"She was down here... I guess she went up."

"Was she alone?"

"I... I said hello, and then I was going through the reservations for tomorrow and okaying a few late departures. I didn't really notice."

Angie's room was on his way to the attic floor. Brock could knock on her door and check on her.

According to what he had seen and learned from Maura, Angie might well have cut to the chase with whomever she had met.

She might be in her room—occupied.

Well, hell, too bad. He was going to have to check on her—whether he interrupted something intimate or not.

Maura wasn't sure what was taking Brock so long, except that he'd be filling Mike and Rachel in on whatever had gone on with Heidi's parents.

She paced her room for a few minutes, then paused as her phone rang.

She answered quickly, thinking it was Brock.

It was not.

It was Angie.

"Maura," Angie said. "You've got to come out—find Tall, Dark and Very Studly, and come on out here."

"Come on out here? Angie, where are you?"

Angie giggled. "Almost getting lucky!" she said in a whisper. "You need to come out here—first. I've found something. Or rather, my own Studly found something for me. Come on, quickly, just grab Brock and get out here."

"Out here where?"

"The History Tree. I have something for you!"

Maura heard a strange little yelping sound—excitement or a scream? She dropped the phone and hurried out into the hallway, just in time to see Brock coming up the stairs at the end.

"Brock, come on. We have to go," Maura said.

"I tried to check on Angie because I didn't see her in the lobby, but she's not answering her door," he told her.

"She isn't there. She's out at the History Tree. Brock—she said that she's found something. She was excited, but then, it was strange—come on!"

She didn't wait for the elevator—she headed straight for the stairs. He followed behind her, calling her name.

"You shouldn't go. I should go alone. Maura!"

He didn't catch up with her until they were out on the lawn, halfway out to the campfire and the trail. He caught her by the arm. "Let me go. You get back in the resort, up in your room—locked in."

"I don't think there's anything wrong," Maura said.

"She wanted me to see something. Brock, you're armed and she said to bring you. She just wanted us both to come."

He shook his head, staring at her, determined.

"It could be a trap."

"Angie sounded like Angie. What kind of a trap would that be? Come on."

"No! You don't know—go back into the resort, into your room and lock the door."

She stared back at him.

"Please, Maura, if we're to go on…"

"But, Brock, I just talked to her. This is silly. I'm with you, and… Please, let's just hurry!"

She broke away from him, but he overtook her quickly. "Maura!"

"What?"

"You can't put yourself in danger," he told her. "Let me do my job."

"Oh, all right!"

"Go!"

She did. And since she knew that he'd wait until he saw her heading back into the resort, she turned and headed for the steps.

Something was bugging her about Angie's call. There had been that strange little noise. And then Angie hadn't spoken again. The line had gone dead.

Irritated but resolved, she hurried back into the resort. She waved to the night clerk and headed to the elevator—too tired and antsy for the stairs.

She walked down the hallway, feeling for her phone to try calling Angie again. She remembered that she'd dropped her phone on her bed.

That was all right; she was almost there.

She walked down the hallway to her room and pushed open the door.

The room was dark.

She hadn't left the lights out.

And neither had she thought to lock the door.

She had no idea what hit her; something came over her head, smothering any cry for help she might have made, and then she hit the floor.

And darkness was complete.

Brock walked carefully through the woods, swiftly following the trail to the History Tree but hugging the foliage and staying in the shadows.

Long before he reached the tree, he heard the cries for help and the sobs. He quickened his pace, but continued to move stealthily.

When he reached the clearing, he saw that Angie was tied to the tree.

She hadn't been hanged as the long-ago Gyselle had been; she was bound to the massive trunk of the conjoined trees, sobbing, crying out.

Brock didn't rush straight to her; he surveilled the clearing and the surrounding areas the best he could in the darkness. The moon was only half-full, offering little help.

There seemed to be no one near Angie. Still, he didn't trust the scene. It made no sense. Girls disappeared. Months later, remains were found.

None had been tied to the History Tree.

He pulled his phone out and called Flannery. "History Tree—backup," he said quietly.

And then, with his Glock at the ready, he made his way forward, still waiting for a surprise ambush from the bushes.

"Brock, Brock! Be careful, he knows you're coming... He knows... He could be here, here somewhere..."

"I'm watching, Angie," he said, reaching her. He found his pocketknife to start sawing on the ropes that bound her to the tree.

When she was free, she threw herself into his arms. "You saved me. Thank God I called Maura. He might have come back. He might have... He would have killed me. Oh, Brock, thank you, thank you."

Mike and Rachel came bursting into the clearing.

Angie jerked back, frightened by their arrival.

"It's all right, Angie. It's all right—who brought you here? Who the hell brought you here?" Brock demanded.

She began to shake. "I don't believe it! I still don't believe it!" she said, and she began to sob.

Maura awoke to darkness. For a moment, the darkness confused her.

At first she had no recollection of what had happened. When she did start to remember—it wasn't much. Someone had attacked her when she'd walked into her room.

She touched her head. No blood, but she had one hell of a headache.

Brock had been right. The call had been a trap.

Angie had called...and there had been that little yelp,

and then the phone had gone dead. But Brock hadn't allowed her to go with him.

Whoever had done this knew how Brock would react. Knew that he would never allow Maura to chance her own life.

She didn't know who it was. Mark or Nils Hartford? Bentley?

Donald Glass himself?

She tried to move and was surprised that she could. She struggled her way out of the covering that all but encased her. It was a comforter—the comforter from her bed at the resort.

She struggled to sit up and realized the earth around her was cold—as if she were in the ground. Struggling, she sat up—but she couldn't stand. The space was too tight. She could see nothing at all.

On her hands and knees, she began to crawl, blinking, trying to adjust to the absolute darkness. Where was Angie—had they taken her, too? Had Brock raced out to the clearing—to find nothing?

If so...

He'd wake the very dead to get every cop in the state out to start looking.

Maura began to shake, terrified. Then, wincing at the pain in her head, she moved forward again.

Brock would search for her, she knew.

She also needed to do her damned best to save herself.

She paused for a minute, listening. Nothing—but it was night. Late at night. She breathed in.

Earth. Earth and...

She paused, and suddenly she knew where she was—

well, not where she was, but what she was in. There was earth, but she'd also touched something hard, a bit porous.

And native to a nearby area. Coquina. A sedimentary rock made of fossilized coquina shells that had been used in the building of the great fort in St. Augustine, that still graced walkways and garden paths and all manner of other projects. But to the best of her knowledge, there hadn't been any at the Frampton Ranch and Resort, unless it had been long, long ago.

Maybe she was no longer near the resort. She didn't know how long she had been unconscious.

She kept crawling, not even afraid of what night creatures might be sharing this strange underground space with her.

And then, suddenly, she touched flesh.

"Who, Angie? Who did this to you?" Brock demanded, his arm around her still-shaking body as they headed back toward the resort. Flannery and Rachel had searched the area, a call had been put out for a forensic team and cops would soon be flooding the place.

"It was—it was Donald Glass!" she said, still sounding incredulous. "He was so polite, so gracious, and he said that he wanted me to see something very special. It was him!"

Flannery, right behind them, pushed forward. "Let's see if the old bastard is at the house. Supreme Being. I'll bet he sure as hell thinks that he's one. What the hell was he going to do? Did he think that Angie would die by herself by morning? Or was he coming back to finish the deed—right where he probably murdered Francine years ago?"

As they neared the house, Brock called to Rachel. "Stay with Angie, will you? I've got to go and bring Maura down."

"Don't leave me!" Angie begged, grabbing his arm.

He freed himself. "I have to get Maura."

Rachel had gotten strong; she managed to help Brock disengage a terrified Angie.

Brock raced up the stairs to Maura's room. He could tell the door to her room was open from halfway down the hall. He sprinted into it.

Empty.

The comforter was gone from the bed; her phone lay on the floor.

The breath seemed to be sucked out of him. His heart missed a beat, and for a split second, he froze.

It had been a trap. And he'd been such an ass, he hadn't seen it.

By the time he raced downstairs, the terrified desk clerk was hovering against the wall and Flannery had Donald Glass—in a smoking jacket—in handcuffs.

"No, no, this is wrong—I've been in my room. Ask my wife! Angie! Why the hell would you say these things, accuse me? I did nothing to you. I opened my resort to you. I... Why?"

Angie was shaking and crying, but Donald Glass was agitated, too. He appeared wild-eyed and confused.

"You meant to kill me!" Angie cried.

"I've been in my room all night!" Glass bellowed. "Ask my wife!"

Marie Glass was coming down the stairs, her appearance that of a woman who was stunned and stricken. Her hands shook on the newel post of the grand stairway as she reached the landing.

"Marie, tell them!" Glass bellowed.

Marie began to stutter. Tears stung her eyes. "I—I can't lie for you anymore, Donald."

"What?" he roared.

Brock strode up to him, face-to-face, his voice harsh, his tension more than apparent. "Where's Maura?" he demanded.

"Maura?" Glass asked, puzzled. Then he cried out, "Sleeping with you, most probably!"

"She's gone—she was taken. Where the hell is she?"

Donald Glass began to sob. He shook his graying head, far less than dignified then. "I didn't take Maura. I didn't hurt Angie. I swear, I was in my room. I was in my room. I was in my room—"

"Get every cop you can. We have to search everywhere. Maura is with those other girls, I'm certain, and they're near here," Brock said.

A siren sounded, and then a cacophony of sirens filled the night.

"We'll get him to jail—you can join the hunt," Flannery told Brock.

"I'll get out to the car with him. By God, he's going to talk," Brock said. He set a hand hard on Donald Glass's shoulder, following him and Flannery out to the police cruiser.

A uniformed officer jumped out of the driver's seat and opened the back door for them.

"He's not going to talk, Brock, get on the search—" Flannery began. "Or don't," he said as Brock shoved

Glass into the rear of the car and then crawled into the seat next to him.

"I don't have her. I don't have her. I don't have her!" Donald Glass screamed. "Don't kill me. Please, don't kill me!"

"I'm not going to kill you," Brock said. "What I need to know from you is anything I don't. Where around here could someone hide women?"

"But I swear, I didn't—"

"You—or anyone else. Dammit, man, I'm trying to believe you! Talk to me."

"Water...please... Don't kill me... Water..."

The flesh Maura had encountered spoke.

"I don't have water. I'm not going to kill you," Maura assured the voice she heard. "I'm Maura Antrim. Who are you?"

"Maura!"

The person struggled in the darkness. Maura felt hands grab for her. "I know you... I know you... I'm Heidi... I'm so scared! I stopped because a car had flashing lights and... I went out to help and there was no one to help, and someone hit me, and... I'm dying, I'm sure. I'm going to die down here. I'm so scared. It's so dark. I don't know... Did they take you, too?"

"Yes, they hit me over the head in my hotel room. You don't have any idea of who did this to you?"

Maura felt the girl shake her head.

"We're not far from the resort—I know that. Not far at all."

"But where...?"

"I think we're in a bit of a sinkhole—covered up

years and years ago—but someone used it as something. They shored up the sides with coquina. But they got us in here—there has to be a way out. Can you still move?"

"Barely."

"Okay, so stay still. I'm going to try to find a way to escape."

"No! Don't leave me!" Heidi begged, clinging to her.

"Then you have to come with me," Maura said firmly.

She began to crawl again, and she felt the earth grow wetter.

They were in a drainage culvert. They were probably right off the main highway, and if she could just find the grating…

Her mind was numb, and it was also racing a hundred miles an hour. Angie had called her because she had been meeting someone. That someone had lured Angie out and let her lure Brock out and, of course…

That someone had known Brock. Yes, she'd thought that right away. Known that he would make her go back, that he'd consider himself trained, ready to meet danger.

Brock would want Maura safe.

Whoever it had been walked easily and freely through the resort, knew where to go—how to avoid the eyes of the desk clerk and the cameras that kept watch on the lobby.

Thoughts began to tumble in her mind. One stuck.

It couldn't be. And, of course, it was just one someone…

It wasn't a society or an organization—but rather someone who had known about it.

She suddenly found herself thinking about the long-lost Gyselle, the beautiful woman running from her pursuers, those who would hang her from the History Tree until dead.

Maybe they had been part of a society. Maybe they hadn't. Maybe they had just…

She saw a light! A tiny, tiny piece of light…

The night was alive. Police were searching everywhere.

Dogs were out, each having been given a whiff of Maura's scent. But while they searched the woods and the house and the gardens and the pool, Brock headed off toward the road.

Donald Glass had spilled everything he knew. No, there had never been a basement; there were foundations, of course, but barely wide enough for one maintenance man. There had been a well, yes, filled in years and years ago.

Outbuildings had been torn down. The wings on the resort were new. There were no hidden houses; the one little nearby cemetery had no mausoleums or vaults…

Where to hide someone?

Warehouses aplenty on the highway. And the drainage tank off the road, ready to absorb excess water when hurricanes came tearing through.

A perfect place for a body to deteriorate quickly.

Donald Glass had been taken off to jail.

That didn't matter to Brock right now. Nothing mattered.

Except that he find Maura.

He reached the road and raced alongside the highway, seeking any entrance to the sunken areas along the pavement.

He ran and ran, and then ran back again, and then noted an area where foliage had been tossed over the drain.

He raced for it.

And as he neared, he heard her. Crying out, thundering against the metal grate.

"Maura!"

He cried her name, surged to the grate and fell to his knees. His pocketknife made easy work of the metal joints. He pulled her out and into his arms, and for a long moment, she clung to him.

And then he heard another cry.

"Heidi—she says there are other women down there… Dead or alive, I don't know."

He pulled Heidi from the drain. She crushed him so hard in a hug that he fell back, and several long seconds passed in which it seemed they were all laughing and crying.

Then, in the distance, he heard the baying of a dog. He shouted, "Over here!" Soon, there were many officers there, many dogs, and he was free to take Maura into his arms and hold her and not let go.

Epilogue

"You know," Maura said, probably confusing everyone gathered in the lobby of the Frampton Ranch and Resort by being the one to speak first. "Sometimes, really, I can still see her—or imagine her—the beautiful Gyselle, running in the moonlight, desperate to live. Legends are hard to shake. And I'm telling you this, and starting the explanation because, in one way, it's my story. And because Gyselle's life has meaning, and legends have meaning, and sometimes we don't see the truth because what we see is the legend."

She saw interest on the faces before her. The employees knew by now that Donald Glass had been taken away. They knew that horrible things had happened the night before, that Angie had been attacked by her host and that Maura had been attacked—but found, and found along with Heidi and the other three missing girls.

Heidi was already fine and home with her parents. The other girls were still hospitalized. For Lily Sylvester it would be a long haul. She'd been in the dark, barely fed and given dirty water for months—and it had taken a toll on her internal organs. Lydia Merkel would most probably be allowed to go home that afternoon, and for Amy Bonham the hospital stay would be about a week.

There was hope for all of them. They'd lived.

The resort guests had all gone. They had been asked to vacate by the police and Marie Glass until the tragedy had been appropriately handled.

The resort was empty except for the staff, Detectives Flannery and Lawrence, and Angie and Maura.

Donald Glass remained gone—biding his time in jail before arraignment. But if things tonight went the way Maura thought they would, that arraignment would never come.

"Thinking about Gyselle brings to mind—to many of us—what happened to Francine Renault. Well, I don't really see her in a long gown running through the forest, but she, too, met her demise on this ranch. And through the years, we suspect, so did many other young women. They didn't all come to the tree. After Francine they were stabbed. Yes, by the same killer. Brutally stabbed to death. As Peter Moore, a cook here back then, was stabbed. It doesn't sound as if it should all relate. One killer, two killers, working independently—or together? All compelled by just one driving motive—revenge."

Blank faces still greeted her. She wasn't a cop or FBI. They were curious, but confused.

"I thought they were random kidnappings," someone murmured.

"Yes and no," Maura said.

Brock stepped forward. "We discovered a longtime association or society. It was called Sons of Supreme Being. They don't—we believe—really exist anymore. So legend gave way to what might be revamped—and imitated."

"I thought the police were going to explain what really went on here," Nils Hartford said.

"I guess Donald Glass did consider himself a supreme being," his brother added sadly.

"Well, he might have," Maura said. "But…there you go. I'm back to beautiful Gyselle, running through the forest. Her sin being that of a love affair with the owner of the plantation."

"I'm letting Maura do the explaining," Brock said. "She's always been a great storyteller."

Maura turned and looked at Marie Glass. "Donald didn't kill Francine, Marie. You did."

"What?" Marie stared at her indignantly. "I did not kill Francine. My husband killed Francine."

"No, no, he didn't. He didn't kill Francine. Nor did he kill Maureen Rodriguez or the other woman whose remains have been found. Donald loved history—and kept it alive. He loved women. You found your way to take revenge on those who led him astray—and, of course, on Donald himself. Oh, and you killed Peter Moore—that's when you discovered just how much you enjoyed wielding a knife."

"This is insane! How do you think that I—" Marie gestured to herself, demonstrating that she was indeed a tiny woman "—could manage such acts? Oh, you ungrateful little whore!"

"No need to be rude," Brock said. "Marie, you were good—but we have you on camera."

"Really? How did I tie up Angie and get back and…"

"Oh, you didn't tie up Angie."

"Of course not!"

"Angie tied herself up," Brock said calmly.

Angie sprang to her feet. "No! I wasn't even around when Francine Renault was killed. Or the cook. Why on earth do you think that I could be involved?"

"I still don't know why you were involved, Angie," Brock said. "But you were. There was no one else in the woods. We've found sound alibis for everyone else here. Oh, both Mark and Nils Hartford were sleeping with guests that night—a no-no. But you weren't one of those guests. And there's video—the security camera picked it up—of Fred Bentley talking to the night clerk right when it was all going on. What? Did you two think that we were getting close? That we'd figure it out— that Marie's hints about her husband were a little too well planted? Then, of course, there was you—wanting to see where the bones had been discovered. Strange, right? But I'm thinking that the bones washed out in the drainage system somehow—and Marie panicked and wrapped them in hotel sheets, thinking she could dispose of the remains with the laundry. And maybe you were hoping that you hadn't messed up somehow. Maybe you didn't know. But for whatever reason, you and Marie have been kidnapping and killing people. Marie getting her rage out—certain she could frame her husband if it came to it. But you…"

"That's absurd!" Angie cried.

"No, no, it's not. We checked your phone records—

you talked to Marie over and over again during the last year. Long conversations. She chose the victims. You helped bring them down."

The hotel staff had all frozen, watching—as if they were caught in a strange tableau.

"You're being ridiculous!" Angie raged. She looked like a chicken, jumping up, arms waving at her sides in fury. "No, it was Marie! I didn't—"

"Oh, shut up!" Marie cried. "I'm not going down alone. I can tell you why—she wanted to hurt Donald as badly as I did. We were willing to wait and watch and eventually find a way to create proof that made the system certain that it was Donald. And those women... Whores! They deserved to suffer. We could have seen that Donald rotted for years before he got the death penalty. There's no record of it—her mother was one of my husband's whores. He paid her off very nicely to have an abortion. The woman took the money—she didn't abort." She looked at Angie. "You should have been an abortion!"

"Oh, Marie, you lie, you horrible bitch!"

Angie tore toward her in a fury.

Rachel stepped up, catching her smoothly and easily, swinging an arm across her shoulders.

She then snapped cuffs on Angie.

And Marie—dignified Marie—was taken by Mike.

She spit at him. She called him every vile name Maura had ever heard.

And then some.

They were taken out. The employees stood in silence, gaping.

Then, suddenly, everyone burst into conversation,

some expressing disbelief, some arguing that they were surprised.

"No," Fred Bentley said simply, staring after them. "No."

"Yes. You saw," Brock told him.

"So, what do we do now?" Mark asked.

"Well, Donald Glass is being released. Right now he's sick and horrified at what has happened. He believed that he caused Marie to be cruel. He never knew he had an illegitimate child, and now he's left with the fact that his child…became a killer. He needs time. He's the one who has to make the decisions," Brock said. "For now, he has said to let you know that you don't need to worry while he regroups—everyone will be paid for the next month, no matter what."

There was a murmur of approval, and then slowly the group began to break up.

Fred stared at Brock and Maura for a long time. "Well," he said. "I will be here. I will keep the place in order. Until I know what Donald wants. I'll see that the staff maintain it. I'll be here for—for anything anyone may need." He started to walk away, and then he came back. "I'm… I can't believe it. Imagine, that cute little Angie. Who could figure…? But thank you, Brock. Yeah, thank you so much."

He turned and left, heading behind the restaurant toward the office.

Brock and Maura stood alone in the center of the lobby.

"Shall we go?" he asked her.

"We shall, but…"

"But where, you ask?" Brock teased. "An island.

Somewhere with a beautiful beach. Somewhere we can lie on the sand and make up for lost time, hurt for those who died and be grateful for those who lived. You are packed and ready to leave?"

"I am," she told him.

They drove away.

Maura could feel the deliciousness of the sea breeze. It swept over her flesh, filtering through the soft gauze curtains that surrounded the bungalow. She could hear the lap of the waves, so close that she could easily run out on the sand and wade into the water.

It was beautiful. Brock had found the perfect place in the Bahamas. It was a private piece of heaven, and no one came near them unless they summoned food or drink with the push of a button. The next bungalow was down the beach, and they were separated by palms and sea grapes and other oceanfront foliage.

It was divine.

Though nothing was more divine than sleeping beside Brock so easily, flesh touching, sometimes just lying together and talking about the years gone by, and sometimes, starting with just the slightest brush against each other, making love.

There would be four days of this particular heaven, but…

"You did talk to your parents, right?" Brock asked Maura.

"Of course! If news about what happened had reached them and they hadn't heard from me…they would have been a bit crazy," Maura assured him. She inched closer to him. "I almost feel bad for my mother—she's so horrified, and she admitted all the messages she'd gotten from you and kept from me... poor thing. And then, I have myself to blame, too. I was hurt that I didn't hear from you—and so I never tried to contact you myself. I thought I was part of your past— a past you wanted closed."

"Never. Never you," he said with a husky voice. Then he smiled again. "But your mom... She is coming to the wedding."

Maura laughed. "Oh, yes. She didn't even try telling me that we were rushing things when I said we were in the Bahamas but coming home to a small wedding in New York at an Irish pub called Finnegan's. And my dad... Well, he thinks that's great. Why wait after all this time? Now or never, in his mind. It's nice, by the way, for your friend to arrange a wedding and reception in one at his place—his place? Her place?"

"Kieran and Craig have been together a long time. Craig is a great coworker and friend. Kieran owns Finnegan's with her brothers—they're thrilled to provide for a small wedding and reception. And you...you don't mind living in New York? For now? Maybe one day, we'll be snowbirds, heading south for the winter. And maybe, when we're old and gray, we'll come home for good. Or, hell, maybe I'll get a transfer. But for now..."

She leaned over and kissed him. "I lost you for twelve years. I'm going to say those vows and move to New York without blinking," she promised. "Besides... Hmm. I'm going to be looking for some new clients— New York seems like a good place to find them."

He smiled, and then he rolled more tightly to her, his

face close as he said, "It's amazing. I knew I loved you then. And I never stopped loving you—and I swear, I will love you all the rest of my years, as well. With or without you, I knew I loved you."

"That's beautiful," she whispered. "I love you, too. Always have, always will." She smoothed back his hair.

He caught her hand and kissed it.

Then the kissing continued.

And the ocean breeze continued to caress them both as the sun rose higher in the sky.

Later, much later, Maura knew that the ocean breeze wouldn't be there every morning. They wouldn't be sleeping in an oceanfront bungalow with the sea and sand just beyond them.

And it wouldn't matter in the least.

Because his face would be on the pillow next to hers, every morning, forever after.

* * * * *

Also by B.J. Daniels

HQN

Buckhorn, Montana

Out of the Storm
From the Shadows
At the Crossroads

Montana Justice

Restless Hearts
Heartbreaker
Heart of Gold

Sterling's Montana

Stroke of Luck
Luck of the Draw
Just His Luck

Harlequin Intrigue

A Colt Brothers Investigation

Murder Gone Cold
Sticking to Her Guns
Christmas Ransom

McCalls' Montana

The Cowgirl in Question
Cowboy Accomplice
Ambushed!
High-Caliber Cowboy
Shotgun Surrender

Visit her Author Profile page at Harlequin.com,
or bjdaniels.com, for more titles!

HIJACKED BRIDE

B.J. Daniels

Prologue

September
Houston, Texas

"**A**nd with the power vested in me, I now pronounce you husband and wife."

Patrick turned from the altar with his new bride, more pleased with himself than he'd ever been. He'd pulled it off—against incredible odds, too.

Finally, he'd beaten Jack Donovan at something. He'd not only gotten the girl—he'd gotten *Jack's* girl.

He took his bride's hand as they started down the aisle. By this time tomorrow he would finally have everything he wanted.

Now it was just a matter of getting Angie out of town—and killing her.

He glanced over at his new bride. Angie *was* a beauty.

Too bad she was so damn rich. And too bad for her that the last thing he wanted was a wife. Mostly, he knew he couldn't keep up the pretense much longer and he wasn't about to let her leave him and take all her money with her.

So he'd come up with a plan to get rid of her on their honeymoon.

She looked at him. He squeezed her hand, reassuring her, just as he'd had to do for weeks. He'd seen her start to waver, becoming more uncertain as the wedding grew closer. It helped that Jack Donovan was locked up in jail and would have a hell of a time making bail at all, let alone getting out to spoil the wedding.

"Angie!"

At least, that had been the plan, Patrick thought as he looked up to see Jack burst into the church, yelling Angie's name.

"Angie?"

The look on Jack's face was priceless as he saw the bride and groom coming down the aisle. *Too late, Jack.*

Patrick felt Angie stumble at the sight of Jack framed in the doorway. The bitch had been *hoping* Jack would stop the wedding! Patrick tightened his grip on her. Amazing the way she trembled, just seeing Jack again. She still loved him—even after all the trouble Patrick had gone to, the weeks of planning and pretending, holding her hand and letting her cry on his shoulder.

He could feel her slipping out of his control as if her blind love for Jack Donovan was even stronger than the drugs and lies Patrick had numbed her with.

Patrick put his arm around Angie—just in case she had any idea of going to Jack—as four security guards cut Jack off. He was a little disappointed Jack didn't put up more of a fight, but then, it was four against one.

By the time he and Angie reached the church door, the guards had restrained Jack in a room out of sight—and hearing. There was no way Jack was getting near the bride. Not today. Angie didn't need to hear any more of Jack's wild stories about being framed. *You lose, Jack.*

Everything was going just as planned. Patrick felt his smile slip, though, as he looked over at his bride. Too bad she didn't appreciate all he'd gone through to get her. He'd always been second to Jack. Just the little friend from the poor family in the old neighborhood. The guy Jack always had to help out when Patrick failed. Well, not this time.

This time he'd outsmarted Jack. But that didn't mean he wouldn't always be second to Jack when it came to Angie. But not for long, he reminded himself.

By tomorrow Angie would be dead. Jack would be devastated—and back in jail for violating the restraining order Patrick had against him.

And Patrick would be rich and free. And there was nothing Jack could do to save Angie. Not a damn thing.

Once in the limo, Patrick poured the champagne and handed a glass to his pale and obviously shaken bride. Did she realize yet the mistake she'd made? Fortunately, he wouldn't have to keep up this pretense much longer.

At his sweet insistence, she took a sip of the drug-laced champagne. Later, when she complained she didn't feel well, they would leave the reception early.

She thought they were flying to Hawaii. Wouldn't

she be surprised when she realized that wasn't the case? By then, though, she would be in no shape to protest.

He glanced over at her, afraid he wouldn't be able to get her out of town quickly enough. Tendrils of her dark hair framed an unusually pale face. Her brown eyes shone with unshed tears and her hand shook as she held the champagne glass to her lips. Damn Jack for showing up.

A stab of anger pierced Patrick's practiced facade. He had bent over backward to try to make her happy, had spared no expense, but she still wanted Jack. He had to turn away, to look out the window. He couldn't blow it now. Just a few more hours of pretending and Angie would be dead and he would be a very rich widower. He did like the sound of that.

He turned back to his bride and smiled sympathetically. "I know how hard this is for you. We both loved Jack. It's…heartbreaking to see him mess up his life like this. Drink up," he said as the limo pulled up to the country club where the reception was being held. "It's almost over."

Chapter 1

Angie woke to the roar of the small jet touching down. She opened her eyes, instantly confused as to where she was. Worse, who she was with. She'd been dreaming about Jack and a wedding. She'd foolishly expected to see Jack in the seat beside her.

But instead it was Patrick. Just the sight of him brought it all back. Jack's lies. Jack's betrayal. She turned away, feeling sick. Out the small window all she could see at first was darkness, then the inky black line of high mountains etched against the night sky. The tops of the mountains gleamed in the moonlight. Snow?

"Where are we?" She sat up straighter, suddenly afraid. "I thought we were flying to Hawaii." The confusion in her mind was scaring her.

"Don't you remember, sweetheart?" Patrick asked, looking concerned.

She'd been forgetting things the past few weeks. A lot of things, it seemed. She often felt as if she were walking around in a fog.

That's what she got for falling in love with Jack Donovan. Hadn't her father always warned her not to mix business and pleasure? She'd broken all the rules she'd lived by for twenty-eight years—and paid the price.

Jack had lied, cheated, broken the law. If that wasn't enough, he'd betrayed her with another woman. *That* she could never forgive.

"We're in Montana," Patrick said patiently, as if speaking to a child.

"Montana?"

"Remember, we decided a cabin in the mountains of Montana would be much more romantic than Hawaii, where everyone honeymoons."

The plane slowed to a stop. She looked out the window and felt a chill run up her spine as she saw that they hadn't even landed at an airport. Instead, the small jet had put down on what appeared to be an old highway surrounded by pine-dark mountains. She could see weeds growing up through wide dark cracks in the pavement, as if the highway hadn't been used in years, and shivered as she looked around and saw nothing but mountains and pine trees.

She didn't remember Patrick saying anything about a change in their honeymoon plans. Nor about flying to Montana right after the reception to stay in a cabin. A cabin in the woods was so…not Patrick.

Her head ached as much as her heart. She felt Patrick take her hand and she wondered if she was losing her mind. She must be. Why else had she married Jack's best friend?

As she let Patrick lead her off the plane, Angie drew in the cold night air, filling her nose with the scent of pine. She felt her head begin to clear a little.

"The car is right over here," Patrick said. "I have champagne chilling just for you."

She could hear a motor running, and moved toward the dark vehicle parked off the highway.

He opened the door and ushered her into a large, warm Suburban SUV. The heater was on. She could hear the whirl of it, feel the waves of heat rising around her. She glanced out into the darkness but didn't see another soul.

"Here, have some of this while I get our luggage," Patrick said, pouring her a glass of the champagne. "Drink up, sweetheart. It's only a short drive to the cabin."

She took the glass he pressed into her fingers as he closed the car door. She saw that he was waiting just outside the car. She lifted the glass to her lips.

He winked. Over the rim, she watched him walk down the road away from her. She knew he'd look back, but she didn't know how, any more than she knew how she'd ended up here.

He glanced over his shoulder, smiled as if pleased with her, then continued toward the plane.

Her lips touched the cold champagne. She shivered and lowered the glass, staring down into the sparkling liquid as if she could read the future in the bubbles.

He'd be angry if she didn't drink it after he'd gone to the trouble. The thought shocked her—not that Patrick would be angry; he was always put out with her when she didn't seem to appreciate the things he did for her—that she could be manipulated like that.

What was wrong with her? She'd never let any man force her to do anything she didn't want to do. Quite the opposite.

But here she was married to Patrick, a man she didn't love. About to drink a glass of champagne she didn't want. About to go to a cabin she had no desire to go to on a honeymoon she didn't care about.

This wasn't like her. At least, not like the woman she had been before she started falling for Jack Donovan.

That's when she changed, wasn't it? Or was it when she found out that Jack had betrayed her? Wasn't that when she started letting Patrick make decisions for her?

She lowered her window and poured the champagne onto the ground. The night air felt good. She turned down the heat and breathed in, as if imbibing sanity.

Patrick started back toward her with the luggage, the bright starlight bathing him in cold whiteness. She stared up at the sky, startled and afraid she was losing her mind. A new moon. She couldn't have agreed to be married on this night. New moons were bad luck.

Instinctively, she reached up to touch the good luck charm around her neck.

It was gone! In its place was something cold and foreign.

Panic filled her. She never took off the talisman. Never. Had she lost it? Or had Patrick talked her into removing it for the wedding? What else had he talked her into?

This marriage.

She opened the car door and stumbled out. She didn't know how this had gotten so out of hand, but she couldn't let it go any further.

"Stay in the car," Patrick said, sounding irritated. "I can get the luggage."

"I don't want to go to the cabin." It surprised her how unsteady she felt on her feet. "I'm sorry, Patrick. This is a mistake. I want to take the plane back—"

The roar of the jet drowned out the rest. She lurched toward the small plane.

Patrick dropped the luggage and grabbed her arm. "Are you crazy?" he yelled at her over the sound of the jet taxiing down the old highway away from them.

She tried to shake him off, but she felt dizzy and weak and her strength was no match for his.

"Most women get cold feet *before* the wedding, not after," he said, letting go of her because there was no place to go now.

She realized that beyond the old road, there were no lights. No towns close by. Why did she get the feeling that Patrick had planned it that way? He'd wanted her alone, just the two of them, because he thought he could make her forget Jack. Had she let him think that was possible? She must have.

"Where is my necklace?" she asked. Her grandmother had given her the amulet to ward off evil spirits, although she'd never told anyone that except Jack. He'd laughed and hadn't believed her. He'd never had to worry about bad luck—until he met her.

"You're concerned about that stupid, cheap charm?" Patrick snapped. "Really, Angie, a woman with your money shouldn't be wearing costume jewelry. Especially the dime-store kind."

"That necklace brought me luck," she said, feeling close to tears, as the small jet roared over them and headed south, the lights becoming dimmer and dimmer.

"Luck? What is it with you and this superstition thing?"

She shook her head. She didn't have the energy to explain it to him. "Just give me my necklace." She remembered now his coming into the bride's room with a present for her. He'd laughed when she told him it was bad luck to see the bride before the wedding; then he'd come up behind her, taken off the amulet and put the bright white gold chain around her neck, a large diamond pendant dangling from it. Against her protests, he'd pocketed her amulet.

She shivered. "I want my necklace."

"So much for my wedding present." Patrick shoved his hand into his jacket pocket and tossed her the amulet.

She caught it and saw at once in the starkness of the starlight that the chain was broken. Her gaze came up. She glared at him.

"It broke when I took it off," he said, sounding angry and disgusted with her. "Do you have any idea how much that diamond around your neck cost me? Oh, I forgot, money means nothing to you."

She leaned against the side of the car, clutching the talisman in her fist, exhausted. "I appreciate everything you've tried to do but—"

"Angie, I'm sorry," he said, softening his tone. "It's late and we're both tired. Look, if you still feel like you've made a mistake tomorrow, I'll take you into

Missoula and you can catch a plane back to Houston, all right?"

She breathed deeply in and out, trying to clear the fog from her brain. She had to find that old inner strength that had got her this far in life. She had to take control of her life again.

He stepped to her and brushed a lock of her hair back from her forehead, his fingers warm against her skin. "I know I'm getting you on the rebound, but I don't care. I thought my love for you would be enough for a while, until… I guess I was kidding myself that you could ever love me as much as I love you."

She closed her eyes, too tired, too confused, too wounded by what Jack had done to her.

"The plane is gone and it's getting so late," Patrick said, his tone soothing. "The closest real town is Missoula, and to get there you have to go down a narrow, winding mountain road. Can we just go to the cabin tonight? It's not far. I'll build a fire. We can have a late supper. I'll sleep on the couch. In the morning, if it's still what you want, I'll drive you to Missoula. I'd hate to drive the road tonight considering I've never been on it before. But I will, if it's what you want."

He sounded so reasonable, so caring. She opened her eyes. She could see his face in the moonlight. How could she have let him think she could fall for him the way she had for Jack? And marriage? Why couldn't she remember his asking her, her agreeing? She couldn't even recall most of the wedding ceremony—except for Jack bursting into the church. The look on his face.

"Angie, it's just one night," Patrick said, his voice thick with emotion. "If I'd known earlier that you felt like this…" He shook his head, picked up the luggage and stood waiting for her to tell him what she wanted.

She felt weak and sick to her stomach. She couldn't remember the last time she'd eaten. Her head still ached and she felt as if she needed to sit down before she fell down. She needed something solid to eat. She needed to get her strength back, to get her edge back.

She looked at him, telling herself this wasn't his fault. He'd been there for her during those horrible days after Jack's arrest, after she'd found out about Jack Donovan's crimes against her. Patrick had thought he could make her forget Jack. Maybe at some point she'd hoped he could.

"There is food at the cabin?" she asked.

He smiled. "Everything we need."

"You'll take me to this…Missoula in the morning?"

He nodded, looking miserable but resigned. "If it's still what you want."

"Thank you. I'm sorry—"

"Let's not talk about it tonight," he interrupted. "You're tired. Get in the car where it's warm. I don't want you catching your death of cold because of me."

She climbed into the Suburban. The heat did feel good. She rolled up her window, leaving a crack at the top to allow in fresh night air, even though she was chilled to the bone. It was a cold that had little to do with the temperature and everything to do with Jack Donovan.

She closed her eyes and leaned back against the seat. The fog seemed to be clearing a little from her mind, as if she was coming out of a long, fitful sleep.

Breathe. And don't think about Jack. Don't think about the look on his face at the church.

She didn't open her eyes as she heard Patrick load the suitcases in the back, then climb behind the wheel, nor when she heard the *clink* of her empty champagne glass as he picked it up from the floor.

"Why don't you have another glass of champagne? It will make the drive go faster and then I will cook you a wonderful dinner. All you have to do is rest in front of the fire."

"I really can't drink any more al—"

"No arguments. Let me take care of you for tonight. Give me at least that."

She heard him pour the champagne. She could almost feel the fine cool spray against her lips. She still didn't open her eyes even as he pressed the glass into her hand. It was just one night. Just one more night of letting Patrick take care of her. Tomorrow she'd fly back to Houston. Tomorrow she'd put her life back together. Tomorrow.

Chapter 2

"Are you sure this is the right road?" Angie asked, growing anxious as the Suburban's headlights exposed what looked more like a trail than a road through the pines.

Patrick turned onto it and started up the mountainside, the beam of the headlights bobbing through the dense woods that formed a wall on each side. "This might surprise you, but I know what I'm doing. Have a little faith, Angie."

Faith. Faith wasn't something she'd ever been strong on. She'd always depended on skill—and the survival lessons her father had taught her.

She tried to relax but couldn't. The rutted road switchbacked upward like a jagged scar cut in the mountainside. The suffocating darkness of the thick pines pressed in on her. Overhead, the starlight glittered in the moonless sky above the pines, like an omen that her luck had taken a turn for the worse.

She squeezed the amulet in her wedding suit pocket, wishing she'd never laid eyes on Jack Donovan.

The pines suddenly opened, and in the clear, cold starlight, Angie saw that the road fell away into a deep, narrow gorge on her side of the car. A twisting ribbon of silver wound its way through the canyon below.

"Take a look," Patrick said as he drove the Suburban along the road's edge.

"Be careful!" She let go of the amulet in her pocket to clutch the grip handle over the door.

"Angie, I thought you'd appreciate this. It isn't like you to be afraid."

No, it wasn't like her. Because she'd always been the one at the wheel. But she didn't see him looking down into the canyon, either.

"I didn't mean to scare you," he said. "It's just that you may never see the gorge again in starlight."

She hoped not. She pressed back against her seat, staring straight ahead at the road. It seemed to climb ever higher up the mountainside.

Out of the corner of her eye, she noticed that Patrick's knuckles were white from gripping the steering wheel so hard. Hadn't Jack once told her a story about Patrick having a horrible fear of heights? So why would Patrick pick a place like this for their honeymoon?

"How much farther is the cabin?" she asked, regretting now that she'd let him talk her into this. How could the road into Missoula have been any worse than this?

Patrick sighed. "I thought you'd love this."

She could hear the disappointment in his voice. "It's spectacular. Just a little scary."

"Only if you were to fall down in there."

She shuddered at the thought and took one last look at the canyon, wondering again what Patrick had been thinking in bringing her here.

A short distance along, the road veered back into the trees, straightening a little but still climbing upward, then leveled out some. Patrick slowed, turned right onto a dirt lane that looked even less traveled. A half dozen turns through the trees later, Angie got her first glimpse of the cabin in the headlights.

"Rustic, isn't it?" he said. "No phone. No electricity. We even have to pump our own water from the well out back." He parked in front, the headlights shining on the small log structure surrounded by dark pines. "Not even a cell phone works up here."

Off to the side, she saw an outhouse with a crescent moon cut in the door. If Patrick was trying to shock her, he was wasting his time. She'd roughed it before—but then, he had no way of knowing that. Or did he?

She looked over at him, anxiety prickling her skin. He'd picked this place because he wanted to make sure they were completely alone! He was afraid Jack would find them.

"I'm surprised this would appeal to you," she said, remembering the gorge and Patrick's fear of heights. Patrick seemed to like the finer things in life. She couldn't imagine him "roughing it."

He flashed her a rueful smile. "I guess you don't know me. Nor I you, as it turns out." He glanced pointedly at the expensive bottle of champagne chilling in the ice bucket next to her. "It seems there are a lot of things you don't like."

She had poured out the first glass and spilled the second, the alcohol making her nauseated. He must have seen the wet spot beside her car door earlier at the airstrip. Just as he must have noticed she hadn't drunk much at their wedding reception. Patrick didn't seem to miss much. Nor did he pass up an opportunity to try to make her feel guilty. Hadn't he realized by now that she would always disappoint him? Telling him she felt sick and didn't want any more would only make him angry with her.

"I'm just not thirsty."

"No, I guess not."

Just before he turned off the headlights, she spotted another vehicle parked off in the woods. An older model Jeep Wagoneer. Someone was here! Someone who knew the road and could take her to Missoula tonight rather than in the morning.

"The cabin owner left us an extra car," Patrick said, dashing her hope in one fell swoop. "We're so far from civilization, he was worried that if we had car trouble of any kind we would be stranded up here."

So they were alone...far from civilization...

Patrick turned off the engine. Silence and darkness settled around them. "I'll go light the fire and the lanterns—why don't you stay here." He got out, taking the car keys with him, and unloaded a large cooler from the back of the Suburban.

She watched him carry it up the steps to the cabin in the moonlight. He put it down, dug out a key from his pocket and unlocked what appeared to be a padlock.

The cabin didn't even have a real lock. A few minutes later, lantern light flickered on inside.

The car cooled down, the engine ticking. It was the only sound. She looked around, seeing nothing but trees and darkness. When she glanced toward the cabin again, Patrick was on the porch, motioning impatiently for her to come inside.

She opened her door and got out. The air was cold and smelled wet. Her head ached as if she had been drinking champagne for days. Maybe she had. She couldn't remember.

Patrick had gone back inside. She couldn't see him. She looked over at the Jeep parked in the trees, then back at the cabin, half expecting to see Patrick watching her. He wasn't—for once.

She hurried over to the Jeep and tried the door. It wasn't locked. The dome light came on. The keys were in the ignition! She quickly extinguished the dome light and pulled the keys, pocketing them.

Relieved, she closed the car door. If Patrick wouldn't take her to town in the morning, she'd drive herself. The thought made her feel a little better. If she didn't feel so weak and tired and sick, she might go now. Except she couldn't imagine trying to find her way to Missoula in the dark.

"Hope you're hungry," Patrick said, as she stepped into the cabin and closed the door behind her.

She could already smell food—precooked, no doubt. The cooler she'd seen must be one of those that also kept food warm. Someone had left the Suburban—and the food—parked off the old highway. Didn't that mean a town couldn't be very far away?

"Starved."

That seemed to please him. "Make yourself comfortable. Rest. It won't be long. I have everything under control."

She didn't doubt that.

The cabin was nicer inside than she'd expected. A fire crackled in the stone fireplace with a large leather couch, end tables and several club chairs circled around the inviting blaze. But the fire did little to take the chill out of the cabin.

She moved to stand directly in front of the grate, warming her hands first, then turning to survey the cabin as she heated her backside. Three rooms. Kitchen, living room and bedroom. Through the partially open door, she could see part of a patchwork quilt covering the antique iron-framed double bed. There was a back door, but it was padlocked from the inside. That seemed odd.

Patrick went out to the Suburban and came back in, putting his suitcase and some other items by the door. She didn't pay any attention to what he'd brought in. She felt chilled and tired and, even as hungry as she was, she wished she could just go to sleep now and skip dinner.

"We're having steaks, baked potatoes, salad and a nice merlot," he said as he went back into the kitchen. He was certainly pushing the alcohol. Did he think he could get her drunk and change her mind?

"Sounds wonderful." She didn't have the energy to argue.

Sitting down on the hearth, the fire warming her back, she watched him add wood to the old-fashioned stove. He took out several foil-wrapped containers and set them on top of the stove.

When she was sure he was too busy to notice, she took off the diamond pendant and put it in her pocket. Quickly threading the amulet onto the gold chain, she clasped it around her neck, buttoning her blouse so it was hidden from view. What Patrick didn't know wouldn't hurt him.

Through the cloth of her blouse she rubbed the good luck charm, pressing it against her bare skin. It felt wonderfully familiar. She closed her eyes, feeling at peace for the first time in weeks.

"There are some clothes for you on the bed. Change while I finish dinner. You'll be more comfortable."

She glanced toward the bedroom. She didn't have the energy to play dress-up. But neither did she have the energy to argue with him about this any more than she did the wine. She got up and walked toward the bedroom, afraid to see what he wanted her to put on.

With relief, she spotted a pair of flannel-lined jeans, a sweater and a fleece-lined canvas coat. It all looked wonderfully warm. She hurriedly changed, noticing that some of her own things were hanging in the closet along with several pairs of her shoes, including her warm winter boots.

She felt a little guilty. It had been thoughtful of Patrick to consider her comfort. The new clothes he had bought her were all the right size and felt good. And he'd brought some of her things from her Houston hotel room—

An owl screeched outside the cabin, making her blood curdle. *"When you hear the screech owl, honey,*

*in the sweet gum tree, it's a sign as sure as you're born
a death is bound to be."* She clutched the amulet at her
neck for a moment, remembering the new moon outside, suddenly afraid.

When had Patrick put her things in the cabin? She
hadn't seen him bring anything into the bedroom from
the Suburban. He'd either mailed the items up here or—

Was it possible he'd been here before tonight?

But he said he'd never been on the road to Missoula
before.

She moved to the chest of drawers and opened the
top one. Several more new items of clothing for her.
Some still had the tags on. She lifted out a bright red
teddy, read the name of the store on the tag. Little Lil's
Boutique? She'd never heard of it.

She closed the drawer and glanced in the closet. At
the far back, she spotted a wadded-up pale blue plastic bag. Squatting down, she reached in and pulled it
out. Printed on it was "Little Lil's Boutique, Missoula,
Montana." Missoula?

Several other plastic bags had been stuffed into this
one. She pulled them out, not recognizing any of the
store names. All of the bags had receipts in the bottom.
She dumped them onto the floor and glanced over her
shoulder, expecting to find Patrick standing behind her.

Why did she think he would be upset to find her
checking the dates? After all, he'd bought the clothing for her.

She picked up the receipts. They all had the same
date on them. Three weeks ago. All signed by Patrick.

The receipts blurred in her trembling fingers. How
was that possible? She'd only agreed to marry him a

little over a week ago. Even now, she couldn't recall why. And she remembered distinctly Patrick promising to take her to Hawaii. She hadn't been to Hawaii in years and the distance from Houston had appealed to her. She'd wanted to get as far away from Jack Donovan as possible, someplace warm and tropical.

Her heart began to pound. Patrick had been planning to bring her to this cabin for *weeks*. He'd bought this clothing and rented this cabin *before* Jack was arrested. *Before* he'd asked her to marry him. He'd been that sure he could get her here.

And he had.

Her head ached, but the fog was clearing, leaving in its wake a growing fear that stole her breath and filled her mind with panic.

My God, what had Patrick done to get her here? And why?

Chapter 3

Jack Donovan swept past the reporters, covering his eyes to keep from being blinded by the camera lights and the flash of bulbs.

"Mr. Donovan! Are the allegations against you true?"

"Jack! How long have you been ripping off low-income homeowners in your old neighborhood? What else is the investigation going to uncover?"

Jack ducked into the back of the black limo parked at the curb and slammed the door on the reporters and their questions. He still couldn't believe any of this was happening and it only kept getting worse.

"Going to that church was beyond stupid," snapped the distinguished gray-haired man sitting next to him, as the limo driver sped away from the jail. "You knew there was a restraining order against you. Do you have any idea how hard it was to get you out tonight? What in blazes is wrong with you?"

Jack Donovan shook his head as he looked out at the darkness. He wouldn't know where to start. "Montie, you've known me all my life. You don't believe these allegations against me, do you?" He turned to look at the elderly man on the wide leather seat next to him.

"It doesn't matter what I believe, Jack—"

"It does to me," Jack snapped. "How can you defend me if you believe I'm guilty?"

Montague Cooke shook his head. "You really aren't that gullible, are you? Lawyers defend guilty clients all the time, Jack."

"We're not talking about any client. Or any lawyer. You've been a family friend all of my life."

"I'm your lawyer, Jack. I was your father's lawyer. It's my job to defend you. Even if you're guilty."

"That's comforting," Jack said sarcastically.

"Someone put a gun to your head and make you go to that wedding?" Montie said sharply.

What had Jack thought he could do? Stop the wedding? Convince Angie of…what? That all the charges against him were fabricated? That she could trust him? Maybe. Maybe he'd just needed to see for himself that Angie was really going to marry Patrick.

Well, he'd seen it and he wasn't even sure that if he'd gotten there sooner it would have made a difference. She'd done it. She'd married Patrick. She was Mrs. Patrick Ryerson now. And he still couldn't believe it.

He leaned back and closed his eyes. The limo smelled of pipe tobacco and leather, a familiar and comforting scent. He'd been riding in the back of one of Montie's limos for almost as long as he could remember.

Still, it felt strange that his father wasn't here. It had

been over a year since Kelly Donovan died, but Jack still expected to open his eyes and see his father sitting across from him, leaning back into the leather as if born to it, long legs stretched out and a big smile on his handsome face. Kelly Donovan loved riding in a limo.

"The point is, you have to quit acting so damn stupid," Montie said, tapping fresh tobacco into his pipe as the limo cruised the streets of Houston. Traffic was light this late at night, and they had temporarily lost the media. "What were you thinking?"

He hadn't been thinking—nor paying attention to his business, not for months—that was the problem. He should have been worried about clearing his name of the charges now against him instead of thinking about Angie, but that wasn't possible.

"I know she didn't want to marry him," Jack said, shaking his head.

One of Montie's thick white brows shot up. "What makes you think she didn't want to marry him?"

"Because. She's in love with me," Jack said, holding on to what he believed to be the one truth in his life right now.

Montie grunted and took his time lighting his pipe. "Who is this woman, this Angelina Grant, that you think is in love with you?"

"You met her that night at the restaurant."

"Just in passing—"

Montie had run into the two of them at a local uptown restaurant. What had they been celebrating that night? Their one-month anniversary? They'd been like teenagers, everything feeling so new, so wonderful.

"I remember she was beautiful."

Jack nodded. Beautiful and funny, sweet and innocent in a way that had stolen his heart.

"But what do you actually know about her?" Montie persisted.

"She's the heir to some fortune. Import-export, I think." It hadn't mattered. He'd fallen for her in spite of her wealth, always having been leery of women with a lot of money. Too much money could corrupt.

"You never asked?" Montie shook his head.

"It didn't matter. Also, she was never involved in the actual business end of it, from what I gathered. Her father died recently, but by then he'd sold the businesses and put everything into stocks and bonds and a trust fund for her, his only heir."

"How nice for her," Montie commented. "How exactly did you meet this woman?"

"In the park this spring. Angie was trying to flag down a cab not far from my office building when some idiot driving too fast practically ran her down. I pulled her out of the way and she bought me dinner." He shrugged. "As they say, the rest is history."

Montie shot him a look. "You saved her life?"

"It wasn't quite that dramatic."

The older man grunted. "So you know nothing about her other than what she told you?"

He knew the important things. Like how her brown eyes sparkled in candlelight, how her dark hair felt running through his fingers, how she made *him* feel. "I know her—all right?"

"Jack, how can you be sure this woman is even rich?" Montie demanded.

"I don't care if she's rich or not," he snapped.

"She could have been after your money."

Jack shook his head. "You saw the way she dressed. She was staying at the Carlton Arms." Montie looked ready to argue. "Anyway, I saw a report from her accountant one day when I was in her suite. It was lying on the coffee table. I didn't really look at it—"

Montie groaned. "She just left it out where you could see it?"

"It wasn't like that." But maybe she had purposely left it there. Maybe she'd wanted him to know she wasn't after his money. "You don't know Angie."

Montie grunted again. "I know she's married to Patrick."

"He was there for her after all this stuff came down about the housing and me." But even as Jack said it, he knew something else had happened. Somehow Patrick had turned Angie against him, talked her into marriage. It wasn't what Angie wanted. Jack had seen that in her eyes at the church. In her expression when he'd burst in before the security guards had hauled him away. Angie loved him, not Patrick.

"So much for her undying love for you," Montie noted.

"She never said she loved me." Jack looked out the tinted side window, the lights of Houston blurring by. "It never got that far."

Montie shook his head. "And you never told her how you felt, did you?"

He'd been planning to, but then there was a fire at one of the houses his construction company was building in his old neighborhood, and the next thing he knew he was arrested for arson and fraud.

"You didn't ever happen to see her social security number, did you? Or the name of her financial advisor?"

Jack frowned. "Why the interest in Angie?" He hadn't been paying attention to anything but Angie that day when he'd seen the financial report. She had come back into the room dressed in a black sheath, a tiny string of pearls at her slim throat.

"She married Patrick and they have both left town. That pretty much says it all."

Jack shook his head. Montie was convinced Patrick was behind the kickbacks and the arson. "I still can't believe Patrick would do something like this."

Montie growled. "Jack, open your eyes. You put him in charge of those homes."

"I know, but it was our old neighborhood where we grew up, we know those people. I never thought he'd cheat them."

The press was having a field day with the story, saying Jack had been taking kickbacks—the difference between the materials that should have been going into the houses and the inferior ones that actually were. And that Jack had burned down a house under construction to try to cover his crime when it looked like he was going to get caught.

Montie puffed on his pipe for a moment. "The buck stops with you since you own the company. Patrick, of course, says he quit when he became aware of what you were doing. I suspect he's the concerned citizen who turned you in. I'm just worried the investigation will turn up more substandard housing down there."

So was Jack. He hadn't been involved in that part of the business in the year that he'd turned the project over to Patrick. They'd built a lot of houses during that time. "I need to talk to Del." Del Sanders was the general contractor on the project, a man who'd worked for Jack's father.

Montie was already shaking his head. "I told you I don't want you going near Del or any of the workers. I don't want anyone thinking you paid them—or threatened them—to lie for you in court. Patrick has already said you threatened him."

"You know better than that."

"A judge and jury might see it differently since you violated the restraining order today at Patrick's wedding."

Jack raked a hand through his hair. He was bone weary, exhausted and sick with regret. He never should have put Patrick in charge of that housing project. He should have paid closer attention to what was going on down there. He should have told Angie he loved her.

"Jack, you have to let me handle this," Montie was saying. "It's a legal problem. That's what you pay me for. We'll get Patrick, don't worry."

Don't worry? What a joke. The hardest part was sitting back and doing nothing. "It's my reputation at stake here."

"It's your *reputation* that's going to get you off with probably little more than a slap on the hand," Montie said. "Sure, there are people who are going to believe you cut corners. You wouldn't be the first contractor to get rich that way. Your only crime is bad judgment for hiring Patrick and letting him run the project."

Even if Montie got him off, his reputation would be tarnished. He would have to forget the housing project, maybe even sell his construction business. The majority of people would think he "bought" his way out of the charges, and he knew it.

They rode in silence for a few minutes, and Jack realized they were almost to his penthouse.

"I tried to warn you about Patrick," Montie grumbled.

Jack glanced out at the city and the darkness, remembering when he and Patrick were kids. They'd been close as brothers growing up in a poor section of Houston, the same part of town where Jack had been building low-income housing for the past year.

"You've always been too trusting, Jack," Montie was saying. "And Patrick has always been too competitive when it came to you. He pretended it didn't bother him when you prospered and he didn't. I'm sure you got him started in his first business, the one he lost—maybe the others, as well. I would imagine he resented the hell out of you because of it."

Jack didn't deny he'd helped Patrick. Why not? Jack had the money. Patrick didn't. And they were friends.

"I saw that hungry look in his eyes when that story came out about you in *Fortune* magazine. He was jealous as hell of you—more jealous, obviously, than either of us realized. You giving him a job overseeing construction of nice homes in your old neighborhood was probably more than Patrick could take."

Jack shook his head. "I thought he'd appreciate the fact that we were building houses for families we used to know, trying to help people who were just like us."

"Just like the way you *used* to live," Montie pointed out. "I have a feeling it isn't something Patrick likes to remember."

"Life can only be understood by looking back," Jack said, trying to remember where he'd heard that.

"At least now you realize what Patrick is capable of," Montie said.

Yes, Jack thought. He was capable of stealing Angie from him and leaving him facing criminal charges. Jack was now in danger of losing his business, his reputation, his freedom... And yet the loss that was killing him was Angie.

"You're sure this was all Patrick's doing?" Jack just didn't want to believe it. "How could he pull it off without the general contractor and the job foreman not knowing what was going on? He couldn't. That means Del and Leonard both knew." Leonard Parsons was the job foreman, someone Del had hired. Jack had only seen the man a few times. Not paying closer attention to what was happening down there was another mistake.

"Jack, I told you. Don't concern yourself with this," Montie said. "I talked to Del. Patrick was running things. Del was pretty much stuck in his office. As for Leonard, well, he said he thought you knew about the cheaper materials being used in the house. In fact, he thought the orders had come directly from you."

Jack swore. "So Patrick had to be the one behind this." He couldn't help but think about the day of his father's funeral, when Patrick had suddenly appeared after a five-year absence. He and Patrick had had a falling-out over a business Jack had helped him start. But when Patrick had shown up for Kelly Donovan's funeral just over a year ago, Jack had been grateful and glad to see him.

He had thought Patrick had changed and wanted to

give him another chance. So he'd given him the job. Patrick had seemed overwhelmed by Jack's generosity.

The limo stopped at a traffic light. Jack realized that Montie was staring at him.

"You still want to believe that Patrick isn't behind this?" He sounded incredulous. "Jack, the man just married the woman you were in love with, framed you and took off. I wouldn't be surprised if he and this Angie woman were in on this together."

Jack scoffed at the idea. "You don't know Angie."

"It doesn't sound like you did, either," Montie said as the limo pulled up in front of Donovan, Inc., a large, glittering monolithic structure in the heart of Houston. The offices for his many businesses were housed on several floors, with his penthouse apartment on the seventeenth floor.

"I want you to lay low," Montie said. "Try to stay out of the public eye. I know you're upset, but don't make matters worse."

"How could things be any worse?"

"If you jumped bail and went after Patrick and this woman," Montie said.

The thought had crossed Jack's mind—except, what would be the point? It wouldn't prove Patrick had framed him. Or prove that Angie hadn't been in on it. Bursting in on their honeymoon would only make him look like a bigger fool—and get him thrown in jail for jumping bail and ignoring for a second time the restraining order against him.

"We'll get the proof we need against Patrick," Montie said. "He isn't smart enough to get away with this.

But you are to have no contact with him. I can't have you violating that restraining order again."

Jack's attempts to talk to Patrick after the arrest had led to the restraining order. Patrick had said he feared for his life for testifying against Jack.

"Patrick has you right where he wants you," Montie said. "Anything you do to fight this will only make you look more guilty."

But how could he not fight it?

"Do the clothes fit?" Patrick called from the cabin kitchen.

Angie leaned against the bed, so shaken her legs felt as if they wouldn't hold her. "Perfectly," she managed to answer.

"Everything all right?" he called back, obviously hearing something in her voice that warned him.

She cleared her throat and pushed herself up, fighting for her old strength, her old courage. "Fine. I thought I'd just rest a while until dinner is ready. I'm a little tired."

"Good idea," he called back to her, sounding more cheerful over the clatter of dishes and silverware.

He didn't seem to hear her come up behind him. He was humming, his back to her, as he put a single red rose beside one of the plates at the table he'd just set.

She watched him turn back to the counter and had to lean against the kitchen doorjamb, she felt so weak and sick. The smell of steak and baked potatoes made her stomach growl with hunger. How long had it been since she'd eaten? She couldn't remember.

Patrick had one of the potatoes split open. He bent

over something on the counter, grinding it with the edge of a glass.

Her gaze went to the reflection in the corner window. He methodically dumped several white pills from a prescription container onto the counter and pulverized them to dust with the bottom edge of the drinking glass, then ground several more.

To her horror she watched him brush the white powder into his palm and then into the open baked potato. Without ever turning in her direction, he topped the potato with sour cream and chives, then set it on the table beside the plate with the rose on it. *Her* plate.

She couldn't move, couldn't breathe. The headaches, the fogginess, the forgetfulness. How long had Patrick been drugging her? From that first night when he'd come to her with the news of Jack's duplicity? He'd made her a drink. It had tasted bitter, but no more bitter than what Patrick had told her about Jack.

Had it all been a lie? Jack had sworn he was innocent, but she hadn't believed him. Because it had been easier to believe Jack lied, being a liar herself.

She watched Patrick pocket the container of pills. He'd manipulated her from that first night. That's how he'd gotten her to turn her back on Jack, to marry him so quickly, to come to this cabin with him. That's how he'd known weeks in advance that she would be coming here with him as his wife.

But why? Why go to so much trouble to—

Oh God.

She stumbled back, bumping into the edge of a bookshelf along the wall.

Patrick turned, surprise flashing in his eyes. He

looked to the table where he'd put the baked potato. She could see the question in his gaze. How long had she been standing in the doorway? Long enough to see him put the drugs in the food? Or just long enough to see him pocket the pills?

"I thought you were going to rest for a while," he said.

Her expression must have given her away. She'd definitely lost her touch. She used to be able to hide her feelings without any trouble. It was one of the first things she'd had to learn.

Whirling, she bolted for the front door, but he was on her in an instant, bringing her down hard on the wooden floor, knocking the air from her lungs. She gasped like a fish thrown up on the beach as he dragged her to her feet.

"This isn't the way I wanted it," Patrick yelled, angrily shoving her backward. "If you had cooperated it would have been painless. All you had to do was drink the damn champagne. You would have been out cold by now and it would be over."

"Why?" she gasped, stumbling back from him.

"Why?" he parroted, shoving her as he advanced on her. "Why? Because I was sick to death of things always coming so easy to Jack. He wasn't getting you and your money on top of everything else."

"You did this for the money?" she cried, the irony killing her.

"Don't tell me you really believed I *loved* you?" He shook his head. "I just wanted to win for once. Do you have any idea what it was like growing up in Jack's shadow? No, a woman like you couldn't understand that any more than Jack could. But now I'm going to be the one with the money, the power. I'm the winner for a change." He smiled. "And poor Jack's the loser."

She stared at him, too shocked to speak, as she inched backwards, trying to stay away from him but running out of room in the small cabin. "You were Jack's best friend."

Patrick smirked. "I was just do-gooder Jack's pet project. He deserves what he got."

Anger bubbled up inside her and she wanted to lash out at him, but she knew he was waiting for her to do something stupid like that. She had to be calm. To think. But her head ached and she felt light-headed from lack of food, from the drugs she now realized he'd been using to neutralize her. "Patrick, you've made a terrible mistake."

"The only mistake I made was in not killing you on the way up here," he said as he advanced on her. "But how would I have explained that—you still dressed in your honeymoon suit? I've put too much into this to have it spoiled now."

She stumbled back, bumping into one of the chairs, as her mind reeled. Jack had tried to tell her it was all lies, but she hadn't listened. She thought he was just lying to save his skin. That was something she could understand. Just like she expected men to betray and disappoint her, didn't she?

She moved around the chair, furtively looking for something to use as a weapon against him. She was too weak to fight him off and they both knew it.

"Patrick, I'm not who you think I am. I'm not rich. I'm not even—"

"Not rich? Nice try, but I'm not stupid. I checked you out. You're loaded."

She was shaking her head. "If you kill me, it will have been for nothing. Those financial reports were fakes. I was just after Jack's money." She was near the door now but he was too close. She'd never be able to get through it before he caught her. Nor could she outrun him even if she did.

"It isn't going to work, Angie." Patrick stepped toward her. "You're a lousy liar. After Jack's money!" He laughed. "You were in love with him. Don't you think I know that? You'll go to your grave loving Jack. But at least *I'll* have your money."

A lousy liar? That was a first. "Patrick, there is no money." She was trapped. She couldn't possibly get out the front door before he grabbed her. Nor would running in front of the fireplace buy her anything but a little time. Either way, she knew he'd catch her in an instant. And no matter how much she protested, he wasn't going to believe that he was killing her for nothing.

"Do you realize what you've put me through this last week, all the whining about Jack, all the reassuring I've had to do? I just wish I could see Jack's face when he finds out about your death."

The raw bitterness and hatred in his voice cut through her like a blade. How could she not have seen this? Because Patrick was more than adept at deceit.

She tried to clear her mind, to think. Out of the corner of her eye, she spotted the ice bucket, the neck of the expensive champagne bottle sticking out, where Patrick had put it on a small end table next to the couch. She hadn't noticed before that he'd brought it in from the Suburban. Just as she hadn't noticed the sediment at the bottom. How could she have been such a fool? Love and betrayal. Falling for Jack was about to cost her her life.

She glanced toward the fireplace tools on the other side of the fireplace, knowing Patrick was watching her every move.

He followed her gaze, just as she knew he would. The poker handle gleamed in the firelight. He smiled, sure she could never reach it before he caught her, but wanting her to try.

She lunged toward the tools.

Patrick gave her an extra second of a head start— no doubt to make it sporting. It was all she needed. He sprang at her, still so sure she was going for the poker that he was taken off guard when she swung around to face him suddenly, her hand closing over the neck of the champagne bottle full of drugs resting in the ice bucket.

He was off balance and not expecting the blow. She swung, aiming for his head. It caught him on the temple, a glancing blow, but enough to drop him to his knees.

She raised the bottle, ready to strike him again, and saw him reach into his jacket pocket. Even before he withdrew it, she knew he was going for a handgun.

She hurled the champagne bottle. It caught him in the shoulder. He let out a grunt of pain as the gun clattered to the floor, and for just an instant, she thought about diving for it. But he was closer and stronger.

She grabbed the ice bucket as Patrick groped for the gun. Using both hands, she hurled it at his head. The bucket hit with a *thud*, making him shriek and fall to his back on the floor as the ice and water cascaded over him.

Just before she turned to run for the door, she saw him try to get to his feet, swaying, blood running down into his left eye from the cut on his forehead where the ice bucket had split his skin open.

Her only hope was that it would slow him down. She burst out of the door, slamming it, frantically fumbling with trembling fingers to padlock the door behind her. The lock clicked closed.

She could hear Patrick banging around inside the cabin. The paned windows weren't large enough for him to get through. With luck, he would try to break down the door—and that would give her more time.

Once he had realized she'd padlocked him in and he couldn't break down the door, he'd go for the back door. That door was also padlocked, but from the inside. It should take him a while to find the right key.

At best, she'd bought herself a few precious minutes. She hoped it would be enough.

She ran to the Jeep, jerked open the door and threw herself behind the wheel, afraid this was another of Patrick's tricks—giving her hope and then snatching it away. She dug the key out of her pocket and shoved it into the ignition. As she pushed in the clutch and turned the key, she prayed it would start. A first. Praying.

The cold engine coughed and backfired like a shot, making her jump. She pumped the gas pedal and tried the engine again, as she heard Patrick crashing angrily into the front door. Then silence.

The Jeep engine sputtered to life, running rough, but running. She slammed the car into reverse, groping for

the headlights switch. As the lights flashed on, she saw
Patrick come barreling around the side of the cabin.

She swung the Jeep around and hit the gas, the tires
throwing dirt and pine needles as she left him behind
in a cloud of dust and darkness. It wasn't until she was
headed down the road and saw the headlights behind her
that she realized the mistake she'd made. Why hadn't
she thought to try to disable the Suburban? She told herself there hadn't been time. Her father must be rolling
over in his grave. Everything he'd taught her—wasted.

The Jeep rattled and bounced as she barreled down
the narrow, rutted road, the dark pines flashing by. She
didn't dare drive too fast for fear of crashing into the
trees. The Jeep couldn't outrun the newer Suburban,
anyway, and Patrick had the advantage: He knew the
road.

Not that she wasn't determined to make this as hard
for him as she could. Even if he caught her, she was
going to do her damnedest to make him work at killing
her. At least she would have that satisfaction.

She tried to remember the road from earlier, when
Patrick had been driving. Behind her, the lights of the
Suburban closed the distance between them. It was all
downhill now—to the big curve and the gorge.

She knew she stood little chance. Not only did he
have the larger, more powerful vehicle and know the
road, but also he hadn't spent the past couple of weeks
being drugged out of his mind. Mostly, though, she
knew that Patrick couldn't let her get away. Just as she
knew with sudden certainly where on the road he would
try to kill her.

He was gaining on her, the blazing headlights of the

SUV growing brighter and brighter, closer and closer, until they filled the interior of the Jeep, blinding her.

With a teeth-rattling jar, the Suburban crashed into the back of the Jeep. She gripped the steering wheel, desperately trying to keep the Jeep in the narrow tracks between the trees.

Ahead she could see where the trees ended—and the gorge opened. Patrick dropped back a little. This would be the spot. The headlights were growing brighter behind her, the Suburban picking up speed.

Her hand went to the amulet at her neck as the black gaping hole of the river gorge opened before her. The lights of the Suburban filled the Jeep and she knew it was only a matter of seconds before he rammed into her again—driving her into the gorge. Angie hit her brakes and swerved.

The SUV crashed into the passenger side of the Jeep. The Jeep rocked under the force, rolled onto its side, slid a few yards, then dropped over the edge into the canyon and darkness.

Chapter 4

Patrick hadn't realized how fast he was going. He laid into the brakes, his heart suddenly in his throat. The bitch was going to take him with her.

At first, it seemed to be happening in slow motion. The brake lights flashing on the Jeep, Angie trying to swerve out of his way. Fool woman.

He had hit the Jeep hard, rattling his teeth, and watched it rock up on two wheels, flop over, slide and drop over the edge.

Now everything was moving too fast. *He* was moving too fast. There was nothing between him and the gaping gorge.

The Suburban began to skid toward the canyon rim. He could see it in his mind's eye. The Suburban dropping over the edge into the blackness of the gorge just as the Jeep had done. Angie's revenge. The bitch.

The brakes on the Suburban were screaming. Or maybe it was Angie. He couldn't be sure it wasn't him as he stood on the brake pedal, fighting to stop, the canyon looming in front of him, setting off his horrible vertigo. The bottomless chasm pulling him—

The Suburban came to a jarring halt, the front tires only inches from the edge of the canyon wall. He gripped the wheel, afraid to move, afraid to breathe.

He hung on, fingers cramping, as he tried to catch his breath. He was shaking too hard to do anything else right now. His chest ached from the pounding of his heart and his pulse buzzed like a swarm of wasps in his ears. He felt physically ill, nauseated and dizzy, and blood kept running down into his eye. He closed his eyes, afraid he was going to be sick.

Too close. That had been way too close. But he'd wanted her so badly. Just the thought that she might get away—

Without looking at the gorge, he carefully eased the Suburban into reverse. He was scared to take his foot off the brake. But he had no choice. He jerked his foot from the brake to the gas. Too hard. The Suburban leapt backward. He slammed on the brakes again, snapping his neck painfully. Damn Angie. This was all her fault.

The engine died. He sat in the quiet darkness, wiped blood from his eye, then slowly cut the lights, popped open his door and got out.

The last thing he wanted to do was go near the edge of the canyon. He had a deathly fear of heights and became violently ill when more than a few feet above the ground. But he had to make sure she was dead.

His shoulder ached where she'd hit him and he was

still bleeding from the wound on his forehead, both spurring his anger. He wanted to hurt her. This didn't feel good enough. Cautiously he stepped to the edge of the gorge and, bracing himself, peered down.

In the starlight, he could see the battered Jeep in the river far below, water rushing over the top of it, through it.

The vertigo hit him hard and he stumbled back, queasy and light-headed. He was disappointed the car hadn't exploded. That would have made him feel better. He told himself that the fall alone had to have been terrifying, let alone the landing, and assured himself she had suffered all the way to the bottom for making this so difficult for him.

A cold breeze came up the sheer canyon wall, chilling him with a thought. What if she wasn't dead?

Impossible. No one could survive a fall like that, could they? Swearing, he edged to the rim of the gorge, forced to take another look.

All he could see was the Jeep. No mangled, dead body that he could make out from here with only stars for light. But he wasn't going down there. He couldn't even if he'd wanted to, which he didn't.

He stumbled back on legs as weak as water. No, he would let the local authorities find her body in the morning. Once he'd gotten rid of the Suburban and made sure he'd covered his tracks.

This wasn't the way he'd planned it. She'd forced him to improvise. Damn her to hell. He'd have to come up with an explanation for his injuries. She had made this so much harder than it should have been. Not that he'd ever killed anyone before.

He wobbled back to the Suburban, trying to reassure himself. He would have her fortune soon. In the meantime he had the stocks and bonds he'd talked Angie into putting in his name before the wedding.

But even better than that was knowing how devastated Jack Donovan would be when he heard about Angie's unfortunate accident. Both thoughts cheered him. *I win, Jack.*

Late the next morning Patrick forced himself to take a quick look down into the canyon. Far below him, he caught a glimpse of the search-and-rescue team scouring the banks of the river downstream for Angie's body, then lurched back to a safe spot to wait.

He was cold and tired, miserable with rage and sick with the damn vertigo. He'd been up all night, forced to cover his tracks. Then, early this morning, he'd driven down to Missoula to report his wife's horrible accident. Since then, he'd had to hang around for hours above this damn canyon, waiting for them to bring up her body.

As the backwoods sheriff approached, Patrick could tell by the look on his face that the news would not be good.

"Well?" Patrick demanded.

Sheriff Jeff Truebow rubbed his stubbled jaw and looked down into the canyon for a moment before speaking. "I'm sorry, Mr. Ryerson, but we haven't been able to find your wife's body yet."

"How is that possible? I mean, where is it?"

"Well, she must not have been wearing her seat belt. I'd imagine her body washed out of the car, and we'll find it downriver."

"How long will *that* take?"

"Oftentimes a body will get hung up in a tree limb or wedged against a rock and won't float up until it starts to…decay. Sorry," the sheriff added quickly, obviously having seen Patrick turn three shades of green.

"What are you saying? That her body might be trapped down there for days?" Without a body, he couldn't get to Angie's money for seven years!

"Hard to say how long," the sheriff informed him. "The water's pretty cold this time of year."

Patrick couldn't believe this. "I can't wait…here."

"No, I guess it's pretty painful," Sheriff Truebow agreed. "On your honeymoon, huh? I'm real sorry. I know how hard this must be on you."

The man had no idea.

"You say she was a sleepwalker?" Truebow asked.

Patrick nodded. "That's what's so horrible about this. She's done this sort of thing before—just got up in the middle of the night and wandered outside. The other times I stopped her before she could leave in the car." He buried his face in his hands. "The worst part is, I took the keys out of the rental car, but I didn't think to check that old Jeep the owner of the cabin had left up there."

"Sleepwalking," the sheriff said with a shake of his head. "I had a cousin who walked out a two-story bedroom window one time and landed in the lilac bushes. Just skinned him up good. Crazy, huh?"

Patrick nodded. The sleepwalking story might sound crazy, but it was the best he could do on short notice.

"You look like you landed in some lilacs yourself," the sheriff commented. "That was a fool thing you did, trying to go down there."

"I know, but when I realized she was missing and the Jeep was gone and then I saw it down in the canyon—" He'd explained his cuts and bruises by telling the sheriff that he'd tried to climb down into the canyon and had fallen. He could just kill Angie all over again for making this so difficult.

He turned away from the sheriff. It was damn hard playing the grief-stricken husband under the circumstances. He had thought it would all be over by now. That Angie would be at a local funeral home. He'd planned to have her body cremated. He would dump her ashes on his way out of town.

"Why don't I give you my cell phone number," he said now, thinking there was no way he was hanging out here any longer.

The sheriff nodded and took down the number in the little notebook where he'd written Patrick's story about poor Angie's accident.

"I'll go into Missoula and find a place to stay," he said. Missoula wasn't large; by Houston standards it was a hick town.

He'd already been to Missoula several times. Last night he'd been forced to drive down there to get rid of the banged-up Suburban and pick up another car. He'd paid cash for the Suburban since it, and not the Jeep, was supposed to have ended up in the bottom of the canyon.

He would have liked to go even farther than Missoula, but he had to at least look like he gave a damn about Angie, and her body had to float up soon. He was running out of money fast. The wedding had cost him a bundle, what with the private jet to Montana and buying cars and jewelry and champagne the bitch then wouldn't drink.

Damn Angie. He hadn't planned on letting her get away with that diamond pendant, either. That had just been for show, just like the wedding. He'd had cheap duplicates made of both the pendant and her diamond wedding ring and had planned to replace the good stuff.

"I'll call you on our progress," Sheriff Truebow assured him.

Patrick nodded and braved one last look at the mangled Jeep in the water below. The search-and-rescue workers had disappeared around a bend in the river. Where the hell was Angie? He felt all the color leave his face and he stumbled back and threw up in the grass.

The sheriff handed him a clean white handkerchief and made sympathetic noises, no doubt thinking it was grief that forced Patrick to sit down on a rock until the nausea passed.

Jack had been making a pot of coffee—out of habit more than desire—when the phone rang. He felt like a zombie, walking around the penthouse, lost. Feeling useless. If he didn't do something soon—

"Turn on the local television news station," Montague Cooke said without preamble.

Jack hit the remote control on his wide-screen TV, afraid of what he was about to see. Patrick's face appeared in some old footage outside the courthouse taken after Jack's arrest.

Fortunately, the news station didn't rerun Patrick's speech saying how shocked he was that his friend had cheated poor people in their old neighborhood. Jack didn't need to hear that speech again.

The screen jumped from Patrick to live footage of a newscaster standing at the edge of a river canyon with pine-forested mountains in the background. Jack turned up the sound.

"…Jeep Wagoneer went off the road at this point and plummeted into the gorge." The camera swung from the newscaster down the canyon wall to what appeared to be a red Jeep in the river at the bottom. "The body of the driver hasn't been found yet. Search-and-rescue workers are looking downstream, believing the body was washed from the vehicle."

Jack stepped closer to the television screen, his heart in his throat.

"Authorities believe the twenty-eight-year-old newlywed was going too fast and either didn't have time to brake before her vehicle went into the gorge or might have been asleep at the wheel. The two were on their honeymoon. I'm Sally Chambers, live, here in Big Pine, Montana, outside Missoula."

"Jack? Jack?"

He lifted the phone to his ear again.

"Oh God—" Jack said, his voice breaking. "Angie was in that car?" He slumped onto one of the stools at his breakfast bar and lowered his head into one hand, still gripping the cordless phone with the other.

Angie dead.

"Jack, listen to me. I don't like the feel of this," Montie said. "Are you listening to me? I think Patrick staged this."

"What?"

"Jack, I ran a check on this Angelina Grant. She doesn't exist. You understand what I'm telling you?"

He raised his head slowly. He didn't understand any of this. "What do you mean she doesn't exist?"

"Obviously Angelina Grant isn't her real name. I'm sending someone over to try to get some latents from your apartment."

"You're going to try to get her fingerprints?" Jack couldn't believe Montie was serious.

"We need to know who she is, Jack. I need to prove that Patrick fleeced and framed you, and my money's on this woman as his accomplice."

"You're wrong," Jack said wearily. What did it matter now, anyway? Angie was dead. How could Montie think Patrick would stage her murder? For what possible purpose?

"Just open the door when my man shows up, and stay out of the way. You hear me?"

Stay out of the way? Jack was damn tired of staying out of the way, standing back, waiting, letting the legal system try to save him. He had to do something.

He walked down the hall to his office and, still cradling the cordless phone against his shoulder, pulled out his atlas.

Angie had lied about her name? Why?

"Jack?"

He remembered their last night together. There was something she had been anxious to tell him. Patrick had interrupted them. And then all hell had broken loose with the arson and discovery of kickbacks and inferior materials in the house.

Had she been going to confess that she'd lied about who she was?

Or was he just kidding himself? He'd been so sure that she was falling in love with him—just as he was her. Could he be wrong about that, too?

Look how wrong he'd been about Patrick. And Patrick had been jealous of Jack's relationship with Angie from the start.

"Jack? Are you still there?"

"What did Patrick say on camera?" he asked Montie as he opened the atlas. "All I saw was old stuff about me and the investigation."

"He wasn't interviewed on camera. They said he was too distraught and had to leave the scene."

"The son of a bitch," Jack said. He hadn't stayed at the scene while they looked for Angie's body?

"Just calm down. I've got my best investigator on this. You sit tight. We'll find out what happened."

Jack flipped through the atlas to Montana. He found Missoula on the map but it took him a while to find Big Pine. It indicated there were no services there, just a wide spot on Fish Creek in the Lolo National Forest. The closest larger city was Missoula. No way would Patrick have thought that a cabin in the woods was the perfect place for a honeymoon. Especially with a gorge nearby, given Patrick's fear of heights. Everything felt wrong about this.

"I've got to go."

"Jack, don't do anything stupid like run off to Montana. You won't find Patrick there, anyway."

"I'll find him."

"Jack, Patrick won't be there."

Still cradling the phone against his ear, he opened his safe and took out all the cash he had on hand. "What do you mean, he won't be there?"

"I told you I'd put my best investigator on this. An hour ago, Patrick bought a ticket to Seattle with Angelina Grant's credit card. His flight leaves Missoula in two hours."

Jack frowned. "He's not waiting for a body to be found?"

"No. And he's using her credit card. You see what I mean? She could be alive and they're meeting up later. If I'm right about this woman, she could be running from something other than this mess with you."

"Did Patrick use the credit card to make a room reservation in Seattle?"

Montie groaned.

"Where?"

"What the hell do you think you can accomplish by chasing after him, Jack?"

"Don't make me have to check every motel in Seattle."

Montie sighed. "It's down by Pike's Market, the Seafarer. You're just going to end up in jail, and this time I won't be able to get you out."

"I'll keep that in mind."

"I'm serious, Jack. Have you given any thought to what you're going to do when you find him?"

"Kill him with my bare hands."

"Wait until we get the prints on the woman. My guy should be there any minute. You don't want to go off half-cocked because I'm putting my money on the two of them being in this together."

No way, Jack told himself. Not the Angie he'd fallen

in love with. "I'll wait for the investigator, then I'll call you from Seattle to see what you've found out." He hung up.

Once Jack had made up his mind to jump bail and go after Patrick, it didn't take him long to get ready. He changed out of his suit into jeans and a cotton shirt, and packed, not sure how long he'd be gone. Or even if he'd be back. The thought surprised him more than he wanted to admit. It wasn't like him. He'd always played by the rules. Faced the music.

But he was going after Patrick and the truth. And he had a bad feeling he wasn't going to like what he found out. If Angie was really dead…well then, he had nothing to lose. He just hated that he hadn't gone after her sooner. Now it was too late…but not for Patrick.

Jack had his bag by the door and a taxi called when the desk phoned up to announce he had a visitor. Jack buzzed up the investigator Montie had sent, a nondescript man by the name of Harvey Ford.

"Where would be a good place to find one of her latents?" Ford asked, getting right to business.

Jack pointed toward the breakfast bar. "I haven't had a chance to pick up." What with being thrown in jail and his maid quitting in disgust because of the charges against him, Jack hadn't been back to his apartment except to shower and change clothes so he could try to stop a wedding.

"You should be able to get a print off that wineglass," he said. Her glass was right where she'd left it when they were interrupted by Patrick's arrival to accuse Jack.

God, Jack wished he could turn back the clock, let Angie tell him whatever it was she seemed so anxious to talk about that night. If only he'd told her that he loved her—before everything else happened.

He stood back while Ford dusted the wineglass.

"There's at least one good one. We've got her."

Whatever her reasons for lying about her name, it wouldn't change how he felt about her.

"What are the chances her prints will even be on file?" Jack said, more to himself than to the investigator.

Ford smiled and shrugged sympathetically as he carefully tucked the glass into an evidence bag and left without another word.

"I guess we'll find out soon enough," Jack said under his breath.

Chapter 5

Patrick was on his way to the Missoula airport when his cell phone rang, making him jump. He hurriedly pulled it from his jacket, hoping desperately for good news.

"How ya doin'?" the sheriff said.

Patrick really didn't have time for pleasantries. "You found her body?" Silence. He heard the sheriff chewing on something. A toothpick? Gum? He had to get out of this backwoods state or he'd go stark-raving mad.

"I'm afraid not," Truebow said finally. "But we did find a shoe."

A shoe? That was good, right?

"It's brown with white stitching. Does that sound like what she was wearing the last time you saw her?"

As if he had noticed what shoes she was wearing when she hit him with the champagne bottle. "I really wouldn't know, Sheriff. I was asleep when she left, remember?" *Idiot.*

"Yes, sorry. I thought you might have recognized it from the description. How about size? These are seven and a half. That sound about right?"

"Yes," he said, not having the foggiest idea what size shoes Angie had worn, nor caring. The shoe had to be hers. He'd talked a maid into letting him into her room at the hotel in Houston and taken some of her shoes, randomly grabbing a few pairs from the back of her closet, ones he thought she wouldn't miss.

He'd put them in the cabin when he'd rented it on his first visit to Montana, long before Angie had any idea she would be coming here. At the time, he hadn't even been sure himself that he could pull this off.

He'd never planned on Angie wearing any of the shoes. But if one of her shoes had been found, that was good news, wasn't it?

Now, if they would just find her body. "All you found was the shoe? That's the only reason you called?"

"No, actually, a thunderstorm blew in up in the mountains this afternoon, muddying up the river. We're suspending the search until the water clears up."

Patrick almost wrecked the rental car as he fought to contain his rage. "How long will that take?"

"Depends on whether or not there is more rain. The thing is, Mr. Ryerson, bodies can travel a long way in that kind of current and get hung up on all kinds of things—old car bodies, tree roots, rocks. Also, we don't know what time for sure she went into the water. She could have left the cabin any time after midnight, you said?"

"That's right."

"So we have no way of knowing how far the body washed downstream, but don't worry, eventually it will come up. They always do. But until then…"

Patrick couldn't believe what he was hearing. "Are you telling me you're calling off the search indefinitely?"

"To be honest with you, Mr. Ryerson, there is just too much river and not enough volunteers. The search-and-rescue team can only do so much. We've got a couple of lost bird hunters we're looking for now. In cases of drownings, the bodies are usually found by fishermen. We had a case just last month where—"

Patrick quit listening. He turned into the airport parking lot and concentrated on the future. Seattle. It would be nice there this time of year. It wasn't the Riviera, but at least it was far from here.

Angie would turn up. Eventually. The bitch.

"Look, Sheriff," he said, interrupting the man's long-winded story. "You have my cell phone number. I can't stay here. There are just too many memories. I need to work. It's the only thing that will take my mind off… this horror."

The sheriff sounded a little surprised but asked, "So I can reach you in Houston?"

God, no, not Houston. He was never going back there. "Actually, Angie and I were relocating after the honeymoon. We hadn't really decided where." He pretended to break down for a few moments. "I'm sorry, but you understand why I can't stay in Montana? I'll be in Seattle for a few days." He repeated his cell phone number. "You'll call me the minute you find her?"

"Of course."

He clicked off and, grabbing his bags, walked toward the airport terminal.

Four hours later, Patrick was sitting under an umbrella drinking a scotch and water at a picturesque little sidewalk bistro in Pioneer Square and going through Angie's address book. He needed to talk to her attorney, her stockbroker and her accountant. He needed to cash in those stocks and bonds and start that whole probate thing so he could get his hands on the rest of her money.

At least he'd been smart enough to take the address book from Angie's purse before throwing the bag into the canyon this morning on his way to town to call the sheriff.

Using the cell phone, he now dialed her lawyer. The phone rang and rang, then an operator came on to say the number had been disconnected.

He called information and double-checked the listing. Directory assistance didn't show anything for a Bob Carpenter. That was odd. Nor was there a listing for Brainard, Benjamin, Carpenter and Harris in New York.

Frowning, he leafed through her book until he found the number for her financial advisor, a man named Ralph Tinsley. As with the first number, the line rang several times—only this time an operator came on to tell him the number had been changed and no forwarding number was listed.

What the hell? He'd heard Angie talking to Tinsley just a few weeks ago. In fact, that's when he'd come up with this plan. He had been damn tired of working for Jack, that was for sure. Then he'd heard Angie on the phone and in a flash a plan had leapt to mind to pay back Jack and get Angie and all her money.

Patrick looked at the name in the address book again. Ralph Tinsley. He was sure that was the name he'd overheard Angie use. Patrick wouldn't make a mistake about something that important.

Sweat broke out on his forehead and he could feel it soak through this shirt under his jacket. He took off the jacket and tried to calm himself.

Angie hadn't had any family—just lawyers and accountants and financial advisors, people who handled all her money. Maybe she'd made a change and had just forgotten to tell him about it. He'd kept her doped up, after all.

In the address book, he found more numbers and names. People with last names that sounded like money, old family friends she'd talked about, friends from college, several close friends he was afraid she'd want to invite to the wedding, friends that might try to talk her out of marrying him.

He'd convinced her not to contact any of them, saying it was short notice and promising to throw her a big party when they returned from their honeymoon so he could meet them all. She'd gone along with it much more easily than he'd anticipated. A little short on friends himself, he'd had to hire guests to fill the church.

He started dialing the numbers of her old friends listed in the book. He was sweating profusely now, his heart hammering in his chest, making it hard to breathe.

He tried all of the numbers. In every case, the line had been disconnected or was wrong in some other way.

Often the person who answered the phone swore he or she had never heard of an Angelina Grant.

He picked up his drink and downed it, the alcohol like a fire running through him. Maybe this was an old address book.

But he knew better. This was the one she had used when she'd made the calls to her attorney and financial advisor to inform them of her upcoming nuptials. Patrick had reminded her to make the calls—and had overheard her end of the conversation as she told them to make the necessary arrangements.

He remembered being amazed that they hadn't advised her to get a prenuptial agreement. Funny, too, that Angie hadn't ever mentioned one, either.

He looked up, motioning with his glass for the waiter to bring him another. "Make it a double."

He didn't like the feeling he was getting. He kept remembering her saying in the cabin what a mistake he was making in killing her.

Jack had caught the first flight out of Houston to Seattle, a nonstop that put him in the city before Patrick. He'd found the Seafarer, had confirmed Patrick was registered and had waited in a bar across the street.

He hadn't had to wait long. Patrick had checked in, then walked down to Pioneer Square where he'd ordered a drink and settled in at one of the tables on the sidewalk. He wore an expression of satisfied arrogance that Jack couldn't wait to wipe off the man's face.

Either he didn't give a damn about Angie and her death, or Montie was right—Angie's alleged death was some kind of scam and she was alive and going to meet up with Patrick later.

Jack didn't want to believe Angie was dead. But he also couldn't stand the thought that Montie might be right about the two of them working together. Not Angie. Angie had lied about her name, though, he reminded himself as he watched Patrick from a coffee shop across the street. Why was that? The coffee shop was almost empty, most customers, at this time of the afternoon, getting coffee to go. No one paid Jack any mind.

Now that he was in Seattle and had found Patrick, he just wanted the truth. About Patrick. About Angie. What Jack wanted was a confession. He wanted his name cleared. And it was all he could do not to go over to Patrick's table and try to beat a confession out of him.

But good sense prevailed. Accosting Patrick in a public sidewalk bistro in front of a dozen people would only get Jack thrown back in jail with little chance of bail. No, he had to bide his time. Wait for an opportunity to get Patrick alone.

From the coffee shop, Jack watched his former best friend order another drink. Patrick was visibly upset. Jack was pretty sure that Patrick had Angela's little red address book and was going through it, trying numbers. Odd.

Patrick was trying another number and seemingly becoming more agitated with each attempt. Who was he trying to reach? Angie?

Jack's cell phone rang. "Hello?" Jack said into the phone, almost afraid it would be Patrick calling.

"Her name is Angelina all right," Montie said on

the other end of the line. He sounded excited. "Angelina LaGrand."

"Who?"

"She's the daughter of Addison LaGrand, granddaughter of Isabella LaGrand. Do you realize what this means?"

"Am I supposed to know those names?" Jack asked, obviously not realizing what it meant, but hoping it meant Angie had a good reason to change LaGrand to Grant.

"Jack, the LaGrands are a notorious family of thieves, con artists, swindlers. Very high-class, mind you. They steal from the very rich and usually get away with it. We're talking confidence men, Jack. In Angie's case, confidence woman."

Jack couldn't breathe. "There must be some mistake."

Montie didn't seem to hear him. "This is exactly what we need to nail Patrick. He was working with a known confidence woman. This is the break we needed."

Jack stared across the street at Patrick. He was thumbing through Angie's address book again, frowning. "It's just not possible." But even as Jack said the words, he knew it was. Angelina Grant was Angelina LaGrand, a swindler and crook. Could it get any worse?

"I'm sending the dossier I've put together on Angelina and her family by express messenger. You'll get it tonight. Read it. If you still think you met Angelina La-Grand by accident, then you need your head examined."

Jack felt numb. "Why me? You said they go after the very rich. I'm not that rich."

"Obviously you're rich enough," Montie said. "The way this family works is they find a mark, study his habits, and then one or more of them work their way into the mark's confidence. When did you meet her?"

"May."

"So it was right after that article came out about you in *Fortune* magazine." Montie swore. "Still think she and Patrick weren't in this together?"

Fortune magazine had called him a "financial genius" because he'd taken what his father had left him and quadrupled it into a small fortune.

He was a genius, all right. Except when it came to women—then Jack Donovan was the biggest fool on earth. He shouldn't be surprised that the first woman he'd really been interested in was a con artist and had wanted nothing from him but his money. So why couldn't he believe that she was in on this with Patrick?

"If this woman is such a crook, why isn't she in jail already?" he asked Montie.

"Confidence men rarely see jail. They choose their marks carefully, reel them in, sucker them and often involve them in schemes that might not be exactly aboveboard. So the marks are either guilty of something or too embarrassed to go to the cops and admit that they'd been hoodwinked."

Jack knew the feeling. He'd been fleeced and framed along with being publicly humiliated and left holding the bag—and all he was guilty of was stupidity.

"Read the dossier when it arrives. I don't want you to have any illusions about this woman. Or what we're dealing with," Montie said, and asked where he was staying.

Jack told him the name of his hotel—one right across from Patrick's.

"I'd bet you Angelina LaGrand is alive and will try to

contact you," Montie said. "If a con works, oftentimes a confidence man will double back and try to play the mark again, for even bigger stakes."

"How could she possibly pull that off?" Jack asked, resenting the hell out of being anyone's mark, especially hers. He might have been fooled once, but twice?

"She could pretend she wasn't in with Patrick, might even come to you for help, tell you she was in danger. This woman is a LaGrand and she's attractive. I would imagine she could convince a man of damn near anything."

Oh yeah, Jack thought. He rubbed his hands over his face. Angie had been incredibly convincing.

"Don't feel too bad. The LaGrands are the best there is," Montie was saying. "You wouldn't believe the well-known people they've swindled. And you're certainly not the first man to fall for a pretty face and a good line. You had no reason not to believe she was as wealthy as she pretended."

The irony was, he'd fallen for her in spite of her fortune. What a laugh.

And to think he'd been considering marriage and a family with her. He'd even been thinking Christmas would be a great time to give her a ring. Maybe sooner, say, Thanksgiving. What a fool he'd been.

"I'm wondering if Patrick knew Angelina before they both showed up in Houston," Montie was saying. "Patrick could have hired her to distract you while he stole you blind and framed you."

Well, if that had been the plan, it had worked like a charm.

"My money's on this accident being a scam," Montie

said, still sounding excited. "I'll bet she meets up with Patrick in Seattle. They are so confident we aren't onto them. Patrick made one big mistake: hooking up with that woman. I'm going to send Ford out—"

"No," Jack interrupted. "Let me handle this."

"Do I have to remind you, you weren't even supposed to leave the state? And anyway, it's a bad idea for you to be the one who catches them together, given your... feelings about this woman."

"If you're right and Angie is alive, I'll find her," Jack said. "I'm watching Patrick as we speak. He's been trying to reach someone on his cell phone and becoming more irritated by the minute."

"Be careful, Jack. And don't do anything stupid."

"No problem," Jack said, and clicked off, wondering how he could be more stupid than he'd already been.

He caught movement out of the corner of his eye. Patrick suddenly stumbled to his feet, overturning the table in front of him and sending everything crashing to the brick sidewalk. He looked stricken, his shocked gaze riveted down the block from him.

Jack looked down the street in the direction Patrick was staring. A taxi turned the corner and started down the block toward him—and Patrick.

Jack's shock turned quickly to anger. Angie sat in the back seat, staring straight ahead as if she didn't see Patrick, but Jack saw the satisfied smile on her lips as the taxi cruised by.

She didn't notice Jack. Nor did she see him leave the coffee shop, hail a taxi and follow.

Chapter 6

Patrick stood staring after the taxi as waiters and guests crowded around him.

"Sir, are you all right?"

He barely heard them picking up the table and the broken glass from the bricks. His ears buzzed and he felt light-headed, as if he might pitch headlong into the bricks himself.

Angie is alive! That's why the search-and-rescue team hadn't found her body. Because she'd gotten away.

Impossible. She couldn't have survived the crash.

Unless she'd gotten out of the car before it dropped into the gorge. He swayed, dizzy, knees weak.

"Here, please sit down. Can I get you something? Another drink? A glass of water?"

He braced himself, palms down on the table that the waiter had righted for him. He felt sick as he watched the taxi disappear into the traffic. He could feel people staring, whispering. He didn't give a damn.

"Sir, are you all right?"

Hell no, he wasn't all right.

"A drink. A double scotch," he managed to say to the annoying waiter. The sidewalk café came back into focus. He sat down, told himself to calm down. He was making a scene.

That couldn't have been Angie. But it was her double, her doppelganger, then. Just a bizarre coincidence. Angie was dead. The sheriff had found her shoe. Didn't that prove she was dead?

A shoe was not a body. But even if she had jumped from the Jeep before it went into the river, how could she have made it down the mountain in the dark last night? She didn't have any idea where she was. And she was wearing only one shoe.

Unless the shoe hadn't been hers—had been left by someone in the old Jeep. He hadn't thought of that.

She could have jumped free of the Jeep, hidden in the trees, walked on the road. Except, there was no moon. But the stars were bright last night. And she was just enough of a bitch to walk out with only one shoe. He had a sudden image of her limping into Missoula barefoot.

He fought to remember every detail, looking for any time she could have escaped the Jeep before it went over the cliff into the canyon.

When she'd swerved! The driver's door had been on the opposite side, out of view. She could have jumped out. Or rolled out. And he wouldn't have seen her.

But the dome light hadn't come on! He was sure of

that. And it would have if she had opened the Jeep's door. So how the hell—

"Your drink, sir."

Patrick took it, his hands trembling.

"You're sure you're all right?"

He waved off the waiter and took a long drink of the scotch. It burned all the way down.

Wait a minute. If she'd survived, wouldn't she have gone straight to the cops? Of course she would have. A woman like her. If Angie was alive, he'd be in jail right now.

The thought calmed him a little. He took another drink. Angie was dead. The woman in the taxi was just someone who looked like her. If he'd seen the woman up close, had gotten more than a brief glimpse, he would know she looked nothing like Angie. He'd only imagined the resemblance—and all because Angie's body hadn't floated up yet.

"Don't lose that cab," Jack ordered as he reached over the seat to stuff a hundred dollar bill into the cabbie's shirt pocket.

"You got it." The driver sped up, swerving as the cab ahead of them slipped into the right-hand lane.

Traffic was bumper-to-bumper this time of the day, with everyone getting off work. His cab followed the other one, several car lengths back, as it worked its way through the downtown area and onto Interstate 5 north, the Space Needle a shining spire in the evening light. The traffic was dense and fast.

It had been Angie in that cab, hadn't it? All that talk of Angie being alive—Jack wondered now if he'd just imagined seeing her. But Patrick had obviously thought it was Angie. The expression on his face had been one of shock. He had looked as if he'd seen a ghost.

Ahead, Jack could make out the woman's dark head in the back of the taxi. She appeared to be on a cell phone—Jack had a terrible thought. What if this too had been staged? What if Patrick had spotted him in the restaurant across the street? What if Patrick's being surprised to see Angie was just an act—one choreographed just for Jack?

Suddenly the cab ahead of them increased its speed, the driver zipping in and out of the traffic.

"He's spotted us," Jack said. Or more likely, given her past, Angie had spotted the tail. "Stay with him and there's another hundred in it for you."

His driver hit the gas, changing lanes, weaving in and out of the afternoon rush-hour traffic.

They were going close to eighty when the taxi they were tailing suddenly cut across three lanes and hit the Aurora exit, causing brake lights to flash across all four lanes.

For a moment Jack's taxi was trapped in the slowed traffic, then the driver started honking and motioning to the drivers to his right as he pulled in front of them.

"Seattle people are so polite," the driver said, as the cars allowed him to cross until he'd reached the edge of the highway—but there was no way he could get back to the exit.

Jack could see the other taxi stopped at a light below the interstate. He tossed the driver the extra hundred and leapt out, sprinting down the grassy incline straight for the cab, praying the light wouldn't change before he could reach her.

She was turned in her seat, staring back up the ramp. No doubt looking for his yellow cab. She didn't see him until he jerked open her door and slid into the seat next to her. He'd caught her. And if she thought he was going to fall for her lies again, Angelina LaGrand was sadly mistaken.

Patrick took a gulp of his drink, still shaking inside as he picked up his cell phone and started to dial Sheriff Truebow's number. Maybe they'd found her other shoe, at least. Maybe the sheriff had some good news for him. He could use it right now.

The number wasn't ringing. He shook the phone. Something inside rattled. Damn. It must have broken in the fall from the table.

Angrily, he threw it down, causing the other patrons to eye him again. *Go to hell.* He picked up Angie's address book. It was wet and smelled of scotch. He tucked it into his pocket anyway, telling himself there had to be a good explanation for the wrong numbers in the book. She probably had a new address book with more current numbers—just like the new checking account.

His pulse leapt. What was wrong with him? He had completely forgotten about their new joint checking account. Just before the wedding, he'd gone to the bank with her, insisted she close out her checking account and move her balance into the joint account he'd set up for them.

She'd had over eight thousand in her account. While most of her money was in stocks and bonds, money market accounts and a huge trust fund, there should still be a nice chunk in their joint account to tide him over. He felt weak with relief.

But it did worry him a little that he'd forgotten about the joint checking account. He'd been so focused on the *real* money. The other had been chicken feed in comparison.

In hindsight, he thought again, it did seem odd that she hadn't even mentioned a prenuptial agreement. But then again, she'd been drugged out of her mind and grieving over her disillusionment with Jack.

Just the thought of Jack fired his anger at Angie all over again. Like Jack, the woman deserved everything that had happened to her.

As he drained his drink, he spotted a taxi coming up the street. He froze. It inched toward him in the heavy traffic. He could feel his heart laboring in his chest. The taxi came to a stop in the traffic right in front of the café.

For just an instant, he thought it was her again. But the woman turned her face toward him. Not Angie. Not even a look-alike. He released the breath he'd been holding and laughed, causing the now uneasy patrons to steal glances at him. He couldn't quit smiling he was so relieved.

Angie was dead. Everything was going to be all right. He got up and headed for his hotel. He'd call the automated number at the bank from his hotel room and have the money in the joint account wired first thing in the morning to a bank here in Seattle.

But first, he'd touch base with Sheriff Truebow. He needed to hear that Angie's body had been found.

* * *

"What the—" the cabdriver let out an oath as Jack jumped into the back seat. The light changed.

Jack looked over at Angie, momentarily stunned by the sight of her, alive, sitting next to him. "Just drive," he ordered the cabbie. "The lady and I have some unfinished business. Although 'lady' might be stretching it."

"You want me to call the cops?" the driver asked, swiveling around to look at Angie. Cars behind them started honking.

"No, that's not necessary," she said. "I can handle this." Her voice had an edge to it that could have cut glass.

"Aren't you the cool one, Angie," Jack said, really looking at her as the taxi began to move along in the traffic.

She smiled at him icily, but her brown eyes flashed with anger. "I'm *not* Angie."

"Right."

She wore her long dark hair up, accentuating her lovely features, her makeup perfect—just like the large diamond stud earrings sparkling at each ear. She was dressed in a dark skirt and matching jacket with a pale silver blouse—all expensive, all fitting her body wonderfully. He would have known that face and body anywhere.

But the dead giveaway was the amulet on the chain around her neck, her good luck charm. Well, her luck was about to change for the worse.

He felt that old ache as he looked at her, but realized there was something different. Probably the fact that she was no longer acting the part she'd played with him. She seemed slicker, more chic and sophisticated, more ruthless. Obviously, things she'd hidden from him in Houston.

"You've been busy, Angie. Conning me. Helping Patrick destroy my business and get me arrested. Marrying him. Faking your own death. And now turning up in Seattle. I can't wait to hear what game you're playing now."

She glared at him. "Who are you?"

He laughed. "Jack Donovan, the man you and Patrick framed. Oh, let me guess. Amnesia? Is that the new game?"

She appeared to be surprised. "Jack?"

"Ah, you *do* remember," he said sarcastically. He felt torn between being glad she was alive, and furious that she'd tricked him into falling in love with her—and all just for his money. It didn't help that she was pretending she'd never laid eyes on him before.

She licked her lips and leveled her dark gaze at him. "I couldn't possibly *remember*, because we've never met."

"So the Texas accent is real?" he said with a shake of his head. "I figured that would be a lie, too."

"I was born in Dallas," she said haughtily.

He nodded, wondering if that were true. Not that he would believe anything she ever told him again.

"Angie, I know. I know all about you, all about your family. I know *everything*, Ms. LaGrand."

"Obviously not or you would know that I'm not Angie. I'm her sister, Maria. Her identical *twin* sister, Maria LaGrand."

"Angie doesn't have an identical twin."

She raised a brow, then opened her purse and pulled out her wallet. From a hidden compartment, she withdrew a photograph and handed it to him. The paper appeared to be old, the edges worn smooth and rounded, the surface cracked and discolored.

He stared down at two smiling little dark-haired girls with Angie's face. Identical right down to their pretty yellow dresses. Except, the one on the right had her leg in a cast.

He must not have looked convinced because she sighed and lifted her skirt to reveal a black garter belt above her silk stockings—and a three-inch scar on the inside of her thigh in the shape of a half moon. "I fell out of a tree and broke my leg when I was five."

She pulled her skirt back down and took back the photo to return it to her wallet. "So I guess you don't know everything about me. Or my family."

"That photo may not be any more authentic than you are. And as for the scar, you might recall that I wouldn't have any knowledge as to whether you have a scar on your inner thigh since you and I have never been that intimate."

She raised a brow as if surprised.

His throat tightened. "What? You normally sleep with your other marks?"

She sighed. "I'm surprised you and Angie never made love, considering how she felt about you."

"I'll just bet."

She met his gaze. "The last time I talked to her, she said she was falling for you and wasn't going through with her previous plans."

"Don't, okay? You helped Patrick frame me. I'm on my way to prison if I can't prove the two of you set me up."

"You're wrong. My sister would never have fallen in with a man like Patrick Ryerson."

"Excuse me? You *married* him."

"Patrick tricked my sister." Anger made her voice as hard and cold as ice. "He killed her."

He stared at the woman beside him, remembering the look on Patrick's face when he'd seen Angie get into the cab at the corner of the street by the hotel. Was it possible Angie really did have an identical twin and Patrick hadn't known about it?

Jack smiled. "You're good."

She nodded.

"You almost had me buying your act. Again," he said. "What's your game this time? You double-cross Patrick? Or is he in on this and just pretending he didn't know you were still alive?"

"You don't get it, do you?" Anger flamed her cheeks. Her eyes snapped. "Patrick murdered my sister. You think it's a coincidence I just happened to be on that street corner, a coincidence that Patrick saw me?" She scoffed at that and narrowed her gaze as she shook her head.

He studied the woman as the cab slowed. She was so damn convincing. He was starting to think he could see dissimilarities between this woman and Angie, as if Angie really did have an identical twin.

He felt the anger return, like a balm against the pain, remembering how Angie had fooled him the first time. He wouldn't be fooled again.

"Enough lies," he snapped, grabbing her. "You're

going with me back to Houston to clear—" His gaze locked with hers. He saw the truth at the same time he felt it. He let go of her as if he'd been burned.

Maria LaGrand smiled a slow, told-you-so smile.

"You really aren't Angie," he said as the cab pulled to the curb and stopped.

"What have I been trying to tell you?" she said, stone-cold serious again. "My sister is dead."

He was shaking his head, not wanting to believe it.

"I'm her twin. I know."

He felt the blow of that news stagger him again as if just hearing of her death for the first time.

The cab had stopped in front of an old brick hotel. He looked out at the building, then at the woman next to him.

"I'm sorry if my sister hurt you," she said.

"She did more than hurt me. She and Patrick framed me for a crime I didn't commit."

"So you say. But if you're really innocent of the crimes, it wasn't my sister who framed you."

"And I should take your word for that?" he asked, the anger back. "Don't even try to con me, all right? I've been conned by the best."

Her laugh sounded so much like Angie's it hurt. "See, you're wrong again. *I* am the best. Angelina was an amateur compared to me."

He hated to hear her say "was." Past tense. "They haven't found her body. Maybe…"

Maria met his gaze, her eyes shiny with tears. She shook her head. "No one could have survived that." She opened her door and swung her legs out.

He started to follow her, had gotten out of the car

and gone around to her side, when he saw the gun. It was small, but deadly enough. She had it hidden from the cabdriver's view, pointed straight at Jack's heart.

"This is where we part company, Jack Donovan. Go back to Houston. Let me handle this. You're out of your league."

"Handle what?"

"Vengeance, of course."

"So Patrick doesn't know Angie had a twin?"

She smiled. "No, few people do. And what could be worse than Angie coming back from the grave to make her killer suffer?"

So that's why Maria had been in front of Patrick's hotel. She'd wanted him to think she was Angie. She hadn't planned on Jack seeing her, too.

"Sorry, but you're not the only one who wants Patrick Ryerson to suffer. Remember, he framed me with your sister's help—"

"Don't be a fool. My sister was in love with you."

"Sure she was. The point is, I'm going to prison unless I can prove I was set up."

"And you thought you could do it by following Patrick to Seattle?" That seemed to amuse her.

"Actually, I came here to kill him, but you distracted me."

She laughed. "You aren't the killer type."

"I might surprise you."

"Don't. If you really are innocent of the charges, then go home before anyone realizes you've jumped bail. Leave Patrick to me." She slammed her door as the cab quickly sped away.

He stared after her, still stunned by how much she

looked like Angie. Stunned also by how much she knew about him and Angie. He figured Maria had been in on the con job Angie had done on him. He realized she could have been driving the car that supposedly had almost run Angie down that spring day by the park. He had thought he'd saved Angie's life that day. The joke was on him. He'd just fallen into her trap. What a chump.

He flagged down another taxi and headed back to the wharf. Maria LaGrand didn't really think she'd gotten rid of him that easily, did she? Not when he knew where she'd turn up next—wherever Patrick was.

Chapter 7

Back at his room, Patrick still felt a little off balance. He couldn't believe he hadn't thought of the joint checking account before this. Seeing that woman who'd looked so much like Angie had thrown him.

It just wasn't like him to forget money. Maybe killing Angie had rattled him more than he'd thought. Especially since it hadn't gone anything like he'd planned and it was his first time. And last, he hoped.

He called Sheriff Truebow's number. The sheriff wasn't in, so he left the number at the hotel where he could be reached. Then he dialed the automated bank number to wire funds to a bank down the block here in Seattle.

He knew there couldn't be enough in the account to live on for long, not the way he planned to live, but it would definitely make things easier for a while. And Angie's body was bound to turn up any day.

Punching in the appropriate numbers, he waited for

the balance, doodling on the scratch pad by the phone, hoping to be surprised—he had no idea how much Angie got from her trust fund each month.

"What!" His pen froze over the pad. There had to be a mistake. Fingers shaking, he hit the star key to have the transaction request repeated.

The automated voice said, *"Your balance of...one dollar...cannot be transferred as per your request."*

He hit the star key again and again until, in frustration, he slammed down the phone and threw it across the room. Of course there was a mistake. One dollar? He'd personally had *two thousand* in his account—let alone what Angie had contributed. And her trust fund check should have gone in there the day before yesterday. There should be thousands of dollars in that account.

He raked his hands through his hair, wanting to scream. Was it possible that Angie had cleaned it out *before* the wedding? That cheating, lying bitch! She must not have been as upset and doped up as he'd thought.

Too angry to sit, he prowled the room, and tripped over the phone cord. As he put the receiver back on the hook and returned the phone to the desk, he saw that the message light was flashing. He must have got a call either while he was on the phone—or while the phone was on the floor, off the hook.

Sheriff Truebow! It could be the call he'd been waiting for. Truebow must have called to say they'd found Angie's body.

Relief washed over him. All his troubles would be over. He could quit imagining that he'd just seen Angie riding in a taxi in downtown Seattle. Even if she'd cleaned out their joint accounts before the wedding, he'd still have the money from the stocks and bonds she'd signed over to him. He could get out of the country until her estate was finalized.

He was thinking about someplace tropical as he retrieved the message, anticipating the sheriff's slow, western drawl.

"Hello."

His heart seized up in his chest at the sound of Angie's voice. He dropped onto the bed, his hand holding the phone jerking spasmodically.

"I can't wait to see you—" Angie's laugh "—soon."

When Jack got back to his hotel, a large thick brown envelope was waiting for him. The LaGrand dossier

He took it up to his room, unlocked the door and dropped the envelope on the bed. Without turning on a light, he went to the window and peered across the street at the Seafarer—and Patrick's room. The drapes were drawn, a light glowing behind them. Through a crack between the drapes, he saw movement every few moments as if Patrick was pacing.

Going to the small courtesy bar, Jack poured himself a stiff drink, then scooped up the file and carried it to a chair by the window and turned on the small light next to it.

He didn't want to read what was inside it. He didn't want to know that everything with Angie had been a lie. Everything Angie had ever said or done. All to get his money. Where exactly Patrick fit in, Jack wasn't sure. But he intended to find out.

Maria swore that Patrick had tricked Angie and killed her, but Jack knew better than to take anything Maria said at face value. He couldn't trust this woman from a known con artist family with Angie's face and body. Why hadn't Montie mentioned that Angie had a sister—let alone an identical twin?

He glanced down at the envelope, knowing he was going to have to read it. He had to know the truth. He had to know why. Why Angie had picked *him*. Had it been Patrick's doing? Or her own? He had to know if Patrick and Angie had been working together.

He opened the envelope and dumped the contents into his lap and began reading, all the time keeping an eye on Patrick's room.

When Jack finished, he shoved all the papers, newspaper clippings and photocopied articles from the Internet back into the envelope, made himself another drink and turned out the light to stare across at Patrick's hotel room window. The light was still on. Patrick still appeared to be pacing.

Jack didn't want to think about what he'd read. It was all there—the truth about Angie, the truth about her family. Except, there was no mention of identical twin sisters. He closed his eyes for a moment, then put down his unfinished drink.

That wasn't all that was missing from the dossier on the LaGrands. It didn't tell him why Angie picked him. Or if she'd been in on it with Patrick.

Jack saw now that there was only one way he would ever get those answers. He headed for the door. He had to see Maria LaGrand again.

Patrick prowled his hotel room back at the Seafarer, more worried about money than about the Angie look-alike he'd seen in the cab.

Antsy, he went to the window and dragged back the

drape. He still couldn't believe Angie had cleaned out their joint checking account. She'd been ripping him off. And all this time he'd thought she was putty in his hands.

He stared down at the street, surprised it was so late. When had it gotten dark? Pools of light glowed under the street lamps and in the windows of the shops and restaurants. A flurry of pedestrians still moved quickly along the sidewalks. He couldn't help looking for Angie. He knew he would continue to imagine seeing her until her body was found. Would imagine she was watching him right now from the shadowed darkness.

He shuddered, the feeling of being watched was so strong. His gaze raked the street even as his mind argued that Angie was in a watery grave back in Montana and not standing out there in the darkness watching his hotel room. He didn't see her, but that didn't mean she wasn't there.

Across the street, diners sat at candlelit tables in the ferny little courtyard along the sidewalk, sipping good wine, eating seafood or grade A prime beef, enjoying themselves while he— He was starting to close the drape when a familiar face caught his attention.

His heart leapt to his throat. Jack! He sat at a table off to one side in the shadows, his candle extinguished. Patrick could barely make out his features, and thought for a moment he'd just imagined seeing Jack, the same way he'd imagined seeing Angie.

But then Jack sat forward, watching the street, watching for someone, then looking up, looking right at Patrick's hotel room window!

Patrick jumped back from the window, pulse pounding. Jack was in Seattle! Looking for him! What was Jack doing here? He wasn't allowed to leave the state.

My God, he'd jumped bail. He'd come after him!

Panic short-circuited his brain, making his thoughts erratic and crazy. He stormed around, only the light by the desk providing any illumination in the slowly darkening room.

He knew he needed to calm down, but all he could think about was the message Angie had left on his phone, the wrong numbers in her address book, the money missing from their joint checking account, and now Jack in Seattle, Jack coming after him with blood in his eye. Patrick was sure of that.

A flash caught his attention. He turned slowly, already knowing what it was before he saw the small red message light on the phone at the desk.

No, not again. He stared at the phone as if it were a snake that could bite him. He'd only left the room for a moment, just long enough to check the hallway and see if anyone was in the elevator because he thought he'd heard someone outside his door.

Slowly, he picked up the receiver, put it to his ear and hit the message button, his chest aching as he waited to hear Angie's voice again, fearing that somehow she *was* alive and coming after him, as well.

Instead, he heard Sheriff Truebow's hick drawl on the recording. "Sorry, I don't have any news for you. The river's still running muddy. I'll call as soon as I have any word. Seems your cell phone isn't working?"

Patrick hung up and began to pace again. If that really had been Angie's voice earlier— It *had* been her voice. Who was he kidding? Angie was alive, and the sheriff and his search-and-rescue team wouldn't be finding any body in the river. Somehow, she'd managed to get away. Oh God. She and Jack were both after him now.

Unless— He stopped pacing, remembering a movie he'd seen where a cassette recording of a woman's voice had been cut and spliced together to trap the murderer into believing she was still alive.

Yes, that was possible. But who would have a recording of Angie's voice and go to the troub— "Jack." The word came out on a puff of air. Jack!

Patrick burst out laughing. Of course, Jack had to be behind this. The look-alike in the cab. The message. Jack had jumped bail, no doubt looking to get even. What better way than trying to make Patrick think Angie was still alive and seeking revenge for her murder? Jack was trying to trap him into admitting what he'd done.

Patrick laughed harder. Now that he was calmer he realized Angie's message hadn't said anything about murder. She hadn't even mentioned him by name. The tape had been so generic that—now that he replayed it in his mind—it was almost comical.

Jack could easily have gotten it off his answering machine from before, when he and Angie were together.

"Jack, old buddy, you had me going there for a minute." He held out his hands. They were still shaking. It had almost worked; he'd almost believed Angie was alive. He'd almost panicked. "Jack, you son of a—"

But how had Jack found him—and so quickly? He slapped his forehead with the heel of his palm. Angie's credit card! Of course.

Unfortunately, he realized he would have to use the credit card again—to skip town. He had no choice, since Angie had cleaned him out and he hadn't had a chance to cash in the stocks and bonds.

It was clear he couldn't stay here and let Jack leave him any more Angie messages. Even knowing Angie wasn't really alive, he still didn't want to hear her voice again. It was too creepy hearing a dead woman's voice like that.

So that meant he had to get the hell out of Dodge. But first, he would take care of Jack.

He glanced out the window. Jack was still at the table, away from the light, watching the street and the hotel. Patrick was surprised now that he'd even seen Jack down there in the dark. If he hadn't had the feeling that someone was watching him…

He smiled and, picking up the phone, dialed 911. Jack wouldn't be following him anymore. *You just can't win for losing, old buddy.*

She spotted Jack about the same time she saw the police car pull up at the other end of the street. She should have known he wouldn't go back to Houston and let her handle this. And to think that at one time he'd been so predictable it had made him an easy mark.

Two officers got out of the cop car and started toward the restaurant. She'd bet Patrick was watching from his room. This had his name written all over it.

She had changed into jeans, a sweatshirt and sneakers, her dark hair hidden beneath a Mariners cap and she wore no makeup and had a backpack slung over one shoulder. She knew Patrick hadn't seen her again.

He would only see her when she wanted him to. Unless Jack made her blow her cover.

She debated letting the cops arrest Jack. At least in jail, he wouldn't be in her hair. But she couldn't be sure he wouldn't just get back out on even higher bail. The last thing she needed was him messing up her plans. But even as she thought it, she knew that that wasn't the reason she couldn't send him back to jail.

Jack was sitting at one of the outside tables farthest from the front door of the restaurant. The other tables were full, the large dark umbrellas folded down for the evening and candles flickering on all tables except Jack's.

The two cops were coming down the sidewalk from the opposite direction. All she had to do was keep them from reaching him. Otherwise, he was on his way to jail.

Piece of cake, since Diversion was her middle name, she thought as she glanced around, spotted her mark and moved in quickly. The two police officers were about twenty yards behind her when she rushed past an exquisitely dressed woman exiting the restaurant and simply bumped into her.

Relieving the woman of her Gucci bag was child's play. Daddy would have been so proud.

Nor did the wealthy matron fail her.

"Help! Help! My bag!" the woman shrieked. "Someone stop him!" She must have seen the two cops then. "Police! Police! Stop that boy! He stole my bag!"

With the bag tucked under her arm, she dove into the traffic, darting between moving cars, to reach the other side at a run. She had a head start and excelled at a quick getaway—and she had reconnoitered the area as soon as she'd found Patrick so she knew exactly where to go to ditch the cops.

She raced down the alley between buildings, leaping trashcans and dodging parked cars and Dumpsters, sticking to the darkness. Not far down the block, she swung over a fence and through the back door of a deli. She ducked into the ladies' room. No one inside the deli had seemed to pay her any mind.

Once inside, she pulled off her baseball cap, shook out her long hair and stripped off the sweatshirt down to the white cotton top she wore beneath. After discarding the cap and sweatshirt in the bottom of the trashcan, she took her purse from the backpack and put on a pair of large silver earrings and a little eye shadow.

She could hear some commotion outside the bathroom door and quickly stuffed the stolen purse into her own bag, along with the cheap nylon backpack, flushed the toilet and washed her hands, then put on her cool, calm and collected expression and walked out to find two policemen banging on the door of the men's rest room.

She showed only mild interest as she glanced at them. She could feel their eyes on her as she entered the busy deli and stood in line, studying the menu on the wall.

Out of the corner of her eye, she watched the cops wait outside the men's room. They seemed both surprised and disappointed when an elderly man came out. The two policemen glanced into the packed deli, evidently didn't see what they were looking for and went back out into the alley.

After a few moments, she pretended to lose patience with the long line and left. Once outside, she hightailed it as quickly as she dared back toward the restaurant.

One of the policemen was inside with the wealthy matron, trying to calm her. The other was moving through the restaurant, obviously looking for Jack.

Jack was gone, just as she had hoped he would be. But she also knew Patrick would be watching from his third-floor hotel room window across the street.

She looked up at Patrick's room. It was dark—no lights on. She smiled up at him, knowing he was standing there, watching her. Leisurely she walked past the courtyard restaurant, slid the Gucci bag from her purse and stealthily dropped it onto the seat of an empty chair across from an honest-looking elderly couple, the purse and her movements covered by the checked tablecloth.

She knew Patrick had seen her. Just as she knew he would follow her. She started down the street, turning at the corner to head toward the wharf and the darkness, drawing in her prey.

Wisps of fog swirled around her as she walked, growing denser as she neared the water. She shivered, wishing she still had her sweatshirt. There were no other pedestrians in the industrial area this late. Only a few cars sped past, headlights piercing the darkness, then fading to black again.

She wanted to look over her shoulder but forced herself not to. She knew why she was feeling vulnerable and it had nothing to do with the soft footfalls behind her. She'd wanted Patrick to follow her, dared him to. He would come to prove to himself that she wasn't real.

She liked the idea of his thinking she was a ghost, and the fog would be ideal for her purposes.

She thought of Jack. No doubt he'd taken off when he'd seen her—and the cops. Maybe he had the sense to catch a plane back to Houston. She could only hope.

She wished now that she'd had Jack arrested back at the restaurant. The safest place for him right now was a Houston, Texas, jail. She feared that moment of weakness would come back to haunt her.

She cut through the now deserted industrial area of the wharf, the fog thick as chowder, the street lamps glowing like diffused sunlight overhead. In the distance she could hear the sound of a boat out on the water, but couldn't see it, couldn't see six feet in front of her.

But she could hear the footsteps behind her, closer now, gaining on her. A few more feet and— She heard a sound off to her right, turned, seeing nothing but blackness in a narrow space between the two buildings.

A hand shot out, closed over her arm. Before she could react, the other hand clamped over her mouth as she was dragged back between the buildings.

"Shh," Jack whispered next to her ear. He could hear the sound of footfalls on the street just beyond them, moving stealthily through the fog and darkness in their direction. He held her to him, breathing in the sweet scent of her hair, her body warm against him.

Jack saw a dark shadow flicker past through the fog. Patrick? It was all he could do not to go after the man. The only thing that kept him from it was the woman in his arms. He had her right where he wanted her.

The sound of footsteps stopped. Silence settled as

thick as the fog. A boat horn sounded. Water lapped at the docks nearby. Jack heard Patrick let out a curse. He was coming back this way.

The footsteps picked up speed, the shadow sweeping past in a blur. Jack listened until he was sure Patrick was gone before he let go of the woman, turning her around to face him.

She'd saved him back there at the restaurant, but right now he wasn't feeling much gratitude. He wouldn't need saving if it hadn't been for her sister.

"Give me the gun you're carrying, Maria," he whispered.

"What gun?"

He grabbed her purse, opened it and dug around for the weapon she'd pulled on him earlier today.

"Don't you believe anything I tell you?" she asked as she leaned back against the side of the opposite building, only inches from him.

"No." This close he could feel her gaze on him, fired with defiance. She was right. No gun.

He looked up at her. The sleeveless, white cotton top she wore accented her curves nicely. So did the jeans. Few places to hide a weapon, and damn distracting. He knew those curves too well. It threw him, seeing them on another woman.

She spread her arms wide against the side of the building. "Go ahead, frisk me if you still don't believe me."

He stared at her, too many emotions coursing through him. Her dark hair curled around her face, falling to her bare shoulders. She looked so much like Angie…

"Well?" she asked softly.

He met her gaze. *Don't underestimate this woman.* He had underestimated her twin and look where that had landed him.

He stepped forward, covering her hands with his own as he flattened her against the rough brick. He saw a spark flash in her dark eyes. Anger? Or something even hotter? What he didn't see was whatever truth he was looking for in all that bottomless darkness.

She didn't move, didn't seem to breathe, as he let go of one of her hands to run his fingers along the top of her hip-hugger jeans, down her long legs to her sneakers. No weapon. Could he be that wrong about her?

She shot him a sly smile.

He let go of her, then, surprising her, he grabbed the front of her shirt and the bra she wore beneath it and pulled, his other hand palm up at her waist.

Her eyes widened, the smile disappearing as the Derringer, warm from her bare skin, dropped from between her breasts and into his palm.

"Well, how about that." It was his turn to smile as he stuffed the weapon into his jeans pocket. "Lying must come as naturally to you as breathing," he said, pressing her to the wall again.

"It's genetic."

"Obviously."

He could almost hear her heart pounding. Smell her perfume rising from the spot where the Derringer had rested, the scent something exotic and potent that dazed his senses. Feel her lush curves pressed against his larger, stronger, harder body.

She seemed to be holding her breath. Afraid of what he'd do next? Or waiting for it?

He reached up to cup her face in his hands, her skin silken cool on his fingertips. He felt her pulse jump under his thumbs. She looked so much like Angie, felt so much like her— Her lips parted, a soft sigh escaping as she closed her eyes.

The kiss was inevitable.

Chapter 8

Jack drew her closer, his mouth dropping to hers. She moaned against his lips and he pulled her to him, deepening the kiss, his body molded to hers.

He felt her tremble against him, her fingers digging into his shoulders as he lost himself in the taste and feel of her, swept away without reason or thought or realization of just whom he was kissing.

Suddenly she shoved him away.

He stumbled back, his heart in his throat as he looked at her, emotions roller-coastering inside him.

The woman in the alley with him wasn't Maria LaGrand! She was Angie! Angie was alive! He wanted to wrap her in his arms, to strangle her, to kiss her, to shake the truth out of her.

He stared at her, his mind racing, battered by conflicting emotions: shock and relief, anger and joy. Angie was alive and she was pretending to be Maria.

The idea came in a flash. Why let her know he knew the truth? If she wanted to masquerade as Maria, he would play along. He wouldn't let on that he even suspected. Not yet, anyway. First he'd get her to help him clear his name. Then, when he didn't have to worry about being sent to prison, he'd deal with Angie.

"Do you think you can just exchange one sister for another?" she demanded, sounding shaken by the kiss.

He shook his head. "It's just that you are so much like Angie…" He shrugged, his pulse still pounding. "I'm sorry. I won't make that mistake again."

She stared at him for several moments. He had a pretty good idea what she was worried about.

"You can see why it's best if you go back to Houston and we don't see each other again," she said, still sounding a little breathless.

He tried to calm his racing heart. What did he want from this woman aside from help clearing his name? Oh, where did he begin?

"I'm not going back to Houston," he informed her. "You and I will just have to get used to being around each other, I guess, since you're going to help me clear my name."

"That isn't part of the plan."

"There's been a change in plans. Otherwise," he continued, "I'm going after Patrick and when I catch him, I know he will try to blame everything on you—" He quickly added, "And Angie. You did help her set me up, didn't you? You and Patrick and Angie. And while I doubt you're worried about your family name being dragged through the mud—"

"I told you—" anger sparked in her eyes "—if you were framed, Angie had nothing to do with it."

"So you say," he replied, ignoring the "if you were framed" part. "But then, I have no reason to believe anything you tell me, do I?" He stared at her, reminded again what a liar she was.

"You're wrong about my sister."

He laughed. "What is it? Some strange kind of family pride that makes it all right for your sister to be a crook who was conning me out of my money, but heaven forbid she would ever stoop to framing me for fraud and arson?"

"I don't expect you to understand," she said, lifting her chin in obvious indignation. "My family are not *crooks*. They only take from those who have stolen from someone else."

"Ah, modern-day Robin Hoods?" he said with a laugh. "Nice. I'm sure that helps you and your family rationalize being thieves, but I didn't steal my money from anyone and your sister came after me."

She raised one fine brow. "I know you claim you're innocent of the fraud and arson charges against you—"

"I am."

"Even if that is true—"

"Angie came after me *before* it had even come out about the substandard housing, *before* the arson," he said. "So that proves she was just after my money."

She met his gaze. "You inherited the money from your father."

"What are you saying?"

She shook her head and looked away.

He grabbed her arm and swung her around to look at him again.

Her eyes filled with anger and defiance as she jerked free of him. "Haven't you ever wondered how your father was able to go from dirt poor one day to rich the next?"

"You think my father *stole* the money?" he demanded.

"I don't think. I know he did," she said, and tried to step past him.

He blocked her exit. "I don't believe you."

"I'm sure you don't," she said. "You don't believe anything I tell you, right?"

"Right."

She shoved past him into the empty street along the wharf and headed in the direction she'd originally come from, almost disappearing into the fog.

He caught up to her. "You're going to drop a bombshell like that and just walk away?"

"What does it matter now?"

"It matters to me."

"Angie is dead," she said, wisps of fog whirling past as they walked. "All that matters now is getting Patrick."

He walked beside her in silence, thinking about what she'd said. Of course she had her facts wrong.

But she was right about one thing. Clearing his name and getting Patrick had to be the top priority right now.

Later… Later he would get answers to all his questions.

Patrick rushed back through the fog and darkness to the hotel, wondering what had possessed him to follow the woman in the first place.

Obviously, she wasn't Angie. Angie was caught underwater on a limb in the Clark's Fork River, waiting for the water to clear so some fisherman could find her.

He had followed the woman only to prove to himself that Angie was dead. He knew the moment he saw the double up close, it would be clear she wasn't Angie. The truth was, he wouldn't mind a little reassurance.

As he neared the hotel, he couldn't shake the feeling that he was being followed. And yet every time he turned around, he saw no one tailing him.

Where are you, Jack? What do you have planned now?

He watched the faces of people coming out of the restaurants and stores, half expecting to see Jack again. Or the Angie look-alike. He couldn't wait to get back to the hotel, get packed, get out of Seattle.

Maybe he could catch a flight out tonight. It wasn't that late. But once he used Angie's credit card, Jack would be right behind him.

"Then again…" Maybe he could use that to his advantage, he thought as he pushed open the door to the hotel lobby and stepped inside. He could set a trap for Jack.

"All I have to do is go somewhere and wait for him to show up again," he said to himself as he entered the empty hotel elevator and hit the button for his floor. "Only this time, I'll make sure the cops get him."

As the elevator door closed, he didn't see Jack or the look-alike follow him into the lobby. He took that as a good sign.

Once in his room, he went straight to the phone and was extraordinarily relieved to see that the message light wasn't flashing. The last voice he wanted to hear right now was Angie's.

He called the airport. There were flights to Las Vegas, Palm Springs, Los Angeles or San Diego tonight. Eenie, meanie, minie, mo. He bought a ticket to Palm Springs. Maybe he would have better luck trapping Jack there. It was smaller. Fewer places to hide.

He wondered what Jack's game was. Did he just plan to try to "gaslight" him? Make him think he was going crazy and somehow trick him into confessing all?

Killing Jack had never occurred to him as part of his original plan. But the thought was starting to appeal to him. If Jack kept chasing him... It would be self-defense, right? Wasn't that why he'd gotten that restraining order against Jack? Because he feared for his life?

Patrick felt confident he could get any jury in the country to believe killing Jack had been self-defense. Jack was a loose cannon. A man who had jumped bail to come after him. A man who couldn't stand the thought of Patrick being with Angie. At least that part was true.

The judge and jury would be sympathetic to Patrick, who had obviously had some bad luck lately. Of course, Jack's attorney would try to muddy the waters by trying to pin Angie's death on him. The husband was always the first suspect. Unless the sheriff was not the brightest bulb in the store.

But maybe Angie Grant Ryerson hadn't really been asleep at the wheel the night she drove off into the canyon. The tire tracks proved she'd never even tried to brake. Maybe she had killed herself over Jack! That would be a nice touch.

What the judge and jury wouldn't know was that, while Jack might want to kill him right now, it just wasn't in Jack Donovan's nature. No, Jack could never kill anyone. Jack just thought that by trying to intimidate him, he could get a confession. *Good luck, Jack.*

So basically, Patrick told himself, he had nothing to fear.

The fog dissipated as Jack and Angie left the water. Buildings rose out of the darkness. Stars twinkled overhead. The moon climbed up through the city, blindingly bright. Jack told himself that he'd make Angie tell him everything. And he'd set her straight about a lot of things. This woman had no idea who she was dealing with. And she thought he didn't, either.

"Help me clear my name and you can have Patrick," he said.

She laughed softly. "I will have Patrick either way." She shot him a challenging look. "So what's in it for me?"

"Mercenary, aren't you? You remind me more and more of your sister all the time."

She glared at him. He could see cold anger coursing through her. It made her eyes blaze, her body seem to vibrate.

"Fine. I'll prove to you that you're wrong about my sister."

"Good luck."

"Do you hate her that much?"

He didn't hate Angie at all. That was the problem. Even knowing that she'd only been after his money, he still couldn't hate her.

"I'm sorry she hurt you."

"Yeah. I'm sure that's what you say to all her marks." She didn't slow her stride as she looked away from him. They were almost to Patrick's hotel. "Angie was going to tell you the truth."

He smiled, hiding his surprise and disbelief, reminding himself of the night she'd said there was something important she needed to tell him. The night they'd been interrupted by Patrick.

"But instead she decided to marry Patrick."

"She was a fool to believe him. Patrick took advantage of her. He…conned her."

"Ironic, isn't it?" he said. "The con getting conned."

"She fell in love with you. It made her vulnerable."

He laughed. "So it was *my* fault."

She didn't answer, just stared straight ahead and kept walking.

He studied her profile, reminding himself who this woman was. A professional liar, a thief. So why did he desperately want to believe her? Because his heart couldn't believe it was all a con. Angie had felt something. But how would he ever know that for certain?

He heard the sound of the traffic on Interstate 5, just a few blocks away. The fog was gone, but the air felt damp. He could see Angie more clearly in the glow of the street lamps as they passed under them.

"Here," he said, taking off his jacket and draping it around her shoulders. "You look cold."

Her expression was one of surprise. And something he couldn't put his finger on.

"I think I understand what Angie saw in you. You're a nice man."

"I used to be," he said, looking into her dark eyes. He knew what he was looking for and quickly glanced away. "Let's find Patrick. I want this over with." He felt her gaze on his face, but he didn't look at her—couldn't.

He would have to be on guard all the time around her, keep her at a safe distance and yet never let her out of his sight.

It would be hell, he thought and smiled to himself. He really did have Angie right where he wanted her.

As Patrick started to repack his suitcase, Angie's address book—scotch-stained and bloated from being wet—fell from his jacket pocket. His stomach roiled at the sight of it. All the numbers wrong or disconnected.

If she'd cleaned out their joint checking account, then maybe she'd hidden her fortune from him, as well. No wonder she hadn't asked for a prenuptial agreement.

Suddenly he recognized that bad taste in his mouth. Fear. Angie's money was now his. But what if he couldn't find it? *Wait a minute.* He knew just the man who could.

He picked up the phone and got the number for a low-life lawyer he'd hired last year by the name of Burns. Lester Burns.

"Ryerson, sure I remember you," Lester said when he'd introduced himself. "I got you out of that scrape in Dallas last year. You never paid me the rest of what you owe me."

"I've been meaning to do that."

"Call me when you do."

"Wait!" Patrick cried. "Do you take credit cards?" He could almost hear Lester smile.

"Give me the number slowly, and the expiration date."

Patrick did, trying not to let his annoyance come

across in his voice. "Now, here's what I need." He started to ask Lester to track down Angie's financial advisor, but realized there was a faster way. "I need to cash in some stocks and bonds and find out how much my wife is worth." He couldn't tell Lester the truth. The man would blackmail him, sure as hell. "I think she's cheating on me and I—"

"Save me the gruesome details, all right," Lester said. "Just give me her name, social and some information off the stocks and bonds. I assume they're in your name. I'll let you know what I find out— if your credit card clears in the morning."

So much for trust. "Angelina Grant." He read off her social security number and birth date. He'd gotten both from the forms they'd had to fill out to get married. Then he pulled out the stocks and bonds and gave Burns that information.

"I'll call you first thing in the morning."

"Eleven. Don't call before eleven." Lester hung up.

Patrick slammed down the phone with an oath and took a taxi to the airport. No sign of Jack along the way. Or the Angie look-alike. So far so good.

Tomorrow he would buy a new cell phone and call Sheriff Truebow to give him the number. He'd call Lester Burns. If anyone could help him it was Lester.

In the meantime… He didn't bother to check out, just went out the back and flagged down a taxi to take him to the airport.

Patrick went straight to an airport bar, ordered a drink and tried to think only about Angie's money, his first big score, but he couldn't relax. Wouldn't relax until Angie's ashes were strewn across Montana. Until he had his hands on at least some of her money and was flying off to Tahiti. Once Lester told him just how much Angie was worth—and how to get his hands on some quick cash—

He heard his flight being called over the P.A. system. As he walked toward his gate, he watched for Jack. And the Angie look-alike. He quickened his step, telling himself that by the time he woke up in the morning, his life could be all wine and roses. Or in his case, scotch and tropical beaches, women in string bikinis and—he smiled to himself—word that Angie's very dead, very bloated body had floated up still wearing the too-expensive diamond pendant and wedding ring he'd given her. A man could dream, couldn't he?

Angie stepped into the hotel lobby phone booth, the door shutting behind her with a soft *whoosh*, and closed her eyes. She fought to still the trembling—worse, the tears. What had made her think she could pull this off?

Years of experience in deceit and lies, she thought bitterly. But her feelings for Jack Donovan had made her lose her edge—and almost cost her her life. The game she was playing now was deadly.

She opened her eyes, the taste of him still on her lips, the scent of him clinging to his jacket, which he'd insisted she wear.

Pull yourself together. It was just a kiss.

What a laugh. No kiss was just a kiss with Jack.

He doesn't know. He can't know.

She turned to look out through the phone booth glass at him. He stood over by a potted plant, waiting, watching her, watching for Patrick. She knew he would die trying to protect her. That's what worried her.

He glanced over at her. Her heart leapt as his gaze met hers. How would she ever be able to pull this off? She should have let the police arrest him. She turned away, took out her cell phone and hit speed-dial.

Maria answered on the first ring. She'd obviously been expecting her call. "How did it go?"

"Fine."

"Fine? What happened?" she asked, sounding worried.

"Nothing. It all went according to plan." Angie had known Patrick would follow her down to the wharf. She hadn't thought Jack would, though. He'd been smart enough to circle around and cut her off. He just kept surprising her. And that was the problem. Like that blasted kiss.

"And Patrick?" Maria asked.

"He's rattled and on the move again," she said. "He didn't even bother to check out, but I had the maid peek into his room. He's gone."

"You're sure Jack doesn't know that we made the switch?"

Angie glanced over her shoulder again at Jack. He was watching her intently. She turned back to the phone. "No. He thinks I'm you. I can handle this."

"Can you? You'll have more than Jack to worry about if Patrick realizes you really *are* alive—"

"You don't have to remind me what Patrick is capable of," she said, recalling his trying to kill her last night. She had hit the brakes and swerved, tucking and rolling as she bailed out of the Jeep. It had been so close that she'd felt the rear tire brush her pants leg. She'd scrambled on all fours into the darkness of the trees, amazed she was alive.

Ironically, the heavy coat and jeans Patrick had told her to put on were the only things that saved her. She had wondered why he'd wanted her to change into them, but realized his plan must have called for her to be dressed in something practical—not her wedding suit. He'd have enough suspicion on him as it was.

She had listened to the shriek of the Jeep's tearing metal as it tumbled down into the canyon, all the time knowing that she could have been inside it.

As she'd huddled in the cold and pines, she'd watched Patrick get out of the Suburban. She'd seen how hard it was for him to near the rim of the canyon, let alone to look down. She'd watched, vowing to get out of the mountains alive—and make Patrick wish he had never been born.

Well, she'd gotten out of the mountains. And now she intended to keep the second part of that vow. As soon as she took care of Jack.

She could hear the clatter of computer keys.

"Patrick used your credit card to book a flight to Palm Springs," Maria said. "He'll be staying at the Rancho Vista del Norte."

He had no choice but to use her credit card, since she'd cleaned out their joint checking account. It made him easy to track. His own cards were maxed out from courting her, not to mention the cost of the wedding and the plot to kill her at the cabin in Montana. That must have cost him a bundle.

"So you got Jack out of your hair," Maria said.

Angie took a breath and let it out slowly.

"Don't tell me you didn't send Jack packing to Houston," Maria ordered.

"He's going back to Houston," Angie assured her. "I'm going with him."

"What?"

Her twin knew she couldn't turn Jack in to the authorities. Wasn't her style, even if she hadn't been in love with him. "I'm going to help Jack clear his name."

A sigh. "How did I know you'd do that?" Silence.

"He thinks I was working with Patrick."

"I know," Maria said. "So you're going to pretend you're me and prove to him he was wrong about you." She chuckled. "What is wrong with this picture? Angie, you don't really think you can change his mind about you, do you?"

"That isn't what I'm doing. I just don't want him believing that I had anything to do with sending him to jail."

"Maybe he belongs in jail," Maria said. "You can't change who you are," she said more kindly. "What does it matter how much you lied to him or how good your motives were? Do you really think he could ever trust you again? Worse, what if you find out that Patrick didn't frame him? What if Jack is guilty of those charges?"

Angie glanced back at Jack again. At one time, she would have argued that she knew the con business so well she could spot a lie at fifty feet. When she'd started falling in love with Jack, she had become a mark herself. And now she couldn't trust her instincts, not when it came to Jack.

"I hate to see you get your heart broken again," Maria said quietly.

Again. Yes, Angie hadn't forgotten the first time. She'd been much younger then, but it hadn't hurt any less. And it had taught her a lesson she'd thought she would never forget. Until Jack.

Wasn't that why she'd believed all the horrible things Patrick had told her about Jack? Because she'd been burned by a man before? Because she didn't have faith in happy endings? And she knew what Jack's father had done. Of course Jack too would be flawed. Of course he would break her heart. And there was the "evidence" Patrick had provided.

"If Jack is innocent, I can't let him take the fall. I suspect Patrick really might be behind this. Worse, that he used me to distract Jack while he was busy framing him." Her heart argued Jack's innocence while her cynical nature held out little hope. But a little hope was better than none.

"You get too close to the truth and you might have to fear not only Patrick, but also Jack," Maria warned.

Angie smiled to herself. Maria didn't realize just how much of a threat Jack Donovan was. Just not in the way Maria was imagining.

She hoped Patrick had left something that they could find to clear Jack. Before Patrick tried to stop them from discovering the truth. They would have to move fast.

"I suppose there is no talking you out of this?" Maria asked.

"No." She didn't deceive herself that she could turn back the clock and change everything between her and Jack. He knew now why Angelina Grant had come into his life. Or at least enough of it to hate her. He would never trust her again. Nor could she blame him—if he was as innocent as he claimed.

"As for Patrick, I don't want you doing anything without me," Angie told her twin. "Let's allow him to think he's gotten away for the next forty-eight hours. I'll take care of things in Houston, then meet you in Palm Springs. Just keep an eye on him?"

"Gladly," Maria said.

"But no more than that. It's too dangerous to move forward on the plan without a backup." Angie doubted even her sister knew just how dangerous Patrick was. You had to look into a man's eyes to see the depth of his depravation. And Angie had. "Just let me know if he runs again."

"Don't worry, I'll be watching him like a hawk," Maria said. "You think forty-eight hours is enough?"

"Any more will be too dangerous if I'm right about Patrick. Promise me, Maria, that you'll stay out of sight," Angie said. She remembered only too well the expression on her twin's face when she'd flown to Montana to pick her up and had heard Angie's story.

Maria had wanted to drive up to the cabin right then and kill Patrick. Forget any plan for LaGrand-style revenge. She wanted vengeance, the clean, simple, permanent kind.

"Promise?"

"Promise," Maria said.

"Why don't I believe you?"

"Because I'm a con artist." Maria laughed. "I told Jack I was better than you."

"You are such a liar," Angie said good-naturedly.

"See?" Maria said with a laugh.

Angie disconnected, still worried Maria might decide to take matters into her own hands. She dialed the airport.

When she hung up, she turned to find Jack standing outside the phone booth. She pushed open the door, wondering how much of the conversation he'd overheard. "Patrick's on his way to Palm Springs."

"Then why did you just book us seats on a jet to Houston?" he asked, making it clear he'd heard at least the last conversation.

"Patrick will be fine in Palm Springs. I want him to think he's safe—at least temporarily—so he stays put. We're going to Houston to clear your name." She'd learned from an early age that nothing was impossible—with the right attitude and the right connections. Her daddy had taught her well.

"Just like that?" He chuckled.

She raised a brow. "Only if you're really innocent."

A muscle in his jaw jumped, his eyes narrowed. "I'm innocent. As for Angie…"

She stepped past him and headed for the door, refusing to take the bait. There was only one way to convince him that she hadn't had anything to do with the charges against him.

"Chartering a private jet to Houston isn't cheap," he noted, catching up to her.

He still seemed to think she was broke and that she'd targeted him last spring for his money and nothing more.

"Vengeance is never cheap." She looked over at him, meeting his gaze. "Sometimes the price can be too high, though."

He met her gaze. "Not in this case."

Chapter 9

As the plane banked over Palm Springs, Patrick looked down and thought it a sparkling jewel—the glittering lights illuminating turquoise pools, towering palms and red-tiled roofs.

He smiled. This was more like it. He felt that old excitement shoot through his blood. This was the life he should have been born to. Not some slummy part of Houston. Not taking favors from Jack Donovan.

Patrick put down his window on the cab ride to the Rancho Vista del Norte and breathed in the dry rich scents of desert night. The cab cruised down the main drag under a canopy of backlit palms.

He thought he might take a late swim in the pool. Tomorrow he would catch some rays, get a good tan. He couldn't wait.

Once he got to his room, he was feeling so good

he decided to call Sheriff Truebow's after-hours number, feeling lucky. Maybe the sheriff had tried to call the broken cell phone. He left his room number, then began to unpack his suitcase, looking for his swimsuit.

The aquamarine pool right outside his sliding glass doors was just too inviting. Majestic palms swayed in the warm breeze, bathed by golden light. He could hear the alluring lap of the water in the pool, the rustle of the palm fronds, the sweet voices of several hotties in skimpy bathing suits as they glided through the water like young playful seals. Oh yeah, this was more like it.

Where was his swimsuit? He couldn't wait to get in the pool. His fingers brushed something unfamiliar. He looked down and let out a startled cry as he jerked his hand back.

It was a woman's brown shoe with white stitching—just like the one Truebow had said was found in the river.

Angie said nothing on the short taxi ride to her hotel but she didn't seem surprised when, true to his word, he didn't let her out of sight for an instant as she quickly packed her things for the flight to Houston.

It was obvious from her expression that she regretted not letting the cops arrest him back at the restaurant tonight.

"I told you I would help you," she snapped at one point.

He smiled. "Angie too told me a lot of things."

"I'm not my sister!"

"As far as I'm concerned, you're the same. Two of a kind. No difference."

"You're wrong about that. Angie and I are very different. Right now, I can't imagine what attracted her to you."

"My money," he said with a laugh. "Nothing but my money."

She groaned as they left her hotel. "You don't have that much money. And I told you, it wasn't about money."

He caught up to her. "Sure it was about money."

"It was about righting a wrong," she said without looking at him as she walked out to hail a taxi.

"Right. Come on, there must be dozens of guys La-Grands could have conned whose fathers were much more crooked than mine. Why me?"

She shook her head, trying hard to ignore him. Good luck.

"Look, I don't know how my father went from rags to riches, but I can't imagine he did something so horrible to your family that it would make you go after his son. My father's been dead for over a year."

She finally looked at him, for an instant her gaze unguarded. Then her eyes narrowed and darkened. Her lips parted. He could see the pink of her delicate tongue, remember the taste of her on his lips. Her eyes locked on his, daring him to look away. Not likely.

Did he just imagine it? Or in that instant when her gaze was unguarded had he glimpsed the Angie he'd fallen in love with? Or did she even exist? Maybe everything about the LaGrands was smoke and mirrors.

"You were right earlier," she said. "We *are* mercenaries. We work as a family on behalf of people who were bilked or wronged, people who didn't get proper justice."

"You're telling me that your family specializes in revenge—for a fee, of course."

Her smile was rueful. "I knew you wouldn't understand." A taxi pulled up. "We have work to do." She jerked open the door and started to get in.

He caught her arm. "Is the truth so hard for you?" he demanded. "Who did my father wrong?"

"We don't have time for this."

"We will before this is over," he whispered as he let go of her, then slid into the dark intimate back seat of the cab next to her. "Count on it."

He gave the driver the address of his hotel. He needed to pick up his suitcase and the thick envelope with the dossier on her family.

Her features weren't quite distinguishable in the darkness. Once a mark, always a mark, he thought angrily. Anger and frustration warred with emotions he no longer wanted to feel for this woman. He told himself that he had never known her—only what she wanted him to see, which was all a lie.

She was lying to him right now, pretending to be her twin. She thought he was buying it, that he couldn't tell the difference between them.

That gave him an advantage he planned to use in his favor, even if he did feel guilty about it. He owed this woman nothing, certainly not the truth. And yet he hated the thought of lowering himself to her level, of becoming her. A liar.

He could tell that once she helped him clear his name—or prove that he was guilty of the charges—she thought she'd be rid of him and could deal with Patrick on her own. Fat chance.

But right now he was more worried about what she may have planned for him. Was going to Houston with him nothing more than leading him on a wild-goose chase? Or was she just trying to cover her own tracks?

He breathed in the sweet scent of her perfume and told himself he could do this, whatever it took. Only, this time, he'd be the one calling the shots.

But even as he thought it, he wondered if Angelina LaGrand wasn't already one step ahead of him and leading him into a trap far worse than any others she'd laid.

"What the hell?" Patrick stared down at the shoe, his throat contracting. How could this shoe possibly have gotten into his suitcase?

He had to sit down before he blacked out. Moving to the glass doors, he pulled the blinds and stumbled over to one of the chairs at the table, dropping down, his gaze locked on the bag.

Of course he had to have put the shoe in there himself. No one else had access to his suitcase, right? He'd packed so quickly back at the cabin in Montana, maybe he'd accidentally put some of Angie's stuff in by mistake.

Right. The other shoe from the river? Like Angie had taken off wearing only one shoe.

Maybe the sheriff had found the shoe, flown to Seattle, come into his room and put it in the suitcase to scare him. Ridiculous.

Jack. It had to have been Jack. But how could Jack have gotten the shoe?

Patrick shook his head as he got up, moved to the suitcase and removed the shoe gingerly. He clutched it in both hands and tried to snap it in half, succeeding only in breaking off the heel.

Angrily, he threw both shoe and heel into the waste-basket and covered it with some crumpled-up brochures and advertising pamphlets from the desk.

There.

But now he didn't feel like swimming anymore. Just moments before, he'd felt safe, content here. Later, after the hotties were out of the pool, he'd get rid of the shoe in the Dumpster in the alley behind the resort. He'd never be able to sleep with that damn shoe in his room.

Once they were on the jet and winging toward Houston, Jack asked, "So what are you planning to do to Patrick?"

She shook her head. "It's better if you don't know."

He'd seen the bruises on her arm earlier. What had happened up at that cabin in Montana? Had Patrick really tried to kill her? Or did she just want everyone to think that? Especially Jack Donovan.

Montie had warned him that Angie might have faked her death. He'd even predicted that she would come running to Jack for help. Show up swearing she hadn't been in on any of it with Patrick.

Except, she hadn't come running to him for help. In fact she had tried to persuade him to return to Houston and let her take care of Patrick alone.

But then again, she knew he wouldn't. So maybe he was playing right into her hands, letting her take him back to Houston. For all he knew, the police would be waiting at the airport to arrest him.

"Just let me handle everything," she said now, and leaned back as if to sleep away the flight.

"Excuse me? My entire life was messed up when your twin waltzed into it, not to mention when she and Patrick ripped me off and framed me. I'm sorry if my being here is inconvenient for you, but I'm part of this. It's my reputation that is shot to hell, my freedom that's at stake. I want to know what the hell you have planned. Start with what's happening when we land at the airport in Houston."

She opened her eyes, glared at him and sat up. "I could have let the cops catch you back in Seattle if my intent was to have you thrown in jail. I could have saved myself the cost of this flight."

"Why didn't you?"

She let out a sigh. "I did it for Angie, all right? Whether you believe it or not, she had feelings for you."

"If you're looking for gratitude—"

"I'm not looking for anything from you. I thought I made that clear. You're nothing but trouble to me. And if I'm not careful, you'll get us both killed. Unless you are still of the mistaken presumption that Patrick isn't a killer."

"There was a time I certainly wouldn't have believed Patrick capable of violence," he admitted. "Now? I'm not sure of anything."

"That's a start, I guess. It helps if you know what you're dealing with."

How true, he thought studying her. "I thought I knew Angie. But the woman I knew wouldn't have married Patrick."

She raised a brow. "When you knew her she wasn't being drugged."

Anger ripped through him. "Patrick *drugged* her? That son of a—"

"It wasn't just the drugs, Jack. What really changed her mind about you was the photographs."

Jack stared at her. "What photographs?"

She didn't answer.

"What photographs?" Jack demanded again. His blue eyes were hard as ice chips and just as cold. Whatever had made her think when she first met him that his eyes were the color of warm denim?

"Photos of you and another woman. In bed."

He stared at her. "What woman?"

"Your former fiancée."

"Constance?" He sounded surprised. "How in the hell did someone get photographs of—" He scrubbed a hand over his face. "The photos aren't real."

She lifted a brow.

"Okay, when were they supposedly taken?"

"Recently."

Jack scoffed. "I broke it off with Constance last spring and I know of no photos—"

"That isn't what Constance says."

He narrowed his gaze at her.

"Angie confronted Constance, and she admitted the two of you had been having an affair—while you were dating Angie."

"That's a lie. I haven't been with Constance since before I met Angie."

But she could tell he was surprised she had—that is—Angie had confronted his former fiancée.

"The photos are quite convincing."

"I want to see them," he said between gritted teeth.

"No problem." She opened her purse, took out a color snapshot and handed it to him. "I found this in Angie's hotel room."

He stared down at the shot of him and Constance in his bed at the penthouse. "Is this all?"

She shook her head. "Angie told me Patrick had the rest at his apartment."

Jack swore and crumpled the photo in his fist. "This photo was obviously taken before I broke it off with her. But what I'd like to know is who the hell shot it."

"Why *did* you break off the engagement with Constance Whitaker?" she asked, way too curious.

He swept her with a look that said it was none of her damn business.

She waited.

"I found out Constance lied to me. Satisfied?"

"That's it?"

"That's it. I abhor liars."

She looked away. "Even liars sometimes tell the truth."

"Right. It's just impossible for people around them to know when that is."

How in the hell had someone gotten photographs of him and Constance? That's what Jack wanted to know. And why would Constance lie about recently sleeping with him?

Well, the second answer was easy. Spite. Constance had been furious when he'd broken off their engagement and had threatened to get even with him. It seemed she'd found a way.

He glanced over at Angie. He forgot sometimes that he had no secrets from the woman beside him. She knew things about him and his family that he didn't even know himself, it seemed. But he promised himself he'd know everything there was to know about her before they parted ways.

He smiled to himself, just thinking about her confronting Constance. That must have been something to see. He wished he hadn't missed it.

But there seemed to be a lot of things he'd missed while she and Patrick were framing him.

He studied Angie, wondering why she'd kept that one photograph. "Tell me how the con works," he said, and saw her flinch. "Tell me how the one you and Angie cooked up for me worked. Really. I'm dying to hear. And we have lots of time before our plane lands in Houston."

And he needed to be reminded right now just how dangerous the woman next to him really was.

Jack settled into his seat, the look on his face making her uneasy. It was clear that he wasn't going to take no for an answer.

"Tell me how Angie set me up that day in the park," he said. "You were in on it, right?"

Her heart ached as she met his gaze. "Yes, I was." The memory of that day filled her with so much regret, it hurt to look at him. What ever had made her think she could pull off this charade? Just being this close to Jack and still lying to him was killing her.

"Well?" he said, crossing his arms over his chest and waiting as if he had all night. He did.

She thought back to that day, the first day she came face-to-face with Jack Donovan in the park. A beautiful spring day in early May.

"Ready?"

Angelina adjusted her earpiece as she glanced out the hotel suite window. "Ready." After all this time, she was more than ready.

"He's on his way down," Maria said into her ear. "Ten minutes and counting."

"Got it." She checked her watch, then glanced across the street at the mirrored steel monolith of Donovan, Inc. It gleamed in the morning sun. Such an easy target. Just like the man behind the building.

She watched Jack Donovan come out the front door, stop to talk to the doorman for a moment and walk south, just as he had every day for the past week. His step was brisk and light. He unbuttoned his suit jacket as he walked and looked around, the sun on his face. Thirty-six, successful and a paragon of virtue, he was a man on top of the world.

She checked the time. Jack Donovan was also a creature of habit. Didn't he know that being this predictable made him an easy mark?

Picking up her purse, she took one last look in the mirror by the door of her hotel room and smiled at the image staring back at her as she made sure her long, dark curly hair hid the earpiece. She even smelled of money, she thought, breathing in the expensive perfume she'd dabbed behind her ears. She ran a hand over the fine fabric of the suit she wore, the gray skirt cut just above her knee, modest but accentuating her legs.

Jack's ideal woman. He just didn't know it yet.

She took the elevator down, in no hurry. She knew exactly where to find him. The same place he was every day at this time. The park. It was only a short walk.

She followed the scent of the lunch cart and saw Jack lathering his daily hot dog with mustard, relish and sauerkraut. He took a big bite, closing his eyes, chewing for a moment, then smiling, making the hot dog vendor laugh.

Jack ate as he walked toward the duck pond, careful to save some of the bun. The ducks welcomed him, all waddling or swimming toward him for the treat he threw them each day. He walked on, nodding, smiling, stopping to throw back a ball to a young boy and his dog.

"This guy is too much," Maria replied in her ear, after Angie had described his movements.

A man who loves hot dogs, ducks, kids and mongrel mutts. She glanced at her watch and headed for the other side of the park, circling from the opposite direction.

She'd walked this stretch at least two dozen times to get her gait down. Timing was everything. And luck, she thought, unconsciously reaching for the amulet she always wore on the chain around her neck, hidden under her blouse today. Her father had taught her to plan for every possible occurrence. But her grandmother knew the importance of luck when it came to a good con. Her grandmother had given her and Maria each an amulet when they were just girls. Angie had never taken hers off.

She glanced at her watch, then up at the next park entrance. "Mark in sight," she said quietly. Jack Donovan was just coming out of the trees. She should intersect with him in one minute.

"Right on time. We're rolling. Good luck."

She kept walking, keeping Jack in sight as the two paths of the park intersected at the busy street. This was where Jack always turned to the left and circled back around through another portion of the park, returning to his office and work.

Today, with luck and years of practice, Angelina planned to change Jack's routine, change his world forever.

As he reached the sidewalk and started to turn, she stepped across the sidewalk and grassy boulevard, pretending to look for a taxi. Being the noon hour, it was next to impossible to get a cab on this side of the park. It was the reason she'd chosen this spot. Along with two lanes of busy bumper-to-bumper traffic, there was a narrow road that cut through the park and merged at this very point. That road had been closed by a repair crew ten minutes ago. Leave nothing to chance.

She stepped out into the street, arm raised as if she'd seen a cab in the traffic. The car came out of the park road, tires squealing, making Jack look up.

He saw her. Even with her back to him, she could feel his gaze on her, his concern for her almost palpable. Predictable Jack Donovan. This was almost too easy, she thought as the car bore down on her.

He tackled her an instant before the car would have hit her, taking her down in the grass along the boulevard. All those years of playing football. Jack Donovan had also stayed in shape.

She'd known that he would save her. The risk this

time had been minimal. After months of study, she knew Jack Donovan better than he knew himself.

"Are you hurt?" he asked anxiously as he pushed himself up on one elbow to look down at her.

She actually did feel a little dazed. This was the first time she'd been this close to him. She'd known his eyes were blue—just like his father's—but they were a light denim like soft, worn jeans. His lashes were like his hair, blond as sunshine.

"What happened?" she asked, trying to sit up.

"Some fool came around that corner going way too fast."

Jack still sounded shaken. It must have been closer than she had planned it.

"I could have been killed," she whispered, and met his gaze.

"Are you really all right?" he asked, concern in his expression, in all that blue denim.

She nodded as he helped her to her feet. "Thank you. I owe you...my life."

He almost blushed as he handed her the purse she'd dropped. "Let's not get carried away. I'm just glad you're all right."

She nodded and looked down. Her suit was grass stained, her silk stockings torn at the knee and one of her high heels broken off. A hole in a stocking was bad luck. She pushed the thought away. Her luck was going fine. Better than fine, she thought, looking up into Jack's handsome face.

"I can't tell you how lucky I feel right now."

He laughed at that, a laugh filled with relief. Then he noticed that she was limping.

"It's just my shoe," she said, and pulled off the broken shoe as well as the other expensive high heel.

"I hope you don't have far to go," he said as his gaze moved from her stockinged feet to her face. He seemed much shyer than she would have thought. He glanced toward the street. "I'll get you a cab."

"Actually, I've changed my mind. I was going to the Institute of Art Museum, but under the circumstances…" She held up her broken high heel shoe. "I think I'll just walk back to the hotel."

"Where are you staying?"

"The Carlton Arms." She looked up at him, knowing exactly what he would say.

"Let me walk you, then—that is, if you don't mind."

"No," she said with a small laugh. "I'd love the company, and maybe people won't think I'm crazy for going barefoot if you're with me."

There was only a moment's hesitation. He quickly slipped off his shoes and socks, stuffed his socks into his pocket, and, his shoes dangling from his fingers, grinned at her. "Let them think we're both crazy. It's spring and I can't remember the last time I went barefoot and felt new grass between my toes."

Angelina was seldom surprised. It was bad for business. But for such a predictable man, Jack Donovan seemed to be capable of surprising her. That should have warned her. Instead, it delighted her.

She smiled up at him. "It is a beautiful day for a walk in the park, isn't it?"

"Do you like ice cream?" Jack asked, sounding as excited as a boy. "What's your favorite?"

She laughed and had to think. "Rocky Road."

He studied her, then smiled. "Rocky Road, it is. By the way, my name's Jack. Jack Donovan."

"Angelina Grant, but please call me Angie," she said, returning his smile.

"Angie," he said, repeating it softly, his smile broadening. "I like that."

Jack held out his hand and she took it as they cut through the grassy park toward the ice-cream vendor.

"Nice work," Maria said in her ear.

Just like that, Angie had changed Jack's routine— and was about to change his life, as well. And not for the better. Even then the thought had given her an odd feeling, one she had little experience with: guilt. Vengeance always comes at a high price, her father used to say. But in the end, all debts must be paid. And Jack, like all marks, was going to pay dearly.

He had bought them each a double-scoop ice-cream cone and they ate them as they sat and talked on one of the park benches. She wasn't surprised when he had asked her to dinner. But she had been surprised when he suggested a small barbecue joint he knew of, instead of a four-star restaurant. Her surprise should have put up another red flag.

But she'd ignored it, blinded maybe by the spring day. More likely, by the man.

Even later, when Jack's friend Patrick Ryerson had showed up unexpectedly at dinner, she hadn't been worried. Patrick wouldn't be a problem because she knew that within no time she'd have Jack Donovan right where she wanted him.

Getting to Jack had been easy. In fact, it had almost been too easy.

She smiled ruefully at the thought. She should have known that nothing was going to go the way she'd planned it. Well, she did now.

Now that it was too late.

Chapter 10

"So it had nothing to do with money," Jack said sarcastically when she'd finished. "It was just a job."

She heard the edge to his voice, part anger, part fear that she knew more about his father than he did. "It is seldom about money, although money is usually the exchange medium."

Jack laughed. "You fleece people. Why don't you just be honest? It isn't about vengeance or settling a score. It's about you taking some poor sucker for everything he's worth. I became your mark because your family saw the article in *Fortune* magazine about me. It had nothing to do with my father."

"You inherited the construction company from your father," she said calmly. "He started with nothing, right? First remodeling one of the houses in your area, then starting his own business as he began buying run-down buildings, getting low-income housing loans and re-building the neighborhood."

Jack's gaze narrowed. "That's right."

"Later, he moved the two of you out of the neighborhood and started building new subdivisions, but he made his money in your old neighborhood, building houses for the poor—just like you started to do a year ago, after your father died—and taking kickbacks from substandard construction and materials."

"That's a lie!"

"Did your dossier mention that I had relatives who came from that Houston neighborhood?" From his expression it was clear he hadn't known. "I had a great-aunt on my mother's side who lived in one of the houses your father built. She was killed in a fire. The fire department found a short in the electrical wiring. That's when it first came out about the substandard materials."

Jack was shaking his head. "If that were true—"

"Your father hired a lawyer, paid off some people and nothing ever came of it. But part of the deal he made was to stop building houses in our neighborhood and never return."

Her dark eyes met his, hers warm as honey. Jack thought he glimpsed regret in that gaze and something far worse, pity.

"It would be smart for you to stay away, as well," she said.

"Don't worry about me, okay?"

"Fine," she said, and looked away. "I just don't think you have any idea how ugly it could get."

"I grew up on the streets of Houston in a rough neighborhood. I was pretty much on my own from the time my mother left and my father…" He stopped and smiled ruefully. "Oh, I forgot, you know all of that." And more. "At least, you think you do."

Jack frowned and looked out the plane window at the darkness. He'd been eleven when they'd left the old neighborhood. It had always bothered him that they never went back. When he'd missed his friends and complained to his father, Kelly Donovan had told him to make new friends. When he'd insisted on seeing old friends, Patrick had been brought to their house in the new neighborhood. Jack wasn't allowed to go back to the old neighborhood. He'd thought it was because the place held too many bad memories for his father. Apparently, if Angie was telling the truth, it did.

"So why didn't your family go after my father then?" he asked.

"Angie and I were only five and my father was busy raising us and making a living," she said.

"Your father had bigger fish to fry," Jack said. "Talk about the pot calling the kettle black."

"The difference is that my father didn't swindle innocent, trusting people," she snapped. "A confidence game only works if the mark has thief's blood."

"Thief's blood?"

"You can't cheat an honest man," she said simply. "A mark must have larceny in his veins. Oh, he thinks he's honest. He's rationalized his behavior to the point where he never admits, even to himself, that he's not. The mark has to be a willing participant. All confidence men do is play upon the mark's weakness."

Well, Jack knew what his weakness was: Angie's

lies. "So after all these years your family decided I should pay for my father's alleged sins?"

"My family hadn't forgotten about your father or what he did," she said. "Vengeance to the LaGrands is a fine art. It can sometimes take years. We have extraordinary patience."

"So it was just a matter of time," Jack said. "You were waiting until I had enough money to make it worth your while."

She shook her head. "One of my distant cousins hired us. He's related to the great-aunt who died in the fire and still has friends who live down in that neighborhood. He saw the article in *Fortune* magazine—and heard you had started building substandard housing down there, just like your father."

He shook his head, more out of disbelief than denial. "So everyone thought the acorn hadn't fallen far from the tree." He was dumbfounded. "Was the plan to ruin me financially?"

"We were going to make you an offer we believed you wouldn't refuse."

"A way to make even more money," he said. "And when I went for that, I'd lose my shirt, right?"

"Right. We would put you out of business for good."

"And make yourself a nice, tidy, little profit," he noted. "Only Angie never made me an offer."

"No." She looked away. "Angie started falling in love with you and having doubts about your guilt."

"Until Patrick convinced her I was even worse than she'd first thought."

She nodded. "That about sums it up."

He could see now why Angie had fallen for Patrick's lies—if what she'd told him was the truth.

As the plane began its descent to the Houston airport, he asked, "What was the name of the lawyer who allegedly got my father off?"

"Montague Cooke."

It was late, dark and raining in Houston. With only carry-on luggage, they caught a cab right away.

Angie felt tense, her skin feverish, nerves raw, fearing the slightest touch or look from Jack would give her away. Their verbal sparring on the plane had left her with a headache. Lying to him about her identity was exhausting. She wanted desperately to reach out to him, to tell him everything.

But she knew her words would be wasted. He had branded her a liar, a cheat, a con. And his disgust of her kept her silent. She'd seen his expression when she told him about his father. *He hadn't known.* She'd stake her reputation on that. And although Jack wouldn't understand this, a good reputation was very important to a confidence woman.

But even if Jack really was innocent—every instinct told her he was—and she could clear his name, she didn't kid herself that he could ever forgive her.

She tried not to think about that, concentrating instead on the task at hand. From an early age, she'd learned to focus on one problem at a time. It had always seen her through rough times before. She knew it would this time, as well.

As long as she didn't forget she was Maria. That wasn't hard because in her mind the old Angelina La-

Grand truly was dead. As soon as things were settled with Jack and Patrick, she was going off the grift. Going straight. Let Maria continue with their family's legacy. Angie was done. Too bad it was too late as far as Jack was concerned.

"I need to make a stop," he said, his head turned toward the passing city streets outside the taxi.

She was too tired for another stop. "You could drop me at a hotel—"

He swung his gaze to her. Even in the darkness of the back of the cab, she could see the hard blue of his eyes. "I told you. I'm not letting you out of my sight. This shouldn't take long and there's no reason to stay at a hotel. I have a perfectly adequate guest room at my penthouse."

She looked away, wondering where they were going first. She hadn't heard what address he'd given the driver. Twenty minutes later, the taxi pulled into the circular driveway of a large brick house in a better part of Houston.

Montague Cooke opened the door in his robe, looking as if they'd gotten him out of bed. Not surprising since it was now nearly two in the morning.

"What in the—" Montie's gaze went past Jack to Angie.

"I need to talk to you," Jack said, and Montie moved to one side to let them both in. "You've met Angelina LaGrand."

"I would advise you not to say anything in front of this woman," Montie said, closing the door behind them.

Jack smiled. "There isn't anything I could say that would surprise this woman. She knows me better than

I know myself. I just need to know one thing. How did my father make his money?"

"Your father?"

"Answer my question."

"He built houses, you know that," Montie snapped. "You woke me up to ask me that?"

"Did you get him out of a mess in the old neighborhood involving substandard construction and another fire that caused some deaths?" Jack asked.

"Lawyer-client confidentially doesn't allow me to—" Montie glanced toward Angie. "Jack, I warned you about this woman."

"He was my father, dammit, Montie," Jack said tersely. "It's true, isn't it? That's what you were trying to tell me the other day. All that talk about how I wouldn't be the first contractor to make my fortune through kickbacks and substandard work and materials." He let out an oath, anger and disappointment like a vise around his chest.

"When did you become my father's lawyer?"

"Your father and I were friends, you know that, from the old neighborhood," Montie said.

"Before you became a lawyer, before he made all his money?"

Montie met his gaze. "What are you asking me, Jack?"

He knew what he was asking, but did he really want to hear the answer? "My father put you through law school. Where did that money come from?"

"I think you already know the answer, Jack," Montie said softly.

Jack stood looking at the lawyer, each breath a labor, his heart hammering so loudly he could barely hear himself speak. "Thief's blood. Like father, like son, right?"

"Jack, this sort of thing is done every day," Montie said sharply. "Your father knew that building nice homes down there was a waste of good money. Those people don't appreciate anything you do for them. Look how—"

Jack was shaking his head as he backed toward the door.

"—those people live. They crowd a dozen people into those houses and live like animals. Jack, your father was no different than other businessmen—"

Jack opened the door and looked over at Angie. The pain he saw in her eyes hurt him worse than his own. Thief's blood. Now, finally, he knew why Angie had come after him.

The taxi waiting outside Montague Cooke's took them to Jack's penthouse. It was nearly three in the morning. Rain drummed on the roof of the cab and the wipers flap-flapped into the silence that had settled like concrete between her and Jack in the back seat.

Jack hadn't said a word since they'd left Montie's. Angie wanted to reach out to him, to say something that would make him feel better, but didn't know what it would be. She could tell that he was devastated to learn that everything she'd told him about his father was true.

"Jack—"

"Don't," he said, and looked over at her. "Just don't, okay? This doesn't change anything between us. I'm not my father. I didn't take kickbacks. I didn't know I was building substandard housing. I'm a fool, but I'm not a crook."

At the penthouse, Jack showed Angie to the guest room.

"I'll be right across the hall with my door open. Leave yours open. Don't worry. Your virtue is safe." His look said he questioned if she had any virtue to lose.

"Do you intend to sleep with one eye open all night?" she asked.

"A man would be crazy to let down his guard around a woman like you."

"I'll take that as a compliment."

"*You* probably would."

She hadn't realized how hard this was going to be. Jack kicked off his shoes and sprawled on his bed. She could see him watching her. She locked herself in the bathroom and took a hot shower, standing under the water, trying hard to forget that Jack was just yards away from her, listening to the water cascading over her.

He thinks you're Maria.

Yes. If only she could tell him the truth. But that would only make proving she hadn't helped Patrick frame him more difficult.

Dressed in silk pajamas and a matching robe, she stepped out of the bathroom, hoping she'd stalled long enough that he was asleep. He wasn't. Both blue eyes were open.

Jack took her in, from her wet hair to the silk that clothed her to her bare feet. She felt her face flush. Desire shot through her.

She moved to her bed, made a project out of turning down her sheets. She didn't look at him, but she knew he was still watching her. She climbed into bed and turned out the light.

He turned out his light without a word.

She wanted to tell him everything. How she'd wanted out of the con because she'd fallen in love with him. How she had been planning to tell him. How vulnerable she'd felt at even the thought of admitting her love for him—and how afraid.

So much so that when she heard that he'd lied and cheated she'd believed it. All her life she had gone after dishonest, corrupt men to con out of their illegally gained fortunes. It had left her distrustful and wary.

She wanted, too, to admit to him how Patrick had conned her. She was glad her father wasn't still alive to see how she'd blown this.

"Jack? Are you asleep?" No answer. "There's something I have to tell you. I'm not Maria. I'm Angie and…" Her voice dropped to a whisper. "I love you."

In the bed across the hall, Jack lay perfectly still, staring up at the ceiling, pretending he hadn't heard, afraid to believe there might actually be a little truth in her words. He wasn't ready to trust her. He wondered if he ever would be.

Chapter 11

Patrick woke the next morning with a start, sitting up in the bed, confused for a moment as to where he was. Palm Springs. That's right. He thought of the shimmering pool just outside the glass doors, the palms, the tanned hotties in their string bikinis, and lay back into the pillows on the bed.

Against his will, the empty wastebasket drew his gaze. Still empty. What did he think? That the shoe he'd taken out to the Dumpster last night would find its way back? He smiled at how ridiculous that was and looked over at the clock on the bedside table to see the time.

His heart stopped. Lying curled up like a deadly snake right next to his head was a silver chain. At the end of it was the pendant that had been around Angie's neck when she'd plummeted to her death in the canyon. Next to it was the wedding ring that had been on her finger—the diamond winking mockingly at him.

Panicked, he threw back the covers and leapt from the bed, staggering backward, his hand covering his mouth for fear he might start screaming. Or throw up. He had to get out of here. But where could he go? She'd found him every place he'd gone.

The wedding ring winked at him again from the bedside table. He frowned and stepped over to the night table, cautiously picking up the ring. Cheap glass. He hurriedly scooped up the pendant. Also glass.

They were the fake pair he'd planned to put on Angie *before* she died. No reason to let her take real diamonds with her. He'd hidden the fake duplicates in his shaving bag. So how had they ended up on the nightstand?

The phone rang, making him practically jump out of his skin. He grabbed the receiver to keep it from ringing again and said hello without thinking that it might be Angie's voice.

"Mr. Ryerson?"

"Sheriff Truebow." Patrick's legs buckled and he had to sit down. "I hope you have some good news for me."

"I'm not sure there is any good news in a case like this," the sheriff said soberly.

"Yes, yes—you know what I mean. Tell me you've found Angie so I can lay my wife to rest," Patrick said.

"I wish I could. But we did find her purse," Truebow said.

Her purse? The one Patrick had thrown into the gorge yesterday morning. "But you still haven't found her."

"Not yet. I'm sorry. The river is running muddy still,

and with a bird hunter still lost in the woods… Can I reach you at this number for a while?"

"Sure," Patrick said, and moved to open the drapes so he could see the pool and the palms.

He hung up and picked up the jewelry from the nightstand, no longer fearing any of Angie's superstition about bad karma. Cheap glass. Definitely not the pendant or the ring that Angie had been wearing. Too bad, though. He would have pawned both pieces if he had them.

He glanced toward the pool. Still no body. Because she was alive? Or because her body was caught in a limb under the Clark's Fork River in Montana?

Looking down at the jewelry in his hand, he figured Jack had either found out about its existence or just stumbled across it in the shaving bag. Either way, it meant Jack was here in Palm Springs. Had even been in Patrick's room.

He felt a chill as he glanced outside. This should have been paradise. He should be lounging by the pool right now. Jack should be in jail in Houston. Angie should be decomposed and floating past a couple of fishermen in Montana. Patrick should have his hands on at least some of her money by now.

He looked around the room, wanting to break something. Smash it to smithereens. His head ached from the fury. He couldn't stand still. Needed desperately to get out of here, out of this town, out of this state, out of this.

But where would he go? He had no money and even Angie's credit card would soon be maxed out. Then what?

He couldn't think, couldn't just keep running. He would call his lawyer in less than an hour. He would get this all cleared up. He took a breath. It couldn't possibly be as bad as it seemed right now, he thought, glancing again toward the pool.

The water shimmered in the morning sunlight, the palm trees swayed in the warm desert breeze and a couple of bikini-clad cuties giggled and splashed at the edge of the pool.

It was paradise. He took his swimming trunks from his suitcase and changed. He'd go for a swim, catch some rays, clear his head. When he came back, he'd call the cops on Jack. Then call Lester for the good news.

Going into the bathroom, he admired his reflection in the mirror. He looked damn good. Angie should have been crazy for him. Instead the stupid woman only had eyes for Jack.

He tried not to think about that as he grabbed a towel, crossed the room and threw open the sliding glass door. As he started to step out, he spotted a woman in a bright-red, one-piece swimsuit standing beside the pool.

Angie. He froze, heart seizing up in his chest. She waved at him and dove into the water.

The next morning it was still raining in Houston. Angie woke from a restless night to find Jack up and dressed and standing at the living room window.

"I want to see Constance first," he said.

She nodded, a little surprised he was going after the infidelity part first. She pulled the silk robe around her as she headed for the bathroom. "I'll get a shower and won't be a minute. Unless you want to go get some breakfast?"

He smiled at that. "I wouldn't dream of going anywhere without you."

"You're too sweet."

"Aren't I, though."

Constance Whitaker was an attorney with Harper, Johnson, Curtis, Whitaker and Whitaker. Angie thought she couldn't dislike Constance Whitaker any more than she had after seeing the photographs of her and Jack together—and confronting her a few weeks before. She was wrong.

"Jack!" Constance said, blue eyes wide with surprise when she saw them enter her office unannounced. She came around her desk, blond and beautiful, tall and slim, carrying herself with an air of privilege.

Angie knew more than she ever had wanted to know about the woman. Constance was from old money and a respected family. She'd gone to the best schools, was smart and enormously successful—and ruthless. She'd lost only one case—the case she'd been working on when Jack had broken off their engagement.

Had she loved Jack that much? Or was Constance Whitaker more upset because their breakup was as highly publicized in the press as their engagement had been?

Jack stood stony straight as Constance embraced him and gave him a kiss on the lips.

She seemed amused when he didn't respond, and turned to Angie. "And who do we have here?"

Before Angie could speak, Jack said, "Don't you recognize her?"

Constance looked at him with total innocence, but

Angie saw a muscle in her cheek jump. "I'm sorry, you'll have to refresh my memory."

"She had a talk with you a few weeks ago about some photographs," Jack said.

Constance lifted one finely shaped brow and flicked her gaze at Angie. "Oh yes. Then I guess we've already met." She turned her attention again to Jack and smiled. "Darling, I hope you're here to ask me to represent you in this little mess you've gotten yourself into."

"Not exactly," Jack said. "Constance, when was the last time you and I were together?"

"What?" Her smile slipped a little.

"It's a simple enough question," he said.

"One that you should know the answer to."

"Oh, I do. I just want to clear it up, in case there is any misunderstanding," he said.

"Jack, are you sure you want to discuss this—" she shot a look at Angie "—in front of *her*?" Her gaze shifted back to him, her look suggestive and sensual.

Angie gritted her teeth.

"I know you couldn't have really forgotten the last time we were together," Constance purred.

"When."

The attorney's blue eyes narrowed, her features hardening. "Nine days ago, Jack. Why? Did you think I'd been counting them? Well, I haven't." She turned and went around her desk to sit in the large leather chair that blocked out the sun from the bank of windows behind her. "I know I'm not the only one you sleep with. It isn't like I think you will ever be happy with just one woman."

Jack laughed, surprising Angie. "Constance, you

missed your calling. You should have gone into the-ater. Oh, I forgot, you're an attorney. You specialize in theater, don't you?"

She leaned back in the chair and crossed her legs. "Jack, I'm disappointed in you. Ripping off people who are desperate for a decent place to live. Stealing from the poor to line your own pockets. And this from a man who hates liars and cheats—"

"I know you didn't do it for money," Jack interrupted. "You're greedy, God knows. But you did this purely out of spite. Payback, right? You couldn't stand the thought that I might have found a woman I actually wanted to marry."

Angie shot him a look. Was he serious? He had wanted to marry her?

"I made the mistake of telling Patrick," Jack contin-ued without looking at Angie. "I had picked out a ring and was going to ask her on Thanksgiving."

Angie's pulse pounded. She tried not to look stunned. Or heartbroken. But she was both. He'd planned to ask her to marry him. The damage was much worse than she'd thought.

But neither Jack nor Constance seemed aware of her shock or disappointment. They were glaring at each other.

Constance had gone rigid in her chair, her cheeks two angry slashes of red. "You got me back into your bed knowing you were going to ask another woman to marry you?"

"You always were a lousy liar, Constance," Jack said with a humorless laugh. "But we both know there is no way I would have invited you back into my bed. No chance in hell."

"Get out of my office," she snapped. "I hope you rot in prison."

"If you were my lawyer, I'm sure I would," he said. "Come on," he said to Angie. "We're finished here."

"Charming woman," Angie said once they'd left the office building and were heading for the rental car, trying to sound like Maria.

"You still believe I slept with her while I was with... Angie?" Jack asked as he climbed behind the wheel.

He looked over at her. There was hope in his eyes, a need for her to believe him.

She didn't want to believe anything that woman said. She especially didn't want to believe that Jack had slept with her nine days ago. "I don't *want* to believe her."

"Well, I guess that's a start." He smiled. "I get the feeling sometimes you're trying to convince yourself I'm worth helping."

"You could be right about that."

He started the car. "Let's see if Patrick left those photographs at his apartment. I assume you still have a key?"

Patrick scrambled out of his room, pushing his way past a horde of vacationers to race to the place where he'd seen Angie dive.

The pool area was cluttered with bodies in swimsuits of every color, both in and out of the water. He kept glimpsing flashes of red material or long dark hair, but when the swimmers surfaced, they were never Angie.

He worked his way hurriedly along the side of the

pool. It was long and curved in a graceful sweep around the side of the building, connecting with yet another pool and another, circling the resort.

He stumbled over the chair of one sunbather, pushed past a half dozen screaming, wet children and leapt over several people lounging at the edge of the pool, feeling their glares.

Where was she? He hadn't just imagined her. Of that he was certain. This was no hallucination. Nor had she been any look-alike. It had been Angie.

He slowed, suddenly afraid he was wrong, suddenly frightened. The hot desert sun lolled in the blue sky above the palms, dazing him with its brightness. He felt dizzy, confused, disoriented in a sea of tanned bodies and a kaleidoscope of bright-colored swimwear.

He glanced around. All the rooms looked the same. Glass and tan stucco. Palms and blue-green pools. He felt lost, like a man who couldn't remember where he'd left his car. Or worse, how to drive it when he found it.

Some kid did a cannonball next to him. Water shot out in a drenching tidal wave, soaking him. He swore loudly, now wet and angry.

As he moved away from the pool, he saw that one of the sliding glass doors to the rooms stood open just as he'd left it, and that lying on the floor where he'd dropped it was his towel.

He had run all the way around the building and was back where he'd started. Relief made him weak. Needing to sit down, he rushed toward his room, stopping short at the doorway.

His heart leapt to his throat. He tried to swallow, but

couldn't. A trail of small, wet footprints led from the edge of the pool directly into his room. *Angie.*

Angie's late-night confession was still killing Jack as she opened the door to Patrick's apartment. It was the last place he wanted to go—especially with her—but he wanted those photographs, wanted them destroyed. As if that would change anything.

"Well, hello, Ms. Grant," said the doorman. "I'm sorry, it's Mrs. Ryerson now, right?" The man obviously didn't watch the news.

"No, I kept Grant," Angie said, smiling. "How are you today, Henry? That arthritis still bothering you?"

"Not so bad today, Ms. Grant," he said, holding the door open. "But thanks for asking."

Jack felt the man's gaze shift to him.

"Will Mr. Ryerson be joining you?" Henry asked pointedly.

"No, I had to come back on business. I'll be rejoining Patrick out in Palm Springs tomorrow," she said smoothly as she walked through the open doorway. Jack followed her with a nod to the doorman.

"Give him my regards," Henry said.

"I will." She swept into the small lobby and went right to the elevator, and stopped to dig in her purse.

"Did you forget something?" Henry asked.

"My keys. Can you believe it?"

Obviously Henry could. He smiled and left his post to go to a small office off to their right. He opened the door and brought out an extra key.

"I'll return it in a few minutes," Angie promised.

"No need. You just keep it," Henry said.

Jack could feel the man's gaze on him.

Angie thanked him and pressed the button for the fifth floor. The doors closed and the elevator began to rise slowly.

"You know about the doorman's arthritis?" he asked, not looking at Angie.

"It's my business to know everything Angie knew," she said.

So it seemed.

"Patrick close to the doorman?" he asked, already knowing the answer.

"I would imagine Henry is calling Patrick's cell phone as we speak," she said. "Patrick pays him for information on the other tenants."

Jack shot her a look.

"Information is often as good as money," she said.

"That sounds like a confidence woman's motto."

"I have it embroidered on a pillow at home," she quipped.

"Where's home?"

She shook her head as the elevator door opened on the fifth floor. "Wherever I am."

"Homey."

She shot him a look. "Like your penthouse is a home."

"I don't spend much time there," he defended, then wondered why he felt he needed to. It was a penthouse, for crying out loud, decorated by a professional interior designer, and she was right. It had never felt like home.

He noticed her hesitate after she unlocked Patrick's apartment. What was she worried about? Something they would find? Or memories from the days before the wedding, when she stayed here with Patrick?

He tried not to think about that as he followed her into the apartment. The air was warm and muggy as if the place had been closed up without air-conditioning for longer than a few days. It was instantly clear that Patrick had planned never to return.

The place was a mess of empty boxes and newspapers, everything he might have valued packed up and gone.

The apartment was small, with an open floor plan: small kitchen, living room, bedroom, bath. It looked as if the place had come furnished, the furniture all big and bulky and drab.

Angie moved straight through to the bedroom. She obviously knew the way. The thought did nothing for his disposition.

Jack could see that the bed had been stripped. He turned away and heard Angie come back out.

"The photos are gone."

He wasn't surprised. As she walked past the couch, she picked up a white blouse. Hers? That's when he noticed the stack of bedding at the far end of the couch. This was where she'd slept? The realization hit him like a brick.

He glanced up to see her looking at him. He tried to hide his surprise, but obviously failed.

"You thought Angie was sleeping with Patrick."

"That seemed the logical conclusion, since they were getting married," he said, sounding as defensive as he felt.

She gave him a look that made him feel small.

"I guess you're out of luck on the photos."

"I think I know where at least the one photograph

was shot from. Constance had the entertainment center built for me." He nodded. "Want to guess who had a carpenter friend of his build it for her?"

"Patrick," Angie said on a breath.

Jack nodded. "He must have known Constance was cheating on me." He shook his head, amazed. "It looks like Patrick knew more about what was going on than I did." The story of his life.

"Blackmail. That must be how Patrick got her to go along with this," Angie said. "That means she won't give up Patrick to us."

Jack agreed. He hated to think who Patrick might have photographed Constance with. Someone significant enough that Constance would still lie to protect herself. "Let's get out of here."

Patrick followed the wet prints slowly into the shadowy room. Angie could still be in here, waiting for him. Or maybe she'd only stopped by to leave him something.

The room was cool and dark after the hot morning sun, and he was still wet from that damn kid splashing him. He blinked, blinded for a moment. There was nothing on the bed. Nothing new beside it on the nightstand. He stepped in farther and stumbled as he caught the heady scent of her perfume.

She *had* been here! He was breathing hard again, each ragged breath taking in the smell of her. The carpet was wet where she'd walked. He could make out her tracks, see where she'd wandered through his room, stopping at the bed and the nightstand, then at the closet and finally the bathroom.

He followed the tracks, seeing the telltale droplets

of water where she'd touched his things. He trembled with rage, cold to his very soul, feeling violated and powerless.

What did she want? Had she taken something? Or left something? What was she doing alive?

The carpet was wet as he slowly moved toward the bathroom, the only room he hadn't checked. The image of Angie's drowned body floating in his bathtub flashed into his mind. He thought for a moment that he heard the drip of the bathtub faucet.

Bracing himself, he peered around the corner of the door into the bathroom. The tub was empty. He gripped the doorjamb, sick with relief. This woman was trying to drive him crazy and it was working.

He was starting to turn back to the room when he felt the dampness on the rug, the tracks headed for the door to the breezeway outside.

He rushed over, opened the door and looked out. No woman in a red swimsuit, though the damp footprints on the terra-cotta tiles were undeniable.

He closed and locked the door, then leaned against it. She was gone. He could almost pretend she'd never been here, if it weren't for the wet spots on his carpet and the scent of her lingering in the air.

Worse, he thought surveying the room, she'd left him something. He was sure of it. And it wasn't a shoe. Or cheap jewelry. No, not this time. Fear gripped him as he imagined a bomb under his pillow. Or a deadly snake. Or— He stepped cautiously toward the bed.

The phone rang, and he clutched his chest. The phone rang again. He hurriedly picked up the receiver.

"Patrick, you son of a bitch."

He jerked back at the vehemence in the voice. "Constance? What the hell are you doing calling me?" he demanded. She knew better than to contact him. Their business was finished. "I told you not to—"

"Jack was here, in my office. Just minutes ago. With Angelina Grant," Constance spat out.

His hands began to shake. "That's impossible."

"I saw them both with my own eyes. He wanted to know about the damn photographs. He knew, Patrick. Damn you, he knew. How long do you think it's going to take him to find out everything else, as well?"

"Settle down," Patrick said, more to himself than to Constance. His heart was racing, he was having trouble breathing again. At this rate he'd have a stroke. "You're sure it was Jack? And Angie?"

"I just told you—"

"The woman was a look-alike," Patrick said, wondering if that were true. But then, who had he seen dive into the pool? Who had left the wet footprints on his carpet?

He tried to focus on the larger problem: Jack was in Houston. Patrick had been so sure Jack would follow him to Palm Springs. Damn. There went his plan to have Jack arrested.

"This woman was no look-alike," Constance snapped.

"I've seen her. The resemblance *is* uncanny," Patrick said. "Jack hired her to try to scare me."

"What?"

"That explains how she cleaned out the checking account," he said to himself, and swore. She must have a fake ID or something. "I knew Jack was behind this."

"Behind what? Patrick, you slimy little weasel. You

told me you'd destroyed the other negatives and removed the camera equipment."

"Calm down," he ordered. "I did." A lie. "I have everything under control. You just keep your cool, damn you. Jack isn't going to find out anything. There is *nothing* to find out. Do you understand?" He took a breath, the sound of his heart too loud in his ears. "How did you get this number?" he demanded, suddenly not sure of anything.

"I saw the news report on television about Angie's alleged death. I called that sheriff up there. He gave me your hotel number when I told him I was your lawyer."

"That was a stupid thing to do," he said. The sheriff would think he was guilty of something, having a lawyer trying to reach him. Damn her.

"Getting me involved in this was a stupid thing to do," she said, her words pelting him like stones.

"I don't remember you kicking up too much of a fuss at the time," Patrick noted. "In fact, you were quite keen on the idea of sticking it to Jack."

"You know damn well why I did it. And I wouldn't have if I'd known you were going to get Jack arrested for arson and your wife was going to take a nosedive off a cliff," she said. "If she's even really dead. Jack introduced her as Angie."

"Yes, you would have. You didn't have a choice," Patrick retorted. "Believe me that wasn't Angie you saw."

"If I find out that you lied to me, you little bastard… You better hope to hell I don't get dragged into this. I know enough about you to get your ass fried." She hung up.

He slammed down the phone. How dare that bitch

threaten him! She had as much to lose as he did. Well, maybe not quite, considering she hadn't been in Montana at the time Angie died. If she truly was dead.

He told himself not to worry about Constance. She was too smart to open her mouth about any of their dealings.

It was Jack he was worried about. Jack was trying to scare him—and it was working. His heart was still banging in his chest. "You expected this," he said to himself. "So stop panicking. There is nothing to find. You covered your tracks. And it isn't like Jack would even know where to begin to unravel all the lies and deceptions you laid for him."

Damn Jack. Why couldn't he have just stayed in jail? Now he was asking a bunch of questions and dragging that look-alike around with him, freaking people out. And that's what worried him, that Angie look-alike.

He took a breath and glanced at the clock. One minute to eleven. Time to call his real attorney, Lester Burns. He picked up the phone, shaking with anticipation.

"Yeah," Lester Burns answered. "Too bad you're not as prompt on paying your bills."

Two things were clear. Lester had caller ID and Angie's credit card had gone through.

"Well, what did you find out?"

"Are you sitting down?"

He was too excited to sit down. Too anxious. "What?"

"What did this woman tell you?"

"That her family made their money in an import-export business and she's loaded," Patrick said.

Lester chuckled. "She's loaded, all right, but not with money. She's a con artist—you know, the kind of crook who fleeces you for everything you're worth. She's very high-class, though—only goes after the cream of the crop. Too high-class for you, so you couldn't have been her mark. How did you end up with her?"

Patrick couldn't breathe. "What?"

"What part didn't you understand? Want me to talk slower? You've been duped. She lied. She doesn't come from money. She comes from a family of thieves," Lester said, and laughed again, obviously finding humor in the fact.

"The stocks and bonds she gave me—"

"Fakes," Lester said. "I couldn't find any money anywhere—at least, not in the name of Grant. Because her name's LaGrand." Lester laughed harder. "Oh, I'm sure she has money, but believe me, you'll never get your greedy hands on it. This woman is a professional. You've been swindled, chump, and by one of the best." Lester hung up, still snickering.

Patrick lowered the phone into the cradle, afraid to make any quick movements for fear he would come apart, fly into a million pieces. It amazed him how calm he was. He felt weightless, numb, almost like he was having an out-of-body experience. He feared he wasn't having a stroke because he'd already had it.

Swindled. Conned. Duped. Angie had tried to tell him he was making a mistake, that she wasn't rich. He had thought she was lying. Oh, she was lying, all right. About everything else.

"Too high-class for you, so you couldn't have been her mark." Lester's words rang in his ears.

Jack had been her mark! She'd said she was after

Jack's money. She had been planning to take Jack for everything and Patrick had bungled into it.

He closed his eyes, his brain nothing but white static, unable to comprehend just how stupid he'd been. Angie must have had a good laugh over his marrying her for her money—that is, she would have laughed if he hadn't been trying to kill her.

She only laughed until the Jeep hit bottom. So he guessed he had the last laugh, after all. *If* she was in that river, he amended, looking down at the wet footprints on his rug.

He slumped down on the bed. No fortune. No reason to have married her. No reason to have spent all his own money to deceive her. No reason to kill her. How could things get any worse?

He lifted his head slowly, knowing the answer to that. Jack was in Houston with someone who looked enough like Angie to fool Constance. And he was in Palm Springs…

He looked toward the pool, his heart already hammering at the thought of seeing the woman in the bright red swimsuit again.

Instead, he saw what Angie had left him.

Chapter 12

Back at Jack's penthouse apartment, he went straight to the bedroom, while she stopped just inside the front door, struck by how much she'd lost. She'd lost Jack. Fallen in love with a mark and ended up being the one taken. She'd almost paid for that mistake with her life. And she had no one to blame but herself.

"I found it," she heard Jack say.

She moved through the living room to the master bedroom. Jack was on the other side of the large entertainment center. He pointed to a camera hidden behind some ornate fretwork.

She stepped closer to inspect the camera. "These don't come cheap." No wonder Patrick was in dire straits right now financially. "It's the latest technology."

"Which means?" Jack asked.

"It's digital and can be accessed by computer much

like e-mail." She stepped in front of the lens, then moved back toward the bed until she heard the soft *click*. "It's motion activated, but since you wouldn't want dozens of pictures of you walking past the camera lens, it's been programmed to focus only on the bed—and to shoot only when there is significant movement."

"I get the picture," he growled. "And you're telling me that Patrick was able to download the photographs without ever coming back here."

"Exactly."

"Did he have a computer at his apartment?"

She nodded. "He must have packed it up when he cleaned out everything else."

Jack raked a hand through his hair. "Too bad. I'd love to take a sledgehammer to it." He reached into the cabinet, ripped the camera out and smashed it under his boot.

"Feel better?" she asked.

He smiled. "Much. Hungry?"

The change of subject threw her for a moment. The same way Jack's grin and the warm faded-denim color of his eyes did.

"Why...yes."

"Good," he said. "Me, too. You like barbecue?"

"What Texas girl doesn't?"

He smiled, a broad, open smile that squeezed her heart like a fist. She was reminded of the man she'd met that day in the park. A man without a worry in the world. The man she'd fallen so desperately in love with.

"Come on," he said.

"This place makes the best barbecue in all of Texas," Jack said as he held the door open for her.

He seemed to be in a better mood after their visit to Patrick's apartment, and she suspected it had something to do with finding out that she—that is, Angie—had never slept with Patrick.

"Jack!" cried the owner, Tiny Durand, from back in the kitchen. "Good to see you! The usual?"

"And some ribs," Jack called back as he and Angie took their usual seat in the booth by the window. The place was empty—it was still early for most people even to be thinking about barbecue.

It had stopped raining. As the waitress slid a couple of sweet teas in front of them, the sun came out, making the late morning sparkle.

An omen? Angie could only hope.

She shifted her gaze from the now sunny day to Jack, and felt her pulse flutter at the look on his face. "What?"

"I was just thinking," he said. "About Angie."

She felt her face flush. Her heart kicked up a beat. "What about her?"

"I'm beginning to understand now why she fell for Patrick's lies," he said.

Her breath caught in her throat. "You no longer think she was in on framing you with Patrick?"

He shook his head. "I think she got taken in the same way I did."

She wanted to laugh and cry and let out a whoop. "What changed your mind?"

"You did."

"Me?" Her voice squeaked.

"You know her better than anyone," he said. "You said all along that she wouldn't have gotten involved in that kind of scheme, it wasn't her style."

"That's true, but why believe me now?" she asked.

He shrugged, his gaze locking on hers. "Like you said, I have to trust you sometime."

She thought her heart would burst. She had to tell him the truth. That she wasn't Maria, she was Angie. "Jack, there's something—"

"I hope you're hungry," he said, as the waitress came over to their table with a large tray filled with barbecue pork, coleslaw and beans. Jack breathed in and smiled. "Nothing smells like Texas barbecue. Or tastes like it, either."

"Jack, I have—"

"Eat," he ordered, smiling as he dished her up a plate. "I've been thinking what we should do next."

"But there's something I have—"

"Whatever it is, it can wait." He handed her a rib. "This food can't."

She took it, her hands trembling at the thought that he already knew.

They ate as if ravenous. Tiny put some country music on the jukebox. The sun spilled in through the window, warming her as she watched Jack eat. His enjoyment of life seemed to show best in food. She was reminded of the days she'd watched him eat hot dogs in the park. The man went at life the way he ate: as if there were no tomorrow. More than ever, she wanted to prove he'd been framed. She couldn't bear the thought that she might be wrong about that.

"You like?" he asked, and reached over with his thumb to wipe a smudge of sauce from the corner of her mouth.

His touch was pure electricity shooting through to

her core. She groaned, closed her eyes and heard him laugh. When she opened her eyes again, he was smiling at her as if he'd never seen anyone like her before.

Angie had been about to tell him the truth. Jack was sure of it. Just as she had last night when he'd pretended to be asleep. Now as he looked at her, the sunlight making her hair shine like burnished mahogany, he wondered why he'd stopped her.

Because it would change things between them and he wasn't ready for that yet. He was having enough trouble with his feelings for her. It was so much easier this way. Mostly, it kept him from kissing her, something he was dying to do right now.

"Did you get enough to eat?" he asked, loving the way she looked sitting there.

She laughed. "Are you kidding?"

He smiled, feeling better than he had in weeks. Learning about his father had come as a blow. Now, though, he knew why he'd become the LaGrand twins mark. Somehow it helped. Having Angie here with him didn't hurt either.

All he needed was proof that Patrick had set him up. He couldn't let himself think past that.

"So can you find out what I need?" Jack asked after their table was cleared and Angie had had him bring in her laptop from the rental car. He might be a genius when it came to business, but he didn't know squat about women—or digging into other people's private lives.

It seemed there wasn't anything this woman couldn't find out through that computer and her remarkable number of contacts across the country—both legit and not. Con artists, it seemed, had a network of friends in both high *and* low places. The true information highway.

"We look at the players," she said, and booted up the computer. "Starting with the obvious. Who had to have known about the substandard materials going into the houses?"

"The construction workers."

She nodded. "Who did they take orders from?"

"The foreman, Leonard Parsons."

She typed. "And who did he answer to?"

"Del Sanders, the general contractor. Patrick was overseeing the housing project."

She nodded and typed. "What did Leonard and Del have to say about the charges?"

"According to Montie, they both thought the orders were coming from me and loyally just did as they were told."

Her gaze flicked up to his. "You didn't talk to them?"

"Montie didn't think it was a good idea," he said.

She arched a brow. "How much do they make?"

He told her and she typed furiously for a few moments.

She smiled over the top of the screen. "Del has to be getting something, but he was too smart to leave a trail. Leonard, on the other hand, seems to have been depositing his share of the kickbacks every week."

Jack shook his head. "Leonard has always been good with the men and seeing that the work gets done, but he's no rocket scientist."

"Obviously. So there is a good chance he'll tell us what we want to know."

He realized that Angie had been right. He was totally

out of his league, but he was now in the hands of the master, he thought looking at her. "Nice work."

She smiled ruefully. "Sometimes it takes a thief to catch a thief."

He wondered how long he could keep pretending this woman wasn't Angie as she smiled one of those smiles that warmed him to his toes. He reached across the table for her hand, wanting desperately to touch her.

The sudden touch of his fingers sent a jolt through Angie. She jerked back, knocking over the saltshaker. Hurriedly, she righted it, pinched up some of the spilled salt and tossed it over her left shoulder without thinking.

She looked up to see Jack staring at her.

His gaze moved from her face to the amulet at her throat and so did her hand. She closed her fingers around the good luck charm and tried to breathe. She waited for him to say something. Anything.

"Jack!" Tiny called from the kitchen and motioned for him to come back.

Jack glanced at her. "I'll be just a minute."

She nodded and swallowed the lump in her throat. He went into the kitchen. Did he just think superstition ran in her family? Or had she given herself away? Wasn't she going to confess anyway? Or had she changed her mind?

She needed to talk to Maria. The cell phone rang three times before her sister answered.

"What are you doing?" Angie asked, worried. She'd had a bad feeling all day that Maria wouldn't wait for her. Maria liked to take things into her own hands. It had gotten her in trouble on more than one occasion.

"Lying by the pool, reading a good book," Maria said, sounding a little breathless.

"How is our…friend?"

"Enjoying Palm Springs. I've seen him by the pool. From a distance, of course."

Angie wanted to believe her sister. Another disadvantage of their profession was a standard assumption that everyone lied. And Maria was very good at it.

"How are things in Houston?"

"Rainy." Angie watched Jack talking with Tiny. She thought she might have given herself away. And she'd changed her mind about telling him the truth. At least for the moment.

"Are you all right? You sound funny."

"Fine."

"Uh-huh. And Jack?"

"He's fine, too. He's a lot tougher than I originally thought," she said, and then could have bitten her tongue.

"He's still a mark, Angie. Don't forget that. Unless you've proven he wasn't responsible for the fraud or arson."

"Not yet." She wanted to argue that Jack wasn't like his father, but she still hadn't found evidence to back that up. All she had was what her heart told her—and everyone knew about hearts: they were worse than marks when it came to being easily corrupted. "You are keeping your distance?" she asked.

Maria sighed. "Would I ever not do what you told me to?"

Angie didn't respond.

"Patrick seems a little agitated. I would suspect he's found out by now that you aren't Angelina Grant, import-export heir, and he's out of luck money-wise."

"He's going to be angry and vengeful."

"I know the feeling."

"Remember what Daddy always said about personal vengeance and anger," Angie reminded her. It could ruin a good con—or worse, get you arrested or killed.

"You think Daddy would have stood back and let Patrick get away with almost killing you?" Maria demanded.

"Patrick isn't going to get away. Not if we stick to our plan. Maria, I'm worried about you."

"Don't worry about me, all right? I'm getting a great tan, keeping my eye on Patrick and waiting for you, little sis. You just clear your boyfriend and get your butt back here so we can take care of this creep."

Clear your boyfriend. Maria wanted Jack to be innocent, too. "See you soon."

Jack watched Angie on the phone. She must have called Maria. He knew her mannerisms so well. The way she cocked her head, brushed her hair back from her face, frowned and tugged at her lower lip with her teeth. He also knew what it meant when she touched the amulet under her blouse. He didn't even think she knew she was doing it.

Her and her superstitions. They made sense now, now that he knew who she was—and what she did for a living. He knew Patrick had found them foolish, childish. But superstition was such a part of Angie, Jack found it charming. Quirky like Angie. Hadn't she told him once that her grandmother had given her the amulet for luck? Her grandmother LaGrand, no doubt. A notorious confidence woman ahead of her time.

But what if she wasn't as good as she thought at

pretending? What if she hadn't meant to, but she'd let him see the real her? What if she'd let him get inside? And at the same time, she'd let herself fall for a mark?

Or maybe he just wanted to believe that he wasn't a complete fool.

He could see how anxious she was as he returned to the table and slid into the booth seat across from her. Was she afraid he knew she was Angie? "Everything all right?"

She nodded. "I just had to make a call to an associate of mine."

An associate, huh. Maria. "And what did you find out?"

She ducked behind the screen of the laptop. "I checked on the fire investigator's report—"

The woman was amazing.

"—and there's nothing in Patrick's background that would indicate he knew anything about arson. So I think it is safe to assume whoever wanted the house burned down paid someone to do it."

He realized something. "You investigated Patrick before you came to Houston, didn't you?"

She nodded.

"Your family doesn't leave anything to chance, do they?"

"No, we don't." She took a breath and continued. "The fire investigator's report suggests the arson was set by a professional but made to look like the work of an amateur." He must have been frowning at her. "What?"

"Sorry," he said. "It's just that you talk about professional embezzlers and arsonists as if they were real professions complete with graduate degrees."

"Where I come from, they are," she said matter-of-factly.

"Just like professional thieves, huh?"

"We aren't thieves," she corrected. "In fact, a good confidence man looks down his nose at pickpockets and burglars and small-time hustlers. Daddy always said, 'If you're going to be a crook, be a confidence man and be the best damn one you can.'"

He leaned back and looked at her appraisingly for a moment. "Daddy must have been really something."

"He was." Her voice broke. "He died last spring."

"I'm sorry," Jack said, feeling awful. "I didn't mean to—"

"It's all right. You couldn't possibly understand."

Angie was right about that. He couldn't understand a man who had raised his twin girls to be confidence women. But he did know how it felt to lose a father. He felt as if he'd lost his twice. Once when his dad died. And again last night when he'd learned how the man had found success.

"How did your father die?" he asked, afraid she was going to tell him that he had been shot by a mark.

"A heart attack, in his sleep."

Jack recalled now reading in the dossier about Addison Grant dying in his villa in the south of France. It was estimated that he and his family had made millions of dollars doing "favors" for friends—for a price.

Millions. It seemed the only truth Angelina Grant might have told him was the part about being an heir to a fortune.

"I'm sorry about your father," he said. "You must have been very close."

She nodded. "My mother died when we were two, so my father raised us with the help of only my grandmother."

"The woman who gave you...and your sister the amulets," he said, realizing he'd almost blown it.

She met his gaze. "Yes." Then she looked back at the computer screen.

There was so much he wanted to know about her and her family. But even if she did tell him, he wasn't sure he could believe it, let alone understand or forgive. He ached for this woman, wanted her more than he had ever wanted anything in his life. But trust was a whole other issue.

"Did you hire Leonard Parsons?" she asked after a moment of studying the computer screen.

"No. Del probably did. Or Patrick. Why?"

"Did you know he was a suspect in an arson investigation at a previous job?"

Jack swore under his breath. "Let's go find Leonard and talk to him."

He took the computer and opened the door, calling over his shoulder to Tiny as they left. He glanced at the cars parked on the street as he and Angie got into the rental car. "You realize Patrick knows we're in Houston by now."

She nodded. "I would imagine Constance called him the moment we left her office."

He looked over at her. It was warm in the car, the sun shining in the windows. He could smell her perfume, just a hint of it. "If there is anything to find on him, Patrick will try to stop us."

"Yes," she agreed, "but then, we've both known that all along, haven't we?"

He'd never met anyone like her. Amazingly he was more attracted to her than ever—even knowing who she was. Desire shot through him. He wanted nothing more than to take her in his arms and kiss her. Oh yes, he did. He wanted desperately to make love to her— and had for months.

It must have shown in his gaze because she turned away as if afraid he just might. What was she afraid of? Giving her real identity away? Or what would happen if they kissed again?

Patrick stared at the sliding glass door, the swimming pool and palms beyond it. A small white envelope was taped to the glass. He hadn't seen it when he'd come in. He'd only seen the trail of wet footprints.

But he saw the envelope now and he knew who'd left it even before he saw his name printed neatly in Angie's handwriting.

He thought his heart would beat its way out of his chest, his skin felt on fire, each breath felt like his last as he moved toward the glass door and carefully lifted off the tape and envelope.

He told himself he didn't have to open it. He could just throw it away. He'd never have to know what was inside. He could change hotels. He could change cities. He could run and keep running. But he knew that with-out money, that wasn't true. He also knew they would follow him, and he wasn't even sure who "they" were anymore.

He looked down at the envelope in his fingers.

Patrick. That's all it said on the outside, but the letters had a mocking tilt to them that made anger boil up inside him.

He ripped open the envelope quickly, fingers shaking, nerves raw, and upended it. The contents fluttered to the wet carpet at his feet. He stared down in surprise.

He wasn't sure what he'd expected to find inside. A note berating him for trying to kill her. A death threat. A few words of gloating. But it wasn't a note.

He bent down and picked up the single slip of heavy paper. A ticket? It was gold with small lettering: "Palm Springs Aerial Tramway. Admit One." On it Angie had written: *Take the last car.*

8:00 p.m. tonight.

Angie was finally making her move. He felt a wave of relief. He could end this more quickly than he'd thought. He would be ready. *I'm coming to get you, Angie. Only this time, I'm going to make sure you're dead.*

Chapter 13

The old neighborhood always took Jack back to his childhood. The apartment house where he'd grown up, the empty lot where he'd played ball, the abandoned old building where he and Patrick had built a fort on the roof.

He slowed in front of the tenement where Patrick had lived and looked up at the second-floor window, remembering Patrick's mother. Mary Ryerson had been a small, kind woman and as close to a mother as Jack could remember. She made tuna casseroles and oatmeal cookies for him and Patrick. She did her best to raise Patrick alone, but as far back as Jack could remember, Patrick had been trouble.

"Boys will be boys," Mary Ryerson used to say and smile ruefully.

But Jack remembered how she would turn her back and wipe at her tears with the corner of her apron.

He realized now how much she must have feared for her son. And with good reason, as it turned out.

Memories flooded Jack of the boy Patrick had been—sandy-haired with a mischievous grin and a charm that captivated everyone. Back then, Patrick had been his best friend in the world.

How could Patrick look back on those days with contempt and resentment? Sure, the people were poor and struggling just as many were today, but it had been a neighborhood where everyone knew each other, everyone cared. Jack had thought he could help bring that back by rebuilding here. He still did.

If he got the chance again. He thought of what his father had done and swore under his breath. Both Patrick and Kelly had seen the old neighborhood only as a way out.

"That's where Patrick lived with his mother, isn't it?" Angie asked, bending down to gaze up at the tenement.

Jack shot her a look, realizing the extent of the research the woman had done on him and the people near him. "As if you don't already know that."

Angie leaned back as he drove on past the neighborhood. He seemed upset. She couldn't blame him. He was a private man who didn't want people knowing anything about him. But she knew plenty.

She knew that he'd taken care of Patrick's mom, gotten her into a nice little house in a safer neighborhood. That he had visited her once a week and paid for her funeral when she died. Patrick never went back to see his mother. He didn't even attend her funeral.

"You were good to Patrick's mom," she said.

"She was good to me." He glanced over at her again and smiled. "You really do want to like me, don't you."

She laughed at that and looked out her side of the car at the passing neighborhood. Liking Jack wasn't the problem. "Sometimes I have trouble trusting people."

It was his turn to laugh.

How did she explain the way she was raised? "In the world Angie and I grew up in, there were few honest men. We came to expect the worst. Humans are often weak. We were raised to use that weakness to our advantage."

"So you look for the weakness. Expect it," he said.

"Yes." She was still looking for it in Jack, wasn't she—and he knew it.

Birdie's was a neighborhood bar, dark and narrow with a dingy linoleum floor and black-vinyl-covered stools pulled up to a long, scarred wooden bar.

Birdie was a large doughy-looking woman whose eyes disappeared in her plump face. She slid two bar napkins toward Jack and Angie and asked, "What'a ya'll have?"

A half dozen of the regulars were already pulled up to the bar, most drinking beer.

"A draft," Jack said, and looked at Angie.

"The same," she said, climbing up on the stool.

The regulars were watching them, some turning on their stools, others eyeing them in the bar mirror. The people in the bar looked suspicious, and he wondered if they recognized him. Or had he just changed so much that he stood out from his old neighborhood and the people he'd once been a part of.

He didn't see anyone who looked familiar. He hated

to admit it, but he'd forgotten a lot of the faces. But he would never forget the look. Desolation. Hopelessness. Defeat. He found that the hardest to take.

He remembered his father's face in old photos. He had never seen anything but hunger in that face. It was the eyes. A determination. Ambition like a low-grade electrical current that had energized his father.

His father had been driven to get out of the old neighborhood no matter what it took. And now Jack knew what it had taken.

He sipped his beer and looked at Angie in the bar mirror.

She winked at him. "Be right back." She seemed to change the moment she slid from the bar stool. There was a loose swivel of her hips that hadn't been there, an easy set of her shoulders, a slow flip of her long dark hair. Even her expression changed.

Every eye in the place was on her, some more subtle than others. Several turned as she went by, smiling at her.

Suddenly she was one of them. She could have grown up in this neighborhood.

Jack watched her in awe. She was a chameleon, changing with her environment. Or maybe her roots weren't that different from his own. Suddenly he sensed that her life had not always been champagne and caviar, expensive hotels and four-star restaurants.

He remembered their first date. He'd taken her to Tiny's, where they'd gone today. Even now, he wasn't sure why he'd taken a woman who looked and acted like she did to a barbecue place. He never took dates there. But then as today, she seemed to enjoy it as much as he did.

Angie disappeared into the ladies' room, and he turned his attention back to his beer, aware that the regulars were eyeing him with even more interest, wondering about him. Mostly wondering about the woman he'd come in with.

When Angie came out of the ladies' room, the regulars stirred, most trying not to look, some meeting his gaze in the mirror, assuming she was his.

He wished it were true.

Angie stopped beside one of the younger men, asked him something and leaned toward him to listen to his answer. The man was rail thin and looked hungover. He appeared at home on the bar stool, although he was not sitting by the other men. He'd been lost in his beer until Angie had singled him out.

Angie said something to the man that Jack couldn't hear.

The man nodded. His eyes flicked to the mirror and Jack, then jerked away.

What the hell was she doing? She laid a hand on the man's arm. He looked nervous, but clearly was enjoying the attention. Basking in Angie's attention was like being bathed in summer sunlight. Jack ought to know.

He heard Angie's tinkling light laugh, then the sound of her approaching. The regulars were still looking at the man at the end of the bar, obviously hoping he would tell them what she'd wanted.

The man turned back to his beer, curling around the glass, looking down at the amber liquid, smiling a little.

Angie slid onto the stool next to Jack, took a long

drink of her beer and licked the foam from her lips, smiling.

"I hate to ask," he said under his breath. He took a sip of his own beer.

"Leonard was in last night, drank too much. Probably still in bed with a bad hangover." She seemed to study her beer. "He lives a couple of blocks from here." She took another drink. "I would imagine someone will try to warn him and if Leonard has anything to hide, he'll run. We'll have to hurry." She drained her beer glass and sighed, leaning into him as she took his arm possessively. Her cheek brushed against his shoulder, and he heard her take a deep breath as if breathing him in.

He put his arm around her, drawing her close for a moment. When he let go he saw the change in her eyes. Just a flicker. She smiled and leaned back, pretending it had been part of her act. He knew better. She was starting to feel comfortable around him. Maybe too comfortable. Just as it had been before all hell broke loose and he ended up in jail.

He threw some money on the bar and rose, calling "Thanks" down the bar. Angie slid off her stool and started toward the door. He was right behind her.

Leonard Parsons lived in an old apartment house that had once been a hotel. The outside door opened onto a dirty hallway that smelled of boiled cabbage and mold. Up six steps, another hall. Door number two.

Jack could hear the phone already ringing and swore under his breath. He knocked. The phone rang again.

"Hey, baby!" Angie called in a high, loose voice. "Open up, it's me."

Jack could hear cursing. Something crashed to the floor. More swearing. The phone quit ringing just an instant before the door opened. Angie pushed Jack back.

Leonard stood in the doorway, a small man with long dishwater-blond hair pulled back in a ponytail, wearing nothing but boxer shorts and a tank top. A diamond stud glittered in one earlobe. He had the phone tucked between his ear and his shoulder, the cord dragging behind him through a disheveled apartment.

"Do I know you?" he asked Angie in a voice that sounded as if he'd just woken up. "Just a minute," he said into the phone as he leaned past her out into the hall and saw Jack. His eyes widened as Jack took the phone from him, hanging it up as he brushed past Leonard into the apartment.

Leonard stared at him, obviously having trouble keeping up. The side of his face was red and wrinkled and he looked as if he'd definitely had a rough night. "Hey!" he said. "What the—"

"I want to talk to you, Leonard."

"Jack. Right. No problem, but you should have called."

"The line was busy." Jack motioned to a chair.

Leonard looked from him to Angie and back. "The thing is, I was told not to talk to you."

"Who told you that?" Jack asked.

"That lawyer guy."

"Well, Leonard, I know you were getting paid to keep quiet about what was going on at the job site, but what I need to know is who paid you to burn down one of my houses?"

Leonard blinked. "Hey, man, I don't know anything about a fire."

He moved past Jack, then did something Jack never would have anticipated in a million years. He dove out the window in an explosion of glass. It happened so fast that Jack didn't even have a chance to grab for him.

The single-pane window shattered, showering Leonard with glass. He hit the ground running, all sign of him gone by the time Jack reached the street—except for the trail of blood drops that ended a block away.

When he returned to the rental car, he found Angie standing beside it.

"I did a star sixty-nine on Leonard's phone and got the name and number of the person who called to warn him we were coming," she said. "Del Sanders, the general contractor on the housing project. The bartender must have called Del."

"We need to talk," Jack said when Del Sanders answered.

"You know Montie said that's not a good idea," Del stammered, sounding nervous, scared.

Jack figured Del had caller ID and knew Jack was calling from Leonard Parsons's phone. "I don't care what Montie said. Where can we meet?"

Silence.

"How about your office," Jack said, suspecting that was the last place Del wanted to meet. Unlike Leonard, Del Sanders wasn't the kind of man to jump through a window. Del was smart enough to know that running wouldn't help. And the man had much more to lose.

"How about Live Oaks Bayou?" Del said. It was the

development he was just starting outside of Houston. "I need to go out there, anyway."

"It should take me about thirty minutes," Jack said, and hung up, feeling sick. He'd already heard what he wanted to know in the older man's voice. Del Sanders was guilty as hell. The question was, who had framed Jack? It was something he knew Del had the answer to.

Chapter 14

Huge old live oaks grew in a thick forest along the edge of the bayous just outside of Houston, except where large earth-moving machinery had plowed a makeshift road through them.

Angie rolled down her window and breathed in the rich scents of earth, trees and water. Nothing smelled quite like this part of Texas.

Jack seemed distracted, frowning as he drove. He hadn't said anything for miles, hadn't said anything since he'd talked to Del Sanders.

Del had worked for Jack's father and had been an old family friend for years. Knowing Jack and how he felt about loyalty and lies, she knew he must be crushed to think that Del might be in on any of this.

The last late afternoon sunlight flickered in the leaves overhead as Jack followed the narrow road deeper and deeper into the darkness of the trees. Ahead she spotted a dirty black pickup parked next to one of the bayous in a small clearing, Sanders Construction painted on the side in block-style lettering.

"I thought Sanders worked for *you*," she said, frowning.

"Used to. He quit to go out on his own about two months ago," Jack said, and glanced over at her as if he was surprised she hadn't known that.

Had she been in on framing him, she would have.

As he parked parallel with the pickup a half dozen yards away, a hot, muggy stillness settled over them.

Del Sanders was sitting in the pickup, but got out now. He waited next to his truck, leaning against it as if he needed the support.

He was a big man, balding with reddish gray hair, his large face florid and head shiny with sweat. He wore slacks and a dress shirt stained with perspiration. A cell phone was clipped to his belt.

He seemed startled to see her as Angie got out of the car after Jack. She noticed that Jack registered Del's reaction to her and frowned.

"You remember Angelina Grant," Jack said, surprising her. But then, he couldn't introduce her as Maria LaGrand, could he. "Del Sanders."

Del shook his head. "I don't think we've ever met."

She took the man's hand. It was moist, and she could feel him trembling. She wondered what was making him so nervous? Jack? Her? The truth?

He obviously knew who she was, just as he'd heard about her marrying Patrick and the accident in Montana.

"Rumors of my death were grossly exaggerated," she said.

Del looked confused and didn't seem to know what to say. After a pause he said, "What's this about, Jack? I really don't think we should be—"

"Del, how long have you known me?" Jack asked.

The question seemed to catch him off guard. "How long? I guess twenty-four, twenty-five years."

The leaves rustled in the huge oaks. Something splashed in the water of the bayou.

Del glanced back over his shoulder.

"Are you expecting someone?" Jack asked.

"No. It's just that Montie said—"

"Right, Montie. Del, I know."

The big man seemed to shrink into himself, his expression grim. "Jack, I don't know what—"

Angie heard the change in Jack's tone. "You remember when I hired you?" He was no longer the Ivy League–educated, wealthy, construction company owner. He was the kid who'd grown up on the rough streets, the kid Del had known as a boy.

"What?"

"I told you what I wanted to do in the old neighborhood, remember?"

"Sure." Sweat was running down into Del's eyes. He wiped his face with his shirtsleeve. "I swear to God, I thought you ordered the changes on the jobs. I thought that's why you hired Patrick to handle things."

"That piss you off, Del?" Jack's voice was low and soft. Angie could hear the pain in it. "Is that why you did this or was it just for the money?"

Del tensed as if expecting a blow.

"You knew damn well I hadn't ordered the changes," Jack said. "You know me better than that."

The silence was dense as cotton batting.

Del swallowed and looked over his shoulder again, his face flushed and sweating. He looked scared.

"Tell me the truth, Del, and I'll fight for the best deal the judge will make you. Lie to me and..."

A sound came out of the older man. A painful groan. He hung his head. "Jack, I never meant—"

"Was it Patrick's idea?" Jack asked.

Del raised his head a fraction. "Patrick?" He mopped his brow with his sleeve, his chest rising and falling as if he couldn't catch his breath. Del began to cry, huge body-shaking sobs that racked his body. "I'm so sorry, Jack—"

The shot came from out of the oaks. A *pop*, then a grunt. Del's eyes widened, blood blooming across his chest. He stumbled forward, grabbed Angie by the shoulders as he tried to stay on his feet.

The second bullet came only an instant later, followed by two more in quick succession as Jack dove for Angie. Del's legs crumbled under him and he went down hard, taking Angie with him.

Jack heard the next two shots; one pinged off the side of the truck, then kicked up dirt near his feet. By that time he was on the ground next to Angie, trying to shield her body from the gunfire.

In the silence that followed the flurry of shots, he heard an engine start up, off in the trees, then the sound of a vehicle roaring away.

As he lifted Del's dead weight off Angie, all he saw was blood. It was everywhere—all over Del, all over Angie. She lay facedown, deadly still.

"Angie! Oh God, Angie!" He rolled her over and into his arms. "Angie?"

She opened her eyes and took a shaky breath. As if the wind had been knocked out of her.

He looked from her face down to her blood-soaked clothing. "Are you hit?"

She shook her head slowly, appearing dazed, looked down at her shirt, then up at him again. "You know."

At first he didn't understand her.

"You know I'm Angie," she whispered.

He wiped a smear of blood from her face with his sleeve and nodded. "I've known since that kiss in the alleyway at the Seattle wharf."

She shook her head, smiling ruefully, then glanced over at the man on the ground next to her. "Del?"

He shook his head and reached for the cell phone clicked to Del's hip, to dial 911.

It was dark by the time Patrick drove the rental car down Highway 111 to the tramway entrance. The steep road wound up Chino Canyon, leaving behind the hot, dry desert warmth as he ascended to a parking area at the foot of the San Jacinto Mountains.

He glanced toward the tramway, not liking what he saw. The lights of a tiny tram car clung to a cable that seemed to drop straight off the side of the mountain. Behind it loomed the mountain, eerily lit to expose rock and creosote scrub. He had to look away.

He felt physically ill already. It was almost as if Angie knew about his fear of heights and was trying to torment him.

Just the thought of Angie waiting for him up there…

made him open his car door and step out. He was surprised at how much cooler it was up here and glad to see there weren't many cars in the lot, glad it was a weekday and not the height of the season. He realized that was probably why Angie had chosen this place to meet.

He glanced up again at the tram car coming down, instantly nauseated. The bitch. If she really wasn't dead, he was going to kill her for doing this to him.

Inside the Valley Station he didn't see Angie, but then, he hadn't expected to. She would make him go to the top, sure as hell. He checked the time and almost immediately heard the boarding call for the last tram.

He followed a half dozen people through a waiting room and into the tram car, needing to sit down. There were no seats. He grabbed hold of the railing along the side and held on as the door closed, and moments later the car slid out of the boarding dock and began to rock as it climbed slowly up the mountain.

He closed his eyes, trying to ignore the woman near him who was oohing and aahing and telling the man beside her that the first tower was the tallest at two hundred and fourteen feet high.

Suddenly the car paused, then rocked wildly before moving forward as it passed that first tower. Patrick's eyes flew open. Behind the car, the Sonoran Desert spread out in glittering lights far below them. He gripped the railing tighter, trying to hold himself up, sicker than he'd ever been.

"It has a vertical ascent of more than a mile," the woman said. "Would you look at that view. Isn't it thrilling?"

He groaned and moved away from her. He didn't want to hear any more about the tram's three hundred pounds of steel cables or the more than thirty-four hundred feet between towers. It was the longest fourteen minutes of his life.

When the car finally pulled into the Mountain Station dock, he stumbled from the car, just wanting to feel earth beneath his feet. He was dizzy and sick to his stomach and couldn't bear the thought of the trip back down.

The Mountain Station facility was huge—and mostly empty. A few people were having dinner in the dining room. Several others were having cocktails in the lounge. No Angie. He looked in the gift shop and theater, then glanced toward the observation deck, eighty-five hundred feet up the side of the mountain.

Angie wasn't here. *Because she is dead, you idiot.*

Then who had gotten him up here? Who was that woman he'd seen by the pool? The one who'd left the wet footprints and the ticket?

Angie was alive. And on this mountaintop. Only this time, she wasn't going to pull a disappearing act on him. If he could find her.

That's when he spotted the message board and saw his name printed in Angie's handwriting.

He still felt unsteady on his feet and nauseated as he pulled the note off and read it. "Take the Desert View Trail. You'll need a flashlight. They sell them at the gift shop. See you soon."

Desert View Trail. He'd rather poke a sharp stick into his eye. But he went to the gift shop, bought a flashlight—a small one that gave off little light—and picked up a trail map, thinking of only one thing: killing Angie. Again.

The night air was at least thirty degrees cooler up here than down in the desert. He felt chilled and still sick as he headed out the back of the Mountain Station and descended the switchbacked sidewalk for two hundred yards. Pine trees rose up into the dark sky, and ahead he could make out what appeared to be a ranger station. The lights were out. No one around.

He checked his map and saw that a sawhorse with a Closed sign had been propped in front of the Desert View Trail entrance. Angie's doing? No doubt. So she wanted them to be alone. He smiled to himself. Perfect.

The flashlight did little to illuminate the dark night as he walked around the barrier and headed down the trail, but he didn't want to give Angie too much of a heads up. He wondered if she would try to jump him. He hoped so. He was ready for her.

But he doubted her plan was to try to kill him. She could have done that in his sleep when she sneaked into his room and left the jewelry. She wanted something from him. Probably a confession that would clear Jack's name. The thought infuriated him. The bitch was still thinking only of Jack.

He moved through the darkness, the trail skirting the edge of the mountainside. Through the pines, he caught glimpses of twinkling lights far, far below them on the desert floor. At one overlook, he shone his flashlight on a marker: View Coachella Valley. He'd rather view Angie Grant.

Excuse me, Angie LaGrand.

He gritted his teeth until they ached remembering how she'd fooled him.

He continued on up the trail, just wishing she would

get this over with. He couldn't imagine how she thought she could get a confession out of him. Beat it out of him? He smiled at the thought of her trying. Trick him? Not likely.

The evergreens grew thicker, the path darker, closing in around him. Through the pine branches he would catch glimpses of stars overhead. He avoided looking down at the valley sprawled below him, so far below him. It reminded him of the canyon where Angie had gone off. Well, where the Jeep had, anyway.

He slowed, still woozy and nauseated, chilled by the night air. He tried not to think how high he was above the desert and suddenly worried this had been a mistake. He'd underestimated Angie at the cabin in Montana, and look how that had turned out. Maybe this had been just a trick to get him away from his hotel room for some reason.

He heard a noise ahead. A soft rustling sound. He pointed the flashlight into the darkness and saw a pine bough move.

Angie.

Cautiously, he moved toward the stand of pines, excited. He couldn't *wait* to see her again.

Suddenly something came out of the darkness and trees at his head; he ducked, throwing up an arm to ward off the blow. At the sound of flapping wings, he slowly straightened and shone his flashlight after it, immediately feeling foolish as a hawk sailed out over the edge of the mountain in the beam of light.

He stood there shaking, trying to still his heart. He'd had too many surprises lately. "Where the hell are you?" he hollered. His words died off. Had he really expected her to answer? She probably wasn't even out here. Might not be on the mountain at all. She could be just jerking his chain.

He thought about turning back, but remembered the trail circled back to the Mountain Station. No reason to backtrack. He had to be getting close to the end.

Was it the altitude up here? He felt even more lightheaded. Maybe it was just knowing that there was an eighty-five-hundred-foot drop just a few yards to his left.

He started up the trail again. All he wanted now was to get off this mountain. There were tram cars going down every thirty minutes. If he hurried…

It happened so quickly he didn't even have a chance to raise his arm this time or duck. A limb the size of a baseball bat struck him in the forehead. He thought he'd walked into the limb—until it struck him again. He pitched forward into the darkness.

The sheriff arrived within minutes after Jack's 911 call. Del was dead. Angie was covered in his blood. Jack had called Montie right after dialing 911.

With Montie's help, he and Angie were allowed to give their statements at the sheriff's department and leave. The sheriff had found tire tracks and spent shell casings out in the woods. They were running the casings for prints.

"It isn't safe for the two of you," Montie said as they were leaving the sheriff's department. "Come stay at my house. I have a good security system and plenty of room."

Jack shook his head. "Thanks, but that would be the first place anyone would look for us."

"Where will you go?" Montie said, sounding worried. "With whoever killed Del still out there…"

"Don't worry. I'll find someplace safe. You've got my cell phone number if you need to reach me," he told him.

Jack couldn't wait to get Angie alone. He wrapped his jacket around her and ushered her out to the rental car.

He found an out-of-the-way motel, paid cash, registered under an assumed name, and ushered Angie straight to their room, where he turned on the shower.

Her bloody shirt was stuck to her skin. She fumbled at the buttons, shaking, her face pale. He suspected violence wasn't often part of the confidence game.

"It's okay, baby," he whispered as he kicked off his shoes and socks, his own clothing bloody, as well, from holding her. Both of them still clothed, he pulled her into the shower.

He wrapped his arms around her, and she leaned against him, burying her face in his chest as the water flowed over them. He had thought nothing could faze this woman but he'd been wrong. Her body began to tremble. He could feel her shuddering sobs. He held her to him and let her cry as the water washed away the blood and her tears.

After a while, she looked up at him, her brown eyes the color of honey. He kissed her under the cascade of water. She wrapped her arms around his neck and pulled him closer, their soaked clothes welding them together.

"Jack?" she whispered, looking up into his eyes. "I'm so glad you're all right. I thought—"

He silenced her with a kiss.

When he released her mouth, she whispered, "Make love to me."

She could have asked him to leap tall buildings at that moment and he would have tried. But there was still so much unresolved between them.

"Angie, I'm not sure we should—"

"I am, Jack," she said, and drew him down for another kiss.

He dropped his mouth to hers. She tasted sweet and spicy, like something exotic and rare. He could feel her unbuttoning his shirt, slipping it off his shoulders, the warm water drumming his bare skin.

He pulled back. The look in her eyes was his undoing. It fired his blood, making his heart pound. With shaking fingers he unbuttoned her blouse, exposing the tanned, freckled skin above her breasts, then the white satin of her bra as the blouse dropped to the shower floor.

He let out a groan at the sight of her, her dark hair a flowing wave under the water, the pale breasts visible through the wet, white-satin bra, dark nipples hard buds, her soaked jeans hugging her wonderful curves.

She smiled at him, a mixture of tears and desire glittering in her eyes, as he reached for her again.

Patrick swam toward the surface, from a deep blackness to a warm, wet one. He surfaced to sound and movement and pain—lots of pain.

He blinked, one eye full of something warm. Blood. He closed his eyes. Opened them again and saw through his one good eye that it was nighttime and he was moving.

Someone was dragging him by his shoulders backward, his heels scraping across the dirt and pine needles. He could hear the person breathing hard from the exertion. Angie. He found some gratification in the fact that he was making her work hard, but he did wonder where she was taking him.

Suddenly she dropped him. He fell hard on his back, knocking the air out of him. Instinctively, he'd closed his eyes and pretended still to be unconscious. His head ached and blood pooled in his eyes. He wanted to touch his forehead where he'd been hit to see how bad the wound was, but didn't.

His listened to her try to catch her breath. She was strong, but not strong enough to drag a man his size any distance. A breeze blew up on his right, drying the blood on his face, and he realized she didn't plan to drag him much farther, just to the edge of the mountain. She wasn't after a confession. She planned to kill him!

As she leaned down to grab hold of him again, his eyes flew open. He got a glimpse of her surprised expression just an instant before he wrapped his arms around her head and flipped her over onto the ground. She let out a satisfying *ooft!* And he was on her in a heartbeat.

She squirmed under him, but she was no match for him physically. He dug the weapon he'd brought and his flashlight out of her jacket pocket. With one hand, he pressed the gun barrel between her eyes. With the other, he flicked on the flashlight and shone the beam on her face.

She seemed amused by his sudden gasp.

Angie. My God, she really was alive!

She smiled up at him. Smiled!

He pressed the gun between her eyes, his trigger finger itchy with expectation. "You're a dead woman this time."

Angie thought she would die if Jack didn't touch her. Her body ached for him. She trembled under the heat of his gaze, the water rippling over her sensitive skin.

But he stood just looking at her, as if needing to memorize her and this moment. Then he reached out and gently rasped his thumb pad across one hard nipple, sending waves of heat through her. She had never wanted a man more than she wanted Jack right now, had never felt such need nor such tenderness.

But she didn't move, didn't touch him. She waited.

His gaze met hers. He groaned again and pulled her to him, his kiss rocking her to her core. He peeled off her jeans and tossed them aside, then removed her satin panties and bra, his lips never leaving hers. He shed the rest of his own clothing, his body more wonderful than she'd imagined.

Finally naked, water flowing over their bare skin, Jack soaped her body slowly, lovingly, intimately. She closed her eyes and reveled in the feel of his wet, slick hands and fingers caressing every inch of her.

His kiss opened her eyes, and she smiled and shyly took the soap from him. She'd never been this intimate with a man. She flattened her palms against him as she lathered his body, and he watched her, his eyes setting her ablaze.

Standing under the spray, they washed away the suds, then he gently kissed her lips, her eyelids, her earlobes. He trailed kisses down the column of her neck to the hollow of her throat over the rise of her breast to her nipple and sucked the hard nub into his mouth.

Her body quivered and she laid back her head and groaned as she pressed her breast against his hot mouth. He moved down her body, leaving a trail of blistering kisses that made her quake against him until she felt him at her center.

He pressed her against the shower wall, this kiss making her bury her fingers in his hair as he took her to the top of a roller-coaster of pleasure, then let her go. She cried out, trembling under his touch.

Turning off the shower, he dried them both, and, skin flushed, they raced into the bedroom to scramble under the covers. The sheets were cool and soft. Her body was alive with sensation as Jack drew her into his arms again.

She could hear rain beating against the window panes and music playing somewhere outside as a car went by. She snuggled against him as his mouth and his fingertips licked across her skin like flames, making her climb again until she thought she couldn't stand it.

He entered her, filling her, completing her. Her heart pounded against his as he made sweet, passionate love to her, lifting her until she was soaring again, higher than she'd ever been.

"Oh, Jack," she cried on a gasp, and felt him shudder, those warm denim-blue eyes gazing down at her, the look in them deep with wonder—and something else. Something that could have been love.

Patrick held the woman to the ground, the gun barrel pressed between her eyes. "I should pull this trigger right now," he said from between gritted teeth.

He wiped blood from his eyes with the sleeve of his left hand—the one holding the flashlight—and cursed her for the hell she'd put him through. How had she survived the first time he'd tried to kill her, anyway?

"You aren't going to kill me," she said, sounding so confident that he almost pulled the trigger. "You're too smart for that."

"What makes you so sure?" he demanded. "You were about to throw me off this mountain to my death."

"Just like you tried to do to me, you bastard."

He smiled at that. He'd been called much worse. And besides, he had the gun and her now. "This time I'm going to succeed, though. Maybe I'll throw you off this mountain since the last one didn't work." That way he wouldn't have to risk someone hearing the gunshot.

"You kill me and how are you going to explain my death again, here—more than a thousand miles from where the sheriff and the search-and-rescue team are still looking for my body?"

Angie had him there. What *was* he going to do with her? He couldn't just let her go. She could have him arrested for attempted murder. Of course, she'd have to prove it—and the fact that she hadn't gone to the cops right away would be in his favor. That and the fact that she was a professional con man. Woman. Whatever.

But she was right. He couldn't very well kill her here. How would he explain that? He already looked suspicious enough in her first death. He couldn't risk her body being found at the top of the Palm Springs Aerial Tramway in California. Or at the bottom. Not even that hick sheriff would believe her body had washed this far downriver.

"There is only one thing you can do," she said.

He glared down at her. "Oh yeah?"

"Who do you hate more than even me?" she asked.

She had to be kidding.

"Jack," she said.

He felt the breath go out of him. Jack. He'd almost forgotten about him.

"What do you think Jack would pay for my return?" she asked, and smiled. "I'll bet you I'm worth a cool million."

Patrick stared at her. Jack loved Angie. He'd do anything for her. Even if he knew she was a con artist, he would still pay a bundle for her safety. And if he were to find out that she was alive and being held by someone like Patrick...

"Oh, I'd say you're worth a hell of a lot more than a million," he said. "Two, three, even five."

"Then I suggest you get off me before you hurt the merchandise," she snapped. "And put that gun away. You're not going to use it."

He wished she wasn't right about that. He slid off her and stumbled to his feet, keeping the gun and flashlight trained on her just in case she tried to jump him again.

"Don't be a fool," she said. "I need you to pull this off."

"You were just getting ready to push me off this mountain," he cried, still a little shocked by that. He'd never suspected she was such a cold-hearted bitch.

"I was angry and not thinking," she said, dusting herself off. "Now that I've had time to think, I realize you're more valuable to me alive. If the ransom demand comes from you, Jack will know you mean business. He won't jeopardize my life by going to the cops or try to dicker on how much I'm worth." She nodded. "It looks like we need each other."

He found himself nodding along with her. Not that he didn't still want to kill her. He couldn't believe everything she'd put him through.

But she was right. He couldn't kill her here. And she *was* worth money. Wasn't that how he'd gotten involved with her in the first place?

His head ached where she'd hit him. Again. He felt light-headed from the tram ride up, and was not in the best mood. "Those stocks and bonds were fakes."

She shot him a "duh" look. "I'm a confidence woman, remember?"

He wiped more blood from his eyes.

"Here, let me fix that," she said, and pulled a bandana from her jeans pocket. She wrapped it around his forehead. "That should stop the bleeding. It's just a flesh wound."

It didn't feel like just a flesh wound. He stared at her as she adjusted the bandana. He still had the cut on his temple where she'd hit him with the ice bucket, and his shoulder was black and blue from the champagne bottle she'd cold-cocked him with. It was all he could do not to strangle her as she tied the bandana in place.

"We can clean the wound back at the Mountain Station," she was saying. "If anyone asks, we can tell them you walked into a tree limb."

"Yeah," he said, and made a nasty face at her.

"Stop being such a big baby. It could have been much worse. You could be tumbling off the mountain right now."

He glared at her. "How did you get out of that Jeep?"

"Luck," she said, and pulled that stupid amulet from inside her shirt.

He saw that it was all she was wearing for jewelry. "Where is the real diamond pendant and wedding ring I gave you?"

"Pawned. How do you think I was able to follow you all over the country?" she asked as she started back through the pines following the beam of her small penlight.

He trailed after her, still holding the gun just in case she tried something. "What about the money you took out of our joint checking account?"

"Don't worry, I haven't spent it all. There's enough to finance our plan."

"Oh yeah? And what is *our* plan?"

She reached the trail and started down it. "Don't worry, I'll come up with one."

He wasn't worried. He had faith that this conniving, devious, scheming woman knew exactly what she was doing. He followed, needing his own plan—a way to get the money and get Angie back into that river. This time her body definitely would get caught in a limb and not float up until next spring.

"The problem is getting Jack to believe I'm still alive," she said as they rounded a bend in the trail. The lights of the Mountain Station shone at the edge of the mountainside a hundred yards ahead.

His stomach roiled at the thought of the tram ride down as he tucked the gun back into his jacket pocket. "Once Jack hears your voice—"

"It won't be that easy. By now Jack knows that my name isn't really Grant and that I'm not really rich."

Patrick nodded. Didn't they all.

"So if I call him from Palm Springs, California, and tell him that I didn't really go off into the canyon…"

He did like the way this woman thought. "We have to get you back to Montana. You have to call from somewhere up there for help. Then I get on the line and tell him I have you and unless he comes up with five million dollars—"

"Five million?" She shook her head. "You're such a greedy bastard, Patrick. Just so you know, we're splitting it seventy-thirty since it's my idea."

He grabbed her arm. "Like hell. I'm doing all the work here."

She mugged a face at him. "Sixty-forty or the deal is off. You need me to make this work, remember?"

Oh yeah, he remembered. But just until he got the money. Killing her a second time had to be easier than the first. Why was he arguing the point, anyway? He planned to take it all once she was dead. "Fine. You'd just better hope this plan of yours works."

"Oh, it will. If you don't foul it up like you did my last one," she snapped, and headed for the Mountain Station.

Jack stirred from a deep, contented sleep to the sound of his cell phone ringing. Reluctantly, he unwrapped himself from Angie's warm naked body. "Hello?"

"Jack?"

He pushed himself up to a sitting position at the sound of Patrick's voice. "Patrick?"

Angie came awake beside him, her brown eyes wide with fear. Why in the hell would Patrick be calling him?

"Did I wake you?" Patrick asked, sounding so casual, as if nothing had happened between them.

"What do you want, Patrick?"

"You sound like you're in a bad mood."

Jack gritted his teeth. "Yeah, being framed and almost killed often puts me in a bad mood."

"Someone tried to kill you?"

"As if you weren't behind it."

"You know, Jack, I'm getting tired of being blamed for everything that goes wrong in your life," Patrick said. "I didn't have anything to do with you being caught for ripping off all those poor people or for burning down one of your own houses or for trying to kill you."

"Right. Is that why you called me, Patrick? To tell me how innocent you are?"

"No, I called about Angie. She's alive."

Jack looked down at Angie. "What are you talking about?"

"Angie—she didn't die in that wreck. How about that?"

Jack held his breath. "How is that possible? I saw it on television."

Patrick laughed, a sound that chilled Jack to the core.

"You believe everything you see on TV but you don't believe me. Really, Jack, you amaze me. Listen to me. I called you because I have something you want."

"I really doubt that you have anyth—"

"I have Angie."

Jack pulled back to look at Angie. "What do you mean, you have Angie?" She moved in so she could hear Patrick's end of the conversation.

"Here's the deal," Patrick said. "A trade, so to speak. You give me five million dollars and I give you Angie."

Angie's nails dug into Jack's arm. He met her gaze. Her eyes were huge, her expression terrified. *He has Maria*, she mouthed.

His heart fell.

"Jack? You still there, old buddy?"

Old buddy. The words grated across his nerve endings like sandpaper. Angie slipped off the bed quickly, dug around in her purse and came out with paper and pen.

"I'm still here," Jack said, reading the scrawled word Angie was writing: *Stall.* "I'm trying to figure out why you'd think I would believe anything you told me."

Angie moved in close to listen again.

Silence. Jack felt his throat constrict. What if Patrick had hung up?

"Okay," Patrick said finally. "I guess I can see your point. Why don't I put her on the phone."

The next sound he heard was Maria's voice.

"Jack, don't do what he—" A cry.

Then Patrick was back on the line. "Well, Jack? You believe me now?"

Jack looked at Angie. She nodded. "Don't hurt her."

Patrick laughed. "Do as I say, Jack. Cross me up, and she really will be dead. You believe me?"

Oh yeah. "Tell me where and when."

"You ever been to Montana, Jack?"

Chapter 15

"You make the arrangements to get the money, I'll take care of everything else," Angie said as she hurriedly got up and started dressing. She knew it wouldn't be easy but Jack could come up with that much quicker than she could. "There is no reason for you to go to Montana. It's too dangerous. I'll take care of it." She stopped when she saw his expression and her heart fell. "You think this is a scam."

"It's crossed my mind." He had pulled on his jeans and now stood bare-chested, his shirt dangling from his fingertips. "Once a mark, always a mark, right?"

She smiled ruefully. She'd just assumed that things had changed between them after making love.

"I'm sorry, but you have to admit it looks suspicious," Jack said. "I'm supposed to pack up five million dollars in two large suitcases and let you go alone to Montana to buy back your sister."

"You won't lose your money, if that's what you're worried about," she said, wishing her heart wasn't hammering so hard in her chest. "You have my word." She saw his expression. "My word. Pretty funny, huh." She fought the tears that stung her eyes.

"I'm sorry, Angie," he said softly, "but I'm going to Montana with you."

"To make sure you don't lose your money."

"No," he said, stepping over to clasp her shoulders in his large palms. "To make sure I don't lose you."

"That's right, you still need me to help clear your name. Del didn't live long enough to finger Patrick."

"It's a little more complicated than that."

She met his gaze. "I don't want you to go to Montana because you think it's too dangerous for me." She and Maria knew how to handle marks who'd gone "hot," the ones who realized they'd been had. "Maria and I have been in situations like this before."

"I'm sure you have," he said, not sounding pleased about that. He studied her for a moment. "Look, if all this—" he motioned toward the crumpled sheets "—was just a plot by you and Maria to get five million dollars out of me, you don't have to go to all this trouble, Angie. Just ask."

She remembered the rough-stubble feel of his beard on her skin, the taste of his mouth, the sound of him catching his breath— She bit down hard on her lower lip, trying not to cry as she quickly busied herself buttoning her blouse so he couldn't see her tears and think they were part of the con. "It's not about money."

Patrick had Maria. Just the thought turned Angie's blood cold. She knew Maria wouldn't be in Patrick's clutches unless she'd planned it that way. And Angie had a pretty good idea what Maria was up to, but she feared Maria didn't know just how dangerous Patrick was—or how unpredictable.

As she bent down to pull on her boots, she surreptitiously wiped her tears before turning to face Jack. "Maria set this whole thing up. She has a plan and it isn't to take your money. It's to get Patrick for you. I would imagine right now she's getting the confession you need out of him."

He stared at her. "How do you know that?"

"She passed me a message on the phone."

He shook his head. "She didn't say ten words."

"She didn't have to. But if you think that I'm not telling you the truth, then we'll wait until Patrick calls back." He would, if Jack didn't show up in Montana. She just prayed Maria would be safe that long. "I can get my own money. I do have money, you know. More than you. It's just not easily accessible."

She started past him, but he grabbed her arm and swung her into him.

"I'll get the money, but I'm going with you. Patrick has already tried to kill you at least once. I don't intend to give him another chance."

She started to argue, but he dropped his mouth to hers, stealing her breath, stealing her words.

The kiss lasted just a few seconds. When he drew back, he seemed to search her gaze. She wondered if he'd found what he was looking for.

"Okay," he said. "Let's hear the plan."

"Have you lost your mind?" Montie demanded when Jack showed up at his office and told him how much money he needed. "You're taking five million dollars to Patrick in Montana?" The lawyer let out a laugh. "This is obviously another of this woman's scams." He shot Angie a look.

"Just help me get the money so it doesn't tip off the court," Jack said.

The older man swore. "Jack, can't you see? This woman has you under her spell. I told you she'd come up with another scam. Once a mark—"

"—always a mark. I know." He was definitely under Angie's spell. "Do whatever needs to be done."

Montie shook his head as he picked up the phone. "You're a damn fool, Jack."

Jack said nothing as he looked over to where Angie was standing by the window. Her eyes were dark with anger, and he suspected it wasn't all directed at Montie. He wished he could take back what he'd said earlier to her. But he'd be an even bigger fool not to suspect this was another con. If not Angie's, then Maria's and Patrick's.

So why was he going along with it?

He studied Angie. She was beautiful—all that dark curly hair that fell to her shoulders, those wonderful brown eyes, that full, lush mouth of hers. Desire stirred deep within him. Oddly enough, what had attracted him to her originally was the same thing that still did: her innocence.

And he knew he was doing this because he believed her.

"By the way," Montie said, covering the mouthpiece on the phone. "The sheriff found Leonard Parsons. He crashed his pickup on a back road not far from where Del was killed. He committed suicide. Sheriff said looks like the same gun Leonard used to shoot Del."

Jack shook his head. "Why would he kill Del to shut him up and then turn the gun on himself? That doesn't make any sense."

"Sheriff said Leonard's leg was fractured in the car crash. I guess he knew he was caught and suicide was the easiest way out. The sheriff found accelerant in Leonard's apartment, the kind used by arsonists, plus they found a wad of cash."

Leonard hadn't been smart enough to get rid of the accelerant? The man was more stupid than Jack had thought.

"What's wrong?" Montie asked.

Jack shrugged. "It just all ties up so neatly. I can't help but wonder if Patrick didn't pay someone to make sure Leonard never talked."

"Patrick obviously knew people who would take care of a problem like that for him." Patrick had done some time in prison in East Texas. But he'd also tried to kill Angie all by himself. If Jack didn't know for a fact that Patrick was in Palm Springs...

Jack looked over at Angie again. He could hear Montie making arrangements behind him. Angie was staring out the front window. She looked worried. About Maria?

He'd only met Maria that one time in the taxi, but he had a feeling she could take care of herself. With Patrick, though?

"You'll have your money before your plane leaves for Montana," Montie said after hanging up. He lowered his voice so Angie couldn't hear. "Why go to Montana at all? Just give her the money and save yourself a lot of grief."

"Can you have the money delivered in the two large suitcases I've left for you?"

Montie nodded and wrote down his flight number. "You must be some woman," he said to Angie as he walked Jack to the door.

She lifted her chin, dark eyes snapping.

"She is," Jack said before she could answer. He put his arm around her and ushered her out to the taxi they had waiting at the curb.

"You trust that man?" Angie asked as they drove away.

"I don't know who to trust anymore," he said truthfully. "But what trust I have is all yours."

"I hope I don't let you down."

So did he. He had a lot to lose. Five million dollars, his freedom if the cops found out he was leaving the state, even his life if Patrick had an ambush planned.

But none of that concerned him as much as the realization that Angie might break his heart again. This time, it would kill him.

Patrick paced the cabin and watched for headlights. What was keeping Jack? In the last call, Jack had insisted on talking to Angie. Like Patrick would be stupid enough to kill her before he got the money? Jeez.

So what was keeping Jack? He didn't think Jack was dumb enough to try to sneak up on the cabin and try to ambush him.

No, Jack wouldn't take any chances with Angie's life.

"Stop pacing, you're driving me crazy," she said from where she was sprawled on the couch in front of the fire. "Get some more logs from the porch."

He turned to glare at her, glad he hadn't even considered staying married to her. "Jack should be here."

She shook her head, not bothering to look up from the magazine she'd been reading. "Jack couldn't possibly reach here for another thirty minutes minimum. I clocked it from the airport."

He stared at her. If she wasn't worth five million dollars… He stomped out to the porch, got an armload of wood and stood listening for a vehicle.

Hurry up, Jack. I'm not sure how much more of this woman I can take.

He regretted that he hadn't let Jack marry Angie. Jack definitely would have gotten what he deserved. A broke con artist with a bad attitude. He smiled at the thought. Too late for that now, though.

He carried the wood back into the cabin and threw it on the fire. He hadn't wanted a fire, afraid it would attract the hick sheriff.

Angie had suggested he tell the sheriff he was back at the cabin, make it sound like he couldn't stay away but wanted to be left alone. He had to hand it to Angie, she was good at this stuff.

"So, come on, tell me how you did it before Jack gets here," she said, putting down the magazine.

He groaned. "I already told you, I never even went to the job sites. I just collected my big salary—"

"Don't insult my intelligence by telling me again that you weren't behind framing Jack."

He wished she would drop this. "Look, if you have to know, Montie's the one who told me about the kickbacks and what Jack was up to."

"Jack's lawyer?"

Patrick nodded. "He told me how Jack's old man had made all of his money—and that Jack was doing it, too." He nodded at her surprise. "That's not all. Montie told me Jack was going to ask you to marry him to get your money." He loved the shock on her face.

"So that's when you came up with your plan to get me," she said. "And turn in Jack."

"Pretty much." He didn't bother to tell her that the plan had jelled when he'd heard her on the phone with her financial advisor.

She laughed. "Montie set you up. He must have known I wasn't who I said I was."

He scowled at her. "What are you talking about?"

"Montie played you." She narrowed her gaze thoughtfully. "But what did he have to gain aside from getting rid of Jack?"

Patrick stared at her. Montie hadn't played him. "You trying to tell me Montie was behind framing Jack?"

"Well, if he is, he's planning to let you take the fall for it," she said, and went back to her magazine as if she'd lost interest.

"What are you trying to pull?" he demanded, leaning over her, angry that she might be right. "You're the only one who's played me. You stole my money, conned me with those fake stocks and bonds, and cheated death. And now you're trying to pull something on me." He grabbed her by the neck. "This time I will make sure you're dead."

She looked up from her magazine at him. "But then you'd lose the five million dollars in ransom money you're demanding from Jack, wouldn't you," she said in a hoarse whisper, since he was cutting off most of her air.

"It almost seems worth it right now." He narrowed his eyes at her and he let up on the pressure. What if she was right about Montie? He was starting to straighten when he spotted the small tape recorder not quite hidden between her and the couch arm, the tiny wheels turning.

He let out an oath and grabbed the recorder, hitting stop. His gaze went to her. For the first time, she actually looked scared. "You were trying to get me to confess on tape." He swore. "What did you plan to do with this? Give it to Jack?"

She laughed, and he thought he'd only imagined that instant when she'd looked frightened of him. "Get real. I was going to use it to blackmail you out of the rest of the five million."

He stared at her as he pocketed the tape recorder, looking for even a hint that she was lying. If he thought for a minute that she trying to get a confession to save Jack he'd kill her. Money or no money.

Chapter 16

The night was black as Angie drove out Interstate 90 to the Big Pine turn off, then up the narrow dirt road, climbing up the mountain through the dense trees.

Clouds scudded across the dark sky, smothering the starlight. No moon. The air was crisp, the breeze scented with the promise of snow.

The night Patrick brought her up here had also been moonless. She remembered the glitter of stars in the night sky. The silver ribbon of river in the gorge along the edge of the road. The anxiety she'd felt, like a premonition.

Just like tonight. She looked over at Jack.

"There are several ways to 'cool out' a con," she'd told him. "One of the oldest is the crackle-bladder. It involves the element of surprise—and fake blood. But with luck, when this is over, your name will be cleared and Patrick will be behind bars."

"With luck we'll all still be alive," Jack had said.

As the trees opened up and she saw the dark cut of the canyon open off to her left, she touched the amulet at her neck. She didn't look down as she drove along the edge. She needed all the luck she could get tonight.

In a few minutes she would come face-to-face with Patrick. Only this time, it wasn't just her life at stake.

She stopped and extinguished the headlights. She'd already taken the bulbs out of the taillights. All of the interior lights were also turned off.

She waited for her eyes to adjust to the darkness. From here on out, she would be following that cut of lighter colored sky that marked the road through the dark pines. She started up the road.

"I will go in first," she said, reviewing the plan again. "Patrick will hear the car engine, but he won't get a good look at me until I enter the cabin. He'll be expecting you—"

"Angie, I've got it down cold, all right?" Jack interrupted. "I don't like it, but this is your show. Yours and your sister's."

He was right. They'd been over this two dozen times. And he'd hated the plan from the start. He'd put his life in her hands. She felt the weight of it, her heart heavy with worry that she would let him down.

"Maria is expecting this," she said. "If you come busting in—"

"I know," he said, his voice softening. "I'll stick to the plan. I just don't want anything to happen to you. Or your sister."

"I know." She touched his shoulder, and he covered her hand with his, squeezed lightly, then pulled her hand to his mouth and kissed her palm, making her heart leap.

"This is where I get out," he said, and smiled, reminding her that he knew the plan forward and backward.

She stopped the car. "You come in ten seconds after the second shot," she said, unable to help herself. Any change in the plan could change the outcome in the worst possible way.

"Got it." He opened his car door and stepped from the darkness of the car into the darkness of the night. "Do I say 'break a leg' or what?"

Say that you love me. "Say good luck."

"Good luck."

He disappeared among the pines in the direction of the cabin. She waited, remembering when she'd stopped in Missoula to buy the unregistered weapons from a person she'd contacted through "friends" in the business.

Jack had picked up a Smith & Wesson Model 19 combat magnum, hefted it in his hand, then loaded six .357 magnum cartridges into the chamber, spun the cylinder and clicked on the safety before stowing the weapon in his jacket.

Angie had stared at him in shock. It was clear by the way he'd handled the weapon that he'd used one before. The man just kept surprising her. Her research on him had shown that he'd never owned a firearm, let alone knew how to use one—information she always obtained before a con.

It was the unexpected that made the confidence game dangerous. Marks could surprise you. With disastrous consequences.

After a count of fifty, she started up the road again, fearing Patrick had some surprises for them.

As she pulled up in front of the cabin, the lantern lights went out inside. She opened her door and got out. She could smell smoke from the fireplace and see the flicker of the flames through a window. Good, there would be some light.

She didn't see Jack, but she knew he was out there.

She climbed the steps to the porch, knocked softly, waited until Patrick said, "Come on in, Jack," and stepped through the door, knowing Patrick would be armed. She was counting on his not firing immediately.

She was counting on a lot of things. For the plan to work, everything would have to happen quickly—within seconds. Every mark reacted differently. She was banking on Patrick being too surprised to shoot.

She wasn't disappointed.

"What the—" That was all he got out. In those crucial seconds, he looked from Angie to Maria and back.

By then, the con was already in play.

"How dare you pretend to be me!" Angie yelled as she advanced on Maria, who got to her feet from the couch in front of the fire.

They struggled for only an instant. The first shot was loud. Maria cried out and staggered, blood blossoming across the front of her blouse as she struggled for the gun between them.

The second shot came immediately after the first. The gun clattered to the hardwood floor. Maria fell back onto the couch. Angie looked down at her chest, shock on her face. There was blood everywhere.

She looked up at Patrick. He was standing, mouth

open, eyes wide, the gun in his hand at his side as if he didn't know what to do.

Angie's eyes rolled back into her head and she slumped to the floor, her body furtively covering the weapon.

"No!" Patrick cried, looking from one Angie to the other. "Dammit, no!" He jerked up the gun and fired off a shot at the Angie on the floor. "You stupid, stupid bitch!"

Jack was moving, counting down after the second shot. His hand was on the doorknob when he heard the third.

"Angie!" he heard Maria cry.

He burst through the door to find Patrick standing over Angie's prone body. All he saw was blood. Fake blood mixing with real.

"Drop the gun!" he ordered Patrick.

Maria was on the couch, Angie at her feet, lying on her side, curled toward the couch, eyes closed, but he could see the rise and fall of her chest. Still alive.

Patrick glanced up, though he kept his gun trained on Angie. "She's still alive. At least, for the moment. But if you were to shoot me, I'm afraid I'd accidentally pull the trigger." He smiled. "Checkmate, Jack. Now drop your gun and kick it over to me. Now!"

Maria sent Jack a look that made it clear she wanted to rip Patrick's head off—but didn't dare move for fear he would finish off Angie.

Jack put the weapon on the floor and kicked it. Except, not to Patrick. The gun rocketed across the wood floor and under the couch. He heard it hit something at the back of the couch and stop. He shrugged. "Sorry."

Patrick was shaking his head. "I thought you played footfall in college?"

"I was a quarterback, not a punter."

"Where's my money?"

"In the car," Jack said. "But first, I want to make sure that Angie is all right."

"Money first," Patrick snapped, pointing the gun at Angie's head. "You're starting to piss me off, Jack."

"I forgot to mention something," Jack said. "I have the suitcase locks wired to an explosive. If they are opened by anyone but me…"

Anger flashed in Patrick's gaze. The arm holding the gun on Angie trembled, and Jack feared he'd gone too far.

"You would have been disappointed if I'd just handed the money over to you," Jack said quickly.

Patrick stared at him for a moment, obviously keeping an eye on both Maria and Angie in case either made a move. "Take a quick look, but if you try anything, I'll shoot Angie first, then you, then whoever the hell she is—" He indicated Maria.

Jack didn't doubt it as he moved forward cautiously. Patrick stepped back a couple of steps, the gun on Angie.

Angie was curled toward the couch on the floor, her back to Patrick. Jack knelt in front of her, his hands shaking as he felt for a pulse. *Don't let her die. Please don't let her die.*

Her pulse was strong. He felt a surge of joy that made his own heart pound. There was blood all over the front of her, though, some of it real, making it hard to tell where she'd been hit.

He found the bullet hole. It was just below her shoulder. He knelt closer, praying it wasn't life threatening. Angie winked at him.

He stared at her. With a glance she indicated her hip. He followed her gaze, pretending to inspect her injuries, and saw the weapon—her body curled around it, hiding the gun. She closed her eyes again.

"All right, Jack, you've seen her," Patrick said impatiently. "She's not dead, right?"

"Not yet," Jack said, getting to his feet. "But she will be if I don't get her to a hospital."

"Then I suggest you trot out to the car and get those suitcases."

"Try not to shoot anyone while I'm gone."

Patrick laughed. "Then you'd better hurry."

Jack went out to the car, popped the hood and dragged out the two large, heavy suitcases. The story about the explosives inside had been a ruse, the only thing he could come up with on short notice.

But once he opened the suitcases and no bomb went off, he knew Patrick would kill all three of them. Patrick had everything to lose by leaving them alive. And he would have enough money to get him out of the country.

Jack carried the suitcases up the steps, across the porch and through the front door, worrying about the weapon Angie had hidden under her. He feared she wouldn't be able to fire it because of the wound to the shoulder. So what did she have planned? He wished he knew.

All he could do was try to provide a diversion. Angie had given him a code word if anything went wrong. Well, things had gone wrong.

Patrick was practically salivating when he saw the size of the suitcases and assessed their weight. "Put them where I can see you open them."

Jack's thought exactly. He set one down and swung the other one up onto the couch next to Maria. He knelt in front of it so he was beside Angie, and studied the locks.

Out of the corner of his eye, he could see Patrick watching him closely, but still holding the gun on Angie. As jumpy as Patrick was—

"Come on," Patrick barked. "I want to see that money."

Jack fiddled with the lock, telling himself that Patrick wouldn't kill anyone until the second suitcase was opened. He popped the latch and felt Patrick flinch, thankful the fool hadn't pulled off a shot without even meaning to.

The suitcase lid rose at Jack's touch to expose layers and layers of large bills.

"Open the other suitcase," Patrick cried excitedly.

Jack heard the cabin door open. "Yes, open the second suitcase," Montague Cooke said from the doorway.

Jack turned to see Montie with a gun in his hand, the barrel pointed at Patrick. He got to his feet.

Montie motioned for the figure behind him to get the suitcases.

Jack recognized Montie's investigator, Harvey Ford. Ford picked up the second suitcase and popped it open.

Patrick cowered, obviously expecting a bomb to go off.

Montie laughed. "No explosives. Just a tracking device so I could find you all."

"Put down the gun or I'll kill her!" Patrick cried. "I'll kill them all."

"Be my guest," Montie said. "In fact, I'd appreciate it, since I'm going to need them killed with your gun. That's right, Patrick, you're taking the fall for all of this."

Patrick brought the gun up and pointed it at Montie, but not quickly enough.

Montie fired. Patrick let out a cry and grabbed his side. His weapon clattered to the floor, and Ford quickly retrieved it, being careful not to add his own fingerprints to the stock.

"Jack, here's the man who framed you," Maria said. "He got Patrick to expose the substandard practices at your housing development and accuse you. He also tricked Patrick into going after Angie. It seems your lawyer knew who she was, probably from the first time he met her."

Jack nodded, keeping his eyes on Montie. "I was afraid you wouldn't take the bait. The only way I could prove you were behind the murders of Del Sanders and Leonard Parsons was to get you up here."

Montie laughed. "Nice try, Jack, but I'm not as gullible as Patrick."

Jack saw Patrick push himself up into a sitting position, his back against the hearth. He held his side with both hands. Blood oozed from between his fingers. His face was white. He looked as if he was going into shock.

"Why do you think I asked you to collect the money for me?" Jack asked Montie, all the time worrying about Angie and trying to come up with a diversion. "I left the suitcases so you'd have a way to track us to this cabin."

"Next thing you're going to tell me is that the cabin is surrounded by cops, right?"

Jack shook his head. "No, sheriff's deputies."

Montie laughed. "Come on, Jack. You're out of your league. You could have made another couple of fortunes—instead of building low-income housing."

"You know when I got suspicious," Jack said as if he hadn't been listening. "It was when you got me out of jail in time to *crash* Patrick's wedding—but not quick enough to *stop* the wedding. You wanted me to violate that restraining order. Just like when you told me where I could find Patrick in Seattle. Just like when you forbid me to talk to Del and Leonard. Why?"

"I have your power of attorney, Jack," Montie said. "If anything should happen to you, I have complete control of Donovan, Inc."

Jack nodded. "You knew about Maria, didn't you? That's why you warned me about Angie trying to con me a second time. You set me up from the first. You just didn't know Angie really *was* alive." At least, Jack hoped she was.

Montie shook his head. "You set yourself up, Jack. Building low-income housing instead of making another couple of fortunes building mansions. Anyway, if it wasn't for me, you'd have lost it all to the LaGrand twins here."

"Thanks, Montie," Jack said sarcastically. He glanced at Maria and knew she was ready. All he had to do was say the word. "Just my *luck*."

It happened in an instant. Maria grabbed the bottle of bourbon next to her on the end table, threw it into the fire and hit the floor next to her sister. The glass bottle exploded, then the alcohol. Flames leapt out of the front of the fireplace in a blinding flash.

Angie came up with the gun in both hands and fired, as Jack shoved the couch back and lunged for the gun he'd kicked under it. The sound of gunfire boomed in the small cabin as his fingers closed over the gun's grip. He rolled over onto his back and pulled off two shots as Montie and Ford lunged out the front door.

Patrick! Jack swung around, expecting to feel the crack of the fire poker.

Patrick was gone. The back door hung open. And over the sound of the last few shots, Jack heard Maria yell, "They're getting away!"

From outside came the sound of a car engine revving, then tires throwing dirt.

Jack crawled over to Angie. "Are you all right?"

She was sitting up, her back against the couch, her face lit by the firelight. She nodded. "Don't let them get away."

Maria grabbed Angie's weapon and went racing out the back door after Patrick. Several more shots were fired, followed by the sound of shattering glass. Then only the roar of vehicle motors dying away in the distance.

Jack didn't give a damn about Patrick right now. All he could think about was getting to a place where his cell phone would work so he could call an ambulance for Angie.

He heard another car engine fire up, then peel out, and he closed his eyes with a groan. Maria was going after Patrick. Damn.

"Go," Angie said.

"Stay here," he ordered her, dragging the throw off the couch to cover her.

She smiled wanly. "No problem."

He stared down at her, knowing what he had to do before he could leave her. "I love you."

Her eyes widened in surprise.

"I should have told you months ago."

She nodded.

"I'm not leaving this cabin until you promise to marry me."

"Jack—"

"Yes or no?"

She smiled up at him. "Yes."

He kissed her quickly. "Good." He got up, grinned down at her. "Good."

Hurriedly, he pulled from his pocket the small flashlight she'd given him earlier for his trek through the trees and took off out the front door at a dead run after them.

Patrick could feel the blood soaking his shirt and jeans, but the only pain seemed to be in his head. The anger made his eyes ache as if his blood pressure was too high.

He stared ahead at the red taillights of Montie's vehicle. The lawyer had used him and now had the two suitcases full of his money, money he'd worked hard for, money he more than deserved considering everything he'd been through. And he wasn't letting it—or Montague Cooke—get away.

The beam of his SUV's headlights filled Montie's rental car. The other guy was driving. Patrick crashed into the back of the car with a feeling of déjà vu. Montie's rental car was no match for the larger SUV Patrick had rented. The car lurched forward. The SUV's off-road utility bumper caved in the rental car's trunk.

In his headlights, Patrick saw Montie turn in the passenger seat. A moment later the windshield exploded, showering Patrick with little cubes of safety glass and really making him mad.

He could see where the trees opened up. Beyond it was the ninety-degree turn and the short stretch of road along the gorge.

The rental car's brake lights flashed on. Down the mountain came the blue flash of lights and the *whir* of sirens. Cops. Behind him, he saw headlights.

Why wasn't he surprised? He was wounded and bleeding and broke and on the run from Jack and all the Angies in the world and the law and Jack still couldn't just leave him the hell alone. No, Jack had to have justice.

It wasn't that hard a decision to make. Montie would hire himself a good lawyer and probably get off. Patrick would get blamed for everything and end up on death row while Jack had not one but *two* Angies.

Patrick pushed the gas pedal to the floor. Montie, at least, would not be getting away with what he'd done. Patrick's only regret was the money. He imagined it floating down river for fishermen to find in the spring.

He slammed the SUV into the back of Montie's rental car, just as it started into the turn, with such force it rattled his teeth, driving the car straight for the gorge.

Patrick laid on his brakes, not wanting to make the

same mistake he'd almost made with Angie and the Jeep. It took him a couple of seconds to realize he wasn't slowing down—and why.

The SUV's bumper was hung up on the rental car, pulling his vehicle with it to the sound of screaming metal.

He grabbed his door handle, throwing his shoulder against the door, hoping he could get out quickly enough.

The door, jammed from the last crash into the rental car, didn't budge.

Patrick looked up to see his fate as the rental car dropped over the rim of the canyon, dragging the SUV with it. *You win, Jack.*

Jack reached the canyon in time to see the two vehicles drop over the side of the canyon into the depths. He closed his eyes, leaning back against a tree, filled with horror and regret.

Then he walked down to where Sheriff Truebow was getting out of his patrol car. Maria had already had him call for an ambulance.

Jack barely remembered the ride down the mountain to meet the ambulance, Angie in his arms in the back seat and Maria driving and Sheriff Truebow following behind.

Jack looked up hours later from the hard plastic chair in the hospital waiting room to see the surgeon coming toward him.

"The surgery went well," the doctor said, as Jack stumbled to his feet, heart in his throat. "We removed the bullet. She's resting peacefully. You can see her in the morning. I would expect a full recovery."

Jack felt his eyes sting as he shook the man's hand. "Thank you."

The doctor smiled and patted Jack's shoulder. "You look like you could use some rest yourself." He glanced toward Maria, who'd finally fallen into an exhausted sleep on the floor. "Identical, aren't they?"

Jack shook his head. "No, they just look alike."

Epilogue

"You're really going through with this?" Maria asked as she straightened the train on Angie's wedding dress.

"You mean the marriage?"

"No, giving up the confidence game."

"Daddy used to say that a good con man always knows when to quit the grift," Angie said.

"I wish Daddy could see you." Maria's eyes filled with tears as she met her sister's gaze in the large oval mirror.

"Oh, I suspect Daddy's keeping an eye on us." Angie smiled through her own tears.

Maria nodded. "You look incredible."

"My maid of honor looks pretty amazing, too, don't you think?"

Maria studied herself in the mirror. She wore an emerald-green velvet dress that was stunning on her.

Her brown eyes shone brighter than Angie had ever seen them. "Sheriff Truebow's kind of cute, don't you think?"

Angie laughed. Maria had invited the sheriff to the wedding after the two had hit it off in Montana. Only Maria could get a date out of a con gone bad.

"Aren't you going to miss it, though?" Maria asked.

"I'm going to miss working with you," Angie said. "But the confidence game?" She shook her head. "Our house is almost finished and Jack will be busy. He thinks he can save his construction company. He has big plans for the old neighborhood. So I will be in charge of decorating the house and getting it ready."

Jack had insisted they hold off on the wedding until he could carry his wife over the threshold of their "real" home.

"Yes, but once you furnish the house, aren't you afraid of being bored to tears?" Maria persisted.

Angie smiled, her hand going to her stomach. "I think I'll be too busy to get bored." She glanced up to meet her sister's gaze again in the mirror.

"Are you telling me you're—"

"—pregnant. I just found out this morning."

Maria threw her arms around her sister. "Oh, Angie, I'm so happy for you!"

"I want my child to have the mother you and I never had," she said. "And the home. Jack knows how much that means to me. Do you know that he ran out this morning and bought a swing set? This baby is so lucky to be getting such a great father."

"And mother," Maria said. "I'm going to miss you."

"We just won't be working together," Angie said. "It isn't like you're leaving Texas."

Maria grinned mischievously. "Sheriff Truebow—that is, Jeff—wants me to come up to Montana for a while. I guess he owns a small horse ranch."

Angie laughed as she remembered Jack joking with the sheriff that Maria would steal him blind if he wasn't careful.

Jeff Truebow, a large, handsome man with an honest face and a quiet manner, had grinned. "I don't have much money."

"That's good," Maria had said. "Because your money isn't what I'm interested in."

The first few chords of "The Wedding March" swelled in the nave next to their dressing room.

"There's our cue—" Maria said, her voice cracking with emotion. "Ready?"

Angie touched the amulet at her neck. Jack wouldn't hear of her taking it off, saying he had never believed in luck until he met her.

She squeezed her twin's hand with her other hand. "Oh yes, I've never been more ready."

As Maria opened the door, Angie saw Jack waiting for her, and for the first time she really did believe in happily ever after.

* * * * *

HARLEQUIN
PLUS

Announcing a **BRAND-NEW**
multimedia subscription service
for romance fans like you!

Read, Watch and Play.

Experience the easiest way to get
the romance content you crave.

Start your **FREE 7 DAY TRIAL** at
<u>www.harlequinplus.com/freetrial</u>.